PRAISE FOR
THE
SLYE TEAM BLACK OPS SERIES

"I could not put this bookdown...Once again Dianna has thrilled my suspense taste buds with an extra dashof spicy romance." ~~After Hours Rendezvous

"Engrossing, thrilling and wonderfully steamy...a pitch-perfect suspense that will keep readers breathless from the first nerve-racking scene to the last shocking revelation."~~The Romance Reviews

"It seems with each book this series gets better." ~~The Reading Cafe

"A FREAKING AWESOME continuation of the Slye Team series by Dianna Freaking Love!!! She did not disappoint." ~~Goodreads

"This is one of those books where your body tenses, you stop breathing and you just can't read fast enough."~~ Amazon

DIANNA

NEW YORK TIMES BESTSELLING AUTHOR

LOVE

NOWHERE SAFE

SLYE TEAM BLACK OPS ROMANTIC THRILLERS

Cover Design and Interior format by The Killion Group, Inc
http://thekilliongroupinc.com

CHAPTER 1

Two Years Ago – near Framlingham, England

Chelsea was late.

Twelve seconds late.

The kind of late that could cost a life.

Josh Robertson forced his grip to relax before he crushed the crystal glass of thirty-year-old scotch. It wasn't as though she'd hit traffic making the fifteen-kilometer drive from Framlingham. Maybe dodge a sheep or two in the road, just part of the country ambience this far north of London.

He expected Chelsea to strut across the polished oak floor of this eighteenth century mansion any minute, chin cocked up as if she owned the place. She could do it, too. Pull off pretending she was one step from British royalty and not a bastard child who made her living as a liaison for touchy deals between dangerous people.

A bastard just like him. One of those little things they'd had in common from day one. Another was an obsessive penchant for being on time.

Always. And she demanded it as a nonnegotiable term for her liaison services.

The second hand on his watch marched on with no regard for his sanity. Something had gone wrong.

Service staff in crisp black tuxedos moved through the elegant party carrying silver platters. One of the staff paused next to Josh. "Would you care for something, sir?"

Yeah. I'd kill for a cellular signal for about ten seconds. Just long enough to check his phone for text messages.

"No, thanks." Without a magic wand, even the best staff couldn't make that happen.

He strolled past floral decorations a foot taller than he was. At six feet, two inches, Josh could see over most of the crowd.

He visually swept the partygoers peppered around the enormous ballroom, looking for Chelsea and Mendelson, the German guy Josh was here to meet.

Still no vivacious beauty with a head of black hair and eyes green as spring leaves.

Ninety-nine seconds.

Frustration burrowed into the center of his skull. He hated stuffy parties, but Mendelson had dictated the location and arranged for the gilded invitation. If Josh closed his eyes, he could be back in the States at the charity ball his adoptive parents hosted for five hundred guests every spring. Same mind-numbing conversations. Same put-me-in-a-catatonic-state Baroque music played by a string ensemble like the ones his mother hired.

Mom claimed the peaceful music kept people calm.

Not doing a damn thing for him right now. His heart hammered like Charlie Watts cutting loose on a drum solo at a Rolling Stones concert.

Come on, Chelsea.

She'd never missed a meeting. She was always on time, even for the occasional casual rendezvous with Josh to scratch an itch.

Hell, there'd never been anything casual about the hot sex they shared. They'd burn hard and fast, like a flash fire. Then go their separate ways afterward. No drama.

The perfect arrangement to keep loneliness at bay.

Not a relationship. At least not in the true sense of the word, but he did care for her. Needed to know she was safe. He'd never had a more dependable informant or go-between. So where was she?

Had Mendelson changed the plans?

Had Chelsea backed out?

No. Not with a man's life on the line.

She had just as much investment in extracting a captured CIA agent tonight as Josh did. The CIA asset had information on a terrorist cell planning to detonate bombs in Los Angeles and Dublin.

In two days.

Chelsea's grandmother lived in Dublin in a nursing home, too ill to be moved without paramedics and a cardiac support ambulance.

Josh's gut snarled at him to get out of this place, disappear before he ended up in the same fix as Chelsea, who might be imprisoned with the CIA agent right now.

Good advice.

That he couldn't follow. His gut didn't get a say this time.

Josh lifted his drink slowly, his eyes trained on the second hand of his watch.

She'd blister his ears for staying. He'd let her if she'd just walk through those beveled glass doors at the entrance.

If the muscles across his shoulders got any tighter, he'd split the seams on this tux the next time he stretched. *Relax a little. Think.* She could handle herself just as proficiently with a weapon—or in hand-to-hand combat—as he could.

Another commonality between them. She wasn't trained as an operative, but she'd gained survival skills on the streets in Liverpool, where failure meant a short life.

His hard-times training had been back in New York as a street rat, but it was nothing like the professional training he'd received.

He and Chelsea had one major difference.

His team of hired mercs was loyal to the US.

Chelsea pledged her allegiance to the almighty dollar and the highest offer. Strictly business with her.

Or it had been until this op when she'd discovered her grandmother was at risk. Her grandmother's nursing home was near the Dublin airport, high on the list of terrorist targets.

Had cool-as-ice Chelsea allowed emotions to rule her actions this once and made a mistake?

If she had and couldn't contact him, there was no way for him to know what kind of trouble she was in, or for him to help her. He should follow SOP at this point and disappear.

Especially after the cryptic warning in her last text. She'd typed that damned XOXO at the end.

When they'd first slept together, she'd told him two things to never forget. She didn't do late, so if she ever failed to show on time, he should not wait for her. And if she sent XOXO in a message it meant she might have to vanish.

Might.

A word that would haunt him forever if he left now.

The sound of a familiar footstep tapping across wood floors reached his ears. He homed in on it, listening as he turned to scan the crowd. There it was, moving toward him. A confident click, click, click that lifted just above polite conversation.

Black hair flashed into view. Halle-damn-lujah. Chelsea headed toward him with her signature smooth gait on a pair of five-inch black heels.

He caught himself before his face revealed the punch of relief slamming his solar plexus. *Showtime.* He shoved cold disregard into his eyes.

What had been the delay?

Shiny hair fell past her shoulders, a long strand dipping to touch the enticing hint of breasts he'd spent hours appreciating on their stolen encounters. She'd showcased them nicely tonight, in a strapless, black sequined dress that sparkled under the crystal chandeliers. Sexy-as-hell body, but that hadn't been what he'd noticed about her when they'd first met. It was the note of Irish in her husky voice that had turned his head.

She wasn't the love of his life.

He couldn't have one.

Neither could she, with their career choices. But even though they sometimes went months without a word from each other, he'd realized tonight that she'd carved a spot in his world he didn't want vacated.

She played her role, too, chilly expression in eyes he'd seen laughing only a day ago. She ignored the admiring gazes snapping in her direction as she moved toward him.

Ludwig Mendelson followed a half step behind Chelsea, shoulders back, body square and thick like wrestlers. His hair was short and too silver for a man only in his forties. Pale skin stretched across a pudgy face punctuated by two unforgiving, ice-chip blue eyes. An inch or so shy of six feet tall, he strode as if the world should drop at his feet and pay homage.

If that were true, he wouldn't need the two bodyguards following close behind, both stuffed into tuxedos tailored for the Hulk.

Mendelson had a reputation for being unpredictable. He'd chosen this party but could've just as easily demanded a meeting at a location that required mountain climbing gear. Josh had the German's file memorized and had come to England prepared to do pretty much anything required to finalize this exchange on Mendelson's terms.

He knew more than he wanted to know about a man with a preference for over-the-top, perverted styles of interrogation.

Just seeing Mendelson walk so close to Chelsea twisted a fist inside Josh's gut, but she'd built one hell of a reputation in the international crime community for arranging meetings like this one, and for swift retaliation against anyone who tried to harm her.

Still, something was amiss, or she'd have been on time.

When she reached Josh, she waited until Mendelson stepped up next to her before speaking first to Josh. "Mr. Taylor, meet my associate, Herr Mendelson."

Offering neither his hand nor any verbal acknowledgment, Josh announced, "You're late."

Mendelson moved his chunky shoulders in a slight shrug then glanced over at Chelsea who didn't bat an eyelash. His German accent matched his blunt face. "Beauty is not a rushed process. Men have always waited for women."

Had she really been the reason for the delay?

If so, had she done it as a signal to alert Josh?

Cognizant of Mendelson's continued scrutiny, Josh swirled his scotch and took a sip. He tinged his words with just enough irritation to hide the concern that brewed in his gut over Chelsea. "I came here to retrieve my client's asset and deliver your payment." He targeted Chelsea with his next verbal shot. "You were chosen as liaison because of your reliability *and* your reputation for being punctual." *Tell me what's going on.*

Any sign.

"You could ha' been on your way if waitin' was a burden," Chelsea warned with just enough venom in her Irish lilt to sell the deadly glint in her eyes.

What the hell was that supposed to mean?

Had she *wanted* him to leave?

She pressed on. "We've all an investment in tonight's meetin'. The sooner we stop natterin' on, the sooner we'll each be enjoyin' the spoils."

Josh leveled Mendelson with a let's-get-to-the-bottom-line look. "Satisfied that I'm here alone?"

"If I were not, you would no longer be standing here."

Meaning Josh would be dead already. Mendelson believed Josh had a transport of weapons waiting nearby to exchange for the CIA agent, so he pointed out, "I can't keep someone mobile in this area for long without drawing attention."

Mendelson smiled with eager eyes. "Then I suggest we proceed with haste and complete our transaction."

"Lead on." Josh lifted his glass in a subtle gesture that said *get on with it, you're wasting my time.* He knew the exchange wouldn't go down here.

Mendelson didn't disappoint. "My car is waiting."

Sucked to be right sometimes.

Following the Mendelson entourage, Josh held his blank mask in place, but unease clawed at the back of his neck. Despite the XOXO message, Chelsea hadn't vanished, but neither could they discuss anything now that the game was on.

He was just glad to know she'd be close enough for him to snatch along with the CIA captive tonight, because he wasn't leaving this country unless he had both of them in hand.

If she needed to disappear, he could make that happen and keep her safe at the same time. His body might take a beating if she didn't see it his way, but he didn't think she'd purposely kill him.

He'd heal and she'd be alive.

All other details could be worked out after that.

Outside the lavish home, attendants rushed through the crisp fall air, opening car doors for late arrivals, and retrieving vehicles for early departures. Josh had driven here in a rented Mercedes, but Chelsea wouldn't be riding with him. That meant no chance to talk before they reached the location where Mendelson held the CIA agent, Len Rikker.

It had taken five days of intense negotiations to convince Mendelson that Josh represented black market weapons dealer Puno de Hierro, known as Iron Fist, who operated out of Nicaragua.

And that Len Rikker was no international spook but one of Puno de Hierro's assets.

Among Mendelson's multi-faceted enterprises, he brokered resources for terrorist operations. Josh's team had tracked the German for twelve days and finally gotten a break when the weapons shipment Mendelson needed as currency for another deal had gone missing.

Thanks to Josh's team who'd stolen it.

That team now waited to move in.

No government would admit to employing mercenary soldiers like his team, but most countries tapped similar off-the-record elite operatives for missions that couldn't be run through the usual channels or couldn't be acknowledged under any circumstances. The CIA would normally turn to one of its own elite military units to extract a captured agent, but they wanted this sterile.

A hands-off operation with none of their assets involved.

Sabrina Slye, who headed up Josh's team, had questioned the "why" behind the agency's decision to send in her people, but the powers-that-be weren't in the habit of answering to anyone.

Much less a merc. She'd turned down the mission until someone way up the CIA food chain had asked her personally to bring home their agent.

And to do it soon, before Mendelson disappeared again.

The German often moved his high-value assets daily.

Sabrina had freedom to execute her operations with full autonomy since her people were considered expendable resources that no government agency would admit hiring and sure as hell wouldn't lift a finger to save.

A young man rushed up to Josh and pointed as a Mercedes rental rolled up to the curb. "Your car, sir."

Right behind Mendelson's sleek black limousine.

Josh continued toward the end of the walkway lit by landscape beacons. The bodyguards took position on each side of the limo's open passenger door where Chelsea paused.

Mendelson's lips tilted with amusement. A pit viper's smile. "I have arranged a driver for you."

A driver who matched Mendelson's bodyguards in size—and grim expression—sat behind the wheel of Josh's Mercedes.

As expected.

If he refused the driver, the deal would fall apart. Everyone involved knew that. But this was all about managing power plays. Josh spun the tables with one of his own. He made a show of looking at his watch. "Your window of time to complete our meeting is running out."

In other words, the weapons shipment Josh was supposed to be handing Mendelson in trade would not remain in the area indefinitely.

Mendelson's gaze turned black as his soul. He ignored Josh and waved Chelsea into the car.

Chelsea glanced back with what Josh could only describe as regret in her gaze and gave a tiny shake of her head that no one could have seen but him.

She couldn't be saying goodbye, could she?

Didn't she know by now that he could help her with whatever was wrong? He had until he closed the deal with Mendelson to stop her from leaving. Josh would be paying half of her fee. She wouldn't normally walk away without her money after coming this far.

That alone proved something was off tonight.

One of Mendelson's men opened the back door of the Mercedes and Josh climbed in. Now that he'd been given an unwanted driver, calling his team on the satellite phone hidden in the driver's door panel of his car was out.

Always have a backup plan.

He'd learned that as a child when he'd been given professional instruction in defensive maneuvers. His parents had lost their only birth child to a kidnapping that had ended badly. They took stronger measures to protect Josh, even though he'd been nothing more than someone else's refuse at age seven when they'd adopted him.

With a subtle movement, he twisted the platinum cufflink at his right wrist, which functioned as a tracking device. His backup plan. That single twist sent a signal that he was mobile, but not alone. Activating his left cufflink in a similar way alerted the team to move in.

Their five-member team had been together for six years, but Josh, Sabrina and Dingo Paddock went back to Josh's days as a kid in a New York City group home, another name for an orphanage.

Once the limo with Mendelson and Chelsea moved off, Josh's Mercedes pulled out behind them.

His driver said not a word during the forty-five-minute ride, with his Mercedes boxed in between the limo and a silver Hummer. A moonless night wrapped the windows, blacking out the view he'd seen earlier of the rolling countryside covered in autumn's golden wash. Colors just as vibrant as a year ago, when Josh and Chelsea had spent a weekend in a renovated crofter's cottage an hour from here. They'd made love under a beech tree while leaves floated down around them.

Sabrina had warned him and Dingo to never get attached, and Josh hadn't before now. Too many years spent alone, watching for death around every corner, had left him numb inside. Or so he'd believed until the first time Chelsea had laughed.

Then she'd made *him* laugh, a genuine, from-the-chest laugh he hadn't experienced since he was a kid.

And now she intended to disappear.

Then he'd spend every day wondering if she'd survived. That was classic Chelsea. She'd never ask for help if it meant putting someone else at risk.

Too bad. Josh refused to let her face a threat, whatever it was, alone.

His driver slowed as the Mercedes passed guards at the entrance to a property. The stone entryway suggested a residence somewhere beyond the short reach of headlights piercing the night.

Mendelson's limo, Josh's Mercedes and the Hummer continued along a curved drive until a two-story stone structure took shape. Temporary lights had been set up, illuminating the yard. Ivy climbed the attractive farmhouse, probably built in the 1700s.

As soon as Josh exited the Mercedes, one of Mendelson's bodyguards from the Hummer met him at his car door. "Lift your arms."

Of course. The pat down.

Josh lifted his hands. When the guard finished, Josh emptied his pockets, showing he had no weapon or phone, nothing that could be used for communicating or killing.

The guard ordered, "Follow me."

Josh's neck twitched with more unease. Chelsea and Mendelson hadn't gotten out of the limo yet.

Trailing behind the guard, Josh assessed what security personnel he could locate outside the lighted area. Smoke trickled from a fireplace at one end of the house, the smell of burning hardwood riding on a light breeze. Two men with rifles were posted on the roof. More were positioned around the perimeter, some barely visible in the shadows.

Ten, so far, counting the limo driver, who had to be armed.

But another five to ten could be hidden.

And not just hired muscle, but deadly operatives.

Josh recognized at least two from the Russian mafia. Mendelson had spared no expense, but was it to ensure the safety of his prisoner, or that this weapons shipment did not get waylaid?

Sabrina and her three-person team could handle inserting past fifteen, maybe twenty guards, depending on how the security was spread around the farmhouse.

At the entrance to the house, another guard—visible guard number eleven—opened a heavy wooden door that swung on black, wrought-iron hinges. The glass lamp on a hall table supplied enough light to see the quaint foyer and a stairway against one wall.

Dried flowers and other potpourri piled in a glass bowl might have freshened the air, but it couldn't combat the stale odor of recently fried fish. Probably cooked by Mendelson's men.

Were the owners away from the property?

Or dead?

The guard by the door nodded at the bodyguard who led Josh up the stairs and down a hall. They entered a narrow room with tall ceilings and old-world character. Dark bookcases were laden with rows of leather-bound books. Two mahogany chairs with tufted green upholstery sat sedately on a Turkish rug, and the scent of pipe tobacco lingered.

A homey picture, which did nothing to loosen the tight muscles in Josh's neck. He ordered the bodyguard, "Tell Mendelson he has five minutes."

Heavy footsteps approached and Mendelson entered the room. "I am here, Mr. Taylor."

Without Chelsea. Shit.

Josh's shoulders constricted further, but he'd stay on task until he had reason to change course. "I'm here. You're here. But my client's asset is not. Are we doing this tonight?" *Tell me you're waiting on Chelsea again.*

"The asset is being brought up for validation." With that partial answer to Josh's question, Mendelson went to a small marble-top table. A flask of liquor and two short-stemmed glasses had been placed on a tray of inlaid wood as though in anticipation of a gentleman's meeting.

There should be a reality show on the eccentric behaviors of insane international criminals.

Mendelson poured two glasses of the amber liquid. "I prefer a good cognac, but when in Rome..." He shrugged and offered the second glass to Josh. "Brandy?"

Josh would rather drink the devil's piss than share anything with this bastard. "Sure."

Moving to one of the chairs that faced the doorway, Mendelson took a seat. "Sit."

"I'm not interested in playing chit-chat, Mendelson."

Mendelson snapped his fingers and one of the bodyguards entered, sans tuxedo jacket and sporting an HK MP7 submachine gun held loosely on a sling over one shoulder, but ready to use.

Josh got the message. He rolled his eyes as though the whole thing merely annoyed him but sat in the other chair.

Where was Chelsea?

He clicked through possibilities. Maybe Mendelson had paid his fee and Josh's, and sent Chelsea away? But why would he?

The sound of multiple footsteps pounding up the stairs reached the library, along with something being dragged. Two guards entered, turning sideways to carry the CIA agent, Len Rikker, between them, each gripping an arm. Gaunt from five weeks in Mendelson's not-so-tender care, and bloody in too many places to count, Rikker's head hung forward.

Josh stood and took a step toward the prisoner who had a distinctive scar at the hairline. One confirmation of the CIA agent's ID. "Lift his head."

A guard grabbed Rikker's mop of scraggly brown hair and jerked his head back, raising Rikker's swollen face into view. Josh studied the eyes and jaw line long enough to give the impression he would walk away if they tried to pawn off the wrong man on him.

Mendelson said, "Satisfied?"

"Yes."

While Mendelson ordered the prisoner returned to his locked room in the basement, Josh used the distraction to twist his left cufflink twice, sending a message to move in.

With the prisoner out of the room, Mendelson put his glass down. "You may have your man as soon as you deliver my missiles. You have thirty minutes, as agreed."

Sabrina and the team required twelve minutes to insert into the secured area undetected and get in position to infiltrate the building to find Rikker. Josh pushed an impatient look at Mendelson. "Need GPS coordinates and a sat phone to call in my transport truck." His nonexistent truck.

"Give the phone number to my man—" Mendelson angled his head at his guard. "He will call with coordinates."

The guard unclipped a satellite phone from his belt and eyed Josh who rattled off the number. Sabrina had someone sitting at a predetermined location two hours away with a disposable phone, and ready to leave the minute the call terminated.

When the guard ended the call, he told his boss, "Done."

A grin spread across Mendelson's face, one that sent worry skidding along Josh's spine. That extra sense operatives developed for survival told him that something had changed, even if everything seemed to be on schedule. He lifted his drink, killed the balance, and set the glass back down, determined to find Chelsea. "Let's get this done. Where's Chelsea?"

"She will be along soon." Mendelson took a sip of his drink. "She is quite unusual. I could find a place in my organization for her. Maybe a personal assistant who could attend to more than negotiations for me." There was the sinister smile again when Mendelson slid a taunting look at Josh.

What was Mendelson up to with this bullshit?

Did he suspect a relationship between Chelsea and Josh? Or was he just testing with age-old bait to provoke a jealous reaction? But that would mean Mendelson knew Josh and Chelsea had been acquainted for much longer than this negotiation had taken.

No way. Josh tested right back. "What are you waiting for?"

Mendelson's gaze turned curious, as if he weighed Josh's reaction. "Then you would not mind?"

That hit too close to be fishing. Josh could count on two fingers the number of people who knew about his non-business relationship with Chelsea. Him and her. Period. "Me? Why would I care?"

"Perhaps I was wrong to believe you placed a high value on her. Either way, I will miss her, perhaps almost as much as you will, but for different reasons."

Noises in the hallway, like someone banging into the walls, turned Josh around.

The second bodyguard stepped into the room with Chelsea in his grasp. Blood ran down her arm and she struggled against a man who outweighed her by a hundred pounds.

She'd gotten in her fair share of licks, based on the guard's broken nose, bleeding temple and torn clothes.

Josh didn't know how it had happened, but they'd both been made.

CHAPTER 2

Screw this. Nothing to lose now. Josh lunged for the bodyguard with a stranglehold around Chelsea's neck.

Mendelson's other guard standing by swung the butt of his weapon and cracked the side of Josh's head with the sharp metal stock.

Stars scattered through his vision. Stumbling sideways, Josh spun around and kicked the guard's chin, crushing jawbone with a satisfying crunch, and knocking him out cold. He snatched the MP7 away before the bodyguard hit the floor, whipping the sling off the man's limp arm.

As Josh gained control of the weapon, Mendelson sighed loudly. "Put the weapon down, Mr. Taylor, or I'll order her death."

Chelsea shouted at Josh. "*Kill them!*"

The brute shoved the muzzle of his Ruger P90 semi-auto pistol against her throat. "Shut up."

Chelsea's gaze met Josh's, holding long enough for him to see the doubt that they'd walk out of here alive. But she didn't know he had a team coming. She only knew what he'd told her to make this exchange happen.

"Go ahead and shoot or put the weapon down," Mendelson suggested. "Either way, we have a bit of a wait."

Lunging against the guard's tight hold, Chelsea shook her head at Josh to not give up the weapon, but he dropped it on the rug and turned to Mendelson. He warned in a cold voice, "You don't want to double cross me."

"Under different circumstances, I might agree, but I feel it necessary to inform you that a cellular jammer has now been activated for this area."

The change in topic cut through the haze of fury threatening to steal the last of Josh's control. "And why would that matter?"

"You will not be able to reach your team even if you could

get your hands on a phone.”

Shock overrode every other emotion. Mendelson knew about Josh's team.

Not possible. Only a select group of individuals were aware that Sabrina's team even existed and those were the ones with whom she contracted missions. National security for the United States and similar departments in countries aligned with the US.

International alphabet spook groups.

Chelsea couldn't have burned him and wouldn't have, even if nothing personal existed between them. She had no motive and knew Josh would use his resources to protect her grandmother. He had a team on site right now, moving the elderly woman out of Dublin, to a quiet country house with round-the-clock care. He just hadn't had a chance to tell Chelsea.

Had Sabrina and the team been burned, too?

How much did Mendelson know?

None of those answers will get us out of here right now.

His number one priority? Warn Sabrina that the mission was an ambush.

“Might as well make yourself comfortable, Mr. *Taylor*,” Mendelson said in a congenial tone.

A new guard ducked his head and stepped inside the already-crowded space.

Huge didn't begin to describe this behemoth.

Nothing about his dark eyes, unkempt black beard and oily brown hair appeared German. Maybe South African, and the MP7 he carried looked like a toy in his hands. Clearly, Mendelson supplied his expensive help with equally pricey weaponry.

Josh shoved everything aside while he focused on first sending a message to his team before they inserted and, next, getting himself and Chelsea out of here. But his mind seemed determined to plague him with more questions. Why hadn't Mendelson killed them yet? Why hadn't Mendelson waited on the weapons before showing his hand? Josh needed more information. "You trade humans for commodities. How can I be of more value than by making a trade for your captive?"

"Oh, but I *did* trade for Mr. Rikker."

He knows Rikker's real name. Not good. How could Josh use that to his advantage? He feigned surprise. "Rikker? That's not the name I was given. I think we've both been played. If that's the case, I'll make a deal for the weapons between the two of us, but the transport won't arrive until I call a second time."

Mendelson's eyes creased with humor. "Let's end this charade, Joshua *Carrington*. There is no transport and no weapons. You and your Slye team are what I received in trade for Rikker. He is being delivered to the higher bidder as we speak." Mendelson smiled with genuine pleasure.

The last trace of Josh's hope sucked away faster than water down a bottomless hole when he heard Mendelson use Carrington, Josh's legal name. How had Mendelson gotten that? Even Chelsea knew him as Josh Robertson. Terror ripped through him at the level of betrayal it took for this to be happening. Something about Mendelson's calm demeanor poked its way into his thoughts. "Why aren't you upset about losing the weapons?"

"Because I don't need them. I *allowed* my first shipment of weapons to be taken and they are being replaced. I made a more advantageous deal for the CIA agent."

What the fuck? It took all of Josh's ability to not react.

Mendelson continued, "As for a truly valuable trade, Sabrina Slye is wanted by many people."

Who had screwed Sabrina? Josh forced himself to sound detached. "Well, hell, as long as I'm dead, at least tell me who sold me out."

"You're of no use to me dead. I will get much information from you and your team before I put each of you on the auction block. As to the person who set this up—I will only share that it was CIA."

Mendelson was wrong on one point.

Josh would likely die, and very soon, because he would not

stand by and let this unfold without a fight. He chuckled with dark humor, as if he'd always expected to be betrayed at some point, and muttered, "Should have expected that out of those bastards."

That drew a gloating smile from Mendelson, so Josh asked, "Mind if I get comfortable while we wait?"

"By all means."

Taking off his jacket, Josh kept an eye on Chelsea in his peripheral vision. She'd stopped struggling, her eyes tracking every move he made, listening intently to how they'd both been screwed by his people. *Not my people anymore.* He jerked his bowtie loose and unfastened the first two buttons of his shirt. When he removed the cufflinks that only his team knew about, he put both metal clips in one hand and rolled them around together as though he played with a pair of dice.

Doing that for longer than ten seconds caused the signal to screech in Dingo's receiver and deactivated the tracking unit embedded in the cufflinks.

Breaking the connection was code for FUBAR, to get the hell out of here now.

He walked over to the tall bookshelf and leaned against it, ticking off seconds in his mind, hoping ten minutes would pass with no sound.

But eight minutes later the first explosion rocked the house, not surprising him in the least. His team was here.

Josh, Sabrina, and Dingo had never left each other as kids and wouldn't now, but he'd tried his best to warn them off.

Mendelson shoved to his feet. Surprise burst across his face. Gunfire rattled outside the house. Windows shattered downstairs.

One of the guards snatched his radio and spoke in rapid German, but Josh easily translated the demand to know what was happening.

And the terse reply that they were under attack.

Mendelson roared, "How did four people get past twenty-seven of the best armed guards?"

Josh knew the answer to that, but not how Sabrina and

company was going to exit past the rest of them now that every remaining guard knew their target was inside the perimeter.

While Mendelson shouted orders at his people, Josh looked at Chelsea, whose gaze shifted into the quiet calm he'd seen whenever she was about to kick someone's butt.

He gave her an imperceptible nod.

Her guard's attention was locked on Mendelson.

Chelsea sagged as though she'd fainted, forcing the guard to move his weapon to hold onto her dead weight.

Josh lunged at Mendelson, shoving him into the behemoth guard holding the MP7.

Mendelson shouted. His guard stumbled back but recovered quickly, knocking Mendelson aside out of instinct to free his weapon hand. The giant shoved a little too hard. Mendelson's head smacked the doorframe and he tumbled to the floor.

The guard got off a shot that ripped through Josh's side right before Josh grabbed the submachine gun and yanked it to the left. He held onto the foregrip with one hand while he battered steel punches to the guard's head, trying for a kill punch to the throat.

Not hurting the mountain of muscle one bit.

Behind the guard, Josh caught sight of Chelsea head butting her captor, who lost his grip on her. She reached between his legs and twisted a fistful of his gonads. He screamed.

She grabbed for the Ruger but missed it as the weapon fell from his hands and skidded behind him.

Josh fought the guard still gripping the MP7 with one hand. He battled to keep the weapon's muzzle pointed toward the ceiling—away from him and Chelsea. A bear-sized fist slammed Josh hard in the ribs. At least one cracked, but he hoped the flood of adrenaline firing through him would mask the pain of the rib *and* the bullet wound until he could get them out of here.

The guard used his extra four inches of reach to grab Josh by the throat. He squeezed, cutting off Josh's air. Pinpricks of light shot through his gaze. He bashed the guard's elbow joint with his free hand. Nothing gave in the hard-muscled arm.

Mendelson was sprawled on his side, still unconscious, with blood running down his face from his head wound. His body impeded any fancy maneuvering in the close quarters.

Josh finally got both hands on the tug-of-war gun. Before he gave it his all he had to break the giant's hold. Lifting his boot, he slammed the guard's kneecap.

Bone snapped. The guard screamed.

Finally, a vulnerable body part on the hulking bastard.

Josh yanked the gun free.

The guard's grip on Josh's neck loosened. He sucked air through his raw throat and swung the metal rail of the MP7's fore-end into the guard's head, bashing open a bleeding geyser.

Chelsea broke all the way free from her guard, the one she'd tried to neuter. She kicked him backward. He hit the floor hard.

She spun around and drove one of her spiked heels through that guard's throat.

Just as effective as a double tap.

The one Josh fought yelled and reached for him again in a haze of pain and rage. Fighting this guy was like trying to take down a Mack truck using his fists.

Coughing from a bruised windpipe, Josh swung the MP7 around and released a fast burst into the guard's chest. "Game over." Or that's what he *would've* said, if something more than a croak had come through his bruised throat. He drew a hard breath, ears ringing from the gunfire in the small space. Choking, unable to speak, he turned to wave Chelsea out of the room.

She took one look at Josh and started toward him.

A movement on the floor caught his eye.

Mendelson had been playing possum, lying on his side, his upper body out of Chelsea's line of sight.

The world slowed to seconds that stretched from one loud heartbeat to the next.

Mendelson lifted the Ruger from beside him.

Josh swung up his own weapon, yelling at the same moment, but only a croaked sound came out.

Chelsea stared, confused for a split-second too long before

she realized what was happening and tried to move.

Both shots exploded at the same moment.

Josh's hit Mendelson in the head. A hair too late.

He caught Chelsea as she folded to her knees. Mendelson's bullet had passed through her chest. Had it hit her heart? Not if she was still moving. Blood spilled out the gaping exit wound. She covered it with her hands, eyes glassy with shock.

He scooped her into his arms, ignoring the screaming pain in his ribs and side. "Hold on," he ground out of his raw throat.

Frightened green eyes stared up at him. "Tried...to...warn you...not to come."

"I know, baby," he rasped. "Couldn't leave you."

He made it to the stairs and looked down to find two armed guards on the main floor with their weapons pointed out broken windows.

He started to lower Chelsea to the ground to free his hands to shoot.

Before he could, the front window and door exploded into the house.

Both guards flew backwards, knocked off their feet. Josh's back hit the wall, but he remained upright with Chelsea gripped tightly in his arms. The sharp smell of burned electronics, smoke, and charred wood flooded the air from the plastique his team had used to blast a way in.

Sabrina Slye burst through the smoke-filled opening like an avenging angel. She took out both of the guards with quick double taps. Black hair was pulled back in a tight ponytail. Her dark molle vest covered in pouches held enough ammo to take down a small city.

Spiked blonde hair totally out-of-context with his olive skin color, Dingo rushed in right behind her and looked up to where Josh stood. "We got burned, eh, mate?"

Josh had never been so happy to hear that Aussie accent in his life. He raced down the stairs to the main floor, gritting against the pain cutting through his adrenaline rush. "Yeah," he croaked. Trying to yell was painful as hell. "The package is gone. Tell you everything later. Where's Singleton? Chelsea needs a medic."

From the way his side burned and the lightheaded feeling threatening to knock his feet out from under him, he did, too.

Dingo produced a second monocular from the vest he wore and slipped the headband over Josh's head. As soon as he pulled the single night vision lens down into place, Sabrina shot out the lamp on the front table, veiling the interior with darkness. Dingo slipped a compact headset with a boom mic over Josh's ears and clipped the small radio to the waistband of his tuxedo pants. No time to deal with the high-tech commo gear the rest of the team wore.

As Dingo did all of that, he explained, his words coming through Josh's headset now. "Changed the plan when we lost contact with your tracker. Singleton's waiting to cover our exit through the woods."

Josh snarled a curse. The team had walked into an ambush and now medical care was out of reach, but he wouldn't put his team at more risk. He told Sabrina, "You four stick with the plan."

Sabrina took one look at Chelsea's wound and realized he was saying he wasn't going with them. "She won't make it to a doctor."

Chelsea coughed and blood trickled from her lips. Her voice was reed thin. "She's right."

"No, she's *not*." Josh gripped Chelsea closer as if he could force her to live by sheer will alone and growled at Sabrina. "Get the team out of here and I'll meet you later."

"How in the hell do you plan to do that dragging *her* around?" Sabrina said in a low voice tight with anger.

"I'll take the Hummer."

Sabrina clenched her weapon with white knuckles and snapped out, "I told you *never* to do this."

Josh had no comeback. She was right and he'd sworn he wouldn't get involved, but he couldn't change what was and he wouldn't abandon Chelsea to make a run through the woods. "Just go and let me handle this."

Another explosion somewhere nearby shook the building.

Had to be Tanner Bodine's handiwork, the only team member Josh couldn't account for right now.

Fury rolled off Sabrina's bunched shoulders. She started issuing orders, no different than back when she'd run their half-pint gang in Queens. Glaring at Josh, she snapped, "Are you hurt, or can you run?"

With so much of Chelsea's blood covering his shirt, Sabrina's question was routine and not because she had any way to determine he'd taken a bullet. Any mention of being wounded would start a new wave of conflict.

"I can run." If he didn't pass out from blood loss.

She turned to Dingo. "We need a path out the front gate. I'll call the other two with the change of plans."

Josh shook his head. "No, Sabrina."

"Shut up and get ready to make a dash to the Hummer or I'll shoot you myself. Stop at the limo then wait for my cover fire."

Dingo had already vanished into the night like the shadow he could be when he wanted.

Josh knew better than to waste breath he didn't have arguing with Sabrina when she had her mind made up. "Thanks."

She ground out a derogatory sound in her throat that he translated as *why did men have to get stupid over women.* Casting another look at Chelsea, Sabrina muttered, "Save your thanks. You're not out of here alive and she's bleeding like a stuck pig."

Blood poured through the fingers Chelsea had clamped over the wound. Her breath came in gasps. "Don't be stupid...leave me..." Her eyelashes fluttered closed.

Josh shook her gently. "Come on, baby. Stay with me."

When her eyes blinked again, he stepped over to the side of the door opening that had been widened with that blast. Gunfire chattered back and forth outside. Bullets pinged everywhere.

Sabrina moved to the opposite side of the opening and took up the position she needed to lay down cover fire to the vehicles. Raising her HK 416 to her shoulder, she said, "Move!" and raked the area outside with rapid bursts of fire.

Josh confirmed, "Moving," and raced out into the pitch black where every light had been shot out. Now the world came to him in shades of grayish green through the night vision monocular. He hoped he was moving fast. His legs felt like lead. Zigzagging as good as he could, he reached the limo and ducked behind it, catching his breath.

His vision swirled. He shook off the dizziness.

A spray of bullets peppered the car and Josh ducked lower, clutching Chelsea to his chest as he waited for Sabrina to reload.

He twisted, watching the doorway for her muzzle flash. The minute she released another burst, he took off for the Hummer. He passed the Mercedes that had been turned into Swiss cheese.

Stars sparked through his vision. Sound withdrew and a black fog rushed at him. He thrashed at it mentally and pushed harder to reach the Hummer. He couldn't lose consciousness now.

Sabrina rushed up beside him, still laying cover fire as she moved. She yelled, "Get in the damned Hummer!"

The shout boomed through his headset, rattling his brain. He growled and drove his legs harder.

She opened the rear door just as he reached the truck. Josh hit the seat with Chelsea still draped over his arms. The door slammed shut.

Sabrina jumped in the driver's seat, all the time talking to her team through their comm sets. "We're in the Hummer. Load up!"

Starting the engine, she threw the truck into gear and made a rock-slinging sweep around the yard. Shots battered the windows and exterior of the truck, not getting through.

Bulletproof truck. *Thanks, Mendelson, you rat bastard.*

Josh pressed his hand over Chelsea's, putting more pressure on her wound. She moved a finger to touch his hand, and wheezed "My grandmother...please..."

"She's safe. I swear it. You'll see her again."

Her pale lips curved, and she drew a breath that gurgled.

"Thank you...for...us."

He kissed her forehead. "Shh. Save your energy."

Tanner Bodine yanked the front passenger door open, running with the truck then throwing his super-sized cowboy body inside.

Sabrina wheeled around hard, heading out of the property. She took one look at Tanner. "How bad?"

"Bullshit bullet in the thigh. You?"

"I'll live."

Josh heard them as if they were far away. He lifted his head. Everything spun again. Had Sabrina been hurt? "Where're you hit, Sabrina?"

"Not hit. Knife wound. Arm. I'm good."

Where was Singleton?

Sabrina slowed the truck just long enough for the rear passenger door across from Josh to open and Singleton to dive in. He scrambled to right himself and tug the door shut at the same time. Right before bullets splattered his side of the Hummer.

Josh said, "Need an IV. Gotta stop the bleeding in this one."

Singleton shrugged out of his Medic's pack and lowered his monocular to look at Chelsea in the dark then raised his gaze to Josh. If not for Josh's night vision monocular, he wouldn't have been able to see the grim concern on Singleton's coffee-brown face. The soft-spoken doctor wielded a knife with unmatched skill whether he wanted to save a life or take one. "I can't, Josh."

"Why not?"

Tanner asked, "Where's Dingo?"

Explosions erupted on each side of the road ahead. Sabrina shouted, "Clearing the way."

A loud thump landed on top of the Hummer then a fist pounded twice.

Sabrina floored the SUV. "Dingo's onboard." She punched the button to open the sunroof, and Dingo's arm appeared, snaking inside for a handhold.

Josh swallowed, damned glad that the whole team had made

it so far, but especially the two people he considered a sister and brother. Now if he could just patch up Chelsea. He ordered Singleton, "Do something, *now!*"

The Hummer slid right and left as Sabrina muscled the truck out onto the road. She yelled at Singleton, "Get an IV into her and Tanner. We'll be at the helo in nine minutes."

That got through Josh's muddled brain. "No. Helo's not safe. CIA burned us."

Stunned silence blanketed the truck. Sabrina found her voice first. "You're sure?"

"Mendelson said CIA traded us...for Len Rikker. He knew your name. Knew it was your team. Knew *my* legal name. We were the currency."

Curses blistered the air.

Pain stabbed Josh's side and he shouted, unsure if it was the wound or the broken rib. He swung around to find Singleton poking at him. "Leave it, dammit."

A figure appeared in the headlights, standing in front of the truck. He fired straight at the windshield.

Sabrina plowed into the idiot. He hit with a hard thump. His body flew up in the air and out of the way. The man obviously hadn't realized the windshield was bulletproof.

Sabrina demanded, "What's wrong, Josh?"

"Nothing."

Singleton answered, "Two things. Josh took a bullet in his abdomen, and we don't have IVs."

"Why not?"

"My pack took a hit. Pack saved my ass, but IV kits were shredded."

"Do what you can for Josh," Sabrina ordered. Her fierce gaze lit up the rearview mirror, accusing Josh of lying to her by omission. "You'll need more than an IV soon. Just hold on for me."

That last part came out weary.

Josh looked over at their medic and saw multiple faces.

Singleton pulled a wad of gauze out of his pack and shoved it up against Josh who gritted his teeth and ground out, "Told you I'm fine. Chelsea needs help."

"You're not fine," Sabrina said quietly. "I *won't* lose you."

Josh had never pleaded for anything, but he was the only one who believed Chelsea could survive. "Shingleton." His chin drooped. He shook his head and worked his lips, trying to stop the slurring. "You got some...give her...jush buy time?"

No one spoke for a moment then Sabrina said, "Tanner."

Tanner shifted around in his seat and looked back at Chelsea. "Ah, hell."

"Tell him, Singleton," Sabrina ordered.

Josh struggled to pull his thoughts together and fight off the fog sucking him into a dark vortex. "Tell me what?"

Singleton had latched his fingers around Josh's wrist at some point, checking his pulse. He should be checking Chelsea's. "Dammit...do somesing."

Singleton spoke in his calm doctor voice, the one he used to talk patients through a disaster. He pulled off Josh's monocular and tossed it away then lifted a small LED light and shined it down on Chelsea's abdomen. "Josh, she...uh."

Josh's chin hit his chest. His eyes followed the light that moved from his blood-covered hand on Chelsea's chest to her pretty neck, then up to her face, and …

Two beautiful green eyes locked open. No, no, *no* ...

Pain reached into his chest and clutched his heart with steel fingers, squeezing and twisting.

Voices ran together in a blur.

Josh lost the battle to keep his eyes open, but he still saw Chelsea's dead gaze staring at him. She'd never laugh again or spend another night with him, saving him from a lonely existence. His mind wandered. Sounds dulled and faded away.

Someone had betrayed them. Had killed Chelsea. Josh would find the bastard who had done this and ... he'd ...

Singleton shouted, *"We're losing Josh!"*

An explosion blasted against the truck, throwing it up onto two wheels.

Josh hugged Chelsea. He was flung against the truck door and the world crashed in on him.

CHAPTER 3

Current Day
Atlanta, Georgia

Josh had no expectations of this being a social meeting.
Sabrina Slye carved no time in her schedule for social.
Not anymore.
She stepped into view with a quick word to the hostess who led her his way.
He leaned back, determined to show a confident front when his insides were getting ripped up from expecting yet another conflict between them. There would be if she tried to take him out of the field again. Not happening.
She wore a sand-colored jacket and skirt that softened the edges of her professional businesswoman façade. But one look at her steel-blue gaze warned she was just as deadly in that outfit as a wolf in a red cape and hood.
He waited as she settled into her seat and their waiter brought Sabrina's Boodles on the rocks. During the brief delay, her gaze snapped around, always cognizant of her surroundings just as he was. No observable threat lurked among the chic downtown Atlanta crowd enjoying a Tuesday night at *Ray's In The City*.
Sabrina's favorite restaurant.
She only came here these days with Josh or Dingo. She must be tired of eating take-out food, or they could have met at Slye headquarters twenty minutes away. Much closer to the airport where Josh's plane had landed an hour ago.
He drummed his fingers against his glass of scotch, ready for a new mission. Something with teeth that required more effort than surveillance and electronic tracking.
But details on sensitive jobs weren't discussed in fancy restaurants.
His gut twisted another turn at that reminder.

On the other hand, she hadn't told him to pack up his cubbyhole in Miami yet. Only that he had to fly back to Atlanta for dinner tonight. What was in the worn brown satchel she'd placed on the table. Could that hold files to a new op?

When the waiter walked away, Sabrina got to the point. "I may need you to stay in Miami."

He stopped tapping his fingers and shifted forward.

That didn't *sound* like screw-his-day news, but he'd wait to hear more before relaxing.

After enduring fourteen weeks stuck behind desks and on computers in Miami under the guise of being an FBI computer forensics investigator assigned to a compact DEA task, he would not go back to that without a fight. A mole within the DEA had been leaking task force information, so the agency had needed someone for a covert investigation—someone with no internal connections.

Mission accomplished four days ago.

Mole identified.

Now the battle started.

He sighed, impatient to get this rolling. "Is this a corporate job?"

"If it is?"

Fuck it. He couldn't outlast her in a battle of attitude. "Just give me a lobotomy without anesthesia instead." For him it'd be less painful.

Corporate protection that carried her name was the public face for a thriving elite security agency Sabrina had opened ten months ago. The contract Josh had just completed in Miami constituted the real bread and butter of Sabrina's business. Those contracts were negotiated behind closed doors at Slye headquarters.

In the basement where the walls were soundproof.

Sabrina accepted government contracts, like this last one he performed for the DEA, on a case-by-case basis so long as they were *not* connected to the CIA in any way.

Just mentioning those three letters in sequence would bring on her death glare.

Shaking his head, Josh grumbled quietly, "I found the task force mole. Corporate security doesn't require my level of expertise. Send the FNG to Miami."

Sabrina could hide her reaction any time she wanted, which meant she intended for him to see just how much calling Ryder Van Dyke the *fucking new guy* pissed her off. "I don't recall asking your opinion on who to send where."

"What's the point of bringing him on if he can't perform?" he argued.

"I didn't say he couldn't do the work." Irritation crackled through her words.

"But you're not sending him, are you?"

"Didn't say that either, Josh."

"Then why—"

"Shut up and I'll tell you."

He'd heard that enough times since they were ratty kids to stand down. He raised his hands in surrender, then dropped them back on the table. Sabrina could send the FNG. Not that Ryder didn't have skills. He'd been an Army Special Forces sniper, but he was new to the Slye team and Josh didn't trust new.

Scratch that. He trusted *no one* except Sabrina, Dingo, and the team that had been with them since the UK disaster.

Which was pretty fucked up, even for someone in his business. But there it was. He worked with *that* team, or he worked solo, for a reason.

"You with me, Josh?" That was Sabrina's patient voice, the one she used more often with him these days.

As if she sensed the rage still burning just beneath his skin. Too close. He'd never sleep again without seeing Chelsea's dead green eyes and never forgive himself for convincing her that the Mendelson job would be easy money.

Nothing Sabrina needed to be burdened with. She had a business to run. Josh let out a sigh. He might bitch about it, but they both knew he'd go back to Miami and do whatever she needed one more time. Dammit. "Why do you need me to stay in Florida?"

"*If* I put you on this assignment, it's because you're still integrated down there."

So, this *was* the DEA again?

Wait. What had she meant by *if*?

She had his attention now. He dialed back his attitude and focused on figuring out what was going on. "When I said *why*, I meant as in what's the problem?" He dropped his voice lower even though conversation crowding the air shielded his words. "I handed the DEA Colbert. How'd the DEA screw this up? Can't they make him talk? Or...did Colbert escape?" Thin, forty-two, seventeen years with DEA, but not overly fit and only transferred to Miami five months ago.

Wouldn't *that* be his luck if Colbert escaped?

"They didn't lose Colbert and he *did* talk. I know you're bored with the surveillance and computer forensic work. This calls for more than that and the stakes are higher."

His ears perked up.

What the hell was going on *now* if the DEA had Colbert in custody? Still hung up on that word *if,* he asked, "What's your hesitation about me when I'm clearly the best choice at this point?"

She took her time answering. "Because I need someone who can get close to the women surrounding our target."

That took a strip off his ego. "You don't think I can do *that*?"

"At one time, you were the best, but after the UK..." Her voice trailed off. "Look, I'm sorry about Chelsea and I'm tired of tiptoeing around the damn subject. She's gone and you're alive, but you don't have the passion for this work anymore. You just go through the motions, which is fine for surveillance and computer investigations, but not for what we need in the field this time. I've dodged putting you back in the position of dealing with female targets of interest, but this can't be avoided."

That smacked him between the eyes.

Josh sat back and thought on the mundane corporate projects she'd asked him to handle since she'd opened her new offices. *While she built up her staff,* she'd said. *Until they had enough trained people in place,* she'd assured him. Lies. She knew him too well. Knew he'd step in to do whatever she needed, no matter what she asked of him. He now realized the real reason she'd handed him those jobs. Sabrina had lost faith in him.

As bad as it was to live with Chelsea's death, losing Sabrina's faith cut even deeper.

He'd never let Sabrina or Dingo down. Ever.

One truth never changed in this business.

A team was only as strong as the weakest link.

He would not be that link.

Folding his hands in front of him, he swallowed. "Chelsea was a personal mistake. One I won't make again. I can do whatever I have to in Miami."

She didn't comment.

No surprise. Sabrina was fair, if nothing else, but brutally honest, too. Decisions about assignments shouldn't be based upon friendship, even one as old as theirs.

Not when lives were at risk in any operation.

He respected that. Respected her.

Sabrina wouldn't accept words. She took responsibility for the entire team to heart. She'd been just as loyal and protective of her band of hoodlum kids back when they were running the dark alleys of New York and sleeping away from their group home more often than in it. She, Josh, and Dingo were closer than blood siblings, but that would not prevent her from making the best decisions for the teams.

A rock formed in his stomach when he realized what he'd been missing.

If he couldn't convince her to hand him this mission, and prove he was fully back, he'd no longer have a place on her team.

Sounded cold, but it wasn't.

And he'd never put her in the position of making that decision. He'd rather chop off an arm than walk away from the people he considered family, but he'd leave on his own before he'd put any of them at risk.

He put on his mission face and returned to the priority topic. "What happened with Colbert?"

Her shoulders relaxed. "Once the DEA showed Colbert the surveillance tape you took of his covert meeting with Salazar's contact person, Colbert started talking."

Salazar had carved a nice niche in the contraband business as the key person for receiving designer drugs from a select group of clients and making the transfer to the groups who got their hands dirty distributing the product. He was a hit-and-run player who was hard to catch because he'd set a meeting with little notice to minimize getting trapped with the goods.

Josh nodded. "What'd Colbert say?"

"He started talking fast and hard about how he isn't *the* mole the DEA's looking for. Said he's just a link in the chain between the real mole and Salazar's drug shipments."

"And the DEA believed that?"

"Not at first, but they do now."

Shit. "Why?"

"I saw a video of the interrogation and I'm convinced, too, but it gets stranger. The DEA busted Salazar last night."

"*Him*?" Josh couldn't believe it. "That fast? Where'd they get intel so quickly?"

Sabrina's mouth twisted with disgust. "*Anonymous* tip came in yesterday morning that Salazar would take delivery of a shipment of Spa Zing, right down to the time and location."

Spa Zing had crept into the United States over the past six months in small amounts. The designer drug had been created to emulate Bath Salts, the street name for a dangerous drug that wasn't illegal *yet,* because the Bath Salts packets were labeled "not for human consumption." It was sold over the counter in head shops, convenience stores, and on the Internet. The chemical makeup only *resembled* stimulants such as cocaine and methamphetamine.

But that crap caused dangerous hallucinations and brain damage when taken internally.

Josh shook his head more to himself than in answer to

Sabrina. "Getting a tip that fast and accurate on Salazar is...convenient." Had someone sold him out? Why? The why always mattered.

"Isn't it though?" She laid her hands on each side of the file, toying with the corner. "Once they had Salazar in custody, he offered to trade testimony for a lighter sentence. He confirmed Colbert as the mole."

"Salazar *knew* who Colbert was even with a go between? Too easy," Josh brushed off.

Easy equaled suspicious.

Josh had discovered Colbert had a gambling addiction, based on what he'd found in the agent's home. That usually meant someone who needed more money than a normal job could bring in. He pulled another person from his mental file. "Hell, I took a close look at Zane Jackson, a pilot working undercover contracts for the DEA, because he'd shown an interest in Colbert. But … nothing jumped out about the pilot."

"I read your report. I didn't find a flaw, Josh. I'm just telling you what's happened after the raid on Salazar's operation was a bust."

Four days ago on Friday morning, Josh had followed Colbert to the outskirts of an historic area in older Miami where Colbert parked along the curb as dark closed in. A lanky guy who kept his shoulders hunched and a hoodie covering his head had climbed into Colbert's car, stayed briefly, then exited.

Josh had sent a text to his team, but the unknown contact vanished into the night.

Someone had ratted out the task force, killing any chance of grabbing Salazar that night.

Instead, a Slye team snatched Colbert and delivered him to the DEA.

Case closed. Or so Josh had thought.

He scratched his chin, trying to figure out the game being played. "Are you telling me we have a *gifted* tip on a bust last night that goes down without a hitch after that first fiasco? Even the DEA's going to know that was a set-up meant to convince them the leaks stopped with Colbert. What'd they get in the bust?"

"Not as much as they'd hoped," she admitted. "A few crates of Spa Zing."

"Who was paying Salazar to distribute the product?"

Her smile turned sarcastic. "You'll love this. Salazar says he's been distributing for Colbert since the first of the year. That Colbert offered him a sweet deal, promising to keep the DEA off Salazar's back. All that drug dealer had to do was handle logistics."

"That sounds like they were dealing direct without a go between." Josh needed a whiteboard to keep up with how this worked. "If that's the case, the DEA should be able to squeeze Colbert for more. Why're you shaking your head?"

"They had Salazar look at photos that included Colbert. He never picked him out. They told Salazar that without a positive ID they weren't going to deal."

Josh considered the players. "What does Salazar look like?"

"Small guy. Swaggers like an arrogant duck and wears his greasy hair in long dreadlocks. Walking cliché."

"The guy who met Colbert last Friday night had to go maybe six feet and moved like a shadow. Doesn't sound like Salazar."

"And Colbert claimed *he* never met Salazar, only Salazar's contact man."

"Someone's lying." Then it hit Josh. "There's a third person?"

Sabrina nodded. "Someone pretended to be Salazar's representative when he met with Colbert and the same person pretended to be Colbert when he met with Salazar."

"That makes no sense. What about the person Colbert claims is the actual mole inside the DEA? How was Colbert contacted and was it male or female?"

"Phone calls. The caller used a mechanical voice distorter so no way for Colbert to even guess at the gender."

Now Josh wanted to return to Miami big time. "Any chance of tracing that phone number?"

"Colbert did trace it. A single-use phone. The next time the mechanical voice called, Colbert was given information on a bust *and* warned about trying to trace any calls."

"Somebody had access to Colbert's electronics." Josh muttered, "We might not get another shot at the mole for a while if he goes underground."

"Actually, the odds are good that we will. Colbert said this mysterious contact person told him there were two more shipments moving soon. Last one would be the most important."

Josh scoffed at the stupidity of some people. "What was Colbert thinking? His gambling debts weren't that much."

"That's not why he did it. Colbert has a thirteen-year-old daughter by a woman he never married. The DEA didn't even know about her. She lives in Portland, Oregon. The baby girl was adopted by a couple, with Colbert's blessing, after her mother was killed in retaliation for someone Colbert put in prison. The mechanical voice caller warned Colbert against going to get his daughter or sending anyone to protect her then warned if Colbert failed to carry out his orders a pedophile would be sent to make his daughter pay for Colbert's failure."

Any hesitation Josh might have had about heading back to Miami vanished with that statement. "Is the girl in protective custody now?"

"Yep."

"That makes Colbert more than ready to deal."

"Nope."

"Why not?"

Sabrina drew a slow breath. "The DEA decided to transport Colbert from Miami to Virginia today. The transport was attacked. Professional hit team. Everyone died."

Fuck. Josh ran a hand over his face. "Was the task force informed of Colbert's arrest?"

She nodded. "This morning. The plan was to get the word out quickly to keep the mole confident, but it backfired. They never expected the hit."

"This smells a hell of a lot worse than just someone in bed with *drug* runners. Why kill Colbert if he couldn't identify the person who called him?" What had Josh missed over the past fourteen weeks? "I'll have to dig further."

Sabrina took a moment before adding, "You would have found something on this second traitor the first time you went through the task force computers *if* there had been anything to find. I don't think the mole is going to leave us an electronic trail. Colbert had been doing his own investigating to find out who put him in this spot. He believed the leaks started when the DEA brought Jackson on board."

"The pilot? Zane Jackson?" Josh sat back thinking. Jackson wasn't technically an agent, but a highly skilled DEA contractor and informant with a Special Ops background. A former fighter pilot who had an uncanny sense for strategy and sniffing out leads.

No one in the Miami office had known Josh's true reason for being there. They thought he was a computer geek. It had been Zane's persistent questioning Colbert's activities outside of meetings that had caused Josh to look closer at Colbert.

Josh snorted and took a step back to reevaluate. "Colbert accused Jackson. Seriously? This from someone guilty of selling DEA secrets?"

Sabrina shrugged. "True, but there's no honor among thieves and one usually knows another. And Jackson had Black Ops training in the Air Force before he opted out. He's tight with a couple of the agents on the task force. Plus, he just got the High Vision air cargo contract."

The DEA suspected High Vision, a legitimate pharmaceutical company headquartered in France, for importing illegal designer drugs for the best part of a year. Josh held up a hand. "I'm not defending Jackson, but the DEA *wanted* him to get those contracts."

"I know. Just had a lengthy conversation about Jackson with my client this morning. Now that Jackson's coordinating the schedules for all those airplanes the DEA handed him–two of which I was told handle a volume of High Vision's legal cargo– he's become more deeply involved in the High Vision case. That means he's in the office for most of the planning sessions. Plus, Colbert showed us a cryptic email sent from Jackson's computer that was highly suspicious."

That was news. Josh opened his mind to evaluating Jackson with this new information.

Sabrina finished by saying, "Jackson has opportunity, but we don't have motive since no unusual funds have shown up in his bank accounts, but … he could be keeping it offshore. Or maybe he's being squeezed by someone else the same way Colbert was."

She had valid points. Jackson hadn't flown much lately, not with his wife so close to giving birth. Josh saw the pilot in passing but hadn't socialized with any of the task force. No reason to when he could find answers from a distance.

That might be why he'd missed a key to another traitor.

Not this time.

Sabrina started unwinding the clasp on the satchel, pulled a stack of files out, and pushed them across the table to Josh. "Based on what we learned from Colbert, we're looking at anyone close to Jackson. Wife, sister, friends. Going through the women might be our fastest route."

"I remember some intel on his wife, Angel. She almost died trying to prove her innocence in a grand theft and was credited with being the reason the FBI caught an international thief. Based on the final report, she sounded pretty courageous."

"Prior to marrying Jackson, Angel had a prison record as a mule for drugs, but it was *expunged*." Sabrina's tone made it clear she questioned the expunged record.

Josh frowned. "When you look at it from a different angle it does make you wonder about Jackson's position and access to agency information." He thought a moment on what this op would require. "Getting near Angel will be tough since she's got one in the oven ready to pop."

"I agree. That alone puts *her* lower on our list. Jackson would need someone who is mobile at any time. With Colbert gone, Jackson would have to go with someone he could trust. He may have figured out that Colbert was snooping and decided to *point* attention at him, set up Colbert to get caught."

Which means Josh had not caught the traitor and had been

used by the suspected mole. He shuffled through the files. "I heard Jackson's sister runs some antique shop in Ft. Lauderdale, but I've never seen her around the office. Don't know how useful she'll be."

"You never know," Sabrina said as Josh opened Patricia "Trish" Jackson's file. Twenty-four. Average height. Grew up in Houston. He pulled out her photo and paused.

Big brown eyes in a dainty version of her brother's face gazed up at Josh. The photographer had caught her waving at someone. Where Zane Jackson could look at you with deadly intent, nothing in this soft, feminine version held a threat.

Sweet came to mind.

Chelsea had looked sweet the first time, too, and she'd been one hell of an operative. That innocent gaze in the photo continued staring at him as he slowly closed the file.

He'd rise to the occasion. Shouldn't be difficult so long as he stuck to his Personal Rule Number One: Never mix business with pleasure. Not again.

Of all the rules he'd decimated, he should never have broken that one.

Sabrina brought him back to the moment. "Colbert spent some time shadowing Jackson's sister after he met her at the holiday office party. He went by her antique shop, trying to hook up with her. She gave him the cold shoulder. He suspected Jackson and wanted leverage if he was right, but Colbert said he wouldn't risk tailing Jackson's sister after he was warned off tracing the cell phone. Wasn't worth putting his child at risk. But he considered the sister's movements suspicious and pointed out that she's the most mobile of Zane's tight group."

Josh put the files down. "We need someone to do more than *tail* Jackson's sister. It has to be someone who can get *very* close to her. I'm your guy."

"I could send Nicholas–"

"Are you serious?" Josh put a lid on his temper, but just barely. Tell Nicholas Ferrari–the self-proclaimed Italian Stallion–that Josh needed help handling women on an op?

Not in this lifetime.

Sabrina's eyes could drill holes through someone when she focused all that visual power like she was doing now. "This calls for *charming* women *quickly*."

"Now you're insulting me, Sabrina. Trust me, Nicholas has nothing on me when it comes to charming women."

"Really? When was the last time you took *anyone* to dinner?"

He was not having this conversation with her. "You're not going there, right? Want me to give you a blow by blow on my last six months?"

She crossed her arms. "Spare me details of your sex life, which I personally think doesn't have a pulse."

He reminded himself that she was like a sister to him. *You don't kill sisters no matter how bitchy they get.*

At this rate, the conversation would go downhill soon. She could be just as hardheaded as him. More so, in fact. "I told you. I've got this. When I'm done with Miami, I'll know everything there is to know about Zane Jackson *and* the women in his circle. Once I do, we *won't* have this conversation again, right?"

Sabrina lifted a shoulder, but finally appeared satisfied. "I *am* sending Ryder down with you."

"Why?"

"Backup for one thing, since this whole thing has turned ugly, and because you can't juggle all those women at the same time."

He ground his teeth and kept his jaws locked. With a product as deadly as Spa Zing coming in and their short timetable, Josh would use the same strategy, but that didn't make it any easier to accept having the FNG tag along.

She snapped them back to the case. "Colbert believed another Spa Zing shipment could happen this week. The deaths of four teens in the past two weeks have been traced to the last shipment that slipped through Miami. One girl tried to punch a hole in her throat with a pen, because she thought she was suffocating from roaches trying to climb out. The other deaths were worse."

Thanks for that visual. "We'll find the leak."

"We *have* to and soon. Our number one priority is to stop that next contraband shipment from being distributed, but..." She held back, thinking, then said, "Just as important...we have to capture that mystery guy who you saw meet Colbert."

"Why's he so important?"

She lifted a piece of paper from the booth seat. "All we got from Colbert was a description of his contact man, but Salazar worked with an artist to give us a rendering of the person he *thought* was Colbert. Colbert's description matches this picture. Neither the DEA nor the FBI could identify him."

As Josh reached for the photo, Sabrina said, "If what Colbert told us is true, we have a small window of time and one chance at capturing this man."

Josh turned the paper around to view.

The air between them grew deathly still.

He stared at the face of the man he'd hunted for two years. Len Rikker, the CIA agent whose freedom had been traded for Sabrina's team. And Chelsea's life.

Sabrina's eyes locked on Josh, watching for his reaction.

She was right. The stakes were high on this job. She would not send anyone who wasn't a hundred percent, especially someone as personally invested as he was in finding Rikker.

Josh shoved his emotions into lockdown and pulled out the skills he used on undercover operations for years. He laid the picture on the table, the epitome of calm. No sign of the rage that roared inside him. He kept his voice matter of fact and controlled. "Son of a bitch has finally surfaced, huh? Catching him would be a bonus. I'll be back in Miami tonight."

She gave it a beat before nodding. "Call for anything you need. Every resource will be made available."

"Will do." And no one would stand in his way.

Sabrina had nothing to worry about when it came to the women on this job.

Josh would seduce Medusa to get his hands on Len Rikker.

CHAPTER 4

Tri-issshh. Wake up, Trish, whispered eerily through her vanishing nightmare.

"Not...yet," she mumbled. Heavy with exhaustion, her eyelids fluttered as she fought waking, then closed tight when she drifted off again.

Come and play, Trish.

"Not...yet..." she groused, mind thick and half asleep. "Go...'way...leave me 'lone." Sleep pulled her under.

Triisshhh!

Trish jolted at the harsh whisper, blinking fast awake in her dark bedroom. She tensed, ready to fight. Who was calling to her? The only sound now was her panting breaths that matched the rhythm of her thumping heart.

The whisper had been so close. So real.

Was someone in the room with her?

She slowed her breathing and lay perfectly still, trying to detect any movement. Had she been dreaming the scratchy voice? Not scratchy, really, but more like a robotic voice.

Her sweat-drenched T-shirt clung to her clammy skin. Maybe the voice had been in her nightmare. Eyes adjusting to the blue glow cast by her nightlight, she scanned the room once more.

Nothing stirred.

No sound. Not even street noise. Trish flipped on the light beside her bed. A few of her geriatric neighbors drove around at midnight sometimes. She'd fallen in love the minute she saw the cookie-cutter houses with neatly trimmed yards and happy flowerbeds. West of North Miami, her quaint, older subdivision offered peace and quiet.

Her safe haven.

Until now.

"You are one step from the looney farm." Her whispered words might be funny if they didn't hit so close to the truth.

She ran trembling fingers through her short curls and worked to calm her breathing. Just a bad dream. Again.

No more sleep for tonight.

She glanced at her digital clock. One tick past midnight. Wednesday had officially started, and April was almost over. Time to begin another day to get through. Dragging her sleep-deprived body from the bed, she headed down the hall to the kitchen for coffee, her sole vice these days.

When Trish straggled into the semi-dark kitchen, she expelled a sigh of relief, glad to escape another nightmare. But she couldn't continue living on so little sleep if she wanted to keep this problem from her overprotective brother.

Zane would soon notice the bags under her eyes.

Still, Trish had no choice *but* to keep this secret. No way would she allow someone to harm her only family.

Leaning her hip against the sink, she instinctively reached to her right where the glass jar of coffee normally sat. Her wrist bumped something in mid-air a foot above the counter. She snatched her hand back and held her breath, flipping the light switch on.

Undercounter fixtures glowed across her kitchen. The coffee jar had been slid back to the wall with a cutting board left in its place.

Her wrist had bumped the handle of a butcher knife stabbed into the thick slab of wood.

The knife blade nailed a piece of paper to the board.

Her mind screeched a denial, refusing to believe someone had been inside her home. She spun, checking behind and around her as she swallowed a sob threatening to rend the silence. Her hand trembled when she reached out to grasp the knife handle. Working it forward and back, she dislodged the tip.

The crisp piece of gray, fine-linen paper bore the same style of typed letters as the other notes she'd hidden in her nightstand.

I should take a Rook to replace the one I lost but knocking over a worthless Pawn in my way first is more fun.

When was the last time you had fun?

Time to come out and play, Trish. Go to your car and find your next instructions. Remember, your brother–or his very pregnant wife–will pay the price if you tell anyone about our game or if you don't follow the rules exactly.

Trish put a hand over her mouth to smother the scream building in her chest.

———*m*———

The Chessmaster smiled when a light brightened the kitchen window of Trish Jackson's home.

Her brother had felled Colbert, another Rook. An inconvenient loss that would mean a complex series of moves for this lowly Pawn. Every move would lead to eventually placing Zane in checkmate ... once Trish was knocked off the board.

But not until Trish fulfilled her purpose.

No one could outplay the Chessmaster.

CHAPTER 5

We need someone to do more than tail Jackson's sister.

Josh ignored Sabrina's voice yammering in the back of his mind. He didn't need anyone to tell him how to get close to a target.

Dawn had just cracked the horizon, with another half hour before sunrise won the battle.

Josh followed Trish Jackson through a seedy part of South Miami. She moved cautiously through an area he'd seen on the news for violence more than once in past weeks. A place known for knifings, shootings, and drug deals, complete with abandoned buildings and busted windows.

Granted, most criminals didn't work this early in the morning, but still.

There was just enough light to avoid falling over sleeping forms of the homeless.

Dark curls slipped out from beneath Trish's white cap and feathered around her neck. It would give the impression that she was a young boy from the back, if not for nice curves filling out her jeans and the feminine shift of her hips when she walked.

Zane Jackson was known for being overprotective of his wife and females in general. What kind of brother sent a woman alone down to this area before daylight to meet someone?

Maybe he hadn't.

Nothing about Trish pinged as a criminal for Josh. In fact, after reading through her file on the flight back last night, he'd had his doubts about her being involved with Zane's illegal activities.

Not one thing in her background jumped out as suspicious.

In the photos, she'd looked ... sweet.

If Zane *was* the mole, his sister could be nothing more than an innocent family member. But Josh couldn't come up with one reason Trish would be in this neighborhood if she *hadn't* been sent here.

Her actions right now made no sense.

When she slowed near a rusted, three-story metal building that had seen better days as some type of factory, Josh tucked into the next dark corner and held his breath against the sickening odor of urine. Trish glanced around once then disappeared to her right into the dilapidated structure.

Josh caught up quickly. The door was missing. He looked through the opening. No one in the first room. He slipped inside what had probably been a reception area at one time and clung to the shadows while he searched for his target.

Trish had continued to an open warehouse area beyond where he stood.

If she was meeting someone, Josh had to find a better vantage point. He eased up a steel stairway that led to another space on the second floor, which was empty except for trash and a busted wood chair. He could see a manger overseeing the workers from this observation point. The wall facing the warehouse had a gaping rectangular hole where jagged pieces of glass stuck out from the molding like giant teeth in an open mouth.

He picked his way through debris, careful not to step on anything that would crunch, and stopped at the right side of the window.

His target stood in the only splash of light sneaking into a warehouse thick with murky darkness where anyone could hide. He reached into the pocket of his fleece jacket and pulled out a low-light video camera no thicker than his finger.

He looped the cord around his neck and zoomed in to focus on Zane's sister.

She carried herself confidently, chin up with attitude and shoulders back, prepared.

For what? Meeting a drug dealer?

More light filtering in from the first hint of daylight grazed the outline of her face when she turned, giving Josh a three-quarter view of smooth, pale cheeks and a heart-shaped mouth.

Unnecessary information, he reminded himself.

Tell that to the part of him that noticed the way her light-gray T-shirt left no doubt that she was a woman. Nothing boyish about *that* body.

She tilted her head up, looking straight toward where he hid.

He sucked back but held the camera so that he could see the image on the small display screen. Her eyes searched for whatever had clued her that she was being watched. *Good instincts.* Beautiful eyes and darkly shadowed as though she hadn't slept much.

When she shook her head over some silent thought and turned away from him, Josh zoomed in on her fingers where they fidgeted with the pockets of her jeans. Telling.

She was nervous.

Or afraid.

Few things bothered him as much as seeing a frightened woman. But he couldn't allow himself to think that way about her, not when she might be a conduit in a sophisticated, deadly drug running operation.

When she flinched at a sound to her left, Josh tensed, pulse ratcheting up with the worry needling him.

What the hell are you doing here, Trish Jackson?

A man burst from the shadows at her right and attacked her, hooking an arm around her neck, and dragging her backwards.

Josh dropped the camera to hang on the cord and reached inside his coat for his weapon.

In the nanosecond that took, Trish had broken free of the man and turned on him. She kicked fast, but he blocked his family jewels and grabbed her arm.

She spun, breaking his hold, and tried to run.

He grabbed her shirt and yanked her backward.

Torn between intervening and doing what he'd been sent here to do, Josh aimed the weapon at the bastard, crazy with the need to jump in and save her. His heart pounded wildly in his chest.

In another couple seconds, he realized she didn't need his help.

Smaller than her attacker, who had to go two-twenty and reached six feet tall where she was five-five, Trish made quick, sharp moves, hands flying in reaction to every aggressive action the vagrant made.

Not a vagrant. Josh knew that for certain.

Curly hair corkscrewed, falling to the guy's shoulders. His dark baggy pants and a ratty T-shirt might *look* like someone homeless, but none of that camouflaged the man's skills.

He was trained. And dangerous.

And he was pulling his punches. He could have killed her at any point, but he hadn't.

Josh moved his sights off the man's forehead. Something was going on here beyond what the casual observer would see on the surface.

Trish broke loose again and spun around. She was fast and passionate about every move. Determinations showed on her face when she rammed her foot into the back of the man's knee.

Hard enough to take him down, but not inflict damage. Not as hard as the strike should've been. Josh would bet his favorite restored Porsche on that.

Still, her attacker hadn't been expecting that move and tried to counter it by throwing his weight on his solid leg, hand flying around in a sweeping, outside block. An instinctive move.

She dodged at the same time, but the heel of his hand cuffed her hard on the chin, knocking her off her feet.

Fuck that. Josh took aim again, ready to shoot the mother if he made one wrong move.

The man yelled, "*Son of a bitch!* Zane's gonna fuckin' kill me, Trish."

She laughed.

Laughed? Had Josh heard that right?

"Ah, shit!" her attacker shouted while extending a hand to her. She took it and he pulled her up.

When she was on her feet, she righted her cap and rubbed at her chin. "Stop your bitchin', Arnie. Nothing's broken and neither one of us is going to tell Zane, right?"

He grumbled something in response.

"Besides, it's my fault for trying a new move on you."

Arnie moved over and took her chin carefully, tilting her head as he surveyed his damage. "That's gonna bruise, babe."

"Makeup will cover it."

He shook his head at her and asked in a voice dripping with disgust, "Was that *real* enough for you? I don't like you down in this area even if you do have moves now."

"I've trained in a contained environment long enough. You're the one who constantly tells me it's not the same when you're in a true threat situation, and you're right. I wanted a place that would put me on edge and test my skills. This showed me that I'm not as on top of it when I'm out of my element. I got distracted right before you attacked. And I let you surprise me. That's bad."

"Yeah, that pisses me off, too," he growled. "And I *waited* for you to be distracted, but didn't expect it, not after the way you've been training. What the hell were you looking at when you *knew* I would show up here?"

"Zane taught me that if I felt someone watching, I should pay attention to it."

"Well, that was me watching you, and you were looking in the wrong direction. And then you fell for it when I threw a screw into the other corner. Always watch your back. Always." He let out a long breath. "Ready?" Then he attacked again.

Josh holstered his weapon, watching as the two continued, with Arnie attacking and Trish fighting him off. She was sweaty in ten minutes, her shirt damp and dark hair clinging to her dirt-smudged face.

But sexy as hell. What was it about a woman who could kick a man's ass that turned Josh on? He didn't know, but there it was. Good news? He wouldn't have such a hard time faking his interest when the time came to get close to her.

Josh stayed for the next hour while Trish and Arnie finished their training session. By the time they'd cleared out, she'd managed to wash away any doubt Josh had about whether she could be a player in this case.

Colbert had been right when he'd called her activities suspicious.

Sweet, his ass.

Trish Jackson was a woman who trained for danger.

CHAPTER 6

Trish tapped her foot against the sandy-beige tile of the atrium. She forced herself to remain calm while she waited on Lead Butt–the name bestowed on the archaic, creeping elevator by the people who worked in this building.

The stalker had warned her against saying a word to Zane if Trish didn't want to end up an only child, but she couldn't avoid coming down here today.

She'd tried.

Standing here felt conspicuous, made her jumpier than walking into that warehouse where she'd met Arnie this morning.

She looked around, trying to tune in to her instincts–use what Arnie called a person's natural spidey sense–but no one strolling through the lobby paid her any attention.

The stalker could be anyone. This had to be a quick visit with Zane.

Besides, she had to finish arranging the new antiques in ReSolution so her shop would be ready for all the business she hoped the television show would drum up. Of course, that would only happen if she were *chosen* as one of two consultants for *Treasured Past,* a local program about antiques that focused on celebrity guests who were collectors. She'd made the last qualifying round and would receive instructions on her final challenge tonight at the banquet being held to promote the show.

She had plenty to do over the next couple hours, which meant she had just enough time to walk in, hand Zane one of the guest tickets she'd just picked up for tonight and walk out. He came to the task force office only when necessary. Being a pilot and owning his own charter business made it tough to catch him anywhere else during the day.

All that plus Zane had a new wife and a baby on the way.

When it came to this crazy stalker, Trish would protect her big brother, for once, after all the years he'd protected her. She didn't need Zane to fight her fights anymore, which was why she'd trained with Arnie for almost a year.

Zane had once told her his Air Force buddy was the best.

She'd convinced Arnie to help her get competent *fast*, and to not tell Zane about the accelerated training schedule so she could surprise her brother with how well she was doing. Zane would ask too many questions, like *why* she suddenly wanted to train so hard.

The defense training had been an outlet for her energy when she'd first gone sober, but after the first stalker note she'd become even more determined.

She hoped the one person *truly* surprised by her new skills would be the stalker when Trish came face to face with him and kicked his cowardly ass. Until that happened, she'd suffer cold sweats at night and train until her muscles quit on her.

What did that maniac chess enthusiast want?

The stupid note Trish had found in her car last night had instructed her to sit very still for exactly seventy-two minutes and to push the rearview mirror away from her face.

Sit. In the dark.

Without making a sound and facing forward.

Every second had been torture. She kept expecting someone to sit up in the back seat or walk up to the car and shoot her point blank or ... she'd imagined a million things, all the while gripping the handle of the fighting knife in her pocket like it was her lifeline.

When her seventy-two minutes finally ended, she'd folded over and fought off nausea, not caring if someone walked up and killed her.

She'd have welcomed the relief at that point, if not for needing to look after her brother–and her sister-in-law, now that the bastard had threatened Angel.

The approaching elevator grunted and whined as it got closer.

Trish glanced at her watch. Tackling five flights of steps was out of the question. Her strappy sandals were perfect with the mauve Jones New York suit from her friend Kellie's consignment shop, but comfort and balance were not among the shoes' attributes.

True to its name, Lead Butt descended and hit bottom with a noticeable clunk. A frazzled young man with a wrinkled white shirt and lopsided tie waited in glum silence to her left.

Trish gave him a critical once over.

Not stalker material.

And you would know this how? she asked herself. Trish glanced at him again.

When the doors opened, he pushed a handcart filled haphazardly with boxes into the left half of the elevator. As she stepped in, the delivery guy hit the tenth-floor button then he squeezed between the cart and the left side elevator wall.

She punched the fifth-floor button and moved over to the right rear corner. The young guy muttered to himself and tried to tidy up his half-ass stacked boxes. He appeared harmless. But then so had Colbert, the computer geek who had cozied up to Trish during a holiday party at Zane's office.

That scumbag had turned out to be a mole in the DEA task force.

News Trish had gotten in an email this morning from her sister-in-law.

The elevator doors almost touched in the middle when a large, suntanned hand shoved between the moving sections, forcing them to bang back and forth twice.

The steel panels groaned open.

One succulent male specimen breezed inside, glanced at the two floors already selected and moved over to the wall on Trish's left. She could smell his fresh shower.

Sleek grooming, sun-tinted blonde hair, and a strong chin. He got her vote for the next sexiest-man-of-the-year magazine award. Plenty of muscle under that button-down shirt with the cuffs rolled up casually.

Sunshine yellow suited him.

She'd seen loads of men in South Florida who fit the criteria for gorgeous, but this one took Super Stud to the limit.

And why was she ogling him when she'd sworn off men?

I haven't sworn off looking.

No vapid gaze of a model on that one. Keen, ocean-blue eyes swept over to her, taking in her suit. He seemed surprised by her clothes.

If they'd known each other in the past, that would make sense, because business suits were a far cry from what she'd worn in her Bohemian days of sandals and ankle-length cotton dresses. But they'd never met. She'd remember someone tall, tan, and delicious who oozed testosterone.

Dangerous loads of it.

Her heart rate picked up and she couldn't tell if it was a reaction to being trapped in this box with two men or standing so close to one with serious bedroom eyes.

She licked her lips and his gaze flicked to her mouth.

Stupid move. A bad memory of being trapped by a man rolled through her mind. She didn't panic, but she did clamp her lips together and consider her escape route.

The doors clanged shut.

Too late.

The elevator began a slow ascent, grinding and squeaking in protest. Just past the second floor, the infernal car screeched and jerked to a halt hard enough to bounce her back against the wall.

The wobbling stack of boxes shifted toward Trish.

Everything happened so quickly she barely had time to cringe, expecting to be pummeled.

A masculine forearm shot across her vision to her right side. His hand slapped against the wall behind her, and his body leaned in close, forming a human barrier against the tumbling cardboard mountain.

The young guy shouted, "*Shit!*"

When Trish realized she wouldn't get pounded, she expelled a sigh of relief on a burst of air. Then she lifted her gaze to find Super Stud's face barely inches from hers.

His voice came out low and sexy as he looked deep into her eyes. "Are you okay?"

She had to shake her mind back to life and find her composure.

Never look like prey. She gave the stack of boxes piled against his arm and shoulder a quick glance. "I should be asking you that."

"I'm fine. They don't weigh much."

Based on the way the young man on the other side of him was struggling to pull the boxes off her human barrier, she questioned his definition of heavy.

She inhaled a deep breath to calm her nerves.

Big mistake. Her nose should be stuck in the opposite corner, far away from the tantalizing scent simmering off him. He smelled like every woman's secret fantasy. The sultry aftershave had to cost more per ounce than her weekly grocery allotment.

Against her better judgment, she angled her face up, thinking to instruct him to step back.

Bigger mistake.

Those blue eyes twinkled down at her. "I'm Josh. And you are?"

Not supposed to be standing this close to someone so hot. Not when men were allowed *nowhere* on her radar right now. As if to go on record as being in conflict with that decision, her nipples chose that moment to tighten.

He smiled, killing off more brain cells in one second than she'd destroyed during her drinking days. He angled his head in question. "I'm only asking for a name."

Attractive, smooth-talking devils had been her downfall for years–at least part of her downfall. After one very stupid, alcohol-laced decision that almost got her killed, she'd stuck mental "Do Not Touch" sticky notes on any sexy male.

But she was no longer that woman who'd been led around by men, starving for approval and confusing lust with love. She'd raised herself from the ashes and stretched her phoenix wings, building a new life. Straightening her back, she lifted herself another inch, which brought her eye level with his chin. He lifted his head, giving her space.

"I'm Patricia," she told him. Boxes bumped and banged their way back onto the cart, reminding her that she owed Josh a thank you. "I appreciate you saving me from a box beating."

His gaze shifted with a different look, one that assessed her from head to toe with a glint of admiration. When he spoke, his voice was husky soft, just loud enough for her ears. "I have a feeling you wouldn't allow a box, or anything else, to beat you. You may be beautiful and…tiny…but you're no pushover. Are you?"

"No, I'm not." That this stranger saw what no one close to her had acknowledged struck a chord deep inside, one that she hadn't realized, until now, that she'd wanted *someone* to notice.

Silly thought. This stranger knew nothing about her.

His smile returned and blood surged through her body to every part except her brain. That had to be the reason she had yet to ask him to back up, so they weren't in so intimate a position.

Or the reason she had the ridiculous urge to know what those lips would feel like on hers.

Forget the sticky notes.

She needed a neon sign for this one.

The elevator jerked into motion and Josh moved back to the wall opposite the stack of boxes that were now under control.

The elevator doors creaked open at the fifth floor.

He stepped over and held his hand out for her to exit first, which she did. Her heart rate kicked up again when she realized he was following one step behind her.

When Trish reached the entrance for the central receiving area of the task force offices, Josh leaned over and opened the door.

Oh, great. A task force agent.

That was enough to kill any lingering hormonal overload.

If there was one thing Trish wanted no part of, it was someone who worked with her brother. She'd been through a learning curve recently and no matter how much the year of training with Arnie had taught her how to think and how to assess situations, she'd failed miserably when she'd misjudged Colbert. She'd thought he was one of the good guys and interested in her for the right reasons. That went to show how she had a long way to go, especially when it came to men.

She walked into the empty room and turned to Josh, wanting to leave this on a friendly, but final note. "Thanks again for your help." *What to say now?* Have a good day? *Lame.*

"Trish? Is that you?"

Thank goodness. Trish relaxed at the sound of Leanne Witherspoon's voice and turned toward the office door that had been ajar, but now opened wide.

The blow-your-mind beautiful daughter of a Florida senator came strutting out in stiletto heels that took her to model tall. Her black trousers were paired with a matching tailored jacket that covered ample D cups as sedately as one could with a figure like hers. Honey-blonde hair and a bubbly personality appealed to the men, but Leanne had a reputation for getting along with women as well.

Trish had heard Zane praise Leanne's intelligence and the way she managed an office full of men, taking no crap from any of them.

Stepping into the hug Leanne offered, Trish said, "How's it going, Sugar?"

"Same old, same old." When they broke the embrace, Leanne chided, "What's taken you so long to visit again?"

"I've been busier than a stump-tail cow in a fly shooing contest." Acquiring her unique inventory, managing the everyday running of her antique business, getting the word out to her growing list of wealthy customers, *and* watching for a stalker was time consuming.

Leanne's gaze moved past Trish. "Hello, Josh."

"Leanne."

"You here for a meeting?"

"Just picking up a few things." He turned to Trish and said, "Nice to meet you."

Saved from having to squash the interest she'd seen in his eyes, she should be relieved, but now that he was walking away, she had a moment of disappointment. Which was ridiculous. *And that would be why all men are off limits at this point.* What was wrong with her today? She turned back to Leanne. "If my brother's busy–"

"Oh, no, he's not. He said he was expecting you. I buzzed him when I heard you out here. Said he'd be right out. I'm glad you're here. Zane keeps bragging on you and your inventory. I've got to get down to your shop soon."

"You should do that. I'd love to show you some of my new consignments. One's a seventeenth century armoire with spectacular detail." Trish launched into a description of the cabinet.

"That sounds just like what I want for my bedroom."

Which was why Trish had mentioned it. One of the things her customers loved was that she remembered their individual tastes and wish lists. She notified them when unique pieces that were perfect fits for their needs were available.

Ironically, it was the single good result of growing up with the dysfunctional need to please every person in the world. She'd gotten extremely good at listening—at paying attention to the details about people—and it had paid off in spades when she'd finally gotten her act together and shifted that need for approval into a client services skill. Zane had told Trish about Leanne's recent move into a townhome she was furnishing with a mix of old and new. Trish had filed that away for the perfect moment.

Leanne's eyes sparkled again. "I can't wait. I'm so excited for you tonight."

"Thanks. I'm nervous just thinking about it." Trish's brain buzzed with anticipation. She had the opportunity of a lifetime. She might be the underdog of the four finalists, but that meant she was the scrapper who would not give up the coveted bone easily.

Leanne's cell phone jangled. She answered, "Witherspoon," listened a moment and said, "Sure, I'll meet you at the front desk and pick it up." Ending the call, she told Trish, "Be right back."

Leanne opened the door to the hall and voices rumbled, becoming more distinct as Leanne left and the door opened wider to the reception area. A man said, "We had to move the meeting to five. Mac's coming in."

Trish recognized that voice as belonging to Ben Trenton, Zane's best friend who worked in the research lab. He'd cut his hair micro-short since she'd seen him a few weeks ago and wore black glasses that gave the thirty-four-year-old an air of authority she'd expect of someone older.

An attractive, redheaded, fortyish woman Trish remembered from the holiday party, but couldn't name, entered ahead of Ben. No taller than Trish, the redhead wore a tailored navy business suit on her plump body. Creamy skin the color of raw sugar and striking, dark-brown Cuban eyes suggested the brassy hair might not be natural. The woman had an air of intellectual arrogance that had grated on Trish the first time they'd met.

Trish had wasted her time trying to engage, uh ... *Rhonda*– that was the woman's name–in a conversation during the party after the woman had commented on her family's aristocratic ancestry. Trish had taken that opportunity to ask about the type of family heirlooms passed down, thinking to make the conversation *about* Rhonda. But the woman had pretty much blown off Trish as though she'd only endured the conversation out of manners more than interest.

Ben caught sight of Trish and grinned. "Hey, Darlin'. How ya doin'?" He crossed the room and grabbed her in a bear hug.

She smiled, relaxing a little more. Ben was like family. "I'm doin' right fine. How's that beautiful baby?"

He released her and his eyes lit with new-daddy happiness. "He's perfect. I've got new pictures, but I don't have time to let you tell me how handsome he is right now."

"Email them and give Kerry a hug for me, Sug."

"I'll do it. I think you know Rhonda Sutton." Ben turned to Rhonda. "This is Zane's sister you might remember from the holiday party."

Rhonda offered Trish a pleasant smile. "Yes. Nice to see you again." Then she switched right back to business with Ben. "You were going to show me those files before the meeting."

"Sure thing." If Ben thought the woman was a bit abrupt, he didn't let on.

Trish cut the woman some slack. Rhonda was out of the DEA office in DC and probably had way more on her mind than chatting with Zane's little sister.

As Ben and Rhonda headed down the long hallway to the individual offices, Zane came walking up that same hallway at a fast pace. Trish took that as a good sign that he needed to get out of there soon, too.

Finally, she could hand off the ticket and get moving. "Hey, Sug."

Zane hugged her. "You look terrific, Sis."

Not that she didn't appreciate a compliment as much as the next woman, but the constant mantra from her only sibling wasn't an honest measure. It was meant to shore up her emotional state. She could waltz in wearing a filthy burlap bag and Zane's first words would still be a positive assessment. What would it take to convince him she was no longer his fragile little sister?

Zane started in on her. "You're too thin. You're not eating right, are you?"

"You just told me I look terrific. So, which is it?"

"Just take care of yourself," he grumbled instead of answering.

She laughed at her grouchy bear of a brother. "Brought your ticket."

"About tonight ..."

Trish didn't like the sound of that. "What?"

Zane scratched the back of his neck, something he did when he procrastinated. "Angel is down with a cold and–"

Trish gripped his arm. "She didn't say anything about that

in her email this morning. Is she okay? Is the baby okay?"

"They're both fine, but she's miserable and can't take any meds because of the baby. She's not getting around too easily at this point, so I need to be at home to take care of her when I get things wrapped up here. That means I can't go with you to the shindig tonight, Honey. Why don't you pass, too?"

She squeezed out a tired sigh, wishing the day would get easier. "You *have* to be kidding to think I'd miss tonight."

"I know this is important to you—"

"That's putting it mildly. This is an *unbelievable* opportunity."

"I know, Honey–"

"No, you *don't* know." She held her temper in check and glanced around, glad they were alone in the reception area, but this was not the place to argue with her brother. Stepping close to him, she dropped her voice for his ears only. "I need at least two solid years, maybe three to get my certification as an appraiser. It takes even longer to gain the respect of other people in my field. This new *Treasured Past* television show is a chance to prove that even though I may not have my certification yet, I *do* have expertise. I can't buy that kind of credibility or exposure."

That didn't even take into account the advertising package awarded the consultants that Trish would never be able to afford if she had to buy it. After having been a burden to her brother for so long, Trish would not lose this chance to prove she could stand on her own and be successful. Prove she had real skills.

Extraordinary skills.

She'd studied under the best when she'd been in her teens. She knew antiques, especially fifteenth century, and had passed every test–so far–the television group had thrown at her.

Zane's eyebrows dropped low over his eyes. "You made the final four. Tonight's just a dog and pony show, right? They'll send you the packet of instructions for the final qualifying round."

Un-freaking-believable. "In my shoes, would you expect

Angel to stay home?"

While Zane tried to come up with an answer for that–*fat chance*–Trish finished her vent. "What kind of message would I send by not even being present for the announcement at this banquet? The free PR alone for ReSolution is invaluable. *And the banquet is a fundraiser for the program's appraisal scholarship program. The producers are the decision makers.* Think they won't notice if I don't show up tonight?"

All at once, she considered another reason he might not want her to go. "Are ... are you saying you don't think I have a chance?"

He frowned harder. "Of course not. You're perfect for this. They'd *better* pick you for one of those two positions."

How could she have doubted his support? "Thanks."

"It's just that you've been running hard and pushing to make a go of the shop and now this television show ... hell." He gave her his best hangdog look. "I can't protect you every minute and I worry about you, okay? That's it in a nutshell."

Oh, no, he was pulling the worry card.

She loved her brother, but she also understood exactly how his mind worked when it came to family. He wasn't happy unless he had the women in his life tucked close where he could watch over them.

Angel was his responsibility now.

Trish was not. "For crying out loud, Sug. I can take care of myself. I would love to have you there, but I'm fine."

"I don't want you going alone."

"I'll be with Heidi and Gunter."

Zane's face took on that bulldog determination. "You said you had to go early, and they won't be there until later. You loaned your car to Bunko for the night. How're you going to get there without a car?"

She'd call a cab, but it would be a pricey ride. Hell, she didn't know, but that wasn't what worried him, and she knew it. She cut to the real issue. "I *don't* need a chaperone."

Zane's eyes filled with a look of pain like the one she remembered from when he'd found her laid up in a hospital, beaten half to death after she'd made a colossal, alcohol-driven mistake.

He said, "I know you're strong, but I still worry."

He was worried she'd drown herself in a bottle again.

She'd fought too hard for every inch of ground she'd gained back from alcohol and wouldn't give it up now. "Trust me. I need to manage these things myself. Okay?"

He hugged her, the same hug that had kept her going through the bad years, his voice gruff. "You're doing great, Sis, and I'm real proud of you, but humor me and let me send someone from the office so I can rest easy with Angel tonight."

She cursed silently, facing defeat. Trish would do anything to avoid causing Angel stress. "Fine."

People were walking up the hall behind Zane, talking in low voices, and Leanne came back into the reception area holding one of those overnight envelopes. She stepped over to Zane. "Glad you're still here. I'm sorry, but I can't go to the banquet with Trish tonight. I was really looking forward to it, but I just got a call that screwed my evening."

"Really? Damn." Zane ran his fingers through his hair.

Trish smiled, ready to grab her victory when a deep voice said, "I'm free tonight."

Zane and Trish turned around to find Josh standing close enough to have heard the last part of that conversation–the part about Zane wanting someone from the office to escort Trish. Josh added, "Sounds like a fun event."

"You don't even know what it is," Trish argued.

Josh shrugged. "I've been bored to death since I got to this town. I'm up for a diversion. You can explain it on the way there."

Trish saw Zane stiffen, his hands clench into fists. *Here we go again.* Back when her brother still lived at home and Trish was a teenager, Zane would *discourage* any boy who wanted to date her. She was not up for this right now.

Leanne stepped over and whispered something to Zane. Whatever she said eased all his tension.

Zane looked at Josh and said, "Great. Thanks."

Leanne gave Trish a conspiratorial wink.

The grin that crinkled Josh's eyes telegraphed some silent victory. As if he knew something no one else in the room knew.

Trish looked up at Zane, who had a strange grin on his face. "Who are you? I can't believe you just agreed to that. Where is my overprotective brother? Did aliens replace him with a sane pod person?"

Zane leaned down and said, "I'll explain later."

She didn't give a flying flip what he explained. She was not going anywhere with a man from this task force who turned her body into a lust machine with one smile. With everything she'd gone through to reach this point, she was not about to gamble that progress by getting anywhere near Josh, or by letting him distract her while she was working.

Not when tonight was so important.

Of course, somebody would have to explain that to her wild hormones. The ones that had been sleeping peacefully until they heard the mention of spending time with Super Stud.

Shaking her head, Trish told her brother, "Thanks, but I've got this. You are not in charge of my social *or* professional life."

Josh asked, "What time would you like me to pick you up?"

Sighing loudly for everyone's benefit, Trish said, "I appreciate the offer, but you'd just get in my way."

His eyes flickered with something dark before he shifted his wide shoulders in a shrug. "If you say so."

"I say so."

Zane started in on her, "Trish–"

She raised her hand. "Discussion over."

As she walked to the door, she heard Zane mutter something ugly and she could swear she heard Josh chuckle.

Trish let it go, feeling pretty good about asserting herself. She enjoyed the confidence boost until she reached her car and slid inside, where she froze.

A pale-gray envelope had been placed in front of her speedometer. Inside was another familiar note.

I know who you went to see today. I'll find out if you told him anything. If not, he's safe, but you still broke the rules when you visited him. Prepare to pay for that.

CHAPTER 7

The bell above Trish's head jingled when she entered ReSolution. Her eclectic gallery was located on Las Olas Boulevard, which carried new art alongside high-end antiques.

Her pride and joy.

Heavy brocade curtains draped the windows, and classical music played softly in the background, welcoming the customer to browse. Hundred-year-old Persian rugs covered the restored wood floor that had been a salvage find. She wanted to give patrons the feeling of entering an estate home.

She loved this place, but she was still so shaken by that last note from her stalker that she couldn't relax into the ambience she'd created with so much care.

Unlike most upscale antique shops, ReSolution had a unique look with select contemporary art mixed in with the classic furnishings. Individual areas of the six-thousand-square-foot shop had been decorated to replicate intimate rooms.

When she'd been in her teens, Trish had envisioned a shop of her own that looked just this way.

That was before she'd lost both parents in one day and learned soon after that she'd been nothing more than a mistake to them. Unlike the son born nine years before her, Trish had been an unexpected inconvenience and a burden.

The dark years had followed.

And those years are now behind me.

For the first time since then, she had a group of people who sincerely cared about her, a chance to prove she belonged, and that she could turn her passion into a viable business.

That she had value.

The door had barely dinged closed behind Trish when a hunched-over, craggy old woman waddled toward her, kept moving and exited without so much as a glance.

Trish suppressed the urge to stick out her tongue. She'd waited on the obstinate woman several times and should be used to the old biddy's cool disposition but getting rebuffed still bothered her.

"Hey, over here," a female voice called to her.

Trish followed the sound to where she found her best friend, Heidi Hildegard, squatted at the rear of the store next to a two-foot-square cardboard box. A compact female with bangles on her narrow wrists and a pointy nose, she had a genuine smile that made everyone want to be her friend. In one ring-covered hand Heidi held up an ultramarine-blue glass dish inlaid with brilliant dichroic slashes.

"You killed it on your last buying trip to Atlanta. This fused glass from that Peachtree City artist is exceptional." Heidi grinned, her nose and eyebrow rings sparkling along with her personality.

"Yeah, Gail Jensen's work is terrific. It's a perfect compliment to our Art Nouveau room."

Bam. Smash. Bam. Trish jumped and jerked her head up at the racket echoing from the back room.

"That's Bunko," Heidi said. You told him to start on the shelves today, remember?" She watched Trish with hawk eyes.

That's right. Bunko. Trish and Heidi had met the twenty-six-year-old man at an Alcoholics Anonymous meeting. Bunko was working hard to change his life, and Trish had been giving him part-time hours, but he came early and stayed late, more often than not.

She ran shaky fingers through her hair. *Settle down or Heidi will see through your everything-is-fine pretense.* Trish hid her nervous fingers inside folded arms. No chewing on her nails.

That left only screaming at the top of her lungs for relief.

Or Arnie's suggestion for stress relief–getting in a ring and kicking someone's butt. Primitive, but it usually worked.

Since neither was an option at this moment, Trish cleared her throat. "Right. I forgot. Too many things on my mind."

"Are you okay? Seem a little edgy lately." Business partner, friend, and housemate, Heidi also qualified as sister. They'd met when Trish had tried AA on and off during her earlier, bleak years. When Heidi emerged into the light, she'd grabbed

Trish's hand, refusing to leave her behind.

Only a real friend would have held on when Trish kept losing her grip and falling backwards. She owed her life to Heidi.

Heidi, Zane, Angel...Trish would never let one of them down again. They loved her and deserved her best.

Frowning, Heidi placed the glass dish back in the box and stood. "What gives, Trish? I heard you moving around downstairs in the wee hours last night. You having trouble sleeping?"

"I'm fine, Sug." First Zane, now Heidi, who would tell Zane the minute she sniffed a problem. And finding a note stabbed with a butcher knife on a cutting board inside her kitchen qualified as a problem.

Thankfully, the original owners of her home had built the second floor as an entirely separate living area accessed by steps up the side of the house, so Heidi was safe from Trish's unwanted intruder.

No one in their neighborhood ever complained about theft or vandalism. One reason she'd chosen the older subdivision. But now she had to put "security system" on her list of things to do and people to contact.

Or would that upset her stalker?

ReSolution had been protected from day one. A basic security system that alerted the police if someone broke in or a fire erupted. God forbid.

Heidi had that I'm-not-buying-it look.

Trish told her, "It's just been a sucky day with having to drive into Miami on top of everything else going on. And after I got there, I argued with Zane."

Heidi's eyebrows arched together like a drifting seagull. "What's bugging him?"

"He can't make the *Treasured Past* banquet tonight."

"Are you serious? Why can't he go? Doesn't he realize how big a deal this is for you?"

Always her champion. "He does, but Angel's sick with a cold and barely getting around. She needs his help. Poor thing.

She can't take anything for the cold because of the baby. And that was no problem, because I *want* him to stay home and fuss over her, but he got pissy when I refused to take someone else in his place."

"You won't be alone. I'll be there."

"I *told* him that, but you know how he is when it comes to women. He better not send someone to act like a bodyguard." Or her brother would land on the top of her butts-to-be-kicked list.

"He loves you."

Yes, but his hovering didn't make Trish's life any easier right now. Just the opposite. "He's smothering me," she grumbled, then admitted, "My fault. With my track record, I don't blame him, but–"

Heidi got all cranky. "Don't even go there, Trish. Your track record has rocked the charts for seven solid months. *Today* is what counts." Her face twisted with a scowl. "Be glad you aren't stuck with Gunter tonight. Ugh."

Trish should feel guilty since she was the one who'd convinced Heidi to take Gunter so he could attend. Gunter's antiques emporium had been top notch, in its day. But he'd been in business since the eighties and had allowed his inventory to turn into a mix of antiques and junk. She had a soft place for the grumpy guy because he'd been the first merchant to introduce himself when she opened her shop. Always interested in how she was doing, he'd made it abundantly clear he wanted to go to the banquet tonight.

Trish appreciated Heidi's sacrifice. "You'll keep Olivia off his back. She won't pay for a ticket, but with her contacts she'll worm her way into the banquet."

"Gunter only agreed to go with me because you were taking Zane. You know he'd rather be with *you*. He's *not* my idea of a hot date. We're like a match made in outer space. Olivia could have him if she was anything like you."

Barely over five feet tall, Heidi made up for what she termed her boring lack of height with spiked platinum hair, four-inch elevator heels and an exposed, pierced navel. Compared to

Gunter's reserved suits and old-world ways, she was a thrill ride, and he was the cart pulled by a donkey.

"Gunter and I are *friends*," Trish replied. She tolerated Gunter's occasional abrupt attitude because he offered business expertise. Not that she could use a lot of his outdated suggestions. But she had so few friends that she appreciated the ones she did have. "He's not a bad guy, but even if he wasn't way older than me—"

"And creepy," Heidi added.

"Reserved. Not creepy. Anyhow, I'm not getting involved with any of the retailers."

"Like being a retailer makes any difference?" Heidi's face broke into one of comic disbelief. "You turn down all men. I can understand business associates, but what's your excuse for the rest of the men in the world? And don't feed me that I'm-too-busy BS. I'd have made time for the hunk who bought the music box for his mother last week."

Clank—clank—clank.

Trish flinched at the vibrating wall behind the register. Bunko claimed he'd been a carpenter at one time. She hoped so. "I can't date yet."

"Not true. You shouldn't get *involved*. You *can* have a life and have dinner with someone."

Shaking her head, she had to make Heidi understand. "I can't trust my instincts yet, sober or otherwise. Shoot, I was interested in a guy I met today who would be the worst possible choice."

"What guy?"

"Some blond Adonis with the task force. Decked out in Armani." The setup Zane had tried to force wasn't a date, but Trish's hormones had been *way* too interested. One evening with a flashy Super Stud like that one today would be the first step in losing all her tomorrows. "You'll love this. He's the one Zane wanted to send as my escort tonight."

"No kidding? Zane was going to hook you up with some *hunk*? Did he have a lobotomy?" Then Heidi paused and waggled her eyebrows. "*But*, if Zane likes him and he's that hot ..."

"Zane sent me a text after I left telling me I was being unreasonable, because the guy was like my friend Brendan. Translation–gay. That explains why Zane was okay with it."

Trish wouldn't have bet on Josh's being gay and she still had a hard time believing it. But Zane said he'd gotten the info from Leanne. Must have been what she'd whispered to Zane in the office right after Josh offered to play escort.

"Oh." Heidi looked more disappointed than Trish had felt on hearing that news. Her friend squinted in confusion. "If that's the case, why'd you say no?"

"I didn't know he was gay at the time, but even so, something about him bugged me." Like how he'd practically melted her panties off by just leaning over her in the elevator.

"He's loony?" Heidi asked.

"No."

"Sadistic vibes?"

"No."

"Too feminine."

Not even. "No. If anything, he doesn't seem gay at all."

Bunko walked out of the back room wearing baggy jeans and an orange Hooters T-shirt. A tribal band tattoo circled the upper part of his thick left bicep. His right arm was sleeved in tattoo art. Shaggy brown hair fell in his eyes.

He asked, "Who doesn't seem gay?"

Heidi took one look at what Bunko had in his hand and huffed, "What are you doing with Trish's letter opener?"

"Needed something to open a package of screws."

She snatched it from him. "This thing is over eighty years old and it's fragile even if it is brass. It's not a freakin' carpentry tool."

Trish appreciated Heidi's concern, but the letter opener's greatest value was sentimental. The desk tool had been a gift from the woman who'd mentored Trish. One of the first professionals to see Trish's abilities when she was a teen. Poor Bunko hadn't meant any harm. "It's not like he hurt it, Sugar."

"I *was* careful with it, Trish," Bunko said in his defense and immediately turned the attention away from him with, "So *who's* not gay?"

Heidi handed the desk tool to Trish and explained, "Some hot guy Zane wants to send with Trish tonight because Zane can't make it. But she won't even consider him for a date even though he's gay."

"That's not fair," Trish argued.

"You'd go with Brendan, right?"

"Of course."

"But you won't go out with someone Brendan would date?" Heidi asked.

"That's screwed-up logic, Heidi."

Bunko squinted one eye. "You lost me with that." He said to Trish, "Didn't think you were dating until you got your one-year AA program coin."

"I'm not." Trish grinned. "See? Bunko understands."

Heidi turned on him with an exaggerated sigh and calmly said, "Those are *guidelines*. Every woman finds her way at her own pace. Trish has made amazing progress."

Bunko scrunched his shoulders in retreat, mumbling, "Excuse the hell out of me."

The only answer he got from Heidi was a smirk, then she wheeled fierce determination on Trish. "As I was saying, you're *nothing* like the woman you were eight months ago. No harm in dinner with a nice guy. I don't want you going from alcoholic to workaholic."

Trish cringed at being called any "aholic" even though it was the blunt truth. Addicts often shifted from one drug to another when trying to go sober, and those addictions sometimes included work, religion, or relationships. Her friend wasn't saying that to slam her, just being honest–a key to beating the liquid demon. Heidi loved her like a sister, but never sugarcoated the truth.

And that was why Trish trusted anything out of Heidi's mouth.

"What if I pick the wrong one?" Trish argued. *Wrong* had been the operative word in her selection of men in the past.

"You won't. I know you and I know what you're capable of and what you've had to do to get to where you are today."

Heidi's strong declaration lit a glow of pride. Trish hadn't spent a lot of time thinking about how far she'd come. Not when she'd worked to get here by making it through one day at a time.

Some days the battle was fought hourly.

Training with Arnie had been a tremendous confidence builder, but Trish still had those moments when alcohol called to her. Like this morning after her most recent stalker contact.

But she hadn't stopped by the bar she knew would be open in the early hours. She'd wanted that drink, but she'd kept the urge locked down.

Hold onto that strength. Trish told Heidi, "Thanks for the vote of confidence, Sugar, but I think I'll stick to my plan. My life's much simpler without men cluttering it up."

The doorbell dinged.

Heidi and Bunko looked past Trish toward the front of the store.

Heidi's eyes rounded in surprise. Bunko squinted darkly at the new customer, then he caught Heidi's reaction and frowned.

That should have been enough warning, but Trish still wasn't prepared to turn around and find Josh–she didn't even know his last name–standing inside ReSolution.

She did not want to face him again. Not after refusing his offer to escort her tonight.

Did that stop him from walking toward her? No. "I can't believe he's here."

"Any chance that's the Adonis from Zane's office?" Heidi asked in a soft voice.

"That's him."

Heidi whispered, "You turned *that* down?"

"Yes."

Bunko snickered. "He's gay."

Trish said under her breath, "Are you sure?"

Heidi made a disgusted noise. "No, he's *not*. That's what all guys say about men who could be Chippendale dancers."

"They're all gay, too," Bunko said, dead serious.

"*Some* gay men are bisexual," Heidi murmured.

Trish hadn't considered that. "Do you think–"

"Who knows," Heidi answered with a sigh. "But that means there's hope."

Bunko emitted a growling noise. "Women."

Josh stopped several feet short of the trio. "Can we talk, Trish?"

"I'm really busy, *Mr....*"

"Robertson, but you can call me Josh."

"And you can call me Patricia."

That evidently amused him, but he continued in a professional tone. "Won't take but a few minutes, *Patricia.*" His gaze swept an admiring glance around the room. "Nice shop you have. Quality selection."

She didn't know what to do with him yet and couldn't get herself to think of him as Mr. Robertson when the name Josh had imprinted on her brain as *Gorgeous Super Stud* along with the smell of his cologne. But he didn't need to know that. To buy a moment, she dug up a cheerful voice and offered, "Why don't you take a look around and I'll be with you in a bit."

His gaze whipped back to her and hung there, clearly assessing her offer before he said, "You won't run out the back door the minute I turn around, will you?"

"Run? From a man? No."

He nodded with approval. "Sneaking out doesn't fit the woman your brother spent twenty minutes telling me about after you *rushed* out of the office."

Zane had bent Super Stud's ear about her, really? This was not going to end the way she hoped. "*What*, exactly, did my brother tell you?"

"He bragged about how you're a savvy businesswoman who faces challenges head on." Josh paused, letting that declaration settle in the silence.

I'd rather beat my thumb with a hammer than make my brother look bad. Fine, she'd deal with Josh, but on her terms.

Trish told Bunko, "Please show *Mr.* Robertson the shop and answer any questions he has."

Bunko nodded, "You got it, boss."

Josh gave a long, drawn-out sigh clearly for her benefit.

As the two men strolled off, Bunko asked Josh in a conspiratorial voice that carried, "Are you bisexual?"

Super Stud shot back, "Hell *no.*"

"Just checking." Bunko slowed his steps and swung around to wink at Heidi then caught up to Josh and started pointing out prime pieces.

Trish closed her eyes. She prayed to be struck by lightning and fried to a crisp. That was the only way she could exit with any dignity. "I can't believe Bunko did that."

"That's our Bunko." Heidi shook her head. "Not one to mince his words or beat around the bush. What a shame about the Adonis."

"No kidding." Trish caught herself before she licked her lips at the to-die-for view of Josh walking away. His shirt pulled taut across those broad shoulders, which looked even wider from the back. Her gaze kept traveling down to a great butt and long legs she'd bet were just as muscular as the rest of him. She ran her hand along her neck and collarbone where her skin suddenly felt hot.

Josh was gay? Life was not fair.

With her attention locked on the men walking around, Heidi said, "Brendan's available. You'll make his year, maybe even his millennium, if you introduce him to that hunk."

Trish blew out a disgusted breath. "There is that."

She should be happy about telling Brendan she had a smokin' blind date for him. And she would be. She'd be *elated* about that, once she got over this unreasonable sense of disappointment, which made no sense if she didn't want to go out with Josh in the first place.

And that was at the heart of the lie.

She *did* want to go out with him. She'd spent what felt like forever content to be alone ... until now. Maybe Heidi was right about dating again. Just not with someone who sent her hormones into a power spin cycle.

The good news? She'd be safe from making a mistake tonight because she'd be in the middle of five hundred people.

With Josh, who was gay.

Her body snorted at that, refusing to hear any input from her brain.

One thing was clear. The time had come for her to cowgirl up and accept the inevitable. "I'm stuck with him tonight, aren't I?"

"Yep." Heidi nodded, her earrings jangling when she turned to Trish. "Unless you want to have Zane so stressed out that he'll make Angel crazy. Or have you changed your mind about loaning Bunko your car?"

"No, I want Bunko to make his AA meeting tonight, and I won't do that to Angel for anything. Might as well get this over with and go throw in the towel." She had to be at the banquet early and Heidi had to stay to close the shop, which was why Trish had planned on Zane being her ride. Stalling, she asked, "Anything come up today or calls I need to know about?"

"Nothing pressing. Oh, before I forget." Heidi stuck her hand in the back pocket of ragged jeans that hung low on her curvy hips. "I found an envelope addressed to you under the door this morning."

Trish reached out to take it without looking, because the men were rounding a corner and Josh paused to stare at her. He lifted an eyebrow, questioning how long she was going to play this game.

Men. "I'll go rescue Bunko so he can finish his work," she told Heidi, then headed to deal with her...escort.

Bunko took note immediately, said something to Josh. As Bunko passed Trish on his way to the rear of the store, he mouthed the words, *told you.*

The door jingled and a middle-aged couple entered. Heidi scooted to the front and greeted them, then guided the couple away from Trish.

That left her to deal with Super Stud.

She still couldn't figure out his interest in taking her to the banquet, especially if she wasn't his flavor for a date. "Why are you here?"

"I'm here to discuss tonight. Are you afraid of me?"

She hadn't expected that. "No. Should I be?"

"No. So what reason could you possibly have for refusing to accept my offer to join you tonight?"

For one thing, just being seen with the walking definition of a hot guy would stir up talk about the old Trish who'd been partying with a few just like him around South Beach last year.

Okay, that was bullshit. Nobody cared.

Or more importantly, *she* shouldn't care what those people thought. She had no reason for refusing Josh, not one she could share anyway, so she gave the only lie she could come up with on short notice. "I'll be focused on other things besides a guest. I just didn't want to inconvenience you."

His lips curved with a smile so sexy she had to keep telling herself it had nothing to do with her, just part of the bad boy packaging. Those blue eyes captured her, pushing everything else from view. His deep voice eased out rich as warm whiskey. "Why would it inconvenience me to spend the evening with a pretty woman?"

She she no longer fell for lines. That one had her doubting her conviction. If he kept looking at her with that hot gaze, she'd go up in flames any minute now. Now would be great for a sound-proof office where she could scream at her ridiculous thoughts. Brendan teased her all the time and women openly drooled when he walked through a room.

She'd never been attracted to Brendan. Enough of this hormonal insanity.

Drawing a deep breath, she had control of her mind again and smiled politely at Josh. "In that case, I accept, and I appreciate your company."

See? She could be gracious.

He nodded and appeared pleased as if he'd finally closed a deal. Maybe he wanted to make points with tight-knit group in Zane's office. "I'll need your address to pick you up."

True, but the devil in her didn't care for the hint of victory once again sliding into his eyes. Did he now think he had the upper hand? "I don't know if that's a good idea. You could be a serial killer."

Josh glanced up at the ceiling in a show of strained patience then lowered his gaze back to her. "Negotiating peace talks between two hostile countries is easier than making plans with you."

For some reason, she enjoyed poking at him. Smiling, she pulled Zane's ticket out of her pocket and handed it to him. "Then you should be glad you only have to endure *one* negotiation."

She'd intended to follow up with her street address then bid him goodbye, which might have happened if he hadn't slipped the ticket into his pocket then taken a step toward her.

Surprised, she backed up and bumped into the hard rear wall of her newly acquired seventeenth century armoire that stood two feet taller than her. Her heart started thumping with the hard beat of a bongo drum.

Josh stopped just inside her personal space–way too close for her peace of mind–and studied her quietly. His blue eyes televised confusion and a bit of disappointment. "Thought you said you weren't afraid of me."

Oh, I'm not afraid of you, Sugar, but I'm terrified by the way my body keeps breaking out pheromones for yours. She put steel in her voice when she argued, "I'm *not*."

His sigh brushed gently across her senses as if he knew she'd lied, but not why. "You know, you might just enjoy yourself tonight if you'd let go of whatever preconceived notions you have about me. I *can* be a lot of fun, given a chance."

Her breasts noticed how close he was and perked up to let him know he'd gotten *their* attention. *They* wanted fun. She inhaled, and his brisk cologne conjured thoughts of what that would smell like on hot skin.

Heat curled in her lower body, breathing life into parts she could not allow to run free.

She put a hand up on his chest. Oh, Mama, was he rock solid

under that shirt or what? Brendan turned heads wherever he went, but Trish had never been attracted to *him* like this. "I have no preconceived notions. But this evening is not about fun for me. It's work. And speaking of work, I really need to get some done before I go home to dress."

Josh covered her hand with his much larger one. "Your address."

His touch might as well have been a topical drug because she rattled off her street address without thinking about it twice and mumbled, "Pick me up at five."

"I'll be there." He gave her fingers a little squeeze then released her and walked away.

She had to stand there until he left.

It took that long for her to trust her legs again. Good grief. What was wrong with her, getting all hot and bothered over a man who was probably laughing his backend off over the mind games he'd just played on her because her initial rejection had pissed him off.

Something Brendan would do, just to prove a point.

Damn it.

People moved into Trish's peripheral view. Heidi gave the couple a business card and a toothy grin as she finished telling them something on their way out the door.

Banging started up again in the back room.

Trish let out the breath she'd been straining to hold. She lifted her hand to brush hair off her brow and realized she still held the envelope Heidi had given her.

When she pulled it into view, a chill crept through her.

The banging continued, rattling the wall. A crash in the storage area sounded as though a picture frame had shattered against the concrete floor.

"Bunko, hey!" Heidi charged toward the back.

Trish ignored the damage and racket. She held another dove-gray envelope in her trembling hands. Fear could be a lethal weapon when wielded properly, something the demented note writer understood very well.

She struggled to open the flap and pulled out the note.

I'll see you tonight. I'll be the one wearing the black lace panties from the top drawer of your oak lingerie chest. Watch for my next move.

CHAPTER 8

Chatton waited for the two international predators seated with her in the room to end their pissing contest and get around to what they wanted from her. They must need her MI6 skills, or she wouldn't have been included in this meeting. It wasn't as though she'd been *invited* to join the three-member Czarion group.

She'd wormed her way in by first discovering these two, and second, by dangling something they wanted in front of them, just out of their reach.

A rare artifact that played into their fanatical beliefs.

Upon casual observation, neither man would be considered physically threatening, but they were both deadly. They each held influential positions in powerful countries and either one had the ability to spark an international conflict in the world theater.

They often underestimated her, which she found amusing, but that was to her benefit, and she *never* underestimated an opponent.

Wayan currently had the floor. Figuratively, since it wasn't a particularly stable surface. He sat on her right, inside the main salon of a ninety-foot yacht floating in the Atlantic Ocean, surrounded by black on a moonless night. Baby-faced and delicate in appearance for someone forty-four, Wayan easily disarmed those unaware of his position within the Chinese Party Chief's inner circle.

He reminded Chatton of the small, saw-scaled viper from Asia.

Inconspicuous and always poised for a deadly strike.

Wayan massaged his chin, a subtle sign of irritation from a man who moved very little in these meetings. "This was not what we agreed on, General. You assured High Vision that we would create a US gateway in Florida. This presents a problem."

"No, it's not a problem," The General rumbled. He leaned his large body on the arm of the sofa, probably to ease his back pain. With that exception, he was still fit at forty-nine, sporting a military haircut and muscular forearms. Coffee-brown skin covered the rigid planes of his clean-shaven face.

"You must enlighten me," Wayan persisted.

"We created a safe route for four High Vision shipments to show them how easy it *can* be to smuggle their designer drugs into the US. Now they know how quickly that safe zone can go away."

Actually, The General–who was not a general, but a high-ranking official in the US Pentagon–had told High Vision, an international pharmaceutical organization, that *Czarion* would secure an open path for moving contraband through south Florida. The Czarion group was comprised of Chatton, The General, and Wayan.

Wayan toyed with his thin mustache, appearing unconvinced. "Are you saying the loss of their last shipment was an *intentional* action?"

"No. We lost an asset, plain and simple. He's been dealt with. I had a team take out the armed transport they used to move him."

Wayan spoke in precise English, a second language for him. "Forgive me if I do not share your positive outlook, General. This sounds as though we have greater problems in Florida." The little guy tapped his steepled hands. "High Vision's agreement to assist with the shipment of our test unit was predicated on their product's safe passage through Florida. Miami, to be specific."

That was as close as Wayan ever sounded to getting his knickers in a wad. Chatton had met with these two enough to know.

She also knew that she could pull details out of a mute captive faster than The General got around to making a point. It didn't seem to bother Wayan, who apparently had the patience to wait for each word to be carved by hand.

The General growled something to himself. "High Vision will hold up their end. I still have a plant inside the task force. An Orion Hunter."

Wayan nodded, looking impressed that The General had a member of that ancient order inside a US law enforcement agency.

He would be. Wayan believed in that crap about the Orion Hunters to the point of obsession.

The General continued his explanation in a tone loaded with arrogance. "I used the loss of their product to our advantage. High Vision now realizes our reach and power. That we can open this channel and shut it down just as easily. Have no worries. I informed them that we possess evidence implicating their Paris laboratories and US holdings, and that said evidence can land in the wrong hands if they so much as *hesitate* in assisting with this shipment for us." The General amended, "Shipment for you, Wayan."

Wayan's thin black eyebrows drew together over his almond-shaped eyes. "Then you guarantee my unit will have safe passage and will be tested?"

Making a weary sound, the General said, "That's where Chatton comes in."

Wayan nodded, appeased for the moment.

Chatton was over allowing these two to continue their cryptic discussion of "the unit." She told The General, "You speak as though it's a foregone conclusion that I'll help with a project you won't even discuss in front of me."

A wise man would take note of the challenge in her voice and cease his dancing around.

The General was just such a man. "Wayan needs three boxes inserted into a High Vision shipment after materials from Paris are loaded. But there can be no link to China or the US on this shipment, only to High Vision. High Vision has been told when to have their loaded container at the shipyard and that no one in their company in Paris or the US can touch it again until we contact them."

Chatton cut in. "What's *in* these three boxes?"

Wayan answered her. "That is not to be discussed."

"With me?" She paused, then flicked a don't-care look at Wayan. "In that case, good luck with your endeavor. I see no reason to get involved."

He was silent for a long time then angled his head to one side. "We allowed you to join with us because you have one of the Orion artifacts, but you have yet to prove your use to either of us."

What he meant was that she'd given them an ultimatum to either bring her into their tight little Czarion group or they'd never see the actual piece. She'd provided proof that she possessed one of five artifacts these two believed would reveal the Orion Legacy, details of a Final Conflict.

Oh, sure. Five artifacts from different countries would bring about the end of the world.

Wayan could spin a convincing yarn of prophecies that had come to fruition already over many centuries. He could also mesmerize a roomful of dignitaries while speaking of peace and honor.

Charismatic and fanatical. Scary combination.

Chatton found their belief in intangible forces and supernatural conspiracy amusing but would never let on. The way she saw it, the only way there could be a Final Conflict was if someone triggered that conflict. Something fanatics in powerful positions–like these two–could do.

Someone had to keep an eye on the world's future and protect her beloved UK.

Wayan must have taken Chatton's silence as still waiting for motivation. "Do you not realize that at some point *you* will need something, and we will bring *our* resources to bear for you?"

"Now that you mention it, there is something I want." She added, "General."

The General stiffened. "This is Wayan's deal."

"But he just explained how we all scratch each other's backs at some point."

Wayan interjected, "Are you not the least bit curious as to what she wants, General?"

The General grunted in her direction. "What is it?"

She had him. "First, finish explaining what you need from me."

"There will be three sealed boxes, ranging in size from six inches square to as long as your forearm. Don't try any of your secret agent tricks to find out what's in the boxes. A deadly toxin is released if anyone tries to open them out of sequence."

Lovely. "You don't survive long in my business if you can't keep your curiosity in check."

He nodded and shifted his bulk again, grimacing. "As I said, there is to be no connection to the US or Asia. The boxes will have labels and packing identical to the rest of the High Vision shipment. You're to insert those three packages into their container *after* it has been secured on the ship."

Did he think she was Houdini or was this some ridiculous test to determine her use to the group?

Wayan's eye twitched. An *almost* smile touched his lips.

Laughing at her? And here she'd given him credit for better survival instincts.

"Now for what you have to do," she said, letting them know by the way she said it that this was not negotiable. "I want the name of the person who killed a British subject while he was skiing in Aspen, Colorado on February eighteenth this year."

"Skiing accident?"

"Shooting."

The General scrunched his black eyebrows together. "If the Colorado authorities haven't found the killer, I'm not going to have a name either."

"I don't care what they have. That's my price."

"Who was this guy?"

"A British diplomat. To protect his identity, he was in the States under pretense of being on vacation. He was actually there to negotiate terms with a US weapons manufacturer for setting up a plant in the UK."

The General's eyebrows jumped at that. "What's his

name?"

"Edward Abbot." His real name had been Edward Abbot Macintosh. Her father's cousin. She intended to use her association with these two to find out who had been systematically killing members of Clan Macintosh, her father's family, since the fifteenth century.

To find the person who murdered her parents.

"What's your interest in this diplomat or his killer?" The General asked.

Chatton smiled sweetly. "I'll show you mine if you show me yours."

The General exchanged a chilling expression with Wayan, then looked at her.

That's right, hardass. She wasn't sharing her secrets if Wayan and The General were going to stay tightlipped on Wayan's "unit."

Leaning forward, The General pushed down against the sofa and stood up. He stretched his back. "Complete this mission successfully and I'll hand you the name."

Wayan leaned forward to open his briefcase that sat on the floor next to his feet. Black shoes with a mirror polish. He retrieved a manila folder and handed it to her. "You will find all the information you need regarding the products High Vision is shipping, the designated cargo ship, a card with a coded message that you will use when you call to arrange a meet point to receive the three cartons. You are to call the phone number provided four hours prior to the ship's departure."

You bloody bastard. A four-hour window to pick up *and* insert the boxes? She'd think this was a trap if she weren't in possession of the artifact these two wanted. She'd made it very clear that no one she knew had any idea where each half of the artifact–a broken Celtic cross–was hidden.

And that would be an issue only if they figured out her true identity. Not a bloody chance in hell of that.

Wayan continued, "The shipment must arrive by–"

"I can read." She stood. "If the cargo ship arrives on time, your boxes will be on time, but I want that name the minute you have confirmation I'm no longer in the States...or I will find whatever is in those boxes."

A tiny muscle tensed near Wayan's left eye. "If that ship does not arrive on schedule or those boxes are not received, the name you want from The General will *never* be available."

This was the dangerous side of Wayan who wanted her to know he had the power to prevent her from ever getting that name. Not because The General was a pushover. No, Wayan and The General would never have teamed up if they didn't know each other's secrets.

But she was no pushover either and breathing the same air as these two was enough to bring out her deadly side as well. Time to go before she forgot why she put up with these two. "Wasting my time with all these ifs. I have your terms. You have mine. Anything else is superfluous."

Chatton ignored Wayan for a moment and opened the folder. The boxes were in Paris. She was floating in the ocean a hundred miles away from the closest airport. They'd all arrived by powerboats protected by a flotilla of armed escorts.

Even if she reached Paris in time and managed to insert those boxes on a container already on the ship, the shipping line carrying that container had a spotty track record for arriving on schedule. Pointing out that she had no control over the operation of a cargo ship would only underscore his arrogance right now.

She closed the folder.

Wayan lifted his chin. "Once the container clears customs in Miami, you must ensure that the correct person takes possession of these three boxes."

"And if not?" She did like to tweak their noses.

The shrug he made was so dainty. "Blood will flow either way."

Would she be aiding a terrorist plot?

What was in those boxes?

Sounded too small to be a weapon of mass destruction, but it could be components of one, or something else equally deadly. Perhaps a chemical agent or biochemical warfare. She believed Wayan's threat.

She didn't have a plan for how to pull this off, yet, but she'd better get one–she glanced down at the shipping schedule–soon. Lifting her head, she looked out the window at the lights of a steady stream of gunboats circling the yacht like steel sharks, three of those boats filled with her people. She told Wayan and The General, "Alert your security details that I'm calling in my helicopter."

CHAPTER 9

Josh parked on the side driveway of Trish Jackson's modest frame home, a two-story structure in a quiet neighborhood that appeared to have been developed seventy years ago. A standout in South Florida where one-level concrete block structures from the fifties and sixties were so prevalent.

At the back corner of the house, a stairway ran up the side to a porch, the entrance to a second living space. Trish's file indicated that her friend Heidi lived here too, so that must be her place.

Josh headed up the walkway, past blooming flowers, to the front door. He could imagine Trish down on her knees, digging in the dirt, and planting. Enjoying herself. Maybe even smiling like she had in the file photo.

Getting a woman to smile was step one in getting closer to her. An easy step any man could accomplish if he understood women at all.

But he hadn't managed it yet with Trish … make that *Patricia.*

He couldn't be that out of practice, right? He reached the three steps leading to her front door, where two concrete urns overflowed with red geraniums. This didn't look like the home of someone willing to unleash deadly drugs on the world, but plenty of dangerous criminals lived in quaint homes.

He knocked on the door, expecting Trish to open it, polite, but rigid again.

Not for the door to fly open with her hiding behind it and saying, "Hurry up and come in. My dress is falling off."

He took in her bare neck and shoulders covered in soft skin that sent his mind chasing the idea of her completely naked. His control slipped a notch until she hissed, *"Jo-osh!"*

She had her hand pressed against the top of silvery material covering her breasts. Not naked.

"Come *on,*" she urged. "I'm in a hurry."

Stepping inside, Josh waited as she gave the door a shove. The rest of her was covered in a shimmering silver gown...that would look great pooled at her feet.

He silently shook himself out of horndog mode and said, "What's wrong?"

"The zipper is caught, and I can't fix it." She turned around and backed up to him.

Her entire back, down to her waist, was exposed.

Heat swirled around the collar of his tux, which was ridiculous. It was just a back. A beautiful sweep of sleek, in-shape, sexy back.

Her fingers clutched the zipper that had stopped just above a sweet pair of buns. She called over her shoulder, "Can you fix it or not?"

Blowing out a breath, he reached for the two sides of her dress. "Let me have it so I can see what's wrong."

There was only one way to fix it and that was to unzip from where the teeth had caught a piece of the material, then rezip. That required sliding one hand between the zipper and her back, just above her ass, so that he could hold the two halves together and work the zipper down with his other hand.

His knuckles brushed skin that was warm and smooth as thick cream. He gave a tug, and the zipper came loose, sliding down quickly to the lacy edge of pink panties.

The spit dried up in his mouth

She tensed and made a little shivery sound.

Zero to hard in three seconds.

"Can you, uh, get it up?" she asked, breathless.

Is the Pope Catholic? If he got any more *up* at this point, they'd *both* know how much he liked pink lingerie. He said, a little terse, "Be still."

"It's hard not to move," she muttered.

Just keep saying things to threaten my control. He hadn't unzipped a woman's dress in a long while and fought the battle not to finish this job and touch the rest of all that skin.

He eased the zipper pull back up slowly to prevent snagging the material again.

By the time he had the dress zipped at her lower back and the tiny hook clasp latched, Trish's shoulders were moving up and down with quick breaths. Meaning she wasn't as indifferent to him as she'd tried to appear at her shop today.

For the first time all day, Josh smiled. This was more like it. He leaned down close to her ear and whispered, "Need help with anything else?"

"No." She practically jumped away and spun around, facing him. Her cheeks heated with two flags of red. Embarrassed. "Thanks for fixing that." She seemed to finally notice him. "You look...nice."

Her eyes said she liked nice. A lot.

See, Sabrina? I've got this just fine. "Happy to oblige any time. And you look amazing."

She gave him an almost smile, something reserved and polite that a person used in mixed company or at family gatherings with inlaws. "Thanks. I'm ready to go."

Reserved meant she'd mentally backed away from him again.

He had his work cut out tonight, but he was up for the task now that he'd seen her respond to his touch. There would be no walking away from her tonight until he'd torn down some of her walls and gotten inside her defenses.

He would accept nothing less than full surrender.

CHAPTER 10

Trish glanced over at the side of the stage again. Josh was still there even though she'd suggested he meander around the banquet area and get something to eat and drink before the masses descended on this event.

"State your name and say *test* a couple of times." Harry Hanover, the emcee for this event, directed Trish to the center of the stage.

She moved to the microphone and did as he asked, squinting as she got used to the blazing lights. Her gaze moved across the roomful of hobnobbers pretending to have meaningful conversations with television celebrities, Miami's crème de la crème.

Trish finished her mic check and the TV station cameraman leaned out from behind his setup at the center of the room and gave thumbs up. Once the emcee told her she was set, Trish walked off the stage and up to Josh. "That's it for now."

"This is quite a production." He looked down at her hands that were clutched in front of her. "Nervous?"

She wanted to sound chic and confident, to tell him she wasn't nervous, but he reached for her hands, lifted them to his lips and brushed a kiss across the knuckles of each one.

Don't sigh. Hard not to when faced with a man whose touch sent electricity sparking along her skin.

She started to pull her hands back until he lifted his head and smiled at her, saying, "You're going to do great."

Sighing was back on the front burner. He had a great smile, an endearing one that made her want to drop her defenses. He was trying to get through to her. Trying hard.

But why? She couldn't help her suspicious mind. She'd been too quick to trust in the past. Everything about Josh was inviting. Easy. Too much so.

She yanked her stray thoughts back under control and eased her hands from his grasp. "Thanks. I am nervous, but I believe

I've got just as good a chance as the others." *I have to keep telling myself that.* "Sounds like there's a lot of people out there. We should probably mingle."

Josh moved aside to allow her to go first, but the minute she stepped away he put his palm against her lower back, and she had to clench her teeth to keep from gasping at the feel of his hand on her skin. Rather than tell him not to touch her, she arched her back a little to create space.

He adjusted, maintaining the contact.

She should tell him to move his hand, but she was afraid her mouth would end up saying she wanted him to move it inside her dress.

When they reached the banquet area, piano tunes twirled through the artfully lit room of candlelight and ice sculptures. A low buzz of conversation built where people in this business clustered in pockets.

Josh snagged a server and asked Trish, "What would you like?"

"Nothing right now." She never allowed anyone to bring her a drink, but didn't want to go into that with Josh. She had to do some moving and shaking, preferably without Gorgeous attached to her back, distracting her. Trish looked around absently. "I'm going to the powder room, and I see a couple people I'm going to speak to on the way so just enjoy yourself and I'll find you. Okay?"

His fingers brushed along her cheek then down her neck. "I'll be right here when you return."

She hadn't been touched in a long time, not like this. It took all the discipline she could muster not to move into his touch. She had to get away from him long enough to regroup. "You're free to move around and meet people, you know. You don't have to be with me every minute."

His fingers touched her chin and tilted it up until she had to face his unyielding gaze. "I'm not interested in meeting anyone else tonight."

It wasn't what he said so much as the way he said it, in a voice that climbed inside her and settled in for the night. Her insides squirmed and twisted around, wanting to make room for him. She didn't understand this strange reaction to Josh.

When his fingers drifted down her neck to her shoulder, she finally said, "Can't believe this."

"What?"

"You. Us."

His fingers paused and he stared at her, thoughts gathering behind his gaze until he lowered his hand. "Thought you had to visit the ladies room."

He pulled back from her so quickly she was stunned, wondering what she'd said to cause the change, but it allowed her to regain her balance. She shook herself out of the mesmerizing stupor his touch had put her in and backed away. "Seriously. Go mingle. I've got work to do, so I'll find you later."

But not until I have to sit down at the table with you, she added silently.

Somewhere that she wouldn't be able to fall under whatever spell had her wanting Josh Robertson.

———*m*———

Watching Trish head across the room, slowing to speak to a distinguished couple on her way, Josh tried to shake off the moment of déjà vu that gripped him. Trish had no way of knowing how her words had hit him like a splash of cold water.

Chelsea had said similar words to him the first night they'd met away from work. She'd said, "Hard to believe."

He'd said, "What?"

"You. Us."

But Chelsea had laughed and jumped in that night with both feet, unconcerned about becoming intimate with an operative. She'd lived for the moment, not caring what tomorrow brought. That's what had convinced him they could carve out a place in time that was theirs. Somewhere he could go and not feel alone.

He'd been a fool to pursue a fool's dream with her. But Chelsea had known exactly who he was and how he operated.

Trish *didn't* know him. Didn't know the danger she danced near.

Doesn't matter. Couldn't matter. She might be the person helping drug runners.

But what if she wasn't? What if she really was what she seemed–a strong, gifted woman who had built her world back from the pit of alcoholism and was as sweet as she appeared?

This was not the time for his conscience to rear its head.

His job was to find out what she knew about Zane possibly being the DEA traitor. Teens were dying from Spa Zing and Len Rikker was at large somewhere here in Miami. Trish might even be in contact with him.

Josh had to get close enough to find answers. He was on track with Trish and knew what to do. He'd gotten through her walls and knew how to get through them again. And keep getting through them until they crumbled. Touching was necessary and often.

Good thing that was easy for him because he *liked* touching Trish. Maybe liked it a little too much, truth told, but he couldn't let up, not when he was clearly making headway. He needed to keep his head about him though. He'd almost fallen into her gaze when she'd spoken those words and emotion had flickered in her eyes.

Think like the operative you are. Cold. Distant. Objective.

Damn straight. When a server stopped by, Josh ordered a club soda and watched Trish until she disappeared through double doors to the hallway that led to the ladies' powder room.

How long would she be gone? She would circle around this crowd to speak to people without him at her side. Was she meeting someone?

What had she said back at the task force offices?

You'll be in my way.

In her way for what? Even though he'd gotten to her just now, she'd tried to get rid of him again. Why?

Charming women had never been a problem and Josh had learned early on that he wasn't an ugly guy. Women liked his looks. Liked his attention. In fact, women he'd targeted on missions in the past had dragged him around the room, showing him off like a fashion accessory.

But he was missing something with Trish. Sabrina had hit too close to the truth when she'd insinuated that he hadn't been with a woman in a while. Once he'd healed from the gunshot wound, he'd gone off alone to shake the garbage out of his head. Sabrina had dragged him back ten months ago, but he still had clutter banging around upstairs.

That didn't mean he'd forgotten anything about women, dammit.

Good thing he had a tough ego.

Because until just now, Trish had done her best to stomp on it. Didn't she trust her own brother? Evidently not since she'd been repeatedly shooting Josh down like a low-flying goose. And just when he'd had her on the line, about to set the hook, the mental garbage had crashed into him again and he'd backed off.

Maybe Sabrina was right. Maybe your heart's not in it anymore.

But then, Sabrina had also suggested sending Nick in Josh's place. *Fuck that.* Josh accepted the glass of soda when the server returned but wished for a belt of scotch. No alcohol tonight. He was about to lay siege to Miss Jackson's emotional fortress and drinking alcohol would be an unwise tactical move around someone recently out of rehab.

"Where's your date, or did she stand you up?" Ryder said as he stepped around Josh and turned to face him, grinning.

Josh said nothing, keeping his thought to himself. *Sending the FNG down to bust my balls is going to cost you at some point, Sabrina.*

"That's some tuxedo," Ryder continued, not paying any attention to Josh's scowl. "Not a rent-a-tux kinda guy, are you?" Ryder wore a decent off-the-rack brand that fit reasonably well on his six-foot frame, doing an acceptable job of hiding the man's bulk. And his weapon.

Josh supposed some women found Ryder's intentional five o-clock shadow, Colgate smile and not-really-styled, sandy-brown hair attractive. Ignoring the FNG's irritating questions, Josh asked, "What're you doing here?"

"Like you. I'm on the clock."

"Where'd you get a ticket?"

"Sabrina. She thought you might like company."

No, she didn't. But Josh wouldn't argue a moot point when he had more pressing things on his mind, like figuring out how to get past Trish's mile-high walls and determining if she had any information on Zane's activities.

Or if she was helping Zane.

Josh waited as a server passed by before he spoke again. "Where've you been today?"

Watching their perimeter as well, Ryder dropped his voice. "Followed Zane since early this morning until he settled at the task force office. After you left there, I went in to introduce myself to Zane as a DEA field operative from Boston in for training."

"Thought you were coming in as FBI."

"Sabrina wanted me to get inside Zane's operation and thought this would be the fastest way."

Thanks for the vote of no confidence, Sabrina. You really don't think I can get what we need out of Zane's sister, do you? It still stung to know that Sabrina had been shifting him to easy work and he'd never clued in.

Shit. She wanted Len Rikker just as much as Josh, and dammit, she was right about one thing. Josh couldn't watch everybody in the office while he focused on the women in Zane's life.

Much as he'd like for the FNG to vanish on the spot, he needed the guy, and he'd share a beer with Satan if it meant getting a lead on the DEA mole. "Are you in with Zane?"

Ryder took a sip of his drink. "Looks like it. I spent some time with him and asked a lot of questions, but I didn't ask him specifics about how his informant division works."

Josh had spent more than three months embedded in the office and had explored every corner of how they ran their ops. He could hold out and let the FNG figure it out for himself.

Or he could get over himself, suck it up and be a team player, which is what Sabrina expected. What she needed from him if he was going to help her build her business. If he was going to convince her he could still be a viable part of their tight-knit unit.

He swirled the drink in his glass, staring into the bubbles and ice cubes like it was a crystal ball. *Screw it.*

Josh turned to the FNG. "DEA pilots fly private cargo charters for Black Jack Airlines, which Zane operates. The actual office for Black Jack Airlines is at Sunshine Airfield. Zane has a dispatcher-manager on site. He comes and goes as a pilot, managing behind the scenes, which means he keeps no set schedule at the task force offices either."

He took a sip of his drink that was sadly lacking in alcohol content and waited for the FNG to process the information.

Winking at a young woman strolling by, Ryder took a drink and said, "I got the scoop on the new courier cover operation he's setting up."

Josh raised an eyebrow, which FNG apparently took as the signal to spill.

"Zane has five vans that look like hell," he said, "but he says they'll run like scalded piss ants. They all have hidden GPS tracking. The DEA figured out similar vans were stolen in a two-mile area down south of the city in Kendall right before each of the last High Vision contraband deals went down. The vans were found after the missed busts. Torched."

A pattern. That was a break. "Who knows about this?"

"Zane, Ben, Vance, *our* boss Macpherson and now me. I'm going to be driving a van for him. The minute we get word of another High Vision shipment coming in, I'll find a place to park in the steal zone and abandon the van."

"You find out anything else?"

Ryder's gaze snuck sideways, clearly scoping out more female scenery. His eyes were bright with humor when they came back to Josh. "Only that you're batting zero with Zane's sister." Ryder scratched his jaw. "Maybe I should take a crack at her. Saw the picture of Patricia in the files. She's cute."

Josh sent a warning glare at Ryder. Just in case the loudmouth didn't get Josh's silent message, he added, "Stay away from *Trish*. I'm making headway with her."

"Not what I heard." Ryder shook his head and frowned in false concern. "I've never had much trouble with women. I'm happy to step in and help. That's what partners are for."

Josh counted to ten, listing the ways he could kill Ryder without getting blood on his tux. "You're misinformed."

"Really? Because Leanne told me about you offering to accompany Zane's sister tonight, but that *Patricia* Jackson wanted no part of you."

How could the FNG know Leanne well enough *already* to have that conversation? "When did she tell you that?"

"Right after she agreed to go to dinner with me this week."

Cocky bastard. "What happened at the task force office was a misunderstanding that's been corrected. I've already informed Zane that *Trish* changed her mind, and she's here. With *me*."

"*Trish–*" Ryder drug out the name for emphasis, "is *here ... now ...* with *you*?" Ryder made a show of looking around as he spoke. "Damn if I see her, bro. Want me to hunt her down for you?"

Want me to rearrange your head so it would look natural when you talk out of your ass? "No."

Ryder's attention moved around as fast as a feather in the wind. When he finally zeroed in on a target, he whistled under his breath. "Man. Take a look at that hot number, would you?"

Josh had already seen the slick redhead someone had addressed as Kellie. She strutted through the crowd. She'd stop, visit, then move on, leaving a trail of tongues dragging the floor.

Nice packaging. Too bad she didn't really do it for him.

Now if she had cocoa eyes and silky black curls...

But until a few minutes ago, Trish had been trying hard to act as if *he* didn't *do it* for her. Then she'd ditched him again.

Why? *There's that question again.* Was it just him or men in general? She'd been very friendly with Leanne. Could that mean that Trish and Leanne were...?

No way. Leanne had notched more than one garter belt with her male conquests in the time Josh had been in Miami. She'd probably add the FNG by the end of the week.

Trish's body had told the tale earlier, when she'd reacted to Josh, but she'd tried to hide it. She had backed away again once he'd stopped touching her and given her space. She'd pretended he didn't affect her.

Josh would prove her a liar as soon as he got her alone tonight. His fingers itched to touch her again, to push his face into that silky hair that smelled like peaches tonight. Visit those pink panties again...and slide them down while he kissed the trail they left.

Damn, he was getting hard thinking about her.

Shit. No pulling off panties. Yeah, that's what he'd do on any normal op. What he used to do all the time to get information. But maybe he wouldn't need to do that with Trish. He should be able to get inside her defenses without seducing her all the way into bed. That way, if she wasn't involved, he didn't have to destroy another piece of his soul.

Ryder snagged a glass of champagne from a passing tray. "I'd have surprised her with flowers when I picked her up at home. Wait. You did pick her up at home, didn't you? That's pretty much step number one in dating."

If Ryder said another word that sounded like a Cosmo how-to article, Josh would have to hurt him. Not right now, but just as soon as Sabrina wouldn't be put in a pinch while Ryder recovered from an ass whipping.

Josh handed off his empty glass to someone carrying a tray and charred his tone with threat when he asked Ryder, "Are you *still* here?"

"I'm giving everyone the impression that you actually have a friend. Maybe Trish will see *me* and come up to talk. I don't mind hanging around to pull in the women."

Josh changed his mind.

Sabrina could hire another FNG to replace this soon-to-be-headless one.

Ryder glanced up, finally seemed to notice the effect he was having on Josh, and said, "On the other hand, you look like you could use some alone time." He turned to walk away but made a parting shot. "You may want to practice smiling before she gets here."

I want to practice basketball slam-dunks with your head.

There she was across the room, that backless silver gown drawing the attention of every male she passed and smoking the redhead, hands down.

Polite smile in place, Trish paused to speak and shake hands, but her dark eyes swept back and forth as if searching for someone.

Me? Not a chance. She'd obviously circled outside the banquet hall to come back in on the opposite side where she thought he wouldn't see her. Josh had no intention of letting her avoid him.

He moved in her direction.

She melted into the human sea, but not out of sight.

He tracked the head full of dark curls floating through the crowd. She zigzagged, stalling out next to the loud circle of men hovering near the bar.

And that damned Ryder was angling a path toward Trish.

CHAPTER 11

"What's it gonna take, missy? I've made you a reasonable offer for that dinky business you're tryin' to run."

Trish fought not to clench her fists. She wouldn't give Big Charlie Larraby the satisfaction of knowing he could get to her. He'd already made two offers to buy her out.

He wanted her location so he could take the spot next door, knock out a wall and make a huge antiques showroom.

She'd burn ReSolution to the ground before she'd sell to him.

"Which offer was that, Charlie?" Trish replied sweetly. "The pitiful one or the ridiculous one?"

He had the good ol' southern boy shtick down, considering Charlie had a business degree from Stanford and grew up in California. Of the four locations he owned in Houston, he'd picked up one from Mrs. Betta Bromley, the woman who had been Trish's mentor during her teens. Mrs. Bromley had owned a premier gallery and auction house in Houston. She'd called Trish gifted and made her feel special for the first time in her life. She'd also taught Trish how to appraise fine antiques and how to spot a fake.

And Mrs. Bromley had detested Big Charlie Larraby, because he'd prey on anyone he considered weak. She admitted once to Trish that she'd acquired a rare piece Charlie wanted and that was the real reason he badgered Mrs. Bromley constantly to sell her business...for peanuts. When Trish's mentor had a fatal heart attack, Big Charlie finally succeeded in his quest when clueless grandnieces and grandnephews were only too happy to sell Bromley's Finest to him for a fraction of its value.

Trish had no proof of wrongdoing, but she blamed Big Charlie for Mrs. Bromley's heart attack and for shutting down Bromley's Finest once he'd gutted the inventory.

Now he wanted to steal ReSolution. Or did he just want to harass Trish?

Could Charlie be stalking her?

God, she hoped not. Just the thought of him being in her house, pawing through her lingerie to find her black lace panties was...she managed to not screw up her face into a disgusted grimace, but ... *ew.* Besides, he'd always been an in-your-face opponent.

Why would he change tactics now?

She'd fought tougher battles and won. So far.

Which only reminded her of how much she wanted a drink right now. Smooth bourbon. That had been her poison. She could smell it in the air.

Charlie hefted his considerable bulk another inch higher and yanked on a belt buckle the size of her hand and snorted–a bull threatening to charge, but too lazy to make the effort. "Listen here, missy. I seen your place. You ain't goin' to make it past a year. We carry the same quality of furnishings as you, but a bigger inventory. Customers want choice. I have eighteen stores to your one. That buys credibility. I can afford national ad campaigns. That's what it takes to survive on Las Olas. Sell it or lose it."

"Chuck, honey," she said in a voice loaded with faux charm. "I hate to disappoint you, but I'm here to stay. However, I do wish you luck with your endeavors."

She left him scowling behind her and walked away, only to encounter Olivia Dent next.

Blow off the snake, land in front of an alley cat.

Olivia cooed, "My, my, aren't we the flashy one decked out in silver?" The sultry over-bleached blond held a martini in one delicate hand with perfectly manicured blaze-red nails long enough to be claws–a fitting image for a feline in attack mode.

"There is no *we* to it, Olivia. You're the queen of flash. I'm just a pale second." Trish smiled to make it sound real and waged a war not to roll her eyes when Olivia preened under the jaded compliment. The woman's scarlet Oscar de la Renta gown cost more than a month's lease payment for ReSolution.

If Kellie hadn't loaned Trish the sparkling gown she wore, she'd have come dressed in her usual business attire. When she'd first met Kellie at a Miami Businesswomen's small business luncheon, Trish had been impressed by the spirited woman's competence. But when the redhead had shown up in jeans with no makeup to pitch in at a women's shelter where Trish also volunteered, they'd bonded instantly.

"Yes, you *are* a pale second." Olivia lifted her head, making it possible to actually look down her nose. The witch probably practiced that in front of mirrors. "I don't know what Gunter sees in you."

"Maybe he enjoys being around a woman who treats him as a friend. You might try that." *Take that.*

Olivia's gaze narrowed for an instant. Long enough to confirm a direct hit, but not deeply enough to induce wrinkling.

Screw her and the broom she rode in on.

Trish smiled graciously and continued on to the bar, doing her best to walk as though her insides hadn't dissolved into a mass of jelly.

What had the stalker meant by *watch for my next move?*
Please don't ruin this for me.

She was having a difficult enough time trying not to think about how close all that free alcohol was and how much she could use something to settle her nerves.

The bartender poured two glasses of wine for a couple ahead of her. Trish eyed the top-shelf bourbon behind him and fought the urge to slide her tongue across her teeth. She pressed her fidgeting hands into fists against her thighs, closed her eyes and swallowed. One minute at a time, if that was what it took to beat the addiction monster.

She could do this.

"What will the lovely lady have?"

Her eyes snapped open, and she unfurled her fingers against her dress. Looking slowly to the left, she came face-to-face with a beaming Josh.

"I can get my own, but thanks." Trish moved up to the bar and requested her usual club soda with a lime. Once she had her drink and they moved away from the bar line, she wondered if Josh had figured out that she'd been avoiding him. If he was gay, she was misreading everything he said and the way he touched her. And it would explain why he'd backed off earlier.

He *could* just be very affectionate.

Every female cell in her body screamed *NOT!*

"Hell of a party," Josh said, his hand at the small of her back again. "Are you excited?"

"I suppose. This has been going on for five weeks. Mostly I'd just like for it to be *over*," she admitted. "I'm ready for the final decision." Answering him would be easier if she didn't quiver at the feel of his palm on her skin.

"When will they make the final decision?"

"Next week." She didn't want to be rude to him, especially when he was being so nice, but he was too freaking attractive in that tux for her peace of mind.

Standing this close to all that hotness just confused her hormones and made her feel stupid for being attracted to him. Plus, Josh shouldn't have to be stuck with her all night.

Not when he could find someone he'd really enjoy.

She moved away from his hand and turned to face him with a polite smile. "Thanks for coming here tonight to appease my brother, but you don't have to hang out with me the whole time."

Something dark shifted in Josh's gaze before he pulled his reaction under control and leaned close. "Are you going to do this all night?"

"Do what?"

"Push me aside."

"I just thought you might like to, uh, meet other people, maybe find somebody you'd enjoy."

He clamped his lips shut. Muscles in his jaw flexed in and out. He lifted up, drew in a long, slow breath and let it out, then gave her a smile the wolf probably showed Little Red Riding Hood before he had her for dinner. "I came here to be with *you* tonight."

She had a hot flash when he said it *that way*, as if he wanted to be alone with her, and in that moment, she wanted to find a place to be alone with him. Had to be nerves sending her hormones way beyond haywire around this guy. If she thought about it, Brendan would toy with her the same way if he didn't know her and didn't care. He was a flirt extraordinaire, and he enjoyed women.

Maybe Josh was no different. If she'd just loosen up and play along with Josh, she might have as good a time as she normally had with Brendan. "My apologies. I'm not trying to push you away. I was only letting you know I didn't expect you to be at my side every second."

"No apology necessary. You're keeping me on my toes. I must need the practice." He broke out one of those high wattage smiles and her body hummed in response.

She'd once been a sucker for sweet talking guys with bedroom smiles who'd seduced her into making stupid choices.

But she couldn't blame Josh for what he was, or for going along with her brother's setup.

Nope. This crazy attraction was all hers and damned uncomfortable. Zane had probably assumed that because Josh was gay, he would be boring. She was not bored.

Trish's body screamed at her that Josh was not only lined up on her side of the straight-gay fifty-yard line, but he was also immediate touchdown material.

There wasn't a thing boring about that mouth of his when all she could think about was what he could do with it besides talking.

Like kissing.

Bad brain. Bad! Rebel hormones had cut off all oxygen supply in an attempt to overthrow her good sense.

Josh took her by the elbow to lead her around the room. "Tell me why you're doing this."

She floundered mentally until she realized he meant the competition, but his easy tone and slow pace relaxed her. "To fast track my reputation in the antiques appraisal community. It takes a long time to build a following and respect for your ability. I'm a little late out of the gate, but I do know what I'm doing." She took a step toward a table filled with hors d'oeuvres.

"Not doing this to be a television star?"

She snickered and turned to him. "No way. This is a behind-the-scenes opportunity, which suits me fine. I want to be the skill in the background, not a celebrity."

He gave her a thoughtful look, as though seeing her in a new light. "Their loss. You're obviously talented if you've made it to this point in the competition, and far too striking to leave in the shadows."

A compliment without calling her cute. Her brain had to be turning to mush, because she could swear he was flirting with her. Her body thought so. All engines were on go.

Where was Brendan when she needed someone to ask about Josh?

She'd never had a thing for gay guys in the past. Her gaydar had been dead accurate. Faced with one of Brendan's stunning friends, her hormones had flatlined.

So why this tingling in her belly just from standing close to Josh? She hadn't felt this way since she was a teenager.

A man who ran a close second to him in the sexy department strolled toward them with a look of recognition that said he knew Josh. The tawny-haired guy might be thirty. He beamed a dazzling smile at her as he spoke to Josh. "Hey, buddy. Introduce me to this delicious creature."

She welcomed the interruption, but Josh didn't appear happy to see his *buddy.* Josh muttered something like, "Again?" then introduced the new guy. "Trish Jackson meet Ryder Brown."

Ryder's smile bumped up in intensity. "Definitely my pleasure, *Miss* Jackson. It is miss, right?" He offered his hand.

"Yes. Nice to meet you." She shook with Handsome Number Two who was clearly flirting and holding her hand longer than necessary, but she didn't feel any more drawn to him than when Brendan teased her.

"Let. Go. Ryder."

Ignoring Josh, Ryder said, "You have soft hands. Seems like there's a saying, soft hands, soft heart."

She laughed at the blatant flirt and withdrew her hand before Josh's gaze turned any darker. "Nice to meet you."

She considered the way Josh was snapping at Ryder and Ryder was laughing, practically busting Josh's chops.

Could this be Josh's life partner? Maybe they were having a domestic squabble and that could be why Josh hadn't wanted to mingle.

Maybe her attraction to Josh wasn't her fault.

Maybe *Josh* was putting out mixed pheromone signals.

A chemical imbalance. Not a clinical theory, but she was going with it. She asked Josh, "Are you two ... partners?"

Ryder said, "Actually—"

Josh snapped, "Not tonight."

What did *that* mean? She waited for Ryder to explain but instead he asked, "What happens this evening, *Trish*?"

Why was Ryder here if he didn't know what was going on? How had he gotten a ticket?

She didn't care and answered, "This is fanfare for the new *Treasured Past* television show. They've narrowed down the field to two females and two males from all those who've applied for a chance to be a consultant on the show. They'll call us each up on stage tonight and give us our individual tasks. Sort of like a final test to determine which two they consider the best."

Ryder started to ask another question, but Josh cut in. "How do they choose the final two?"

"We're given an item from our area of expertise. We've been providing written appraisals of items for weeks now that will be compared, because first and foremost, a consultant has to be capable of assessing real value. Then it's up to us to find an individual who is a private collector and convince that person to come on the show as a guest host."

"How much time are you given to find this guest host?"

"Twenty-four hours to book a guest who has to come here next Monday for filming."

Ryder sounded enthusiastic when he said, "That sounds tough, but you must be damned good to have made it this far."

"We'll see." Trish pretended not to notice the glare Josh shoved at Ryder since Ryder ignored it. She explained, "The key is showing the producers who has resources and can bring in celebrity collectors. Finding an expert knowledgeable on unusual or rare antiques and artifacts is one thing, but a celebrity who can draw viewers is a challenge."

Crossing his arms and looking like he belonged in jeans and outdoors instead of a stiff party, Ryder asked, "Does the celebrity win money?"

"Yes and no. The guests do engage in competition against pros, but in these first four pilot programs the money won will be awarded to the celebrity's chosen charity."

"Do *you* know celebrities?" Josh asked, curious, not challenging.

"I know *collectors,* and some are celebrities, but I don't know anyone well enough to pick up a phone so I'm a little apprehensive about that part," Trish stated. "I mentored under a woman who taught me knowledge was more powerful than money. She was a brilliant businesswoman and knew everyone of consequence in this business."

Ryder was listening, but also tugging at his sleeves every so often. He didn't wear a tux as comfortably as Josh did. Not that he was a slouch. Anything but. Ryder should be modeling clothes, but something rugged. Not evening wear.

Nothing distracted Josh. He wore a tux with the ease of a second skin while still giving the impression that he would look extraordinary in anything. Jeans. Tattered shirt. Boxers.

Ryder quipped, "Sounds like a reality show."

Trish had thought so, too, in the beginning and wouldn't have signed up to do this if she hadn't been given a nudge. "Sort of, but without all the drama."

She sure hoped that was the case.

On that point, her life had to stay drama free for any chance of being chosen for the show. She'd signed papers that clearly stated in heavy legalese that the show would boot anyone with negative press.

Josh was speaking in a low, terse voice to Ryder. "Don't you have somewhere *else* to be?"

Ryder shook his head and continued smiling at Trish, clearly set on aggravating Josh. "Do *you* get anything besides a consulting contract if you win? A car? Vacation?"

"I have an antiques shop on Las Olas. My name and business would be listed in the credits for each show, but the consultants receive a signing bonus, plus a major advertising package comes with winning a position. I'd have a thirty-second commercial spot played during each program, and one in the Good Morning Florida show for three months, plus a drive-time ad spot on three radio networks." She'd be able to get her business off the ground and pay back what Zane and Angel had loaned her. "I'm working on my appraisal certification. All of this would help move me forward."

"Do you work with anyone international?" Ryder asked.

That struck her as an odd question. "No. I'll be happy to build a local and national clientele."

"But your expertise is in fifteenth century European history and antiques, right?"

She couldn't hide her surprise. "How'd you know that?"

"Heard someone mention it. You're a hot topic in this place." Ryder boosted his rating with another smile and added, "I'm not familiar with that era. Maybe I could–"

"*Give* it a rest, Ryder," Josh finished for him. He leveled a threatening gaze at Ryder. "We won't keep you from catching up with someone *else*."

Trish could practically feel the friction between these two and, for some reason, believed she was part of the problem. Eager to get away, she looked around and caught sight of Heidi in the area of their table. That gave her the perfect opportunity to scoot away without leaving Josh alone. He and Ryder could work out their issues on their own.

Trish said, "Excuse me, gentlemen. I see my business manager."

She got six steps away before a warm hand touched her arm. Josh had caught up with her. His deep voice whispered close to her ear. "Not trying to get rid of me *again*, are you?"

Warm breath danced across her face, feathering her skin. "Of course not. But I thought maybe you two had something to, uh, talk about."

"No, we don't."

That sounded pretty final. She kept moving toward the VIP tables. "What does Ryder do?"

"He's with the DEA. Assigned to the Miami task force."

Ah. Guess that's how Leanne put two and two together about Josh's being gay. Trish would never have figured it out, because Ryder didn't strike her as gay either. She'd been off the market for so long that she was rusty at reading male signals. Obviously, they must be a couple.

With that last bit of doubt removed about Josh, Trish accepted that the best she could hope for with Josh was friendship, which should be *all* she wanted.

And would be, *if* he kept his hands off her. Not that he wasn't being a gentleman, but his fingers grazing along her back sent heat spiraling into places it shouldn't.

When she reached the VIP table that had eight elegant place settings with name cards, four of which were her group, she smiled. She'd come pretty far to be here today.

Josh pulled out the chair in front of her name card. "What's that smile about?"

She laughed. "Back home, we'd say this was walking through tall cotton."

He studied her with a strange intensity then leaned close and murmured, "You should laugh more often. You're stunning."

How was it that Josh could make her feel like the only woman on earth? Why couldn't she have met someone like him a long time ago?

You did. Brendan. Gay, remember? Shoot. It was easy to forget when Josh looked at her that way. Brendan had teased and flirted, but she'd never had this intense urge for something more with Brendan the way she did with Josh.

When Josh slid into the chair on her left, she stole another quick sniff of his masculine scent. Would he smell that good all over?

If he does, you won't be the one finding out.

She wasn't sure she could be friends with him after all. But was this all in her mind, or was he encouraging it by the things he said and the way he kept touching her?

Was her reaction accidental or was he intentionally trying to confuse her? She turned to him. "Are you flirting with me, for real flirting?"

"Yes."

What?

He added, "Is it working?"

Answering that truthfully would make her a candidate for a Fool-Of-The-Day award. He had to be yanking her chain. "No, it's not."

Sharp blue eyes full of turbulence stared at her while something menacing swirled behind his gaze, then calmed. "Liar."

He'd said that one word with the force of a challenge.

Her lips parted in shock. Was he serious?

Or...could *he* be the stalker?

Her stomach quivered with the possibility, but she couldn't come up with one logical reason for why he'd want to stalk her. They'd never met before today, and he worked with her brother.

Josh gave her another smile, but this one smacked of bad boy. Zane had told her in their text conversation that Josh was FBI and temporarily assigned to the DEA task force. Maybe Hot Guy FBI Agent just had a warped sense of humor and enjoyed watching women fall all over his hotness.

"Hey," Heidi called out as she came up from the opposite side of the table.

Relieved to have backup, Trish glanced up at Heidi and smiled. Her friend had agreed to wear something sedate for the evening. Heidi's version of sedate was a gold sweater, gold stiletto heels and black spandex pants swooping low enough to expose her glittering navel ring. Another Kellie outfit.

"Where's Gunter? I thought he'd be here by now."

"Had some last-minute something come up." Heidi shrugged, walking around the table to Trish's side. "Said he'd meet us at the table."

Josh stood when Heidi reached the chair next to Trish. He offered his hand. "We weren't introduced today. I'm Josh Robertson."

Now I feel rude on top of confused for not making introductions. Sitting between where Heidi and Josh stood, Trish leaned her head back. "This is Heidi Hildegard. Heidi, you remember *Mr.* Robertson from today, right?"

"Sure. I remember Josh." Heidi let go of his hand and glanced down at Trish with an evil look in her eyes.

Trish knew that glint and sent Heidi a glaring eye message of *don't encourage him.*

Heidi made a laughing sound that Trish interpreted as *loosen up and have fun,* then she headed for her seat two places to the right of Trish.

Gunter made a frazzled entrance, dashing up to the table. "Sorry to be late. Good Lord, Patricia, you are a vision."

He was the only man who could grumble a compliment. Standing behind his seat, Gunter turned to Heidi. "You look lovely too, Miss Heidi."

Heidi lifted one eyebrow, curled a half-smile and raised her index finger–a Heidi hello.

Wheeling back to Trish, Gunter finally noticed Josh and gave him a hard appraisal.

Might as well get this introduction over, too. "Gunter, Zane couldn't make it. This is Josh Robertson. He works with Zane." She told Josh, "And this is Gunter Weiss of Dynasty Treasures, a wonderful shop in our area that offers...classic antiques." That sounded better than saying Gunter had been around since before electricity. He wasn't keeping up with the times, but he was her friend and deserved respect.

Josh stood, accentuating the vast differences between the two men, from Gunter's being six inches shorter to Josh's being over-the-legal-limit handsome.

They shook hands, but Gunter's cool, "Nice to meet you," left little doubt of just how much he didn't care for Josh.

The rest of the table guests began taking their seats for dinner, including Xavier Gomez, a slender brunette who was also competing to be a consultant. Xavier caught Trish's eye and they shared a discrete wink and a wave. Even though they were competing against one another, they'd hit it off early on. Trish politely acknowledged Xavier's three guests.

With introductions made all around, Xavier's group settled into a conversation on their side of the table, but Trish noticed that her friend's stunning, black-outlined green gaze strayed to Josh repeatedly.

When Josh looked away for a moment, distracted by the server filling water glasses, Xavier mouthed a silent "OH. MY. GOD!" across the table to Trish.

Trish gave her a conspiratorial grin, and shook her head a little, but Josh turned back around before she could clue her friend in that nothing was actually going on.

Xavier caught a pause in conversation on her side and smiled over at Trish. "Where's your brother? I'm surprised he would miss this. I've seen him at every one of these functions so far. So sweet."

Trish smiled to cover the tiny, unintentional hit to her confidence. Her friend would hate knowing she'd caused it. *Sweet.* Just every now and then, Trish resented being the "sweet" one. "His wife is close to delivering their first baby and needed him tonight."

Call it female vanity, but Trish had been compared to Xavier more than the other two competitors, who were male, and she always ended up being the "cute" one, in contrast to Xavier's voluptuous beauty that was usually described as "sexy" or "hot".

Josh had been flirting all night, throwing her off her game. Trish decided to turn the tables on him. She placed her hand on

Josh's arm and told Xavier, "When Zane had to bow out, Josh, uh ... volunteered."

Trish prayed he wouldn't pull away out of sheer surprise after she'd worked so hard to keep him from being here with her.

Obviously curious, Xavier shifted the power of her exotic green eyes to Josh. "Are you a collector or a dealer?"

"Neither. I'm new to the antiques world."

"Trish is great," she said. "Don't tell Charlie, but I think she's going to win."

Trish grinned and shook her head. "You're nuts." They'd been playing the "you're going to win...no *you're* going to win" game since the second round. Xavier's specialty was seventeenth century, and she'd spent a year mentoring with Big Charlie, which put her chances pretty high in this competition. In fact, Xavier had quietly tipped Trish off to the reason Big Charlie was after ReSolution–for expansion on Las Olas.

If Trish wasn't chosen for the female slot, and if nothing came of this TV show except a bit of exposure, Trish would always be glad for the effort she'd made because it had gained her Xavier as a friend.

Josh beamed a smile at Trish, then grinned at Xavier, and Trish saw her friend's eyes widen.

Trish needed to find a private moment to tell Xavier that Trish had only been playing and not to read too much into Josh's behavior one way or the other, that Josh wouldn't be interested in sex with Trish *or* her. But when Trish considered the possibility of either one of them tempting him, she had to admit that Xavier was at least Josh's equal in the beauty department.

Not wanting to take the joke too far, Trish removed her hand from his arm and sat up straighter in her chair. She was just glad the competition was based on brains, not beauty. That meant she at least had a chance.

Josh hooked his arm over the back of Trish's chair in the same proprietary way she'd taken when she'd touched him.

She held her breath. What was he going to say to Xavier?

"I'm definitely interested in acquiring something of value, and Trish has agreed to tutor me *privately*. That's an offer *no man* could pass up."

The man was outrageous and pulled it off.

Warm tendrils squirmed in her heart at his last line.

Bless him. Too bad he worked with her brother and was not in the market for a woman. He sure could put on a great show.

She'd bet there wasn't a woman at the table who didn't believe he expected one-on-one time with Trish. She got hot just thinking about the possibility. Her body felt too tight in her skin.

That could be because Josh's fingers were slowly massaging her shoulder.

Xavier cocked her eyebrow, gave Trish another "holy shit" wink then returned to talking with her guests.

Trish glanced at the stage, where the emcee stood with the producer and pointed to the upper back corner of the room, where a technician aimed and focused a follow spot. Trish just wanted this night to end. She was holding herself together, but walking up in front of so many people, being stared at, judged, talked about, gave her the jitters. So many strangers and...

A feeling of being watched hit her.

Trish froze. She glanced around left then right and across the room. Everyone appeared busy with conversation and food at their respective tables. She tried to shake off the creepy feeling, to convince herself it was nothing more than an over-imaginative mind fed by lack of sleep and a stalker's intrusion into her life.

But Zane's advice about always listening to her instincts shot to the forefront of her mind. He'd told her to trust the feeling and take measures to protect herself.

But she was sitting in the middle of a room with over five hundred people and would soon get called on stage. Anyone could be watching her.

Was her stalker here? Was he in the middle of all these people?

Was it even a man?

She hadn't thought about it, just assumed it was a man. But the stalker could be a woman. Maybe someone she trusted? Like Xavier?

Trish wiped the idea from her mind. Why would Xavier stalk Trish when she already had a better chance at winning because of Charlie's support? Xavier was her friend.

If Trish let paranoia get any more of a foothold, she'd be suspicious of everyone she knew, from friends to family.

Trish took a deep breath and ignored the sensation of something crawling up her neck. *Get through tonight and focus on making a good impression.*

Maybe the stalking was just someone's elaborate, sick joke. She prayed the stalker was not here to destroy this one chance to launch her business in an economy not favorable to luxury items.

But antiques were all she knew, all she'd ever wanted to do. If ReSolution didn't make it...

She couldn't think about that. Heidi said negative thoughts lead to negative actions. *No negative thoughts.*

Josh shook her out of the dark place she'd gone when he asked Gunter, "How long have you been in Ft. Lauderdale?"

A server removed dishes as Gunter went into an oration about how he'd come to Miami first then moved to Ft. Lauderdale after getting married. By the time he finished naming notable people who had shopped in his store, he'd covered the past two decades.

Trish caught him taking a breath and grabbed at any change in subject. She'd never heard him mention a wife before. "Are you divorced?"

"The woman was a blood sucker," Gunter stated flatly, as he picked at his dessert. "I make a habit of getting rid of anything that reminds me of her. You married, Robertson?"

"No. Don't think that's in the stars for me."

"A case of too many women and too little time?" Heidi piped up, clearly testing him.

Trish shot her a warning glance that Heidi ignored.

"More like not husband material with the type of work I do."

"What exactly do you do?" Gunter asked.

"At the moment, I'm working in computer forensics for law enforcement in Miami." Josh shrugged. "But I tend to get shuffled around. Have no idea where I'll be sent next. That's the beauty of no ties. They can use me wherever needed."

Heidi asked, "How long will you be here?"

"Not sure, but probably one or two more weeks."

Trish only had to lift her eyes to look into Josh's with him leaning so close to her. "Where's your home?"

"Atlanta, but I'm rarely there."

He'd leave Miami soon. She should feel relief, right? They wouldn't see each other after tonight anyhow, so no more fantasy attraction.

But she'd spent more time with him today and this evening than she had with any man in too long to think about, and now she had the strange feeling she'd miss him.

Heidi might be on to something about dating again if spending time with one man affected her this way.

Gunter stood. "I'll be back in time to see you go up." He tossed down his napkin and disappeared through the doors that lead to the restrooms.

"Ladies and gentlemen," the television spokesman said, drawing everyone's attention to the stage. He launched into thanks for all who had attended, and for the money being raised for the scholarship program. Then he started thanking the investors.

He would call the contestants next.

Trish took a deep breath to calm her nerves.

Her cell phone vibrated in her purse. She'd left it on vibrate in case Zane called. Angel was close enough to her due date that she could go into labor at any time. Opening the clasp, she hit the button to stop it from making more noise and peeked at the text:

Now would be a good time to visit ReSolution if you don't want to lose it.

Your move.

Trish's hand shook. What was the stalker going to do?

CHAPTER 12

Josh had heard the buzz of a cell phone and glanced over at Trish as she opened her purse.

What could be important enough for her to check her phone when the guy on stage would call her up in a few minutes? She couldn't be any more visible, sitting up front at this VIP table under the scrutiny of hundreds of people.

Trish stared at the phone that was shielded inside her small bag.

Her face had lost all color.

He put his hand on her wrist.

She flinched and looked up, eyes wide with fear, but she recovered quickly and mumbled, "Sorry. Gotta go."

Now?

Before Josh could ask what was going on, Trish leaned toward Heidi. Being observant, Heidi put her hand on Gunter's chair and turned toward Trish, mouth open and confused.

Trish whispered, "When they call my name, go up in my place. Tell them I had an emergency. It's not Angel. I'll explain later."

Heidi looked ready to argue until Trish said, *"Please,"* with so much emotion Josh would have thought someone was dying.

Her friend nodded, but said, "You need a car."

Josh leaned over. "I'm driving her." He didn't know what was going on, but she wasn't leaving without him.

Trish turned back to him, ready to argue.

He leaned close and whispered, "The longer you talk the more attention you'll draw."

That prompted her to look around where heads were turning her way. She paled even more.

He cursed softly and said, "Head straight for the door and don't slow down, so you'll cause as little distraction as possible."

She was up and out of her seat like a shot with him right behind her. When they reached the lobby of the hotel hosting the event, Trish got several steps beyond the closed doors and swung around. "Thanks for coming out here, but I'll have them call a cab so you can stay."

Here we go again. He'd fished out his valet slip and handed it off with a hefty tip for the eager runner. "I'm not interested in staying if you aren't here."

"Then go home." She said it the same way someone would shoo away some mutt bothering her.

He'd be ready to hunt down a bottle of prime scotch and call it a night if she weren't acting so suspicious. He bit down on his irritation and told her, "The whole point of Zane's wanting someone to accompany you tonight was so that you wouldn't be alone. I heard your phone buzz with a text. What's going on?"

What color had returned to her face in her dash out of the banquet room faded away again. "Nothing."

Did she really think he'd believe that? "Based on us standing out here right now and you walking away from something as important to you as this banquet, I'm not buying that. And since I get the impression that text was a crisis of some sort, you should probably get moving soon."

Her eyes got even larger. "I'm sorry but I *have* to go. Do whatever you want." She turned and raced over to the valet stand and started rambling about needing a cab, hands animated.

Trish was still waiting on a cab when Josh's Porsche convertible pulled up along the curb and the kid jumped out, leaving the engine running.

Josh walked up to Trish. "I'm going to follow you until I know you're home safe, so you might as well ride with me."

She hissed a sound that couldn't mean anything nice. "Oh, all *right*." By the time she stepped over to the car, the valet had her door open. She smiled at *him* and got in.

Josh shook his head as he walked around to the driver's side. He produces transportation immediately when she's in a panic and the kid with the fat tip gets the smile.

Sliding behind the wheel, Josh said, "Where to?"

"ReSolution."

He dialed up a jazz station on his satellite radio to fill the conversation void while he drove, and to hopefully calm her down.

This was the opportunity he'd been looking for to get closer to Trish and find out if she was connected to the mole.

But the music failed to soothe her. The closer they got to ReSolution, the more Trish twisted her hands in her lap. Josh went for the direct approach. "Was there a problem at your shop?"

"Not really."

"Want me to call Zane?"

"*No!*" She spread her fingers out over her lap and took a breath. "Sorry, I didn't mean to yell at you, but I don't want to bother my brother. He's home with Angel and she's not feeling well and ... anyhow. I don't need his help. I can handle this."

Was she kidding? Just look at her. She wouldn't have left that banquet tonight short of being forced out at gunpoint, but one text sent her racing out of the room.

And she was terrified.

Of what or whom?

Vulnerable...and prepared to face something frightening all alone.

In that moment, Josh had to fight off the urge to protect Trish from whatever scared her. To demand that she tell him the truth about that text. But he couldn't *be* the guy who protected Trish, since she might be communicating with the mole, and especially because it might be Zane.

Was that why she refused to contact her brother?

Because he'd sent her a task to do or a message to pass along?

　　　　DIANNA LOVE

This was not the time to get protective around Trish Jackson. This was the time to exploit her vulnerability. To use every weapon in his arsenal to find the mole and Len Rikker.

Wasn't that what Sabrina wanted? The ruthless Josh who could seduce any secret out of a woman and walk away? The Josh who never let a woman get to him?

He remembered the cold bastard he'd had to be in the past, the one who could succeed where others failed. For some reason, the idea of unleashing that on Trish left a bad taste in his mouth.

He didn't want to take advantage of her while her guard was down.

Every time he looked over and took in her pale skin, he wanted to shield her from danger.

Sabrina was right about one thing. He hadn't put the UK behind him.

Teenagers are dying. It was time to harden his heart and get the freaking job done. Josh pulled up alongside the entrance to ReSolution, where all was dark and quiet. Streetlights shone along the sidewalk in front of upscale stores with professional window dressings.

Trish reached for her door handle, and he put his hand on her arm, softening his voice to preserve his role. "Don't get out until I come around."

She sat there a moment. "Josh, this doesn't concern you. Please go home. Heidi will be here as soon as she gets out of the banquet."

"Let's go inside your shop and check it out. Make sure everything's okay."

"No. Just *leave*." She reached for the handle, opening the door, and climbing out on the sidewalk.

He was just as quick and met her on the other side. He'd never had this tough a time with *any* woman. Mr. Nice wasn't working. Maybe Mr. Pissed Off could get a straight answer. "Why have you pushed me away all night?"

"You're really taking this escort thing for Zane too far."

Subtle hadn't gotten through. Maybe direct would be better. "Did you ever think I might be here for a reason other than because I work with Zane? That I might *want* to be here with you?"

She gave him an incredulous look. "What?"

This would be funny...if it was happening to the FNG.

Flashing lights came rolling up in front and behind Josh's car. What now? He took in the approaching police cars and asked, "Did you have a break-in?"

"Not that I know about." Her gaze followed his, fear climbing back into her eyes at seeing the police. Why?

"If this isn't about a break-in, then what was the text you got?"

"I can't talk about it." She lifted a hand to her neck. Her fingers trembled. This was the same woman he'd seen walk confidently through a rotten Miami neighborhood and hold her own sparring with a guy twice her size. What could frighten her when she'd been training to meet a threat alone in a dark warehouse?

If she was acting, she deserved an Oscar, because watching her was calling up every ounce of Josh's ingrained need to find the threat and kill it.

Officers spilled out of the cars and walked up to them. The first one, Officer Vasquez who had a soft middle and dark eyes that missed nothing, asked Josh, "Are you parked in front of this business for a reason?"

Josh put his hand on Trish's back. "This is the owner of ReSolution. Is there a problem?"

"We had a call of suspicious activity here. How long have you been here?"

"Just pulled up right before you did."

"See anyone or anything suspicious?"

"No." *No one except Trish Jackson*, Josh added silently.

Vasquez shined his flashlight toward the display windows, but the majority of ReSolution's glass front was covered by drapes. He asked Trish for her ID. Once the officer checked that, he asked Josh, "And who are you?"

"I'm her date, but I'm also FBI with a task force unit in Miami, and I'm carrying my service weapon." Josh waited for that to register. No reaching into his jacket and surprising the suspicious officers with an accidental flash of the shoulder holster under his arm. "Would you like to see my ID?"

"Yes."

Once Vasquez had confirmed Josh's ID, he eyed the shop again. "Might as well check out the premises while we're here."

Josh could tell Trish was going to refuse the inspection, which would only ping the officer's curiosity. He didn't need any more complications right now and told Trish, "Good idea. Why don't you unlock and clear the security alarm?"

With a sigh of irritation, she dug the key out of her purse. When she pulled the door open, no alarm sounded.

Trish hurried over to an illuminated panel that showed the system was powered but not activated.

She stood there, staring at the box as if something was amiss.

"Guess someone forgot to set it tonight," Josh said, stepping up next to her as the officers came in behind him, flashlights beaming across the interior.

"No, I–" Then she caught herself and snapped back into the moment. She reached over to flip a switch. Soft light flooded the showroom area.

The policemen spread out, checking high and low.

Trish watched them with intense attention.

Josh watched *her*.

The minute one of the officers headed into the back room, Trish took off in that direction.

Why would she be more concerned over that area than her showroom? Was she worried that law enforcement would find something to do with her mysterious text?

Josh stayed with her step for step as she reached the back room and turned on those lights too. The officer disappeared into a room Josh guessed was a restroom.

Trish looked all over the room with frantic movements, squatting as much as she could in that slinky dress to see down low and standing up with her head tilted back to take in the tops of shelves.

Would she be searching haphazardly if she *knew* what she was looking for?

She caught Josh watching her and stilled.

The officer stepped out of the bathroom. "Is anything disturbed, ma'am?"

"No. Everything looks okay to me," she said a bit too brightly. "I think we're good. I appreciate all of you coming down here." She turned to leave the room and missed her step next to Josh.

He grabbed her by the shoulders to keep her from stumbling. "Are you sure?"

"Yes. They can go," she said, as in right now wasn't fast enough.

Josh turned and walked out to the showroom where the other three officers were standing together, talking quietly. They looked up as Trish and the last policeman joined them.

Vasquez eyed their clothes and asked Trish, "What brought you down here tonight?"

She was struck mute so quickly you'd have thought the guy had asked her the meaning of life.

Josh gave a negligent shrug. "She forgot some files she'd planned to take home tonight, so I suggested we just swing by and pick them up."

She raked a shaky hand over her hair. "That's right. Files."

Trish was either poorly trained or exceptionally skilled.

Josh had to figure out which.

Vasquez nodded, making a note on his pad then he asked, "You have any trouble with employees?"

"No, I have great people," she answered too quickly and with just a bite of defensiveness

That pricked Josh's curiosity even more about the police visit. "What type of suspicious activity was called in?"

"Drug related."

Trish went from nervous to wet-cat mad in two seconds. "Not in *my* shop. I don't tolerate *any* drugs. *Ever*. None of my people even drink alcohol."

That was overkill. Did she really expect Josh to believe Heidi and Bunko didn't drink just because Trish didn't?

But the officer's head bobbed with another perfunctory nod that could mean he believed her, or he was just pacifying her. "Got it." He shoved the notepad into his pocket. "Guess we're done. Let us know if you do have any problem."

"Thank you." Trish gave them a polite smile and clasped her hands behind her back. Nice trick to hide her nerves.

Once all four officers were out of the store, the tension in Trish's shoulders deflated.

Josh took in the illuminated security panel. "Why was your alarm off?"

"I must have forgotten to set it."

He didn't believe her. "Do you do that often?"

"Sometimes." She murmured that lie and turned toward the counter in the back of the showroom, to the right of the entrance to the storage room. "I'll be right back."

She was still searching for something. He followed her, watching for the slightest indication of anything different. Behind the counter was a desk and chair, the sales transaction area.

She'd almost passed by when she halted sharply. The desk was as tidy as an operating table.

That made it easy to spot the black chess piece sitting in the center of the clean surface.

A rook had been carved from onyx and had an inlaid gold band near the top. Was that a message? If so, who had left it and what was the message?

Trish's face went from confused to a light bulb moment. And not a bit happy about whatever she'd realized.

She snatched the piece off the desk in a tight fist.

He wanted to shake an answer from her, but now was the time to charm her, not threaten her. "Are you missing a piece from a set?"

She wouldn't meet his eyes, a prelude to lying. "No. This is just...I'm a big chess fan. People leave these all the time for me."

Right. Just as often as he was asked to be the next pope.

He had to be careful with his next move. She'd been trying to shut him out all night. He'd bet that chess piece was tied to her text and her rush to get here. Someone had sent a message with the police tonight. "You ready to go home?"

"I'll wait on Heidi. You go on."

"I'll wait with you."

"Why?"

"Because I'm not the kind of guy who leaves a woman alone at night if something's off, and because I promised Zane–"

"I know, I know." She rubbed her head as if just talking was sapping her energy. "Okay, you win. I'll text Heidi and tell her to meet me at home." When she dropped her hand, she jutted her chin up in determination. "Then you can go your way and I'll go mine."

Not a chance, sweetheart.

Not until he found out what that chess piece meant.

CHAPTER 13

Why couldn't Josh see that she was at the end of her frayed rope?

Josh took the last turn toward her house in north Ft. Lauderdale, and Trish watched the headlights of his Porsche sweep across the first frame house on her street.

When he reached her driveway and pulled in to park the car, he said with more authority this time, "*Don't* get out until I come around."

"Don't give me orders."

"Do you fight everyone this way, or just me?"

Why *was* she fighting him? Because he'd had her on edge all night. The man was gay, but he'd sent her constant strange signals that had her body twisted with need. Then he wouldn't let her go to ReSolution alone when she had no idea what the stalker was doing.

Or what danger she might have been leading Josh into.

She was too tired to fight. "I'll wait."

"Thank you." He walked around the car, a dark shadow moving with a smooth stride. Then her door opened, and he offered her a hand. She took it, and that sizzle of energy she'd been experiencing since they'd first met in the task force office slid along her senses as he helped her out of the car.

No point in trying to tell him goodbye here.

Knowing what little she did of Josh, she wouldn't be surprised if he wanted to come inside and check out the house. Were computer techs trained in defense? They must be, since he'd mentioned a service weapon. She had pepper spray and could defend herself against a physical attack but finding that black chess piece in ReSolution had unhinged her confidence.

She'd had no chance to examine it closely with Josh hovering, but she was pretty sure that rook was from an infamous chess set that had belonged to a famous serial killer in 1867. The set had been stolen from a private collector several years ago.

The serial killer had once been a promising chess champion before being imprisoned for murdering an opponent. When he escaped, he'd used the pieces as a calling card, systematically killing everyone he'd fingered as being at fault for putting him in prison.

"Careful," Josh said, taking Trish's elbow as she started toward the front door. He guided her with an odd mix of gentleness and strength that had her wondering what he'd be like as a lover.

Crap. Exhaustion had sent her mind on one heck of a trip to Fantasyville.

Josh noted, "You should have a security light out here."

"I do." She looked up at the spotlight controlled by a motion detector. "Must be burned out."

A warning tapped at her shoulders. That bulb had been replaced ten days ago. Had someone...

Stop jumping to stalker default. Every blown bulb wasn't the result of terror tactics. Besides, Josh was with her. Whatever training he'd had, she'd noticed serious muscle when she'd touched his chest at the shop earlier today.

For this one moment, she experienced something she hadn't enjoyed in a long while. She felt safe.

This man had persisted in accompanying a belligerent date to attend what had to be a boring event for him, then faced law enforcement at her store. *And* he'd helped her out by speaking up when she couldn't form a reasonable reply for why she and Josh had gone to her shop in evening clothes that time of night.

He'd come to her aid when she was reeling from the latest threat, expecting the shop to explode into flames at any moment.

Josh had been tolerant throughout the entire evening. More than that, he'd been giving her far more consideration than she'd given him.

She'd been the date from hell.

But he said the most bizarre things. Like just before the police showed up when she was sure he'd said he was *interested* in her.

Why would he toy with her that way? Especially at that moment when she was obviously distressed?

They reached the front door that needed a new coat of gray paint, which probably meant the shutters did, too. Unlocking the door, she stepped inside and hit the wall switch for the lamp.

That worked.

The burned-out spotlight was probably a fluke.

"I'm home and safe," she said, turning to Josh who stood too close behind her in the doorway. It even smelled safe with the welcoming scent of a winter mix potpourri.

Josh loomed over her just inside the doorway. "Aren't you going to invite me in for coffee?"

That was *not* a question about coffee. Any female would recognize that as a date wanting to come inside to get cozy.

Enough was enough.

She tossed her purse on the sofa. Out of patience and dead on her feet, she was done with this game. "Why would you want me to do that?"

He lifted his palm to her cheek. "Because I've been waiting all night to be alone with you."

"This is ridiculous," she muttered. "Are you going to tell me you're actually *attracted* to me?"

"No. I'm done talking." He cupped her face and kissed her.

She turned to stone, shocked beyond words. He sure as hell wasn't talking. He tasted warm and masculine. Everything about this kiss said skill and he used his lips the way an artist wielded a brush to create a perfect work of art. But something was missing.

The passion of an artist going for a one-of-a-kind.

This felt more like a reproduction. But damned sexy for a knockoff.

Trish grabbed the lapels of his tuxedo. He did look hot in a tux. Smoked that guy Ryder.

Ryder? Josh's partner. What kind of idiot was she?

One who thought this was a real kiss by a man really interested in her.

She broke away and backed up. "What was all *that* about?"

He scrubbed a hand over his face, mumbling, "What the hell?" Crossing his arms, he stabbed a dark look at her. "Are you going to tell me you weren't enjoying that kiss?"

"No, I can't say that."

"Or that you're not attracted to me?" he continued.

"Nope. Can't make that claim either, even if it does make me sound like an idiot."

"Why would that make you an idiot? What *is* the problem?"

She couldn't help it. Her mind had hit overload. She grabbed her head and started laughing. "What's wrong with this?" She spread her arms wide to indicate the two of them. "Nothing other than you being ... *gay*."

"What the fu ... are you serious?"

Angry Josh was a scary version of hot Josh. She hesitated then gave up. What was the old saying? *In for a penny, in for a pound.* "Yes, I'm dead serious so I don't understand why you kissed me."

When he could finally speak, his words came out chillingly soft. "I'm. Not. *Gay!*"

"Really?" She struggled to come up with something to say, but all that came out was, "Are you sure?"

He took two steps and pulled her into his arms, cupped her bottom and snugged her up against him. Close. Stomach to hip close. He said in a deep voice, rough with arousal. "Would I be this turned on if you *weren't* my type?"

Holy crap that was some erection. She didn't think he could fake that, and the next question was–why would he?

Heat coiled and started a slow burn in her womb. She stared into a fiery blue gaze that refused to let her go. "Guess not," whispered from her lips.

She ran her tongue over her lips.

The moment stretched tight as a piano wire then snapped when he lowered his head. He kissed her again, but not so softly this time.

This kiss packed a punch. Loaded with pure seduction.

His mouth took possession of hers, leaving no question that she was being kissed by a man who enjoyed women.

A man flush with passion and bent on creating a masterpiece.

She gave in to the longing that she'd fought against all day and pushed her hands up his shoulders, feeling the solid muscle. His tongue swept inside her mouth, brushing hers in a tangled dance.

Her breasts ached to be touched.

Her body had struck up a dialogue with his, and her body was liking this part of the conversation.

Kissing her deeper, his hand slipped between them to cup her breast. His thumb raked across the hard tip, dragging a desperate sound from her. No question he was aroused, and the impressive thickness pressed against her.

She shivered, wanting that. Wanting him.

His mouth teased the skin along her neck and shoulders, "You are so damned beautiful."

Trish smiled, lost in a sensual haze.

A car door slammed outside. Who ...?

Crap. Heidi. "Josh ... uhm ... we have to stop, Sugar."

He lifted his head, eyes sharp with hunger. "Why?"

"Heidi's home, and she's going to want answers."

The sigh that escaped him came from down deep. He released her and stepped back, breathing just as hard as she was.

She started straightening her dress.

Her mind took the conversation back from her body, and with that, sanity returned. She'd been kissing Josh as if naked would be next in her vocabulary. He had to get out of here. She couldn't be getting naked with anyone.

Heidi didn't bother to knock. She bounded in the front door, stopped, and crossed her arms. That pose warned no one was going to bed until she got answers. "What happened? I got your text."

Trish jumped on that opening to explain her hasty exit. "The police had a call about suspicious activity at ReSolution. They met us there."

The hard lines smoothed out on Heidi's forehead. She dropped her arms and came over to Trish. "Oh. Everything okay?"

"Yes. False alarm." Trish hated lying to Heidi by omission, but she still didn't know why the stalker had sent the police or left that black rook. The stalker's notes had mentioned Zane and Angel but made it very clear that anyone Trish spoke to about their little game would be at risk. For that reason, she could not share any of this with Heidi. "I'll walk Josh out and be right back."

Heidi gave Josh a once over, as if questioning his presence then nodded. "I'm grabbing a shower and changing, but don't go to bed until we talk," she said, making sure Trish knew she wanted more than a quick explanation. "I told everyone at the banquet you had an emergency. They made appropriate noises of concern and gave me your sealed packet of information."

Trish could tell Heidi hadn't been happy about using the "emergency" excuse but had given Trish the benefit of the doubt that she did have an emergency of some sort.

"I'm not going to bed any time soon. Thanks for standing in for me." Trish had until Heidi finished her shower to come up with a story that sounded believable.

Heidi said goodnight to Josh and disappeared back out the front door. Trish heard her double-timing up the steps to her apartment.

What had been one sizzling moment was now awkward as Trish herded Josh toward the door. Once they were both outside, she pulled the door almost closed. What did she say to him now? "Look about what I said–"

"Did you *really* think I was gay?"

"It didn't make sense. But Zane said–"

Josh covered his eyes with a hand then dropped it. "I've heard how overprotective he is but telling you *that* just so you'd keep your distance was one ballsy move."

Trish hesitated to tell Josh that Leanne was the one who'd said he was gay. That might cause bad feelings at the task force. She'd ask Leanne about it next time she saw her, but first she had to smooth this over for Zane.

Since Josh assumed Zane had made that up, Trish said, "My brother means well."

"I still don't understand how *you* could think–"

She held up her hand. "In my defense, I might not have been sold on it if I hadn't met Ryder."

"What did *he* say?" Josh tensed just as he had when Ryder had stood next to him.

"He didn't say anything," she rushed to explain before this caused even more problems within the task force. "I thought he was your partner. You know ... life partner."

Josh's lips parted with confusion then he threw his head back and laughed, a real, heart-felt sound. She had the strange feeling that he didn't laugh often or hadn't in a while because of how it came out almost like relief. He was a physically beautiful male but seeing his eyes light up that way exposed a relaxed side she found far more attractive.

His laughing slowed to a chuckle. "Glad we cleared that up."

"Shouldn't have happened to begin with. I feel like a fool."

Josh angled his head, a quirk at his lips. "You have a look that says, little sister paybacks are hell."

"You have no idea."

"I sort of do. Let's not tell Zane," Josh suggested. "That way he won't be a nuisance."

"A nuisance for what?"

"For us seeing each other."

Hold everything. "No. I'm sold on you being a super stud, okay? But I'm not dating right now."

"Why?"

Did he have to question everything she said? "I'm not ready to date again."

"Because of your rehab program?"

After so many hours spent in AA meetings and rehab, her chest shouldn't get tight when somebody said it out loud. It wasn't a secret, but she still struggled with the stigma. "Not sure how you know that, but yes, that's the reason. I'm not ready to get involved with anyone."

"That's perfect. I don't want to get involved either. But I'm going to be here for another two weeks, and I'd like to see you again."

"Josh, I'll be blunt. I'm not sleeping with you."

He was just as blunt. "I didn't ask you to."

Well, damn. What was she supposed to think after that kiss went atomic?

Cupping her chin with his fingers, he leaned down. "What do you say we just get to know each other? No pressure for you, and I won't have to spend my entire time here alone. I'll call you tomorrow." He kissed her lightly on the lips and walked to his car.

He proposed a relationship that sounded like hers and Brendan's, except Brendan's quick goodbye kisses were more like Zane's, a brotherly touch on the cheek that she didn't feel all the way to her toes.

Josh sure as hell didn't kiss like a brother.

There had to be a catch to his offer. Nothing could be that easy.

Not when it came to men like Josh Robertson.

She watched the taillights of his Porsche fade as he drove away, thankful he'd been with her tonight when she had to face the police. Trish slapped a palm against her forehead.

When did you get the crazy idea that you were out of danger?

There was no way she could see Josh again. Not with a crazy stalker watching everything she did. She couldn't be responsible for the safety of one more person.

Her body disagreed with the decision, but her body only cared about getting up close to all that hot male again. After all she'd done to push Josh away, Trish liked him.

And that was the biggest problem of all.

It bugged her to think about him with another woman, but she couldn't face herself if anything happened to someone that sweet and considerate.

He'd have to find someone else to keep him company.

CHAPTER 14

Sabrina waited for the hostess to mark her dinner reservation off the list. The trendy restaurant fit the upscale Alpharetta area north of Atlanta, but the drive for those who worked downtown had to be a bugger every morning.

"Your other party has not arrived yet," the young lady said. "Would you prefer inside or the veranda?"

"Veranda."

The hostess cringed slightly but started gathering up what she needed.

Sabrina had dressed in black jeans, a turtleneck sweater and leather jacket for sitting outside in chilly evening weather. And to conceal her weapon in an easily accessible place.

Temperatures hovering just below sixty would make sitting outside unpleasant for most people, and so, prevent civilian casualties if the meeting went bad.

Lifting menus, the hostess led Sabrina past tables covered in white linen and surrounded by pods of people enjoying meals and conversations.

With no other patrons on the veranda, Sabrina had her choice of tables, just as she'd planned. And just as she'd known, the outside tables offered an optimum location for a sniper shot. Before the shivering hostess left, Sabrina told her, "Please let the server know that once my guest arrives, we need some time to chat, and to give me at least fifteen minutes before coming to the table."

"Absolutely."

No point in ordering food that would very likely not be eaten.

Where *was* this snitch?

The only reason Sabrina had even considered this meeting was because Burton claimed the snitch had significant intel on her operation in Miami and he would only share it with her in person.

Burton, a DEA contact she'd known for close to ten years, had vouched for the snitch. But Burton would not give her a name. He said he'd given his word and she'd understand the reason he was being so cryptic once she'd met the man.

So, as far as she was concerned, Burton should understand the reason she had a sniper in position to take out any threat the instant she gave the signal.

She'd chosen this location because it was the only place that provided a clear shot without threat to civilians. She sat in the corner with her back to the brick wall, trying to figure out who might be her guest for lunch.

Then *he* appeared.

Every thump of Sabrina's heart pounded in her ears.

She might kill Burton. If she survived.

Her guest came forward slowly. No sudden moves. She'd never considered him attractive so much as a forceful personality that had its own brand of magnetism. Nose too wide, square jaw, rugged mouth of a man who loved as hard as he lived. Coarse brown hair that barely touched his collar and the length changed often, just as his now clean-shaven face was sometimes covered with a beard. Not quite six feet, he carried his weight in attitude as much as the lean muscle she knew lurked beneath that camelhair sport coat.

The bronze-colored shirt had been an intentional choice.

She'd once told him that she liked him in autumn colors, liked how it brought out the gold in his hazel eyes. Silly words said late at night.

Stupid, stupid mistakes committed time and again starting five years ago.

She'd spent the last two of those years planning ways to kill him.

So why was she allowing him to breathe her air for one more second?

The answer to that lay buried so deep in her chest she didn't want to dig it up and crack open a door to emotions she could never trust again.

Gage Laughton stopped at the edge of her table. "Sabrina."

She said nothing, staring up at him with hatred burning through her. All she had to do was touch her right earring, right *now*, and his head would explode in the next second.

That would ruin a few appetites for those sitting too close to the windows.

Gage pulled out a chair carefully, his eyes on her, clearly aware of his precarious position as he sat. Every movement was deliberate and should be. "I wanted a chance to talk to you."

She was glad for the turtleneck sweater that hid her involuntary swallow. Hurt and anger crashed around in her heart. When she knew she could speak without any hitch in her voice, she said very softly, "I warn you to take care with your words. The only reason you are still alive right now is because neither Dingo nor Josh has his finger on the trigger covering me. *They* wouldn't wait for my signal to fire. Keep your hands where I can see them."

"I understand, but this is important to both of us."

Pissing her off always helped bring the situation into focus. "You flatter yourself to include me in anything significant to you."

Her strike hit true. Pain grazed his eyes, but she refused to be touched by it. He'd played her once, sacrificed her and her team. To be honest, she didn't want him dead. Yet. Not until she found out why he'd betrayed her trust in the most brutal way possible.

"I *didn't* betray you," he said as if he could hear her thoughts screaming at him. "We've been investigating–"

"For *two* years?"

"Yes."

"Who picked up Len Rikker that night from Mendelson?"

"We don't know. We're still digging for answers and looking for Rikker. I want to know who burned you as much as you do."

She scoffed. "No, you don't, because if you did you would send every assassin in your arsenal after him. You're two steps from the top of the CIA and you want me to believe that you don't know who was dealing with Mendelson and where

Rikker went? Has it not occurred to you that I might be less gullible than I was before?"

He leaned back, chagrined. "I never thought of you as gullible and I did *not* screw you over, Sabrina."

She remembered that voice, the one so coated heavily in honesty that it had finally broken through her barriers once. Not again. "I have no intention of eating with someone I find disgusting. If you have no intel, I will permit you to walk away *alive* this one time as long as you never try to speak to me again."

Misery lined his eyes and the grim tilt of his mouth, but to his benefit he recognized a lost cause even if he didn't accept it. "I do have intel. And don't blame Burton for this."

"I don't, but if you gave a rat's ass about US teenagers, or the shipment of Spa Zing Burton's people are trying to stop, you would have handed over what intel you have to *him*."

"I wouldn't have kept it from him if you'd refused the meeting," he admitted. "That's why I asked him, as a favor, to not tell you it was me. I knew you wouldn't meet with me otherwise."

"That's easy to claim now that you're here."

"I know. I'm hoping what I have to tell you will show that I'm trying to help you."

She didn't respond. Wouldn't give him an ounce of understanding.

Taking a deep breath, he started explaining. "I know you have a team in the Miami task force, but you may need to send more agents."

She snorted at that. "You think I'm stupid enough to give you a second shot at my people?"

A muscle pulsed in his neck, the only sign his patience had a limit. Too bad. She had less.

"Hear me out, Sabrina. Then do as you will. Burton's people are focused on High Vision's designer drug shipments, not the real danger coming to south Florida."

"And that would be?"

"We don't know yet."

"Then what makes you think there's more going on than drug running?"

"Because Len Rikker is down there."

She'd been toying with her keys and only years of control kept her from clenching the key ring. "We know."

That surprised him. No physical twitch gave him away. It was the way he looked up calmly at her. This was a man whose control could not be broken easily.

She knew. She'd enjoyed wrecking it at one time.

Nodding slightly, he continued, but did not ask how she knew about Rikker. "We just found out that he's stateside. I believe the mole Burton is after is in contact with Rikker."

Lifting an indifferent shoulder, she said, "Still nothing new."

"But the code name for Rikker's contact might be."

Ask him or not? She wanted to throw his words back in his face, but the mission had always come first. Josh and Ryder needed any intel she could find no matter the means. "Yes, I'd like to know that."

"The contact is called Chessmaster."

Gage hadn't tried to negotiate. Just gave up the name. She'd think on that later. "Male or female?"

"Don't know. We cooperate with other agencies, but we all horde information."

"Especially spooks." She should have kept that in mind two years ago.

"Guilty as charged ... but I did not hold back on the UK," he argued.

"We're not here to discuss *that*."

He nodded again, keeping his fury contained. "*We* have to find Rikker."

Every muscle in her body tightened at his easy use of "we," as if there was still a *we*.

Barely lifting his fingers off the tabletop to stall her reply, he explained, "Rikker's presence is the reason we know there's more going on than contraband shipments. Burton believes the FBI has had recent breaches in classified information similar to what's happening in the South Florida DEA. He and I both think there's a cancer seeping into the agencies. Your team is the only neutral player in all this."

She absorbed the significance of that. *If* it was true. "What do you think Rikker's presence means?"

"I'm going to share classified information with you that I have to trust you to not pass along, even to your own people. Burton doesn't know this."

This was a first.

She'd always had to report back to Gage, every detail on an operation, any intel, but he had maintained limits on what he would share with her.

He watched her with eyes searching for an opening, some small crevice he might ease into. The silence grew and expanded as he waited to see if she would give her word, something she'd taught him she did not give lightly.

She'd grown up on the streets where a person's word was currency. Hers came with a titanium rating.

This man didn't deserve her vow of honor, but she had to put her team first. They couldn't miss this chance to find Rikker. "You have my word."

"Thank you."

Why had he said that? So unnecessary and it gave the impression he'd extended an olive branch that she'd accepted. "Your time is almost up. Don't confuse cooperation with trust."

A feral turbulence built in his gaze, but in a blink the steel shutters slammed into place. "Rikker was not in the UK to uncover a terrorist plot against the US or Ireland two years ago. That's why no bombing ever happened in either country after Rikker went missing. He was tracking an organization called The Orion Hunters. A bunch of people who believe that five rare artifacts will predict the final world war that destroys world powers."

She'd almost lost Josh for that bullshit?

If Josh were here right now, he'd rip Gage's head off his shoulders. Chelsea had died to protect two countries and to save a CIA agent. None of which had been necessary. "You sent me and my team on a fool's run? Put my people in jeopardy for some ridiculous group looking for artifacts?" She was leaning forward, hands gripping the arms of her chair.

"No, dammit," Gage bit out low and sharp, hunched forward, too. "I had no idea either until I started ripping people apart to get answers. I couldn't find you, couldn't find word of any of you for months." He looked away, staring off for long seconds then back at her. "You vanished. I thought ... I thought you were dead."

His voice remained steady, but her ear was tuned to catch the moment of emotion that broke through.

She didn't want to hear that or give credit to the anguish gripping his words. Forcing herself to calm down and sit back, she took several breaths while her gaze roamed over the empty veranda. On the other side of the windows looking into the restaurant, friends chatted and laughed.

No idea that two cold-blooded killers sat so close to them.

"Sabrina."

One word said with so much emotion she had to take an extra moment before she brought her gaze back to him. *Stick to business.* "So, what are you telling me?"

His gaze dropped first. He gave another of his little nods, pulling his control in with tight fists, then his game face returned. "The Orion Hunters have been around for a very long time, but then so have a hundred other groups anchored in conspiratorial myth. It took me most of the past two years to piece together enough to figure out that Mendelson had captured someone he believed was connected to these Orion Hunters. He had no idea just what he'd caught."

"A double agent?"

"Possibly. That's the simplest explanation, but nothing is simple about any of this. As far as I'm concerned, Rikker's been a traitor for a long time, but we have proof now. Digging for any lead on him turned up a deadly pattern. He's been in the vicinity multiple times prior to major terrorist attacks. We established his presence at each one, but the thing that makes no sense is that the outcome of every attack benefited a different faction, some that were vicious enemies of the ones who'd benefited from the last attack. It's like he's freelancing for any group who picks a victim of the week."

The picture came clear in her mind. "You think he's involved in terrorist activity in Miami."

"We have evidence of at least three occasions when he was on site for six to twelve weeks prior to an attack. Hundreds killed and maimed in a subway attack and an apartment building bombing. Sixteen young missionaries died in a bus sitting next to a building in Dublin. The building had a suspicious massive electrical overload and exploded."

"How do you know he was involved in each of these?"

"We have surveillance footage showing him on site every time, but we never get the evidence until after he's gone. He has to be found."

"My people will find him *and* his contact the Chessmaster."

"That's why I want to work with you." Gage paused, then added, "I've got intel and I'm willing to share."

No pleading. Gage didn't plead, but that last part about sharing had come out with a tinge of hope that pinched her heart. An organ she'd disconnected from her brain two years ago.

Gage added, "I just want him alive."

That killed the moment.

She stood up. "You wanted him alive the *last* time and we put everything on the line to deliver."

"My people didn't screw you."

She countered in a low harsh voice. "Someone in your agency did and *you* were my handler. That makes you responsible."

Gage played the card he'd clearly been holding back. "No one has bothered you or your new corporate security company because I'm keeping the agency off your back. But I can only do so much, Sabrina. Fail to turn Rikker over and you'll be considered an enemy of the state."

She leaned down, placing a hand on the white tablecloth and kept her voice soft. "I'm not working with anyone but my own people. When we find Rikker, and we will, the only questions he's answering are mine. Stay out of my way, because anyone who crosses me will be considered an enemy of my *team* and a threat to our existence." Sabrina stood straight. "Sit very still with your hands on the table for five minutes. You so much as twitch a finger, and they'll carry you out of here."

Sabrina stepped around the table and headed out of the restaurant.

CHAPTER 15

That kiss got way the hell out of hand.

Dangerously out of hand. Josh cruised along the beach highway with no destination in mind. He couldn't think of one that would bring clarity to his muddled brain.

The goal had been for him to get close to Trish Jackson quickly. Mission accomplished and a helluva feat, too, now that he knew what had been going on inside her head the whole night.

It had damn near been mission failure when he'd almost lost control of the situation. If Heidi had shown up another minute later, she'd have walked in on a half-naked Trish.

Maybe all naked.

Son of a bitch, he still wanted her.

Kissing her that first time had been about getting inside her defenses. He couldn't claim that had played any part in the second kiss that had been way too real, raw honesty he hadn't intended to ever let out of its cage again.

Not after Chelsea.

He downshifted and accelerated around a truck poking along.

His *job* was to manipulate the enemy.

But was Trish the enemy? His gut was saying she'd given too freely in that moment.

What if that chess piece meant nothing and Trish was *not* involved with the mole?

If that turned out to be the case, encouraging her to see him again and taking advantage of this attraction would be using her in the worst way. Doubt gnawed at his conscience, but he couldn't allow beautiful brown eyes and a sweet smile to sway him.

He couldn't do sweet again. Couldn't let it influence his judgment.

Duty came first and he would do whatever it took to catch Len Rikker.

This is who you are. Accept it. There was no room for guilt in his world. Guilt was reserved for people who had the luxury of following conscience.

For people who expected to, one day, live a normal life.

He'd made a pact with Sabrina and Dingo. Len Rikker and the people responsible for burning their team had to pay.

Josh would not let them, or Chelsea, down.

But could he hurt Trish Jackson and walk away without leaving a part of himself behind?

He shoved that concern aside for the moment and called Sabrina. Once he confirmed they were on a secure line, he launched into his report. He started with Zane's agreeing for Josh to accompany Trish tonight, covered Trish's strange text then explained what happened at ReSolution.

Sabrina interrupted. "What did the police find at Trish Jackson's shop?"

"Nothing. It could have been a prank call, but I have a feeling it's tied to something strange Trish found after they left."

"What?"

"A chess piece carved of onyx with a gold band."

"No *shit?*"

He sat up straighter. Alert. "Why's that important?"

"It might be the connection we're looking for. I've been waiting on your call to tell you what I found out today. The mole's code name is Chessmaster."

He should be thrilled to hear that, but in a moment of honesty he realized he hadn't wanted Trish to be a part of all this. "How do we know that?"

A pause stretched long seconds before Sabrina said, "I received some unexpected intel today. That chess piece *is* significant. Trish Jackson either *knows* who the Chessmaster is or..."

"She *is* the Chessmaster," Josh finished.

"Exactly."

Josh shoved his disappointment aside and told himself this was great news even if he did feel miserable. "I'll have a definitive answer in a day or two."

"We may need it sooner."

He slowed to pull off the highway and park along the beach. When he cut his engine and headlights, abrupt silence gave way to the ocean's soft roar along the dark shoreline. "What's happened? Have we gotten word on a shipment?"

"No, but we have bigger problems than bath salt getting into the states."

He didn't want to think about something worse than drugs that caused a young man to go from a promising future to becoming a lunatic who laughed hysterically one minute and screamed in terror the next, over, and over. "What?"

"I'd say it's a terrorist attack, but no one knows enough to define what we're looking for. Rikker is tied to three deadly attacks in the past year, so far. Significant body counts in each attack, but a different group claimed responsibility in all three incidents. None of these groups work together so there's no way to know who he's working for this time."

Josh propped his elbow on his car door, tapping his thumb on his cheek. He could think of only one agency that would have information on Rikker. "Where'd you get this intel?"

"That's not important."

If that were the case, why be evasive? "Are you in contact with the agency again?" They both knew *which* agency he referenced.

He got his answer when she said nothing. Josh swore viciously. "And you believe *them*?"

"In this situation, yes."

"Why would you even listen to anything they have to say?"

"Because he shared information no other agency has. I took one for the team."

Josh caught her damning slip. "Wait a minute. Back up to the *he*. He who?"

She cursed lividly. "Not important."

Josh stomped the floorboard. "Bullshit. I don't fucking believe this. Did you really meet with *him*?" He didn't give two shits about protecting Gage Laughton, but he'd given his word to Sabrina to never mention Gage's name when they were on any electronic device, no matter how secure.

She wanted to kill the bastard as much as Josh and Dingo did. Or she *had* wanted to at one time. What had changed?

"You have a job to do," Sabrina said with the bite of a winter storm. "Either do it or tell me to send someone else. No part of your assignment involves questioning me. Got it?"

"Yeah, I got it," he snarled right back. "I'll find that bastard Rikker and the Chessmaster. But don't think in your wildest moment that I'm handing him over to your *buddy*."

"We'll discuss it when you have said target in hand."

No, we won't. "You forget the deal you made with me and Dingo?"

"You can be such a bastard. *Of course not.* We get our shot at him before anyone else no matter what."

Their agreement hadn't included *anyone else* before today. He answered with enough sarcasm to ensure she didn't take his words to heart. "You're the boss."

"And you're the asshole. Now that we're through playing footsie, back to the op. I'm sending down an additional team, but they'll be in the background. Anything else?"

"No."

The call ended with a click.

Josh couldn't believe she was going to hand Rikker over to the CIA. Screw the agency.

They claimed not to have had any part in trading Sabrina's team for Rikker, but Josh believed Mendelson who'd said he made a deal with someone in the CIA. If Rikker was walking around free and the agency had no idea where he was, that meant Rikker was the only one who could tell Josh who'd burned his team. If Rikker had been found at terrorist operations since then, Rikker was clearly the enemy.

The CIA could have that bastard after Josh was through with him, but there wouldn't be a lot of discussion going on if he delivered Rikker minus most of his head.

Some days he hated everything about the spook world.

Most days.

The last two years of misery and a burning need for justice came crashing down on Josh. He knew what he had to do tomorrow, no ifs, ands, or buts.

Searching for some objectivity, he got down to basic facts. Trish could be a sophisticated operative or working in sync with one. He'd come up against some of the best in the world of spooks, and they could put the A-list in Hollywood to shame.

He'd determine whether Trish was the Chessmaster's contact person or the actual mole. Then he'd make the call for a Slye team to snatch her and hand Trish over to Sabrina.

CHAPTER 16

Trish hugged her mug of coffee and leaned on the counter in the showroom of ReSolution, trying not to accept defeat mentally before it had been delivered to her. Her brother would say, "Can't win 'em all, honey."

She didn't want them all. But she had to have *this* one. *Needed* this consulting position, or she had real concerns about making it through a full year with ReSolution.

If she didn't, everyone would just chalk it up to another Trish failure. Except this would be a really, really expensive one.

The naysayers were probably booking bets on how long she'd last without drinking. Her biggest customer draws right now were consignment pieces she'd acquired since gaining recognition in the preliminary rounds of this competition. Those would go away first if she stumbled.

One mistake would cost her everything.

No longer walking around in an alcohol-dulled haze, she couldn't face another failure. Sobriety sharpened everything, but most of all her emotions. She wanted this win.

Just once, she wanted to kick ass on her own merits, and not need anybody to pick her up and carry her to the finish. Was that too much to ask?

She'd aced everything the television group had handed her so far, but now she stared at what they expected next, detailed neatly in her packet of instructions. This had all seemed doable yesterday.

While the couple she'd helped earlier still strolled around the showroom, Trish studied the forms in her packet. With the fifteenth century as her specialty, she had to find someone knowledgeable about the famous Amber Room. Her first thought was to wonder whether the show had a bona fide artifact or not, but that might be the real test–the ability to differentiate real from bogus.

Many collectors of World War II items were familiar with the Amber Room's history, but to evaluate an actual piece required someone with exceptional ability.

Oh, and that person had to be a celebrity.

Trish had come up with one celebrity guest who *might* give her an edge over Xavier in this last round.

A soft jingle from the front door drew her attention. The female of the young couple waved at Trish and said, "Thanks for the background on that armoire. Love your shop. I made notes for when I come back."

"Thank you and have a nice day." Trish didn't like pushy salespeople, so she gave customers space to meander. She'd always been a people person and enjoyed spending time with everyone who came in.

Well, almost everyone.

Her least favorite customer entered as the couple left.

Calling the old woman a customer was a stretch since she had yet to spend anything except time.

Decisions, decisions. Arrange inanimate metal sculptures–guaranteed not to give Trish grief–or attempt to assist the elderly woman she'd privately nicknamed Pruneface, who lived for ruining an otherwise promising day? *Suck it up and be the better person.*

Trish sidled over to where Pruneface scowled at Heidi's jubilant display of hand-cast sterling-silver flatware and color-splashed dishes that added flair to quality antiques. Pruneface browsed through ReSolution for the third time in two weeks. For what purpose, Trish had no idea, because the old bat had yet to find anything that met with her satisfaction.

Patience. The woman walked bent over as if she suffered from some form of osteoporosis.

"May I help you?" Trish asked, infusing a heavy dose of peppy tone.

Pruneface cocked up her garish face. Thick makeup covered her haggish features. Severe rouge slashed her cheeks and poorly applied, rust-colored lipstick had been stroked across her perpetual frown.

"You don't have any antiques with pelicans," the old biddy stated in a gritty voice.

Guilty as charged. Trish kept her smile plastered in place. Easy to do with her teeth clenched. She couldn't take much more abuse this week. If the old biddy wanted pelicans, she'd send her to Gunter's shop.

"You might want to check out Dynasty Treasures about two blocks down. They have some wonderfully eclectic pieces." *And if Gunter didn't move into the twenty-first century soon his struggling business was going to be left behind.* But he did possess sets of extremely rare, handcrafted antique silver place settings from around the world, some of which had belonged to royalty.

Who knew, maybe Pruneface was an eccentric millionairess who would love Gunter's shop and bring enough friends to put him on the cover of Forbes.

Sure, and Florida would never get hit by a hurricane again.

"You're right." The old woman smiled, well, sneered was more like it. "That place sounds like it has a better selection."

Trish thought she recognized something in the woman's voice that she couldn't pin down, but she dismissed it. No way to forget someone this gaudy and irritating.

Bad enough that Pruneface had managed to further deflate Trish's already sagging attitude, but the blatant slam against ReSolution was akin to making a derogatory remark about a person's only child.

Some people lived to offend others.

Trish kept her I-will-not-be-baited smile in place. "I'm sorry we couldn't help you. I hope you find what you're looking for at Dynasty Treasures. The owner is a wonderful man."

"Hmph." The hunched figure tottered around and shuffle-stomped across the floor and out of the shop.

"Nice dismissal, but sending people away isn't going to help our bottom line," Heidi said, emerging from the storage room.

"Yeah, I know, but she wasn't going to spend money here. She doesn't like me or our merchandise," Trish grumbled. She swung around to find her friend holding a long cardboard box.

"It's not you," Heidi said. "She hates life in general."

"You're probably right, Sug. What's in the box?"

Heidi's face broke into a cheery smile. She removed the lid. "Found this outside the delivery door in the back. Looks like you got flowers."

Trish took the box containing a dozen yellow roses in a vase and carried it over to place on the counter. She pulled the small envelope off a plastic holder.

Small, dove-gray envelope.

She heard a buzzing in her ears and felt the room tilt a little.

Heidi's eyes were bright with anticipation.

Trish didn't want to open this in front of her, but she had no choice. When her hand shook, Heidi grinned even more, no doubt misinterpreting Trish's tremble as excitement.

When she got the card free of the envelope, she made a show of reading the message out loud. "Thanks for a great time. Your secret admirer."

Heidi snorted. "A little hokey, but sweet."

Hammering started in the back room. Bunko building the shelves.

Heidi rolled her eyes and walked away, muttering, "I don't know that we're saving any money with him playing carpenter."

Trish waited until Heidi was out of sight before she lifted the card to read the actual text:

Roses are yellow for a little hello. I've done something nice for you. Now you will do something for me little pawn. Keep your phone handy.

This stalking had to stop.

She wiped her mouth with a shaky hand and licked her lips. The buzzing in her ears got louder. One drink would calm her nerves. She could almost taste the bourbon and craved that first hit when the alcohol drenched her stress.

Don't think about drinking.

Maybe she should go to an AA meeting tonight.

She'd missed the last few because she'd been traveling, and crazy busy with the competition.

When Heidi stepped out from the back again, Trish shoved the card and envelope into her jacket pocket. "How long before Bunko is done?"

"Are we talking days or millennia?"

Glad to have a different topic, Trish forced a chuckle out of her tight throat. "Come on, Heidi, give him some credit."

"He's only supposed to be part-time. Every time I turn around, he's here."

Trish was starting to think Bunko's interest in ReSolution had more to do with Heidi than the little bit of money Trish paid him. "Don't you think he's nice?"

Heidi's gaze drifted toward the back of the shop with a warmth Trish hadn't seen before, then Heidi shrugged. "He's okay." She glanced over at the unfinished forms Trish had been working on. "What rare antique did *you* end up having to find talent for?"

"A panel from the Amber Room."

"That's great, right?"

"I guess so," Trish hesitated, then said, "That room was considered the eighth wonder of the world before it was destroyed."

"Then why do you sound concerned? You should have this nailed." Heidi grinned.

True, and Trish had spent plenty of hours studying the history surrounding that room. "It's not the panel that has me worried. The producers are testing to see how extensive our resource database is and how adept we are at convincing celebrities to come on the show. I dug through my old files from when I was working with Mrs. Bromley."

"Did you find someone?"

"Maybe. Senator Dixon has been a long-time collector of artifacts surrounding World War II. I surfed the net this morning and found an article on him from last year where he said that he has a particular fascination with the Amber Room so he's a good fit, but that doesn't mean he's an expert or that he'll be charismatic on camera." Which made him a risky choice.

"Have you called his office?"

"Yes, and it took a few tries, but I finally reached his assistant. I was told the Senator's schedule was booked for months."

"But you didn't talk to the man himself, did you?"

"No."

"He might do it. You have to at least get past the gatekeepers and find out for sure before you give up on him."

Heidi was right, but Trish couldn't see why the Senator would consider this when he was so busy. She'd been hoping to ask one of the celebrity collectors she'd researched whose ratings had dropped in the last few years and who might need the publicity. "I have to do something. Xavier has the edge with Big Charlie in her corner. He'll give her access to an international database and pull out all the stops to help her win."

"Screw Big Charlie, and you can run circles around Xavier when it comes to knowing your stuff. She depends too much on her looks."

Trish smiled over Heidi's unwavering support. "Xavier's got her certification, and she's my only rival since the producers are choosing *one* female and *one* male. If she comes up with a strong celebrity guest, I'm screwed."

The door jingled at the same time Heidi said, "Uh oh." Her eyebrows jumped up and down.

"What?"

"He does not look happy. Maybe you should have sent *him* flowers."

Trish turned around to find Josh bearing down on her. "Crap."

"So, you know why he looks that way, huh?" Heidi asked then added, "Think I'll supervise the shelf building."

"Heidi..." But she was gone.

Trish crossed her arms, refusing to let Josh know her insides turned to jelly every time she relived last night's kiss.

Now was the time to be firm and send him away, not melt in a puddle of longing at his feet. Especially now that she knew he was definitely available, and their chemistry could power all of Miami.

Josh's long strides ate up the distance from the door to her. He had on an open-collar cream shirt and dark sport coat with khaki pants. She had the urge to brush her fingers through his windblown hair.

Bad idea. No hair touching. No kissing. When he reached her, she said in her most curt tone, "What can I do for you?"

"You could *start* by returning a phone call or the texts I've sent."

"I was busy." *Avoiding you.* She'd hoped he would get annoyed enough that he'd give up and move on to someone more promising. She hadn't trusted herself not to fold if she talked to him. Sad to admit that she had no more self-control than that, but he brought her erogenous zones to life with just a look.

"No one is *that* busy unless they work the emergency room."

He had a point but admitting it would be incriminating. While he was here, he could answer a question she'd been worrying over. "Did you discuss last night with my brother?"

"Yes. I told him we had a wonderful time, and you were going to help me choose antiques for a sunroom back home that I plan to redecorate. Somewhere I could work on my watercolor art." His eyes twinkled with humor.

"Are you an artist?"

There was the scowl she'd seen last night when she'd asked him if he was sure he wasn't gay.

Josh made a growling sound. "No, I'm not an artist and don't have a sunroom. I was just reinforcing what your brother believes."

"Did Zane mention that another friend of mine does have a sunroom I helped redecorate?"

"As a matter of fact, he did. Somebody named Brendan." Josh watched her face. "Who is he?"

"A friend," she repeated. "Did you discuss anything else?"

"No, Zane left in a hurry. Leanne said he had to fly out with one of his new pilots."

Leanne.

Trish would bet money that Leanne could figure out how to reach the Senator. "Is Leanne in the office all day?"

"I have no idea, but she'll probably be back for a meeting at five. Why?"

She didn't want to start up a new subject when she needed Josh to leave so she could contact Leanne. "Just curious. You never said why you were trying to get in touch with me."

"I *originally* wanted to take you to lunch, but that passed two hours ago so we're down to dinner. I was thinking we'd ride over to South Beach tonight, eat dinner and take a walk."

Why did he have to be so charming and sexy and determined *now*? Why couldn't he have shown up in her life down the road after she felt like she was ready for this? "Sorry I didn't get back to you before lunch, but I'm not available."

"Now? Or ever?"

He just had to push her. "Ever."

"Why are we going to do this again?"

The bell rang again and a man with an Alfred Hitchcock profile entered, glanced around, then meandered off to the right.

Trish had stuck her head past Josh, letting him know she had more important things to do than discuss dinner with him. When the customer disappeared behind tall furniture, she told Josh, "We're not *doing* anything and that's the point. I appreciate your offer to get together with no pressure, but I'm going to pass."

"And here I thought you'd want to show your appreciation."

"For what?"

"Me suffering through the third degree with your brother on how last night went. Zane wanted details. All of them."

Like the police showing up. He didn't say it, but that's what he meant. And she'd forgotten about that...

Okay, that wasn't exactly true. She hadn't *forgotten* really. It was just that watching police snoop through her shop for a bogus drug dealing tip had fallen down her worry list behind the stalker, the competition and Josh's four messages.

Trish asked, "What'd you tell Zane?"

"That you managed to look elegant and professional at the same time last night."

She refused to let him slide inside her defenses with his smooth charm. "You know that's not what I mean."

He took a step closer. "You mean did I rat you out on the police visit? No."

When he put it like that, she did sort of owe him, dammit.

But what if the stalker saw her with Josh and targeted him?

On the other hand, what if Zane found out about the police being sent to her shop for drugs? Zane would show up and suffocate her with round-the-clock protection.

And wouldn't that go over big with the stupid stalker?

The stalker had probably sent the police to her shop to punish her for going to see Zane. A second warning might not be as benign.

Keeping Zane away from ReSolution was paramount, second only to keeping him away from *her*, period.

The longer she stood here arguing, the less time she had to contact Leanne without chancing Zane's being nearby when Trish called.

Josh had found the perfect way to manipulate her into dinner. Would he *really* keep his hands and lips to himself if they went for a walk on the beach?

Do you really want him to?

That had to be her hormones talking. Mouthy bunch.

She finally said, "Okay. What time do you want to go?"

He muttered, "I asked you to dinner. Not to clean my apartment.'"

Agreeing wasn't enough for Super Stud? He expected enthusiasm, too? She gave smiling her best effort. "Sorry. Long day. Dinner sounds wonderful."

The look he gave her said she hadn't convinced him, but he let it pass. "I'll pick you up here at six." His gaze ran over her and paused at her face. He reached up and touched her hair, toying with the curls. "You don't mind the top down on my car, do you?"

His finger moved from her hair to her neck where he stroked lightly down the side of it.

She hadn't known a straight line of nerves ran from her neck to her breasts, but her nipples puckered. Breathing became difficult. Thinking was even more taxing. "Um..."

When his fingers slipped around under her chin and lifted gently, he leaned down.

Her lips parted. Her body ached, waiting for more of his touch. Just as he got close enough to kiss her, he moved his mouth to the side and kissed her cheek. His voice came out low and rough. "Don't even think about standing me up. See you at six."

With that threat hanging in the air, he walked out of the shop.

Trish stood there, trying to regain control of her body that was on high alert for sex and wanted to send her after Josh like a heat-seeking missile. She had to find some way to discourage him from any more dates.

Because he had *mistake* written all over him. She liked being with Josh, loved the way he kissed and the feel of his hands. But he was leaving in two weeks and, if that wasn't deterrent enough, he was with the task force. She loved her brother, but she didn't want someone who had to keep what he did a secret. She wanted a man who would share his world with her.

Nothing good could come of her and Josh getting to know each other better.

But right now, she was running out of time to line up a celebrity collector for the television show. She hurried to the sales desk where she grabbed her cell phone to text a message asking Leanne if she had time to talk about something confidential today.

Leanne sent back that she had a window of time at quarter after four if Trish wanted to come down then. Trish started to send back that she'd rather talk by phone but considering that

Leanne worked for the DEA and her father was a politician, Leanne might hesitate to answer Trish's questions over a cell phone about how to reach a senator.

She sent another text asking when Zane would be back, and Leanne replied that she didn't expect him until five-thirty.

That was plenty of time. Trish confirmed the meeting.

And prayed that Zane did not return to his office before Trish left. She had to declare her celebrity guest by six today or forfeit her position.

Leanne would help her. Had to. If Xavier got the television position, Trish's chances of keeping ReSolution out of Big Charlie's hands wouldn't be worth calculating. She could not lose this shop. This was the reason she got up every day and fought her demons.

Thinking of demons, she thought again about the stalker.

Her fingers trembled when she ran them through her hair. Would the stalker know that Zane wasn't in the office?

CHAPTER 17

The Chessmaster stood on top of a ten-story building and waited for a sat phone call to go through. The view of downtown Miami sprawling in all directions beneath overcast skies included the DEA task force offices two blocks away.

When The General answered his phone, the Chessmaster first made sure they were on secure lines before addressing the coded message The General had sent an hour ago. "What do you want?"

The General's rough voice complained, "Is that electronic filter necessary? It's not like I don't know who you are, and I hate listening to the sound."

"Yes. It's necessary." Because The General would be taping this conversation in hopes of using it as leverage or blackmail. Not happening. "The sooner you get to the point, the less you'll have to endure the sound."

With no choice, he moved ahead. "There's a contraband shipment coming in tonight. We have to ensure that High Vision's product makes it through this time."

"I know. One of our people in the agency caught word of it on the street."

"What about the distributor?"

"I thought Salazar had been grabbed. He disappeared for two days but came back on my radar last night when he moved product for someone else. He must have gotten spooked after that last bust went down and he barely escaped. High Vision could make this easier on all of us if they chose better people."

"They won't need Salazar after the next two shipments."

That sounded like a change in plans the Chessmaster hadn't expected. "Why?"

"Don't ask questions about things that are not your concern. You just need to implode the task force. How're you coming along with that?"

You don't want to be insulting me, General. "Everything is on track. I told you, the key to taking down the core group in the task force is discrediting Zane Jackson and pointing the evidence in his direction. That's working."

"It's taking too long. Can't you come up with a more expedient way?"

"Not if you still want the core group destroyed without any suspicion of a set-up. Jackson's not an agent, but he's close to two agents. Been best friends with one since childhood. Between that and his military black ops experience, he's privy to enough of the operations to make him the perfect patsy. Especially once I finish breaking his sister. She has no idea who is stalking her."

"You don't think she'll fold and run to him for help?"

"No. She loves him too much to risk his life. And she's stronger than I expected, which plays into my hand. The more I toy with her, the more determined she is to protect her brother. She'll keep dancing to my music with no idea that I'm leading her to her death, or that Zane will be held responsible for killing his sister."

"An ambitious plan, *if* you can pull it off."

If had never been part of the equation. "I can do my part as long as your man does his to get the information to Salazar. Speaking of your man, when will I hear from him?"

"He can't help with tonight's contraband shipment."

"You told me when Colbert was snatched that your man could fill in."

"I'm telling you differently. If you have a problem performing, say so."

The Chessmaster considered several responses before choosing one that had a payoff. "Nothing a future favor can't fix."

"We can work that out." The General coughed and grumbled like a bear in pain. "My man will be in touch to discuss shipment number six. As soon as that unit clears customs, he'll contact you about plans for activation."

"How soon?"

"Days."

"Good enough. Anything else?"

"Just one more thing. I had checks run on all the agents in the task force again after Colbert was caught. I wasn't convinced Zane Jackson fingered Colbert on his own. I think one of them could be there undercover, maybe still hunting for the leak."

The Chessmaster hadn't been any more convinced than The General, but Zane had played a part in drawing attention to Colbert. Could someone be inside the task force in a covert position? Besides present company, of course. "Who?"

"Josh Robertson. That's all I have. He checks out as FBI, but I know a false identity when I see one. He might be an agent pulled out of black ops just to find you. Regardless, he has to be dealt with but not until after this unit is tested."

Damn. The General was right, because eliminating Robertson now would upset the Chessmaster's carefully arranged game board. "I should be able to come up with a way to take him down *with* Zane and Trish Jackson."

"You're one of the sharper Orion Hunters I've met," The General commented with a hint of admiration in his voice. "Impressive strategic planning."

"Sharp? At my IQ level, that's an insult. This isn't about impressing you but getting what I want."

"Hand me a successful operation and I'll hand you the keys to the kingdom."

He'd better, or The General would suffer the consequences of disappointing a *clever* opponent.

CHAPTER 18

Trish kept checking over her shoulder all the way down the hall to the task force offices. She poked her head inside the door.

Zane's truck had not been in his favorite spot in the parking garage a block away, but Trish still worried he'd just appear. Coast was clear. She walked in and called out, "Leanne?"

"Come on in. I'm on hold."

Trish went into Leanne's office and closed the door. When Leanne looked up, Trish whispered, "I'm a little early."

"That's okay." Leanne waved her to a basic gray side chair, then finished requesting a file to be sent electronically and hung up her landline. She wore burgundy pants and a white jacket trimmed in black, another classy outfit that suited her lush figure.

Showing off perfect teeth behind ruby red lips when she smiled, Leanne put her pen down. "What's up?"

"I need some advice."

"What kind? Men?" Leanne's eyes widened with mock surprise.

"No." Trish laughed. "But now that you mention it, I do have a question. Did you tell Zane that Josh was gay?"

Leanne grinned. "Yes, I did."

"But he's *not*, Sugar."

"I know." Leanne arched a conspiratorial eyebrow.

"Then why did you lie to Zane?"

"Because your brother's reactions are so extreme when it comes to you or Angel that it's absurd. When I couldn't go to the banquet, I knew he wouldn't want you going alone or with an eligible man. The only male he *might* have considered asking was Ben. You wouldn't have wanted Ben to go when he has a new baby."

"You're right," Trish admitted.

Leanne shrugged. "You've been working your buns off and deserved to get out for a night. When Josh spoke up, I figured

Zane would be more inclined to agree if he thought Josh was gay. He's gorgeous and you know how guys always think *any* hot-looking man is gay."

"You'll love this." Trish relayed what Bunko had said about Josh and the Chippendales dancers. She and Leanne erupted in give-me-a-break laughter.

"Anyhow," Leanne said, catching her breath. "With Josh rarely in the office, I figured Zane didn't know him well and would buy into the gay thing easily enough, which he did. I would have told you yesterday, but you left too fast, and I got sucked into a meeting right after that. You obviously figured it out."

Not soon enough. "Now it all makes sense."

"Josh seems sweet and sexy as hell," Leanne added. "How'd the date go?"

"Wasn't really a date, but we had an interesting night."

"That's great. By the time Zane figures out the truth, it'll be too late for him to interfere."

Trish felt the need to clear up any confusion. "Josh and I are *not* going to be an item."

"Why not? You don't like *him*?"

It did sound insane when Trish heard it that way. "The problem isn't him. It's me. I'm just not ready for a relationship."

Leanne's eyes warmed with understanding. "I hear ya."

"What are you going to do when Zane finds out the truth about Josh and blows his top?"

"Give him my prom queen reaction." Leanne slapped her hands up against her cheeks and made an exaggerated shocked face.

It was so hilarious to think of Leanne doing that, Trish busted up again. She couldn't recall the last time she'd enjoyed laughing so much. "Good luck with that."

Lowering her hands to her desk, Leanne winked. "Your brother's a marshmallow when it comes to women. He's no real threat."

"I agree, which reminds me of one more question in that direction, sort of." Trish debated for a moment, but Leanne made it so easy for her to share things and she knew Leanne would give her a straight answer. "If you knew a woman who was being stalked and she had a good reason for not going to the police, what would you tell her to do if she knew the identity of the stalker?"

Leanne gave her an odd look at first, then she frowned with serious consideration. Her eyes filled with concern. "We're not talking about you, right?"

"No, of course not," Trish lied.

"Is it a dumped boyfriend or something?"

When she caught the unease in Leanne's voice, Trish realized it was unfair to expect guidance without sharing more information. "My ... friend ... thinks he's a ... business competitor." Could be Big Charlie.

"Ah. I get it." Leanne nodded. "I had a stalker once at a gym. I think it's a passive aggressive personality because they sneak around when they're trying to intimidate you. He was aggressive only when other people were watching so I waited for him to leave one night and caught him alone in the parking lot."

"Oh, my God. Did you kick his ass?"

Leanne shook her head. "With my training, I could have, but that would have gotten me disciplined by my agency. When I confronted the guy, I called him on what he was doing and warned him what would happen if he bothered me again. I told him I had plenty of evidence, which I did, that my *friends* at the DEA would be happy to review. Those men are spineless. They'll back down when someone gets in their face."

"I hadn't considered that," Trish murmured.

"But tell your friend that still doesn't mean to take any chances," Leanne warned with the tone of an older sister.

"I will." This new information gave Trish something to think about.

"Now, what did you need to talk about?"

Trish explained the details of the competition and that she'd tried to get through to Senator Dixon. "I'm hoping since your dad's a senator you could tell me how I can convince Senator Dixon to interrupt his busy schedule to fly down for something as frivolous as this television show. I can't come up with a reason for him to do this that has merit in *my* mind."

Leanne leaned back in her chair, tapping a pen against her palm. "You have to think about motivation for how a senator from Chicago would benefit by an event in Miami when he's not in the middle of a campaign period." She paused to smile sheepishly. "But my dad says a politician is *always* in campaign mode."

"The only thing I have to offer him is a chance to win money that will be donated to his favorite charity."

Leanne studied on that then sat forward quickly and snapped her fingers. "That's it."

"What is?"

"Dixon has a tough time gaining the female vote. He comes across as not sympathetic to women's issues. Makes you wonder how he found a wife," Leanne joked. "Give him a reason to earn goodwill with women and he might come in."

Trish hadn't looked at this from Dixon's political perspective.

Leanne paused, a sly smile crossing her lips and her eyes lit up then she frowned.

Trish prodded. "That looks like you have an idea. What is it?"

"Well, it *might* be a good idea, but it's devious."

"I like it already." Considering that she was running out of time, if devious was expedient, Trish was in.

"First, figure out a women's charity to donate to that could use the exposure, maybe even something local. Then call Dixon's campaign manager and tell him you have an opportunity for Senator Dixon that would raise awareness among female voters, but you have a deadline to meet and need to firm up a name."

"That's actually the truth."

Leanne paused to move her mouse and click a couple of times, her eyes going back and forth, reading. "Here's Dixon's campaign manager and contact information."

Trish grabbed a sticky from Leanne's desk and a pen, writing as Leanne rattled off the information. "Got it."

Raising an excited gaze to Trish, Leanne said, "Here's the clincher. Tell him no problem if Senator Dixon isn't available, because your producers will be fine with Senator Witherspoon taking his place instead."

Trish stopped writing. "Really?"

"Of course not. I love antiques, but my dad doesn't know squat about them." Leanne laughed. "*However*, Dixon and my dad have always had a friendly rivalry from back when they played college ball against each other. Dixon knows my dad isn't an antiques buff, but he'll assume that I'd help my dad with this. I'm thinking if he has any wiggle room in his schedule and this is presented as a challenge that comes with a chance to do a high-profile event where money is donated to a women's charity, he might just agree."

"That's a great plan."

"I can't say for sure it'll work."

"It's better than what I had when I walked in here," Trish admitted, relieved to see a real possibility when she'd thought all was lost.

Leanne leaned forward with arms propped on her desk. "But do me a favor and don't ever tell my dad I helped you with this. It'll be bad enough to hear him gripe about Dixon getting one up on him without catching hell for conspiring with the enemy." She snickered. "Whenever I want my dad to do something–like losing a few pounds recently–I tell him Dixon could do it. My dad gets all huffy, but he rises to the challenge. From what I've heard, Dixon is the same way if my dad is involved. Men are so easy some days."

"You and your dad are really close, huh?"

"Oh, yes." Leanne got quiet and her eyes softened. "Even closer after my mom died four years ago. She'd been battling cancer for a long time and not really getting better, but we didn't expect her to go downhill literally overnight. It took a while to realize it was a blessing to have her out of pain."

Trish had never envied something like Leanne's beauty, but she'd be lying if she didn't admit how much she wished to have had a relationship that close with her dad. "You're fortunate to have a great dad and he's lucky to have you."

"I agree. We'd do anything for each other."

Checking her watch, Trish stood up. "I hate to run, but I *am* on a deadline to get someone booked for my segment of the show. I can't tell you how much I appreciate your help today."

Leanne stood, too. "No big deal. I'm excited about this opportunity. Hope it works out with Dixon, and Josh, too."

Trish let that last part go. She was jazzed to put this plan into motion *and* get out of the building before she ran into Zane. Outside, she rushed to her car but stayed in the parking deck to make the call to Dixon's campaign manager while she was stationary rather than risk dropping the cellular call.

After waiting on hold, she was put through to a man with a nice voice. When she'd finished laying out her offer, pausing for effect, then adding the part Leanne had suggested about offering this opportunity to Senator Witherspoon, the campaign manager said, "Give me fifteen minutes and I'll call you back."

She felt a jolt of adrenaline at the positive sound in his voice and started her drive home.

When her phone rang five minutes later, she answered cheerfully. "Trish Jackson."

"Well, well, Missy. How ya' doin'?"

"What do you want, Charlie?" Trish would hang up if another call came through and not even feel rude about it.

"I'm over here with your buddy, Gunter. He's not interested in my offer unless you sell out, too. Do I have to keep pressing my position?"

Gunter might benefit by selling to Charlie, but she didn't want his decision predicated on hers. What had Charlie said to squeeze Gunter into a corner? "What Gunter does is entirely up to him. I'm not interested."

"You sure you want to keep pushing me, Missy?" Charlie said that so softly it raised goose bumps on Trish's skin. Could Charlie be the stalker? If so, why had he terrorized her that night she had to sit in the car?

To break down her confidence.

Constantly threatening Zane might just be a way to insure she didn't tell her brother what was going on.

Would Charlie back down if she confronted him about the stalking? Was he just being passive aggressive? It might be time to do what Leanne had done and meet Charlie alone, but not in a dark parking lot. Just somewhere he had no audience that fed his need to show off and be arrogant.

What if he *wasn't* the stalker?

Worst case, he'd laugh at her. How much worse could that be than this? She was tired of being harassed by the blowhard. "Tell you what, Charlie. I do want to talk to you, but it has to be alone."

"Now you're talkin', sweet thang." He chuckled.

The smug dog. "Come by my shop at six tonight and–"

"Can't do that. You want to talk to me, you gotta come to *my* place and I can't meet until six-thirty."

"That's too far. I have plans tonight."

"I'm not talkin' 'bout my offices. Hell, I don't want to fight traffic back there today either. I got a warehouse not far from you. Won't be no one around but the two of us by that time."

She didn't like the sound of that even if she had been the one to set the terms of this meeting.

He must have caught her hesitation. "Parkin' lot is lit up and it's a safe area." He gave her the address. "I can leave the back door unlocked. But if you don't feel right when you get there, just call me and I'll come out to walk you in."

From anyone else, that would have sounded chivalrous. Not a chance from Charlie. He'd love for her to call him like some damsel in distress. That day would never happen. The warehouse location was a decent area. She'd carry pepper spray to deal with anyone who walked up to her in the lot, and she'd take her fighting knife, just in case. "I'll be there at six-thirty."

"Lookin' forward to negotiatin' terms with you."

Let the fool think she was going to sell.

That way he'd be waiting all fat and happy, literally, which would catch him off guard when she asked him if he was stalking her.

She'd just hung up the phone when Dixon's campaign manager called back, saying, "Senator Dixon has a cancellation in his schedule. He's available for your event, depending on if we can work out the timeline. Email me the particulars so I can make arrangements and firm up the details."

Holy crap, she had a celebrity guest.

She replied in a calm, professional tone, hung up the call, and laughed, shouting *"Yesss!"* at what she'd just pulled off. Her moment of joy lasted for the next mile, then traffic bogged down. She had to get back to load her information into the computer page for the show before six.

And she had to bail on dinner with Josh. She wouldn't get home from Charlie's until half past seven at the earliest. She lifted the phone, hoping she got Josh's voice mail.

CHAPTER 19

Ryder hung up his phone and dropped it on the desk in the hotel suite his team was using as an operations headquarters. Showtime.

As soon as Josh got off his call.

Josh held a mobile phone to his ear and leaned against the wall next to a window that looked out over the parking lot. He'd been as distant and snarling as Sabrina had warned. She'd also said Josh was the best person for showing Ryder how she ran her operations.

Squeezing blood out of a rock was easier than getting information out of Josh when he had a hard-on for someone.

Like he has for you. What was this guy's problem?

The voice mail Josh listened to caused a jaw muscle to twitch, then disappointment crossed his face briefly before he punched the off button. He turned to Ryder, who shared his news first.

"Salazar says a High Vision shipment is coming in tonight. He hasn't heard from the mole yet, but he doesn't expect to until very close to the exchange time."

A chilly silence stretched while Ryder waited on Josh to ante in on tonight's game.

"Trish canceled our dinner plans," Josh said, the words coming out tight and angry.

The cancellation didn't surprise Ryder after what he'd learned about her possible connection to the Chessmaster, but he could tell Josh hadn't expected it. Ryder asked, "What was her excuse?"

"She said she had an unexpected business meeting come up for six-thirty, and she can't get out of it." Josh shoved his phone into the pocket of his sport coat and stepped over to the window where twilight was taking over the city.

"But you don't believe her?"

"No."

"The timing works."

"I know." Josh turned around then, his face hiding whatever had bothered him a moment ago. "Tonight's op is a go. Let's run over this once more."

Ryder started to remind Josh that this wasn't his first rodeo, but it would be a waste of breath. "Zane won't be back until eight, so I'll be able to grab one of the vans without him knowing until he gets back. By then, if this goes down the way we expect, my taking a van without his knowledge won't matter."

"Is Salazar set?"

"Yeah, but he doesn't know anything about us dropping a van in the steal zone. Dingo is covering the area, putting a boot on any van that matches the profile so ours is the only one available." Turning Salazar loose in hope of drawing in this Chessmaster was a gamble, even though they could track him the whole time. "Nick will watch the van once I abandon it, then I'll double back and team up with him. Once the van is boosted, we'll stay with it while the team closes in on the meet location."

"Odd for Zane to be gone on a night with a bust."

"I thought so, too, but he may be doing this to have a strong alibi after Colbert was grabbed. If anything, it points toward him using his sister if he's the Chessmaster."

Josh nodded. "We'll know better after tonight. That GPS unit under Salazar's skin still pinging?"

"Yep. Crazy how well that little gadget works. That Dingo's a genius."

"Don't tell him unless you're outside so there's enough room for his ego when it inflates."

Had stiff-ass Josh just made a joke?

A knock sounded at the door. Josh checked the peephole and opened up to allow Nicholas Ferrari and Dingo Paddock to enter. They had keys but walking in unannounced with armed agents in the room could be detrimental to their health.

Josh asked them, "What have you got?"

Dingo moved with wiry strength that could outfight heavier muscle based on speed alone. Strange-looking dude with spiky blonde hair and skin that had been baked a toasty tan. He shed a denim jacket and answered Josh. "Nick and I been shadowing Jackson and his mates, Ben and Vance. Boring buncha bastards."

Nick had a mask of perpetual brooding and a reputation with the women, but Ryder didn't see it. Dark and Mediterranean looking, and as tall as Josh, Nick stood with arms crossed as if he waited on instructions, when in truth Ryder doubted Nick could be instructed. Based on the rumors Ryder had heard, Nick gave new meaning to rogue on his best days.

Time to get moving. He stood and pulled on a tan-colored utility coverall with the name "Sonny" sewn on a patch that had been stuck on with Velcro. The coverall had false seams on the side that were velcroed shut. They could be torn open easily to access his weapon. He brought Nick and Dingo up to date as he dressed. "Trish Jackson just canceled on dinner with Josh."

"The weasel runs toward the trap," Nick murmured, a smile haunting his lips that Josh answered with a hard glare.

What was the problem between those two?

Like I give a shit? Ryder didn't share his business with anyone and stayed out of everyone else's. When Josh glanced over at him, Ryder said, "Where're you headed next?"

"To follow Trish. If your bust falls apart then it's very possible that she'll be going to meet with the Chessmaster, or to meet with a person she'll send to Salazar with Colbert out of the picture."

"What if she does neither?"

"I talked to Sabrina on the way here. No matter what, she wants Trish brought in tonight and handed over to DEA interrogators."

Dingo asked, "What about her brother?"

Josh's hard gaze swept all three of them. "He's to think she's disappeared, gone off the wagon. We're to feed him enough doctored information to make him believe it. With no idea what Rikker is up to and an attack imminent, we need Zane out of step to make a mistake. His sister wouldn't be this deep in this mess if he wasn't as well."

Ryder checked the magazine on his HK USP Compact .45 and shoved it into the holster at his hip. Two extra mags went into wristbands inside his coverall sleeves, one on each wrist. He inserted his ear bud next and clipped the radio mic to the inside of his collar and ran the wires to his compact radio unit. Then he tested it with Dingo and Nick. With that done, he exited first.

The other three would depart separately.

On the way to Zane's cargo office at Sunshine Airfield, he returned the call he'd been putting off for as long as he could.

"Thanks for calling me back," Terrence Van Dyke said as soon as he answered.

Ryder felt a moment of guilt at putting off the call to his brother. Half-brother, but even that wasn't accurate. Terrence's father was Ryder's uncle, who'd adopted Ryder when his mom died in childbirth as an unwed mother. Ryder simplified by calling Terrence his little brother since he'd been born a week later.

Ryder explained his tardiness in replying with, "Didn't have time until now and I only have about ten minutes."

"I understand and–" Terrence covered the phone while he coughed.

Hearing the sound dumped another load of loser-brother guilt on Ryder's shoulders. Terrence had been *sickly Terrence* since their teens. Terrence's mother had sent her only blood child to specialist after specialist and doted on him, which only caused Hubrecht Van Dyke to criticize what he saw as a weakling even more. Hubrecht ruled with a mighty fist that crushed foolish dreams and anyone he perceived as weak.

Ryder had intervened on Terrence's behalf time and again with the Van Dyke patriarch. Someone had to.

When Terrence recovered from his coughing fit, he said, "Sorry. Where was I? Oh yes, I hate to impose on you since I know you're busy and you have such a difficult job and–"

Ryder kept from snapping at him, but his brother rambled when he was nervous. "What do you need, Terrence?"

"Right, right. Get to the point. I need some help with one of father's competitors."

Growling at this moment would only send Terrence into a fit of rambling or coughing again. Ryder had sworn off ever setting foot in the Van Dyke compound in Atlanta or joining the Van Dyke empire again. He'd done his time in his father's company during school, escaping when he joined the Army. He and his father differed on many points. Pretty much *all* points. Let the money-hungry bastard solve his own problems.

But this was Terrence asking. Ryder maneuvered around slow traffic, closing in on Sunshine Airfield. "What do *you* need?" he asked, emphasizing *you* so Terrence would know who Ryder was willing to help.

"To convince J. K. Kearn to return to negotiations with father. I tried, but Kearn won't even take my calls."

J. K. Kearn manufactured a small line of unusual close-combat weapons and had one he was in the process of bringing to market that was rumored to replace one of Van Dyke's more popular, and highly profitable, products. Ryder silently cheered the man for one-upping the arrogant Hubrecht Van Dyke.

He sighed, realizing that was not helping Terrence. "Kearn won't be happy to hear from me. Not after I turned down his generous offer before I went into the Army. How do you think I can help?"

"You said last week you were going to Miami. Are you there?"

"Yes."

"Kearn is at his winter home in Belle Glade this week. I know it's over an hour north of you, but I thought maybe with your skills that you could...get to him."

"You want me to break into his home?" Ryder had only told his brother he was in security work, but Terrence knew about Ryder's Special Forces training and that he'd been a sniper. A job he'd embraced until...

Terrence laughed. "Heavens no. I meant that you're clever enough to figure out how to get past his watchdog assistant and talk to Kearn. I'm betting he still wants to hire you and would be willing to talk to you."

That didn't mean Ryder wanted to meet in person, regardless of whether Kearn was in the area, so to speak. Much as Ryder hated to do anything to help his father, he couldn't say no to Terrence. "I'll give it a try."

"Thank you so much. Are you coming home any time soon?"

The hopeful note in Terrence's voice dug a claw into Ryder's chest. He sucked at being family. He sucked at any relationship. "Not right now."

"Alright." One word loaded with sadness.

Turning into Sunshine Airfield, Ryder tried to think of what he could say, but he'd never been good at fixing hurt. Seeing a red Dodge truck at the airfield saved him from having to try. "Hate to go, bro, but I'm in the middle of something. I'll call you back if I get in touch with Kearn."

"That's fine." Terrence hung up.

Ryder parked next to Zane's truck and reached for his door handle when he saw Zane's Titan aircraft parked outside the hangar. Fuck a duck. Zane was back early. Way early.

That turned a simple plan into FUBAR. How was he going to get a van out of here with Zane present? And why had Zane come back earlier than expected?

Ryder could think of one reason. Tonight's shipment.

CHAPTER 20

"Trish, glad I caught you. You're still going to the retail convention in Atlanta this weekend, right?"

"Yes, but I can't talk long, Gunter." Trish grimaced at the familiar voice and grabbed the stack of mail she'd been ignoring for two days. If she had to waste time on the phone with Gunter, she could at least accomplish something, even if it was only opening envelopes. "I'm leaving soon for an appointment." She searched her desk for her letter opener, but it was nowhere in sight. Heidi would have a fit if Bunko had it again. Watching those two circling each other was becoming entertaining. She checked the clock over her desk, abandoned the mail and picking up her purse, she headed toward the front of ReSolution. "I'm late," she said.

Speaking of leaving, would the stalker know if she left town?

Gunter would not take the hint and hang up. "I'm finishing up paperwork. Let's meet after your appointment."

No, no, no. Dealing with Big Charlie would push the limits of her patience for today. Should she ask what Gunter had discussed with Charlie? If she opened that discussion, she'd never get off the phone and still have to talk to Gunter tomorrow about tonight's meeting. "I'm too beat to meet tonight. Why don't you call me tomorrow?"

"Sounds serious. Is there anything I can help you with?"

Nosy man. Trish stretched her neck for some relief. Gunter meant well, but sometimes he was a headache. She might as well tell him who she was meeting since Big Charlie had already bragged, she had no doubt, after he hung up from their phone call.

She said, "I'm meeting with Big Charlie."

Gunter was quiet for several seconds. "Are you going to sell to him?"

She did not want to get into this right now. "We're just

talking, and I'll fill you in tomorrow, okay?" Time was dwindling. "I really have to go."

"Very well. Olivia needs an escort tonight to some function. I suppose I'll take her after all. Talk to you tomorrow."

For once, Olivia was actually helping Trish.

Trish set the alarm and locked up. Twilight gave way to full dark by the time she arrived at Big Charlie's warehouse. Plenty of security lights illuminated the rear loading area. Everything looked safe enough.

But she felt like a glowing target in her pastel-yellow blouse.

Her imagination would be the death of her.

The walk-in door at the top of the steps next to the loading dock was unlocked, as promised. She gave the steel door a yank and peered inside the dimly lit building. Took a minute for her eyes to adjust to the single string of lights left on when the warehouse had shut down for the day.

She didn't expect Charlie to greet her but called out in a half-hearted voice just in case he was within earshot. "Charlie?"

Stepping further inside, she eased past a tall, chain-link enclosure and found a wide walkway stretching down the center of the warehouse. To the right were offices with large glass windows covered on the inside by blinds.

Light leaked through the closed slats.

Now that the time had come to confront Charlie, her nerves threatened to send her running.

Jittery, she dug deep to find the anger that had sent her on this mission. She mentally ran through the threatening notes and menacing phone calls.

That did little good. Fear still clutched at her throat.

The liquid demon beckoned her to leave, go to the closest bar and relax for just one night, drown her worries.

One drink would make all of this go away for a while.

She swallowed against her dry throat. *Alcohol is poison to you*, Heidi's voice argued in her head. Facing Heidi and Bunko's disappointment when she showed up hung over tomorrow would be worse than facing her own fears tonight without a drink.

Trish lifted a fingernail to nibble on and then snatched it back.

Put this meeting with Charlie off and the same problems would be here tomorrow. She would end this today if Charlie turned out to be the stalker. He didn't scare her physically. He'd never had a history of being dangerous, as far as she knew. She drew on the confidence she'd gained from training with Arnie, plus she had pepper spray. She'd changed her mind about bringing her knife. No way would she let Charlie get that close.

She marched toward the office then knocked lightly.

No answer.

Charlie expected her. He was probably on a phone call.

One twist of the knob and the door opened to soft lamp lighting.

Big Charlie had his arms folded on the desk and his head down, looking as if he rested.

She stepped all the way into his office. "Charlie?"

The smell struck her hard.

She froze. Bile rose inside her, a scream stuck in her paralyzed throat.

Blood ran across the desk and trickled down the side where it pooled on the floor.

The room started spinning.

CHAPTER 21

Trish and Colbert?
Okay, fine.
But Trish and Big Charlie?
No way.

Josh had called the Atlanta office with the coordinates on the warehouse, and immediately gotten the owner's name from Amanda, who was manning her souped-up laptop for the duration of tonight's op. Amanda had mad skills, could find out anything on anybody, and Sabrina had snaked her from MI6 four months ago. *Thank God.*

Josh had run background checks on everybody he–or Ryder–had seen Trish speak with at the TV banquet but hadn't gotten half the dirt on Big Charlie that Amanda had found on Trish's business competitor in a ninety-second data search.

Still, no links to drugs, the underworld, or terrorism. Hell, no links to anything other than an expensive 900-number porn habit. No obvious connection that would finger Big Charlie as The Chessmaster.

At this point, Josh had a headache from trying to make the puzzle pieces fit and fight off the gut feeling that he was missing something critical–that Trish didn't fit the role he kept trying to cast her in. He parked the sedate gray sedan–a rental kept at the hotel headquarters for his team–a block away from Big Charlie's warehouse. He loved his retro Porsche but knew better than to drive an easily identifiable vehicle while tailing a target.

He'd watched at a discrete distance after Trish had driven down the access to the rear of the building, tapping nervous fingers on the steering wheel as he'd waited on intel.

He had to know what he might be walking into, and whether he might need backup.

Was Trish a recovering alcoholic, struggling to regain her life?

Or was she a professional agent working Josh like a skilled con artist by portraying the vulnerable but untouchable female? There *were* a few holes in Trish's past, and while nothing had seemed like an obvious connection, he couldn't now ignore that she'd associated with some shady characters in the past.

But Amanda had uncovered the most telling part earlier today.

Trish had no significant assets to match her family's name and wealth.

Of course, as Josh knew better than most, that could mean something entirely different than it appeared on the surface.

But it *could* mean that she was exactly what Sabrina insinuated. A skilled operative.

He shut the car door, shoved his keys in his pocket and followed on foot. The office hours displayed on the front door of Big Charlie's warehouse indicated it closed at six.

What was Trish doing here? From what he'd been able to discern, she couldn't stand the man.

Josh had spent a chunk of his investigative time playing devil's advocate. These operations called for cold, objective thinking. He excelled at it. Or had at one time.

He'd been trained since he was ten to think of everyone he didn't know as an enemy.

His parents–the only ones he knew anyway–had lost their only birth child to a kidnapping. When they'd adopted Josh, they were determined that no one would ever harm another child of theirs because of their money.

Josh's adoptive dad, a technology industry magnate, had a brother in the CIA, the person who, three years after the kidnapping, had first observed Josh as a punk kid running the streets of the Upper West Side of New York, going up against opponents who were bigger and badder when he was still wet behind the ears.

Josh's future uncle–the one he'd called Ty before he'd ferreted out the man's real name–had been undercover and playing the role of street bum when he'd first encountered Josh and taken an interest.

Josh had tried to pick Ty's pocket for the few dollars Ty had begged from passersby.

Yeah. He'd tried to pick the pocket of a homeless man. Tried being the operative word. Josh had been after food money, but even desperate he couldn't do it. He'd stolen the money, backed a few steps away, then he'd turned around and put it back.

Ty had seen potential in Josh, then Sabrina and Dingo, offering them payment for intel when they delivered.

Ty had convinced his richer-than-God brother to take in a wary kid with no manners who wanted only to stay in his group home with two other brats, Sabrina and Dingo. Ty had guessed right–that the childless couple had plenty of love left to give, even though they couldn't bring themselves to have another baby. Josh hadn't made it easy on anyone, but the impossible happened when Ty was proven right.

Once Josh's parents decided to keep him, they'd raised him with bodyguards, the best private tutors available, and pre-set play dates with the kids of trusted friends.

All the while, Ty had funneled money and opportunities to Sabrina and Dingo, watching over them from a distance, then helping them find their way into the intelligence community.

Trips out for Josh were always scheduled. No chance a date could take him as far as first base with a freaking security detail in tow.

It had been a privileged, orchestrated, strange upbringing.

Except when they'd handed him over for short stints to Ty, who'd taught Josh all he needed to know about how to protect *himself* when the bodyguards were absent. Josh had trained with Ty for one month, four times a year, until the summer when Ty didn't come home from his latest mission.

Josh had made Ty a promise. He would shield his identity at all costs. Ty had told Josh that there were no guarantees in life, and no person was promised tomorrow, but made Josh promise to never put his parents through the pain of having their money cost them a child again.

Josh took everything Ty taught him to heart, and by the time he was eighteen, could ease his way into any social setting, take on any persona from uber-wealthy aristocrat to street thug.

Which was why, once Josh became an adult, he'd been more at home in a clandestine life than in the social world where his parents lived.

Josh had gone underground and never re-emerged.

When Josh reached the loading area at the rear of Charlie's warehouse, hair prickled along his neck. All of his instincts sharpened, on alert.

Something was wrong.

At the corner of the building, he leaned around to find...no Trish. Her late-model Dodge sedan and a Cadillac sport utility were in the parking lot, along with two panel trucks. The kind normally used to deliver furniture.

He was damned tired of feeling one step behind her. Josh surveyed the deserted loading dock and eased over to the steps that led to the service door.

———*m*———

White panic froze over Trish.

Breathe. Breathe. Move. Do something, for crying out loud.

Big Charlie could be dying. Maybe he was already dead.

Don't hyperventilate. She whimpered at the idea of touching him but forced herself to move into the wide office toward his still form.

He was huge. Maybe he was breathing under all that body. Bile ran up her throat at the sharp coppery smell permeating the office. *Don't throw up.* Her body shook so hard her teeth jarred. She extended a trembling hand to check his throat for a pulse.

None. She snatched her hand back.

Maybe he was too fat to find one. She felt like she was moving in slow motion. She got her hands under Charlie's shoulder and strained to lift him up to a sitting position, grunting with the effort.

She felt his bulk shift and jumped away.

Big Charlie lay back in his chair, eyes wide open in horror and a knife shoved through his throat.

Oh, dear God.

Tremors racked her body. She lunged for his desk phone and dialed 9-1-1. The operator answered. Trish cut her off with, "Send an ambulance to Big Charlie's at—"

A shadow fell across the desk in front of her. She shifted into defense mode. She swung an elbow around that hit a solid body and she heard an "umph" just as something hard struck her head.

Pain flashed through her temple. *Crap.* Arnie would be totally pissed because she hadn't watched her back. She threw her hands out to break her fall, but she fell anyhow into a black, empty void.

CHAPTER 22

Vicious pounding in her temple brought Trish slowly back to consciousness. Something wet and cool was draped over her throbbing forehead. Icy cold pressed against her aching head. Noises filtered in and out between painful stabs.

Voices murmured. "Trish. Come on, honey, wake up."

Honey?

Zane was here. Oh, thank goodness.

"Trish, open your eyes," a low, concerned male voice coached.

Like a good girl, she obeyed, but Zane wasn't the one urging her to rejoin the living. Worried cobalt-blue eyes stared down into hers. They belonged to Josh, not Zane. But she wasn't complaining. His palm was on her face. His thumb stroked her cheek. Comforting her.

She tried to lift her head a fraction. Pain lashed through her skull. Trish groaned and raised a hand to her head.

"Whoa." Josh intercepted her fingers, pulling her hand down and gently pushing her back onto soft cushions. "I've got an ice pack on your head. Just lie still."

Ice pack and a major headache. What had hit her? A train?

"Is Miss Jackson awake?"

Trish flinched at the loud voice.

Josh cut a feral look at someone behind her. "No," he said softly. "Keep your voice down."

She seconded that motion.

"Josh, whaz going on?" she mumbled.

He shifted his concerned gaze back to her and spoke softly. "Someone hit you. Did you see anyone?"

Before she could answer, the voice from behind her spoke again, his voice low, but terse. "I need to ask her some questions."

A dangerous glint slashed across Josh's face.

Until now, Trish had thought he was too nice to be a DEA–

or an FBI–agent, but she'd seen the same fierce reaction in Zane when someone crossed him. A look that promised painful retaliation.

Some loudmouth had just pushed Josh too far.

"Don't move," Josh whispered. "I'll be right back, okay?"

"'Kay."

He made some adjustment with the icepack and patted her hand. She felt the cushions underneath her shift as he stood. She was on somebody's sofa. He walked out of her line of sight, and she focused on a picture on the wall, trying to recognize the image.

Or whose wall the painting hung on. Late renaissance period. Well preserved...

Oh, God, this place smelled disgusting.

A terse conversation rumbled behind her. She didn't catch any distinct words, just extremely angry tones of at least three or more men. They snarled at low volume for over a minute.

When everything quieted, Josh was back. A surprising relief filled her at the return of his touch. Why was he here? She wanted to ask, but didn't have the energy to care, just glad for his warm touch.

"Where am I?" Trish asked.

"You're at Big Charlie's warehouse."

She squinted in concentration. Big Charlie's? Oh, yeah. She had a meeting with Big Charlie. She came in the back door, called out, no answer. Then went to the office and found...

"Oh, my God." She clenched his hand for support. "Josh, Charlie is hurt. I called 9-1-1–"

"Shhh. I know." He cupped her cheek again, his fingers splayed across her face. His gentleness silenced her until she flashed back on the blood dripping from Big Charlie's mouth. The puddle of it on the floor. Was that the sickening odor she smelled?

"Is he going to be okay?" she asked. "I couldn't find his pulse. He had a knife..." Her heart pounded and her head thumped with each beat.

Josh hesitated before answering. "He's dead."

"Oh, God." She started panting and swallowed against the bile threatening to race up her throat again. "I need to sit up." At his frown, she insisted, "Please, help me up or I'm going to throw up." Might anyhow.

He removed the ice pack and slipped an arm behind her, raising her to a sitting position slowly. Then he shifted her legs around until her feet were on the floor. She squeezed her eyes tight to stave off the flood of tears threatening at the rim of her lashes.

Josh settled next to her. His arm curved around her shoulders. He held the icepack gently against her head.

Trish breathed a couple of shallow breaths and opened her eyes. She found the source of the other voices.

A team of police officers—one or two might be detectives—and two paramedics were congregated between the door to the warehouse and the lump at Big Charlie's desk that was covered by a white sheet. Blood had congealed on the floor, giving off the smell of death.

She wrapped her arm around her middle, fought to keep her revolting stomach from adding one more humiliating misery to her day. The police wouldn't appreciate her contaminating their crime scene.

Josh cupped her chin and inched her face around to his. "Don't look."

"Why aren't they taking him away?"

"They need a special gurney to handle the weight."

"Oh." She focused on Josh's face. "The detectives want to talk to me, I guess. I'll answer their questions now," she whispered. She would not fall apart in front of an audience.

Josh studied her as if he debated on allowing her to speak to anyone. He didn't have a choice and they both knew it. A man had died. The police would want answers.

Trish didn't have any.

Josh tipped his chin up at the detective who must have read the motion as the invitation he'd been waiting for.

How had Josh held the detective off until now?

The man who stepped forward first introduced himself as

Detective Vickers. He knelt, eye level with Trish. "Miss Jackson," he began. He made an obvious effort to keep his voice at a low decibel, though the sound came out rough as rusty cans dragged against pavement. "What happened?"

She chewed on her lip, struggling to recall exactly what had occurred. "I had an appointment with Charlie, and he couldn't meet until after business hours, so I got here around six thirty. He'd told me the loading dock door would be unlocked and it was. I saw the lights on in this office–"

"Did you see anyone in here?" the detective interjected.

"No. The blinds were drawn. I called out and knocked on the door, but nobody answered. I figured he was on the phone so I opened the door and saw–" Oh, God, would she ever forget the blood? Charlie's body not moving. She'd known he was dead but couldn't accept it. Stuck on that image, she lost her line of thought and her eyes glazed over.

Then she realized Josh was rubbing her arm with his free hand, soothing her.

"Take it easy, Trish." He had her tucked up against his chest. His heat cloaked her raw nerves like a gentle balm. She wanted to curl up in his arms and go to sleep, forget everything, drift into another world.

But life didn't work that way. Someone had killed Big Charlie and had slammed her as well. The sooner the detective got information, the sooner they could go after the murderer. More than anything she was ready to get away from the wretched smell.

"Uh, I tried to check his throat for a pulse, but I couldn't f-find one. I thought, maybe, I couldn't feel one because he was so heavy." Her voice trailed off again. She breathed hard and continued. "I dialed 9-1-1 and think I gave them an address before I was hit."

"Did you see who hit you?" the detective asked.

"No."

"Do you know who would want to kill Charlie?"

"No."

"Who knew about this meeting?"

"No one ... well ..." She hesitated, and the detective's body clenched. Crap. "I told Gunter–he owns Dynasty Treasures–but he was on his way to see Olivia Lackey to escort her to a function. He didn't like Charlie, but he wouldn't do this. Gunter wouldn't hurt a fly. Right, Josh? You met him." At no response, she shoved her gaze to Josh.

He worked his jaw a moment and said, "I don't know, but we'll find out." Angling his head to Detective Vickers, Josh asked, "Any more questions?"

"Yes. Miss Jackson, what were you meeting Charlie about?"

About threatening me and Zane.

About stalking me and trying to steal my business.

Okay, neither of those were intelligent answers. She didn't know that Big Charlie was the stalker. She needed something neutral, quick. Even Josh waited silently, reading too much with his intense gaze.

"Business." Close to the truth. She held her breath.

"Can you elaborate?"

Why did this feel like an NCIS episode? She dug her nails into the sofa cushion and tried again, careful to stick close to the truth.

"Charlie made a couple of offers to buy my shop. I told him we'd discuss it."

"So, you were going to sell your shop?"

"No, just discuss it."

The detective shifted back on his heels. He seemed neither satisfied nor convinced by that answer.

"Detective, Miss Jackson has been through a traumatic event," Josh interrupted. "She's told you what she knows. I've told you that the front door was locked when I arrived. Since you found it open, I would have to think the assailant killed Big Charlie, hit Miss Jackson, and fled through the front door. Have you located what he used to hit her?"

"No, but we intend to continue searching."

"I'd like to get Trish to the hospital," Josh said.

"*No!*" Trish gritted her teeth as soon as the loud word

popped out of her mouth.

"Yes, you are going to the hospital," Josh argued in a hard voice.

"I want to go home."

"You could have a concussion."

Trish raised her hand to her head and this time carefully touched the goose-egg-sized lump. "I've always heard the lump means the swelling is going to the outside and not the inside. Isn't that so?" she said toward the paramedics who had stood throughout the exchange as silent spectators.

One of them answered, "We're not authorized to make that diagnosis."

"I'm going home." She sent Josh a silent plea with her eyes. She did not want to go the hospital. They'd call Zane. He'd have to leave Angel.

Josh huffed out a sound of frustration. "Against my better judgment, I'll take you home. But if you show any signs of a concussion or getting sick, you're going to the hospital."

The detective stood and moved over to the desk.

Someone from outside the office called out, "The coroner's here."

Uh-uh. She was not watching them load that body. "Josh?"

"We're going." He removed the ice pack and got to his feet.

She gripped the sofa on each side of her legs, prepared to push up, but his hands cupped her under the arms and lifted her until she could stand, then pulled her against his strong, solid body.

Taking deep breaths in and out to keep her stomach from erupting she asked the detective, "Am I free to go?"

"Not yet."

She felt Josh tense and put her hand on his arm. "It's okay. I want to do whatever I can to help them find the person responsible for this." She raised her gaze to Detective Vickers. "What else do you want?"

"You said this is the first time you've been here, right?"

She stopped herself before nodding this time. "Yes."

Vickers lifted a bag from the desk. "Can you tell me if this belonged to the victim or not?"

Trish stared at the bloody weapon.

"That looks like my letter opener."

CHAPTER 23

That looks like my letter opener.

Josh played Trish's words over again in his head as he led her through Charlie's warehouse that had turned into Law Enforcement Central. Granted, she got points for being truthful, but what the hell? If not for Josh having told Vickers that Big Charlie and Trish were part of an ongoing FBI investigation, Trish would be on her way downtown to be held until the fingerprints were run.

Gaining her freedom had involved a second conversation with Vickers, and Josh's claiming he was taking Trish into his custody.

Now Josh just had to convince Sabrina that Trish was more valuable to them free than locked up. He couldn't hand her over to anyone, not like this and not now, when his insides were screaming that she was not the enemy.

That she was the one in danger.

When he'd found Trish on the floor, with blood oozing out of a head wound, his first thought had been to get her out of there and to safety. He'd had a moment of total disregard for his mission, something that had never happened before.

If Ty was standing here today, he'd tell Josh that the last person to trust was a woman. He'd point out that everything Trish had done to this point was suspect.

He'd also warn Josh against letting his dick make decisions. That had been an ever-present mantra on the long list of Ty's advice.

Don't let the small brain convince you to do something stupid.

Like convincing the detective that Trish was part of an investigation when there was *no* FBI investigation involving her or Big Charlie.

If Vickers discovered that before Josh got a chance to talk with Sabrina, who could hopefully work her magic to fix this, the task force mission would be blown to pieces.

When Josh reached the loading area at the rear of Charlie's warehouse, hair prickled along his neck. His instincts sharpened, on alert. Could the killer still be around?

More law enforcement spilled into the building, moving in the opposite direction that Josh guided Trish. He kept his arm around her body since she shook from shock and injury, but she was determined to leave under her own power.

She wobbled every couple of steps. Face colorless and eyes glistening with unshed tears, she was holding herself together pretty damned well for what she'd been through.

Who had killed Big Charlie and why?

Was there a chance Big Charlie had something to do with the DEA mole?

Or was his death a message to Trish?

Josh's curse came out half growl.

Trish turned to him, said nothing, and made her way down the steps outside. After all she'd been through in the last hour, oddly enough it was the sight of the gurney being rolled in for Charlie's body that buckled her knees.

She stumbled and his heart caught on the next beat.

Fuck this. Josh caught her behind her legs and lifted her against his chest.

"Put me down," she hissed, too miserable sounding to have any punch. Then she swallowed. "Josh."

"Don't push your luck. It's enough that I'm taking you home when you should be in a hospital."

When he reached his rental car and leaned down to settle her onto the passenger seat, her eyes drooped.

"Wake up, Trish."

She blinked at his sharp order.

He buckled her in, not pushing the hospital again. Yet. When Josh slid in behind the wheel, Trish asked, "Where's your Porsche?"

"In the shop."

She accepted that lie without question then asked, "Why were you at Charlie's warehouse, Josh?"

How could he explain that without telling her she was part of an investigation? Until he knew for sure, he had to keep playing this role. "I drove over to your shop, and you passed me, so I turned around and came back. Followed you here."

"Why?"

Always stay as close to the truth as possible. "I wanted to know if you really had a business meeting. Or if there was ... someone else."

"Oh." She fell silent as he drove away from the busy scene. When she spoke, her voice trembled. "I can't be insulted that you didn't believe me about this being a business meeting when I have you to thank for being here. You might have scared off the person who attacked me." She turned slowly, flinching at the movement, and gave him a sweet smile. "Thank you."

He didn't deserve the honesty pouring out of that face. Not when he was actively working toward proving her brother was another task force mole. Plus, he'd just implicated her with the police as being a suspect in an FBI investigation. On top of all that, he didn't deserve her appreciation when he'd almost shown up too late.

She could have been killed.

With every new deceit, he felt more like a new species of vermin around her. Could Sabrina be right? Had he lost his ability to be objective and stay emotionally detached around women?

Or just around this woman?

He mentally buckled down, determined to act like the operative who had handled far more dangerous missions than this one.

Trish was still a potential suspect.

He took in said potential suspect. She was hunched against the window with her gaze fixed on her lap and her lips pressed tight.

She took a breath that shuddered through her as if she held

herself together by sheer will. She swiped her cheek.

He hadn't seen a tear fall, but the motion splintered his heart. Because he couldn't place her squarely on one side of the law or the other.

Josh turned into her driveway and parked behind Heidi's lime-green VW Bug. He laid a hand on Trish's arm. "Wait for me to come around, okay?"

She straightened up. "I can walk."

He shook his head. Stubborn, independent woman. "Fine but wait until I get there." She did and Josh held on to her as she turtle-shuffled to the door. He'd agreed to let her walk, but not fall flat on her face. Inside the house, he got her to the sofa and swung her legs up so she could recline against a pillow he placed at the end.

She was vulnerable. This would be the perfect time to chip away at her walls, get inside her defenses. He should take advantage.

Maybe he could find a puppy to kick while he was at it.

He leaned down and kissed her lightly on the lips. "How are you doing?"

She put her hand on his cheek. "Better now."

Heidi yelled from the back of the house, "Trish, is that you?"

Josh stepped over to answer in the direction of the hallway. "Yes, she's here." Heidi came bounding around the corner into the living room then jammed to a stop when her eyes lit on Trish.

"Hey." Trish waggled her fingers.

"What happened to you?" Heidi dashed over to the sofa and wrapped Trish in a careful hug.

Josh suggested, "If you'll get an ice pack, Heidi, I'll fill you in."

"Sure, hang on, I'll be right back."

Once Trish had a bag of frozen peas placed gently on her head, Josh explained the sequence of events to Heidi.

"Why were you at Big Charlie's?" Heidi asked, her frown fierce.

Josh waited, curious to hear what Trish would tell her friend. This would be the perfect time to find out more than Trish would say to only him.

"It's a long story. Can we talk about this later?"

Heidi twisted her mouth to one side and must have read more from Trish's statement than Josh was able to gather. "Sure, we'll talk later."

Damn. Thwarted by telepathic female communication.

The phone rang and Trish tensed. Heidi moved to answer the landline on the end table, but Josh intercepted her. "Let me." He lifted the receiver. "Hello?"

"Hi, I'm a reporter for–"

"Miss Jackson has no comment," Josh said.

"I'd just like to ask her about the murder–"

"What part of no comment confuses you? Goodbye." Josh turned to Heidi. "Do you have an answering machine?"

"In the kitchen."

"Turn it on and just let the recorder answer all the calls." He clicked the ringer off on the phone.

"The media?" Heidi said. "Is this going to turn into a zoo? Are we going to be able to handle this ourselves?"

"Oh, my God," Trish moaned, lifting a hand to cover her eyes.

Josh hurried over to her. "What's wrong?"

When Trish uncovered her eyes, misery hung in her gaze. "I just got confirmation for my celebrity guest earlier today. The media will..." She couldn't talk, swallowing against tears that threatened to flow, but she still choked them off.

"Oh, honey," Heidi sat, kneeling next to Trish and patting her shoulder. "We'll figure it out."

Trish shook her head, chewing on a corner of her lip. "There's nothing to figure out. My guest will back out and even if he didn't, which he will, the show will probably boot me. Our agreement gives them the right to terminate at any point if we cause negative publicity."

"But you didn't," Heidi argued. Then the phone rang again.

"Shit." Josh told Heidi, "Follow my lead and stick with 'no

comment.'" When she hurried to the kitchen and answered the phone there, he sat down next to Trish and rubbed his finger lightly along her jaw. "You don't know what will happen until tomorrow, so don't stress about it tonight."

Trish nodded. Her red eyes filled with hope for a moment that made his heart hurt for her.

His cell phone rang. Josh stood up and fished the phone out of his pocket. When he answered, he had to pull the receiver away from his ear.

"What the hell happened to my sister?" Zane roared.

"Zane, she's fine."

"*Fine*? Detective Vickers just called asking questions about Trish and said she was hit on the head hard enough to knock her out cold and she didn't go to the hospital. *Let me talk to her!*"

Josh shot a look at Trish.

She mouthed the word "no." She didn't look up to dealing with anyone, including her brother. Maybe *especially* her brother.

Josh told Zane, "Trish is resting. She didn't want to go to the hospital, and she doesn't seem to have a concussion."

"So now you're a doctor?"

"No, but she's an adult who can make her own decisions."

Trish gave Josh a wan thank-you smile.

Zane said, "Tell Heidi I'm on my way over."

That must have been loud enough for Trish to hear. She looked panicked and shouted a hoarse, "No!"

Josh put his hand on her shoulder to keep her from jumping up, then rubbed the tight muscles, calming her. He nodded that he'd handle it, but why did she not want her brother here?

"Look, Zane, Trish is okay, and Heidi will take care of her tonight. She's had a bad day to say the least. I think she needs rest more than anything. Why don't you talk to her tomorrow? I'll tell Heidi to have her call you as soon as she wakes up. Okay?"

"Hell no, none of that is okay. Dammit. You told me you could keep her safe when she was with you."

Man, if Josh didn't feel worthless, that did it. He should have gotten to her sooner.

Zane didn't say anything. Josh could see Trish's brother storming around wherever he was with the phone clutched in his hand tight enough to crush it.

Trying to slow down Zane and get some intel, Josh said, "Thought you were still gone."

"My wife had what she thought were labor pains and the doctor wanted her to go to the hospital, but she's fine. I came home early to check on her."

If that was true, then neither Zane nor Trish had been involved in communicating information on the drug deal tonight. Had the DEA bust gone down after all? Josh couldn't find out anything until he spoke to Ryder, Dingo or Nick. He suggested to Zane, "Why don't you stay with your wife. I'm not leaving Trish if I think there's any chance she should go to the hospital and, like I said, Heidi is here."

A growl rumbled through the connection. "Okay." Anguish came across in that one word. "I don't want to leave my wife alone. Don't mention Angel's hospital visit to Trish. I don't want her any more stressed. Call me in the morning and tell Heidi to call me *tonight* if they need *anything*. Dammit, Trish should be in a hospital."

Josh overlooked Zane's ordering him around in the face of her brother's worry. "I agree, but you have to believe me when I say it would have been a battle."

"Yeah, I know my sister. I can't believe she walked in on that scene. We'll talk tomorrow," Zane repeated, sounding beaten.

If Zane was not the mole, this had to be killing him.

Josh had thought more than once that Zane's overprotectiveness toward his sister was completely at odds with sending her into any kind of danger. The idea that Zane and Trish were both putting on an act *this* convincing struck him as unrealistic. But if Zane was not the mole, Josh's investigation had taken a huge step back.

"Will do." Josh closed his cell phone and sat down opposite

Trish in an overstuffed chair. "Your brother's pretty concerned about you."

"I know," Trish said, her eyes darting away from him. "I wasn't ready to talk to him. Thanks for keeping him from coming over."

Heidi stepped into the room. "Either of you hungry? Trish, you probably need to eat."

He wouldn't get any more help from Heidi. She was clearly not willing to push for more details until Trish was ready.

Trish answered, "I don't think I can eat right now."

Josh turned to Heidi. "Maybe aspirin for Trish."

Heidi and Trish said "no" at the same time.

He blinked, realizing just how hardcore an approach Trish was taking by avoiding *any* drug, even aspirin, because of being in AA. That raised another doubt about her as an accomplice to the mole. What woman so adamant about her recovery would willingly aid drug dealers?

Was that a legitimate doubt or one borne of feelings she stirred in him?

"Let me know when you're ready to eat," Heidi said, effectively getting Josh out of an uncomfortable silence. "I've got some laundry to get started and I'll be back."

When Heidi left, the phone rang again, but cut off after two rings. The voice recorder must be working.

Josh leaned forward, elbows on his knees, chin on his steepled fingers. He hated to be the person who had to do this, but he had a duty to get answers and Trish was at her most vulnerable for questions. Better him than Sabrina.

"Trish, just what were you really doing at Charlie's?"

The pink tip of her tongue flicked across her bottom lip. She adjusted the package of peas and stared at the ceiling.

"Business, like I said." She rubbed her forehead with one hand, her eyes squinting sharply as if the slightest movement hurt.

"I don't believe your meeting was just about business."

"I don't know what you're talking about." Her eyes strayed to him, then away. Guilty.

Josh wished he could forget about the mole, forget about getting answers and give her the comfort she needed. Wished he could tell her this would all be okay tomorrow.

But if a Jackson sibling was guilty, nothing would be okay again.

Damn, what was she hiding? He'd have to come up with a better reason for not handing her over to Sabrina than just his opinion that Trish was innocent. He couldn't honestly say she was. Josh pinched the bridge of his nose. If he didn't hand her over and Sabrina thought he was shielding Trish, Sabrina would send in a team that could take Trish from him.

Trish had to help him, dammit. "Look Trish," he said, more of a no-nonsense tone this time. "It's time to come clean."

"Yeah, Trish, and *I'm* not buying any BS," Heidi announced from the doorway to the kitchen. She stood with a small sheet of gray paper clenched in one hand.

Trish's eyes bulged. "Where'd you get that?"

"From your jacket. Who's threatening you?"

CHAPTER 24

Fear for Zane fingered through every nerve in Trish's body. She stared at the stalker's note in Heidi's hand. "Why were you looking through my pockets?"

Heidi stormed over to the sofa. "I'm doing *laundry*. I found it when I checked the pockets of your jacket. What's this note all about?" she demanded.

"Give it to me." Trish reached for the paper, gritting her teeth against the pain behind her eyes. "That's mine."

Josh leapt up from his chair. "No, let me see it and you stay still, Trish."

Heidi handed the slip to Josh, then glared at Trish.

Under his breath, he read aloud, "Roses are yellow for a little hello. I've done something nice for you. Now you will do something for me, little pawn. Keep your phone handy." Josh seared her with a ferocious glare. "What the hell is this?"

"Nothing. Give it to me." Trish pushed up again, head spinning, and almost fell off the sofa.

Josh moved fast. He had her by the shoulders, gently pushing her back down. "Whoa. Easy. Don't panic. We're going to talk about this, but I want you to stay calm."

Calm? This was a disaster.

"Trish, fess up." Heidi had never sounded more serious. "Don't give me that 'not now' look or I'm calling Zane."

"*You can't!*" she yelled, and the sledgehammer in her head paid her back, big time.

"Okay, okay, take it easy, like Josh said. I'm not calling anybody...yet. But you have to tell me what's going on."

Trish closed her eyes and tried to will the day away. Unfortunately, her genie powers were as nonexistent as her luck. She had no choice. Josh would tell Zane even if Heidi didn't. She had to make them realize they couldn't do that.

Opening her eyes, Trish took in an anxious set of gray eyes with an eyebrow ring and a troubled pair of stormy blue ones waiting patiently on her.

She had no choice but to trust him. "Okay, I'll tell you about the notes, but you have to both promise not to tell Zane."

"Notes? As in plural?" Josh tipped his head back and stared at the ceiling, frustration clear in his every move. He dropped his chin forward and nailed her with an accusatory stare. "You've taken independence to an unbelievable level."

"Zane should be the *first* person you tell," Heidi agreed.

"Would you both please sit down? Hurts to bend my neck back to look up."

Heidi dropped on the floor, cross-legged, next to her.

Josh pulled up an ottoman and settled on the edge.

The house phone rang again. Trish had lost count and hoped it was the same person. Not every news outlet. "I've been getting notes and I got a text from someone."

"Text." Josh uttered a sound of disgust. "All right. First, what's in the other notes?" His monotone words didn't fool Trish. He was furious, but to his credit she could tell he was working extremely hard not to yell or upset her further. She said, "Heidi, if you'll go look in the lower drawer of my nightstand, you'll find the other notes."

Without another word, Heidi sprinted to the back of the house.

Josh leaned close. "Why haven't you told anyone?"

"I couldn't."

"You *wouldn't*. There's a difference."

"No, I *couldn't*." She'd wanted to share this with someone, but the stalker had convinced her that anyone she brought into the mix would be in danger.

"Here they are," Heidi announced on her return, handing the pile to Josh as though there'd been an unspoken agreement that he was in charge. He flipped through each one, his jaw working from side-to-side as he read. He placed them on the floor and turned to Trish. "Now the text."

As Trish related the message from the night at the banquet, then told them about the voice in her room, and the knife in the cutting board, Josh's visage darkened more with each recitation.

No one uttered a sound when she finished.

"That's all of it," Trish prompted, glancing from Heidi to Josh. She waited on a response, any response. *Come on, guys, say something.* Anything was better than the silent treatment.

Josh stood. "I'm going to check your bedroom to see if I can find the speakers that fed in that robotic voice." He walked down the hallway.

"I can't believe you didn't tell me," Heidi said. The disappointment in her friend's words pained Trish more than her throbbing head. "I live here, too, you know. He was in your *house*, Trish, and I didn't even know."

Shit. What had she been thinking? In her effort to protect the ones she loved, the last thing Trish had meant to do was hurt them.

"I'm sorry, Heidi. It wasn't because I didn't trust you, but I didn't want you or Zane harmed."

Heidi gave a nod. "I heard the washer stop. Let me throw the clothes in the dryer and I'll be back."

Trish leaned back, letting her eyes close...just needed a moment.

"Wake up, hon."

Trish's eyes flew open at Heidi's soft order. "Sorry, I didn't think I'd nod off."

Josh came back down the hall. "Do you realize what kind of danger you've been in?" He started in on her as soon as he rounded the corner. "I found a remote camera in your fancy curtain rod, and a speaker hidden inside your lampshade. That's with a five-minute sweep. I'm going to do a more thorough check later and sweep the rest of the house."

Chills raced up Trish's arms. The stalker had a camera *in her bedroom.* He'd seen her naked. She really wanted to use one of Arnie's best moves on that miserable creep.

Josh continued, "This is not an amateur job, so I doubt we'll find any fingerprints. And Big Charlie's murder could be tied to this stalker." He began pacing. "There's no telling how many times you've been in the stalker's sights." His voice began to rise.

Oh, boy. Josh was revved up. From the look on his face, Zane's short fuse temper had nothing on Josh in a fury.

She was pissed, too. She'd been dealing with the damn stalker nonstop for weeks with no way to stop the insanity without putting Zane at risk.

He stopped short. "What was your plan, Trish? Just sit around and wait until this maniac came after you?" He leveled a gaze harboring reprimand at her, then shook his head. "Of course, it was. You don't accept help from anyone."

"That's not true," Trish protested. She'd been wrong. The silent treatment was better than this humiliation.

"Yes, it is. But that's changing right now," he warned.

"What do you mean?" Trish eased up against the sofa arm, desperate to be on a more level playing field.

"We have to bring the police in on this."

"No! Didn't you read the note that threatened Zane?"

Josh disagreed. "Don't underestimate your brother. He's capable of taking care of himself."

"Yeah, Trish," Heidi concurred. "And Zane will be crazy when he finds out what's been going on with you."

"That's just my point. He's got Angel and the baby to worry about. He won't watch out for himself. He's always had to fix my problems. Not anymore." Trish folded her arms across her chest to send a clear message that she wasn't budging. She would not give them a chance to speak until she got her piece said.

"And now this, this...person has threatened Zane's life, and Angel's. I don't even know what the stalker wants. I can't risk something happening to Zane and I *won't* bring any police into this until I find out who is behind the notes and what they want."

"You don't have *any* idea who the stalker is?" Josh asked.

Trish let out a small breath of relief when his focus moved to the stalker. "No. That's why I went to Big Charlie's tonight. I thought *he* was."

"Why?" Heidi wanted to know.

"He had motivation. He's been after me to sell ReSolution. Then he called today and said he was over at Gunter's place. I think Gunter might want to sell out, but Charlie had me convinced that Gunter's deal depended on me selling. I didn't want that responsibility."

"Was Charlie a chess player?" Josh asked.

Trish should've known he'd remember the chess piece she'd found on her desk. "Not that I know of, but that's part of what got me thinking it was Charlie after he called from Gunter's place. Anyone with Charlie's background in our business would recognize that piece as being part of an infamous set a serial killer once used as a calling card. I thought Charlie might've had it planted in my shop just to rattle me."

"When did all this start happening?"

She understood where Josh was going with his questioning and gave him what she'd put together. "Right after I made it into the final round of the competition. That's why I thought it might be business related, but Charlie had always been an in-your-face kind of threat, so I didn't seriously consider him as the stalker until today."

Heidi scrunched up her face. "Did you really think he was capable of getting a note inside your locked car?"

"Not him, but he could have hired someone with his money."

"Guess you're right," Heidi conceded.

"That timing can be attributed to coincidences," Josh interjected. "As of tonight, Big Charlie's off the list."

Trish perked up at a thought. "Using my letter opener as the murder weapon isn't coincidental."

"True," Josh agreed. "Which means that someone had a grudge against you *and* Big Charlie." He rubbed his forehead with a palm. "We need a plan."

Trish shifted the position of her arm supporting the half-thawed bag of peas. She was all for figuring something out and really liked the "we" part if Josh's plan didn't include telling Zane. "But what I've told you stays in this room."

"Give me one good reason not to tell Zane about this," Josh

challenged with everything from his tone to his stance.

"Because I can't..." She paused to hold her composure, but she had to make him understand. "I can't live with the guilt...if anything happened to Zane." Her voice dropped to a whisper as her throat closed off. "He's the one person who wanted me when no one else did."

Lines creased Josh's forehead. He glanced at Heidi who said nothing, then back at Trish who explained, "My parents planned for Zane, but not me. I was an unwanted oops. They provided for me, but our relationship was polite at best. Zane was the one who made me believe I counted. He made it clear that he wanted me as his sister and gave me all the love he could to make up for my parents. Then Angel came along and put her life on the line for me and Zane. That's what you do for family. I would sacrifice everything for the ones I love." She glanced over at Heidi. "For *everyone* I love."

Heidi gave her a sad smile. "Back at ya."

Trish's blunt words must have gotten through.

Josh's face eased from fury into a frown of concentration.

Heidi moved over close to Trish, placing her hand on Trish's knee. Trish covered it with hers, glad to know her friend understood. The last thing she'd ever do was hurt Heidi but protecting Zane at all costs came first.

Of all people, Heidi would understand that.

Josh stared out the front window.

Trish didn't believe anything beyond that room had captured his attention. He was weighing his decision. She waited anxiously until he shared it. No man before, except Zane, had ever been there for her. But Josh had been her anchor more than once in the last two days. A harrowing two days that made her feel as though they'd known each other longer. She'd never considered a man other than her brother trustworthy enough to accept his help, especially after allowing one to lead her into a trap that almost killed her.

But Josh could have let her go alone last night when she left the banquet, and he didn't have to intervene with the detective tonight. Now he was listening and giving her words consideration.

When he turned to her, his face gave away nothing. "Trish, if we don't bring in the authorities there could be consequences beyond anything happening to Zane."

She understood he meant that she would be in danger. "I'm willing to take that risk."

"That's what I was afraid you'd say. Okay, here's the plan. For *now*, I won't tell Zane or the authorities–"

"Thank you, Josh." Her heart was in her voice.

"Hear me out before you thank me. You're not to be alone at any time while we figure out who is behind this."

Being dictated to by anyone grated on her after all she'd gone through to finally be responsible for herself. "I can be careful, but I can't have someone with me every minute. I have to travel to a convention Saturday."

"That's off the table."

"No, it's not." Now Trish was seriously ticked off. "Leaving town isn't going to make any difference. If anything, it might get me away from the stalker for a while."

Josh thought on something a moment before telling her, "You don't understand. Detective Vickers released you into my custody tonight."

"Custody?" Trish thought back over the killing. "He really thinks I'm a suspect? I told him the truth about the letter opener."

"And he's running fingerprints right now from the ones you gave him before you left. I'm betting there'll be a match."

She covered her stomach with her hand, feeling sick. This was going to destroy any hope she had for even staying in the competition. Why work so hard only to watch everything she wanted to end up destroyed before her eyes? She whispered more to herself than anyone, "I have to go to this conference. I'm one of the speakers."

"They'll get over it," Josh tossed back casually.

"That's easy for you to just sit there and say. You've never been the underdog trying to build a business and your reputation at the same time." She hadn't meant to sound so bitter, but she was tired of life beating her down every time she tried to take a step up. Control of her life was slipping through her fingers, and she had no idea why. As an FBI agent, Josh had the authority to lock her up if he thought she might flee his custody.

But more than that, her fear for Zane's life had armed Josh with the power to manipulate her into doing whatever he wanted.

He said nothing in response.

No wonder. She sounded like a bitch after all he'd done for her. "I'm sorry to sound unappreciative. I'm not myself right now. But if I back out at the last minute, they'll blacklist me and won't ask again. It'll do serious damage to me professionally and I can't afford that."

Understanding filled his eyes when he took her in with a long look. "No apology needed. You're right. I wasn't putting myself in your shoes. This convention is that important?"

Was he considering letting her go? "Very important, especially now that I'm probably out of the competition." The outlook for ReSolution would still be dismal, but she was not giving up her dream without fighting every step of the way.

"We don't know that about the television show," Heidi pointed out, then looked over at Josh expectantly. "You should be okay to travel in another day."

He rubbed his neck and shifted his shoulders as if the muscles were knotted and tight. "You can go–"

"Thank you," rushed out of Trish on the breath she'd been holding.

"–but not alone," he finished. "I'll get your itinerary tomorrow."

She could live with that and knew when to stop fighting. Detective Vickers would never have allowed her to leave. If Josh had not pressed to have her released into his custody, she might be sitting in a jail cell. His willingness to help her and not tell Zane reached a part of her other men had never cared about.

Trust couldn't be freely given–it had to be earned.

Josh had just earned a fair share of hers.

"Another thing," Josh continued. "You are to tell me when you get a note, text, phone call, dream, passing comment on the street...anything that is out of the ordinary. Got it?"

"Got it, but I think you're going overboard."

"I'm not even going to acknowledge that in the face of what happened tonight. If you want Zane kept out of the loop, then I want you protected at all times."

Just what she did *not* need. Another overprotective man in her life. But his concern for her safety sent a wave of comfort through her. She'd fought off Zane's smothering attention and had avoided men for so long that she hadn't expected Josh's strength to feel welcome, but it did.

Josh swung his attention to Heidi. "What's your schedule tonight and tomorrow?"

"I leave for the shop at 8:30 in the morning. Trish can stay home tomorrow."

"Wait a minute. I didn't agree not to work," Trish complained.

"Yeah, and *I* didn't agree not to tell Zane," Heidi deadpanned.

"You wouldn't." No one understood better than Trish the rock-hard will Heidi possessed.

"Oh, yes, I would, because I think Zane can handle himself. So, if you want *my* cooperation as well, you stay here tomorrow and rest."

"Dammit."

For that she got a Heidi victory grin.

"Fine," Josh answered then gave Heidi his cell phone number. "I'll trade with you in the morning, Heidi."

Trish couldn't believe it. Her world had been taken over by a short she-devil and a sexy FBI agent. She'd play their game tonight and rest–in fact that sounded pretty good–but tomorrow *she* was calling the shots again.

"I'm going up to make a pot of spaghetti at my place and bring it down," Heidi said, rising from her perch on the floor.

"Are you staying for dinner, Josh?"

"No, thanks. I have an appointment tonight."

Heidi nodded and was out the door.

Well, damn. Trish had wanted them both gone a minute ago. Now she wished he'd stay. Josh had an appointment. What kind of appointment this late at night?

She asked, "Business?"

When he didn't answer right away, she started to backtrack, but he said, "Yes."

She might have believed him if he hadn't taken so long to answer. A date? Not likely, based on his reasoning for following her to the warehouse, but, bottom line, either way was none of her concern. She'd been the one to reject his offer time and again. But even though she didn't think there was someone else, the thought of him spending time with another woman struck a nerve that felt dangerously like jealousy.

She'd never suffered that around any man.

Or this thumping ache in her heart because he was leaving.

After recent days spent stressed out over the stalker and now having walked into a murder scene, she began to question why she'd denied herself a few pleasures in life–like the company of a man who didn't try to ply her with alcohol.

She'd accepted loneliness as a trade-off for sobriety to the point she'd convinced herself she was better off alone. But that was a lie. Avoiding men had been safer than risking a decision. Living that way had been easy until she'd met Josh.

She wanted to be in his arms. To feel him.

Dangerous ground.

He worked for the FBI. He was leaving in two weeks. Had a no-strings lifestyle he clearly liked. She could not keep letting him deeper inside her heart.

But she still wanted him to hold her.

As if reading her mind, he got up and moved over to the sofa where he sat on the edge facing her. He studied her with a lost look in his eyes. He skimmed his knuckles along the side of her cheek.

A tear escaped before she could save it with a blink.

Josh lowered his head and kissed the tiny drop away. His lips moved to hers and he covered her mouth in a sweet kiss. Trish dropped the frozen pea ice pack and ran her hands up his chest, around his neck, ignoring the throb in her head in favor of the momentary escape. Hungry for his touch, she returned the kiss with the depth of her appreciation.

His hands soothed over her back then pulled her closer until he had her in his lap. She molded to his body. His mouth kissed her with care, teasing with his tongue. He gave her what she needed right now more than anything.

To feel cared for and cocooned in a safe place.

Josh's kiss heated. His lips moved over her cheek and down her neck. She shuddered against the warm rush of arousal.

Forget comfort. She ran her fingers over his chest again. Muscles tightened. He made a sound, something low and hungry that woke a matching need inside her.

When the kiss ended, she dropped her face against his chest, feeling the thump of his heart against her cheek.

Cradling her head, he kissed her hair. "You have no idea what I thought when I found you on the floor and saw all that blood." He rubbed her back, soothing her as no man had before.

"I'm glad you were there," she whispered back.

"You're sure you have no idea who the stalker might be?"

"No."

His cell phone buzzed. He moved a hand, checking it then moved his hand back to her shoulder, rubbing gently as if distracted. "Why would he target Zane?"

Hair lifted along her neck at that question that sounded more like business than curiosity. "I don't know."

He held her quietly for a little longer, his chest rising and falling with slow breaths until he finally said, "I want you safe. Promise me you won't take any chances."

"I promise."

"I have to go, but I'll see you tomorrow. Call me if you need anything." He moved Trish back to the sofa and rose, then leaned down and kissed her one more time.

Trish hugged him, thankful to have a man who honestly

cared about her. A man who would act only in her best interest for once.

Josh was a man she could trust.

CHAPTER 25

I would sacrifice everything for the ones I love. Trish's words played over and over in Josh's mind. She'd meant what she said. He had no doubt that she'd put her life at risk and lose ReSolution if that's what it took to protect Zane and Angel.

Josh would do the same for his parents, or for Sabrina or Dingo, but what about Chelsea? If he were honest, he knew he wouldn't have walked away from his team and black ops work for Chelsea. But she wouldn't have walked away from what she was doing for him, either. That's why the relationship with her had been convenient and tidy.

Love had never been a part of that equation.

He'd cared for Chelsea, no doubt. Maybe he'd even loved her in a way, but still, it had been a friends-with-benefits arrangement.

After listening to Trish's impassioned declaration about protecting those she loved, what Josh and Chelsea had shared now sounded cold and empty. Nothing more than affection and a deal that would have filled a few lonely days in his life.

But that was the life he'd chosen. It didn't come with honest relationships. Or a woman who loved the way Trish did.

So why were her words digging into his chest?

Josh parked his rental car outside of the team's hotel suite headquarters. He had no idea what rental vehicles Nick and Dingo were driving, but Ryder's black pickup was parked two spots over. Josh had to talk to Sabrina before he met up with the rest of his team.

He'd used the drive from Trish's house to sort out what he'd learned.

Trish was not the mole, and a stalker was fixated on her. References to chess in the notes and the black rook Trish had found in her shop pointed at one person.

The Chessmaster.

He dug out his phone. As soon as Sabrina answered, Josh

filled her in on everything that had happened, summing it all up with, "Trish is the Chessmaster's pawn, and I don't think she has any idea that her stalker is linked to the DEA mole."

Sabrina said, "You may be right, but that doesn't mean Zane is innocent until we figure out how everyone is connected."

"But would Zane terrorize his own sister?"

"He may not be the Chessmaster, but there has to be a reason Trish is being stalked. That points a finger at Zane's involvement. And he returned early tonight."

Trish's brother had sounded sincere when he told Josh he'd come home early for his pregnant wife and that could be confirmed. Probably had been by now. If Josh argued in favor of Zane at this point, Sabrina would become suspicious of Josh's ability to be objective.

That she'd have a point didn't make it any better.

Sabrina broke him out of his thoughts by saying, "This is perfect."

"What is?"

"You kidding me? I would have thought you'd be the first to realize that Trish is the perfect bait. She's clueless about what you do and she's in your custody. I'll make some calls and keep Vickers off your ass."

What? He clamped his jaw shut to keep from yelling at her that he was not putting Trish in danger.

Wouldn't *that* go over well.

Sabrina would demand he back away so she could put someone else in his place. That was a battle he didn't want to have with her. He wasn't going anywhere and realized the quiet gap that had ensued meant she expected him to buck her plan.

He snorted as if she'd said something ridiculous. "*Of course*, I plan to use Trish as bait." He paused after that screaming lie. "I thought you were excited because you had more intel."

That must have convinced her because Sabrina launched into strategizing. "Give Trish enough space for the Chessmaster to stay in contact and set up a tap on Trish's cell phone so we can intercept the texts."

"I'm on it," he said, as if the idea was already in motion, then moved on to a new subject. He didn't want to wait on Ryder to fill him in on tonight. "What'd you hear from the team?"

"Ryder thought he was screwed when he ran into Zane Jackson at the airfield much earlier than anyone expected."

"From what I understand, Jackson came back early because his wife went into premature labor."

"That's what Jackson said, too, but Ryder used that to his advantage. He told Jackson he'd gotten a tip and wanted to borrow a van to see if it panned out. Zane gave him the okay and left. Told you Ryder was going to be an asset."

Score one for the FNG, but Josh wasn't interested in hearing Sabrina sing Ryder's praises. "What happened tonight?"

"Ryder's van got heisted, as planned. He and Nick followed it to a new meet spot. Dingo observed the DEA team at the place Salazar was supposed to have picked up High Vision's contraband, but no baddies showed. Ryder called the DEA team and informed them he'd tracked the van to the new drop point. The team showed up and made the bust."

"So does that mean the next shipment will be that all-important last one?"

"I don't know," Sabrina answered, taking a minute. "We're going to have to move forward based on thinking the next shipment is *the* one and that it's not going to be drugs. Rikker didn't make contact this time with Salazar."

"Who contacted Salazar with a tip on the DEA bust?"

"He told the DEA his contact was a street kid who said he'd been grabbed with a sack over his head and instructed to deliver a message to Salazar. Kid said the person's voice sounded like a machine. He was given directions, then told he'd be dropped on the sidewalk a block from the meet point and to count to twenty before he pulled off the sack or he'd die."

But the Chessmaster had been outsmarted tonight. Something Sabrina had mentioned raised a new concern for Josh. "Do you think Rikker's moved on already?"

"No. He was on site for weeks to months before each of

those three prior attacks. If he wasn't involved tonight, I'm thinking it's because he suspected a trap, which it was. Don't forget that Rikker is former CIA. He wouldn't just accept that Salazar had gone missing because he'd been spooked when his people were captured during the last bust."

"I'm not as quick to use the word *former*," Josh countered. "But I agree with your thinking." If Sabrina took offense to Josh's insinuation that Gage Laughton had given her a load of bullshit, she didn't say. He hoped she was right about Rikker staying in the area.

"Sounds like you've gotten close to Trish in a short time. Nice job." Sabrina let a couple of beats pass then added, "You're good with this bait setup, right?"

He still wanted to hurt someone over the terror Trish had been enduring. His chest was tight every time he thought of her in danger and the idea of dangling Trish as bait was ripping his insides up, but when he answered Sabrina, his voice was as hard and smooth as polished marble. "Sure. Why wouldn't I be?"

"Good. Call me if anything changes."

Josh got out of the car. On his way across the paved lot, Trish's face haunted his mind. She'd been an easy read at his mention of an appointment tonight.

She thought he was leaving her to see another woman.

An insignificant betrayal compared to the truth—that he and his team would be using her. He was disgusted at his role, which made no sense. This was what he did and who he was. But he had a real concern about this bait plan ending badly.

He'd see it through, but he'd make damned sure Trish was safe the whole time. The danger would be doing that and keeping an emotional distance from Trish but getting involved with a woman had made sense only once in his life. He couldn't be with a civilian. Chelsea would never have expected to know all his secrets. She would've been content with living on the periphery of his life, and he would have been as content with a slice of hers.

Trish was the kind of woman who would expect full

disclosure. The kind that Uncle Ty had warned Josh to not *ever* get involved with, because this business punished a man who did. Uncle Ty would roll over in his grave if he knew how much Josh had wanted to stay with Trish tonight.

Trish pulled at him, but she'd never fit into the neat little relationship design Josh had thought to have with Chelsea. No woman could know his true identity. Over the years he'd shielded himself, first so that his parents' money wouldn't make him a target, but later he'd put layers of protection around his identity so that an enemy could not retaliate against *him* by harming those he loved.

Back in the UK, Mendelson had thought he was clever when he'd called Josh by his legal last name of Carrington. But that was only the name he claimed as a legal identity, something that would not lead back to his parents.

He'd accepted the limitations of the undercover world when he'd entered it. Duty always came first.

His work was the only life he'd ever have. The sooner he got that straight, the easier this mission would be to complete.

Sounded good on paper, until his conscience reared its ugly head and laughed at him.

CHAPTER 26

A blade of sunlight slashed through barely parted drapes, sparking pain in Trish's temple. Her head throbbed, but not as badly as yesterday.

She'd survive this–had survived worse headaches from hangovers. Aspirin would be nice.

A shot of Woodford Reserve would, too.

Her sleep-heavy gaze paused on a note propped against the lamp on her nightstand. White, not gray. Her pulse calmed.

Heidi's scrawled handwriting told her to rest some more, and she'd be in touch about lunch.

Trish pushed up to a sitting position and waited until stars stopped showering past her eyes and her head eased to a dull ache. She made the trek to the bathroom and cursed whoever had created mirrors.

God, she looked awful. A purplish welt decorated the side of her face at her hairline. She hadn't blow-dried her hair after showering last night. Dragging a wiry brush through the tangle of black curls would be masochistic torture. Pass.

She washed her face and brushed her teeth. Changing from the bikini panties and sleeveless cut-off tank top that stopped just below her breasts would take more energy than she could muster. After carefully finger-combing her hair, she pulled on a short silk kimono and trudged down the hall. She threw a quick look at the front door, glad to see it bolted.

No boogieman coming in that way.

No sizzling blue eyes in the living room either.

She deliberated between being disappointed Josh had a late-night *appointment* and relief he hadn't returned to see her this morning as promised. This way she could regroup. Staying a step ahead of him when she was on top of her game was tough enough. Today she felt more like she'd been sidelined after getting hit by a two-hundred-pound tackle.

Trish sniffed the air.

Could it be? The rich aroma of fresh coffee beckoned her. Bless Heidi. She deserved a BFF award.

Trish shuffled to the kitchen with her gaze going to the almost full coffee pot. Yawning, she stretched and twisted, then leaned her head against the cabinet and poured a cup of the steaming brew.

Staying home alone would do her good. She had to sort out her feelings about Josh and figure out how she was going to convince him to let her function without him hovering.

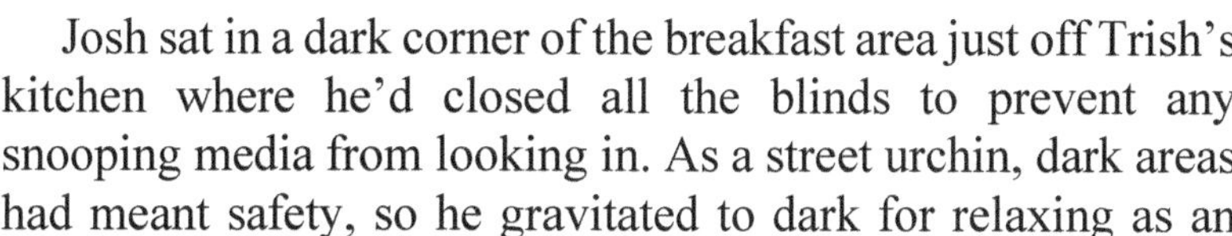

Josh sat in a dark corner of the breakfast area just off Trish's kitchen where he'd closed all the blinds to prevent any snooping media from looking in. As a street urchin, dark areas had meant safety, so he gravitated to dark for relaxing as an adult.

This *had* been restful until Trish appeared in the kitchen.

Josh almost dropped his mug of coffee. He'd heard her coming up the hall and hadn't called out for fear of frightening her.

No chance of calling out now. He couldn't breathe.

She had on a kimono. Sort of.

The thing was shorter than a miniskirt and gapped open and...

Air had locked in his lungs the minute all that exposed skin wandered into view. Where were her clothes? Not that he was complaining, but damn, the woman was practically stripped.

Finishing the job wouldn't take much.

He'd volunteer.

When Heidi had let him in earlier, Josh had thought the breakfast area would be a safe zone to wait for Trish to wake up. No such thing as a safe zone with this woman. A red alarm light should flash before she entered a room to warn a man of imminent attack on his peace of mind.

Trish poured her coffee, then paused to stretch and the kimono dropped down on one shoulder. Her skimpy shirt rode

high, then higher, and she shifted until he had a nice view of
her sweet bottom.

A perfect place for each hand.

He flexed his fingers, trying not to think about all that
creamy skin so close.

His body clenched at the idea of touching so much softness.
He let out the breath trapped in his lungs before he passed out.
Now what was he going to do? The longer he sat here like a
voyeur, the deeper in trouble he'd be as soon as she discovered
him. But, man, was she hot. With her mussed hair and sleepy,
half-awake look, she could have just rolled over from a
draining night of lovemaking.

She yawned. Well, a yawn would have been all right, but
not the torso-twisting stretch that followed. Now he had a nice
side view. When she lifted her arms above her head and arched
back, the slip of material she wore for a shirt skimmed closer
to uncovering a handful of breast.

He remembered exactly what a handful of Trish had felt
like.

Sitting here was getting damned uncomfortable.

If she extended her arms up another inch, both nipples
would flip out below the taut edge of material.

A jackhammer pulse thrummed in his crotch. He tried to
swallow but couldn't with his throat as parched as an Arizona
butte in August. He gave the back door exit consideration. If
he slipped out and walked around to the front, then knocked,
she'd never know he'd been in here the whole time.

Yeah, that might work.

Except for the dog. Heidi said a pet called Dazzle was in the
back yard. Well, hell.

The doorbell chimed.

Trish turned her head toward the front door and frowned.

No, Trish, don't answer the...

She abandoned her cup, heading for the front door.

And killing his chance for a clean getaway.

Damn. Josh jumped up, rushing after her. *What the hell is
she thinking?* Half asleep, she *wasn't* thinking. She had no idea

who was at the door. Regardless, whoever kept ringing the doorbell was *not* going to see her dressed like that.

Her hand touched the knob.

"*Don't* open that," he ordered, a step behind her.

She shrieked and swung around, falling backwards into the corner with her hand over her chest and snapped, "Where'd *you* come from?"

"Happy to see me, are you?" Josh reached the door and snatched it open to a grinning man who might as well have had MEDIA tattooed on his forehead.

"Go. Away," Josh warned, "or I'll have the police pick you up for trespassing." He stopped short of slamming the door out of consideration for Trish but shut and locked it. Then took a breath and looked over at her.

His gaze traveled down to her navel ring.

That pumped another jolt of happy juice into the erection he was trying his best to keep turned away from her.

Her lips were soft and plump, begging to be kissed. He wanted to accommodate them.

Josh closed his eyes. *Try thinking like a man who's here to protect her.* Not some hound trying to get her flat on her back. He opened his eyes to find Trish still tucked in the corner, but she'd wrapped the kimono across her body and tied the belt.

What a shame.

She stared past him at the kitchen. "Where were you?"

Screwed, but not as much as I am now. "Sorry to scare you," he said. "Heidi let me in. I was in the breakfast nook, off to the side, catching a few Zs." *Change the topic now.* "How're you feeling?"

"Oh, uh, fine." She sidestepped toward the hall. "I'm, uh, going to go change. I'll be right back." She left the room. More like raced from the room.

Thank you, God, for small miracles.

If she'd stayed another minute, he'd have kissed her, starting at her navel.

He needed to get laid, but he hadn't been interested in any women he could've easily *had* in a long while. The pisser was that he only wanted one woman right now. The one he *had* to keep his hands off of for any hope of remaining even marginally objective on this mission.

One benefit of scaring her half to death was that she hadn't asked him where he'd gone last night.

Josh returned to the relative safety of the kitchen, still in a painful state of arousal. Had to deal with that first.

He thought about standing naked, chest high in snow. Thinking about that had worked in the past.

A minute went by. Nope. Not helping so far. Superimposed on the snow was the image of Trish, clad in next to nothing.

Apparently, the vision was permanently etched in his mind. Trish mere inches away and wearing less material than he used to clean his laptop screen.

He started writing computer code in his mind, which worked as well as counting sheep most nights. His body began to relax. When she came back out, he'd be ready. He'd have everything under control.

She'd just caught him off guard. Wouldn't happen again.

Trish dashed into her bedroom and shut the door. Her heart pounded against her chest. Josh had scared a year off her life, but that had nothing to do with her blood pressure shooting off the charts. She slumped to the bed.

Get a grip. He hadn't even touched her this time.

None of her body was going to settle down with Josh still out there, alone, looking like ten shades of wonderful.

How did he do that this early in the morning?

She needed to get her head on straight. Last night her heart had said she could trust Josh, but she'd been shaken. Vulnerable. In the cold light of day, common sense and hard experience reasserted itself. Handsome men, especially those who came from money, and Josh obviously did, were nothing but dangerous. They all had hidden agendas. Hadn't she learned that in the most brutal way imaginable?

She'd been so easy when she was younger. Some sexy guy

with a flashy lifestyle would start flirting, buy her a few drinks, and she'd follow him home. Not because she truly loved him, but because of her pitiful need to *be* loved.

The one who'd beaten her to within an inch of her life hadn't even *had* money. He'd just looked the part. But she'd been so drunk by the time he took her to a cheap hotel that she hadn't even protested. Then his idea of rough sex involved her spending the next two weeks in a hospital.

Love was for family only. She was never going to be a pity case again. No man was worth risking the life she'd fought to rebuild.

She'd carved that belief into her stone-dead heart and embraced it daily ... until Josh kissed her. With every touch, he chipped a sliver of stone away.

If she let him, Josh could be the man to break through and get his hands on her heart. The thought scared her to her toes.

He'd awakened a longing to be with someone–with one kiss.

And she'd loved every minute his mouth had devoured hers.

No man had ever kissed her with so much passion. That's when she knew she'd stepped into trouble. Maybe Josh was trustworthy and maybe not. The issue wasn't that she couldn't trust *him*, but that she couldn't trust herself to make a wise decision.

Her conscience smacked her around, arguing she couldn't keep grouping all men together. Zane was honorable. Ben was a great husband and father. Even Bunko was one of the good guys.

Why discount Josh so fast?

She didn't have an answer.

Damned conscience.

Josh had stayed at her side the night police had shown up at ReSolution and he'd stepped in to protect her from being arrested last night.

He kept showing up when she least expected him and doing things that pecked at her heart, a constant tapping to let him in.

He made her want something more...something special.

Heidi had said it was time Trish recognized the strength everyone else saw within her, but that was the image Trish *wanted* them to see. She hadn't fooled Josh. He'd seen past her bravado.

He'd offered a no-strings-attached arrangement.

Could she do that?

Just a little practice run spending time with a man her brother knew who would be gone in two weeks? Nothing too serious.

That could work in her one-minute-at-a-time life.

At some point she'd have to face the fallout from last night. Hiding out here was cowardly. She walked over to her closet and dug for an outfit that would boost her confidence. The day she'd left rehab she promised herself she'd face her fears and doubts head on. She hadn't realized that would encompass a stalker and murder, but other women dealt with crisis and so would she.

Jeans? No. Dress clothes? No.

She looked at the peach dress that had a sexy swish to it. Wearing that downstairs might be dangerous.

I could have been killed right along with Charlie last night. How much more dangerous could it get? She didn't want to wake up one day and find her life was over and she'd been too afraid to take a chance again.

Josh had been trustworthy thus far, so she would give him a little faith.

It wasn't as if he'd been trying to jump her bones. What had he told her that first night when she said she wouldn't sleep with him? *I didn't ask you to.*

A man like Josh didn't come along very often. *Seize the damn day and start living again.*

Decision made and feeling more in control, Trish dressed, freshened up with a dab of mascara and suffered through a quick hair brushing. A splash of her favorite cologne and she exited the bedroom, ready to face her fears.

Please don't make me regret trusting you, Josh.

CHAPTER 27

At the sound of Trish's muffled footsteps against the carpeted hall, Josh relaxed back against the kitchen counter. He could handle a few hours alone with her.

He'd survived plenty of dangerous operations.

How tough could it be to keep from touching a female he was protecting? Even a smoking hot one? Besides, after what Trish had been through, the one thing she did not need was a man in her house pawing her.

"I'm back," Trish announced, strolling into the kitchen.

The vision walking toward him turned his mind to mush.

She wore a peach-colored dress that drifted to mid-calf and clung in the sexiest way. Those lovely breasts were back.

Covered, but not hidden.

Nope. Right up front. Accessible.

All that soft material reminded him of marmalade. He loved marmalade. *Sweet and tangy, spread across her thigh...*

"Josh?"

She stopped right in front of him. Close enough for him to smell her powdery scent.

Her nipples peaked. Ah, hell. No bra.

Josh cleared his throat and stood up straighter. Tried to back up, but there was that counter behind him.

Trish put her hand on his chest, sending a hot ripple through his muscles. "Sorry about yelling at you, I was just surprised to see you, but I'm glad you're here."

She sounded breathless and that drove him crazy.

"Me, too," he mumbled.

"When did you ... come?" she asked innocently.

Come? Perspiration beaded at the back of his neck. *Move, dammit. Stop thinking about that thin layer of material.* The only barrier between him and paradise.

"Was that someone at the door?" Weak, but all he had. He put his hands on her shoulders and gently moved her back so he could sidestep around her. "I'll check it out."

The confused look on her face was nothing compared to what was going on in his chaotic mind.

Had she just given him a green light?

What if she had? She was off limits.

How in the hell was he going to keep his hands away from her for the next two hours when everything about Trish said *touch me*?

She was likely just feeling vulnerable after last night and needing comfort. What he had in mind couldn't be construed as comfort ... except that she'd be noodle limp when he got through with her.

You are such a dog. He was *not* going to take advantage of her no matter how hard he was. *Again.*

The woman was killing him.

He made a show of moving the blinds in the living room enough to look outside. Just as he'd seen ten minutes ago, the news people were hunkered down in cars parked along the street.

They'd persist until the police he'd just called showed up to run them off.

He heard the back door open and close, followed by excited yapping. A streak of fur blasted out of the kitchen and down the hall.

Josh stepped over to see *what* she'd let into the house.

Trish entered the living room laughing. She stopped a couple of feet from him. Man, she was attractive from any angle, but damned beautiful when she smiled.

She whistled and called, "Come here, boy." The blur ran back up the hall and around the living room twice but stayed this time.

Josh took one look at the dog—he assumed it was a dog—and asked, "What is *that*?"

Trish sent him a frown filled with the promise of physical harm if he made a derogatory comment.

"This is Dazzle." She smiled down at a conglomeration roughly the shape of a Wire-haired Terrier. "Aren't you, precious?" She melted for a multi-colored animal whose coat was a mass of black and tan streaks of fur sprouting out between tight clumps of burnt orange corked curls. The mutt gave her a hairy, crooked-tooth smile.

Trish squatted, clapping her hands together.

Dazzle leapt into her arms. She ran her hands all over him, massaging his shoulders, patting his stomach, and hugging him to her breast.

The mutt lapped up her adoration. What male wouldn't?

Josh considered telling Trish he was just as much of a Heinz 57 as that patchwork beast. He needed a rubdown and a hug too.

"Dazzle is an adventurer," Trish said, looking up at Josh with a big grin. "When he was about two months old, he survived a hurricane to find me and Heidi."

Adventurous or not, that beast had captured Trish's heart– an organ she hadn't seemed to think a man worthy of touching, from what he'd observed.

Warmth rippled through him at the pleasure on her face over an anomaly of nature.

He wanted to do that. Be the one to make her smile and feel her hands touching him. Be the one holding her throughout the night.

Where had *that* foolish thought come from?

He didn't know, but the longing had kept him awake most of the night. If he ever started on that body, he wouldn't stop until he'd tasted every inch.

Only a masochistic fool would stand here and torture himself.

Trish lowered her dog to the carpet where she stood, and the mutt danced at her feet.

Josh took a step toward the kitchen, anywhere he didn't have to watch the way Trish's hair curled around her slender neck or see her tongue slip out between her lips.

"Dazzle, do you know how nice Josh is?"

The mutt danced back and forth.

Josh paused to see if the four-legged fur storm could do a

trick.

"Show him how smart you are. Let Josh know how much you appreciate him taking care of your mama."

The wiry length of fur spun in a circle.

"Not that. Tell Josh thank you."

Her dog flipped an about-face and leapt high against Josh's chest. He caught the ball of energy with a grunt, then lowered the mutt back to the floor.

"No, Dazzle, not that high." Trish giggled a happy sound that came out rich and womanly instead of girly. She raised a hand to her forehead as the dog sped away to some unknown target. "I'm sorry, Josh. We're still working on that one."

Recovering his balance after being hit by the canine missile, Josh smiled. He hadn't heard her laugh much since he'd met her and was reluctant to give up this relaxed moment with her.

She lowered her hand to her mouth and nibbled on her knuckle. "Is your offer still good?"

"What offer."

"Spending time with me over the next two weeks."

He'd made that offer to keep the door open for seeing her again and had no idea if he'd be here for two full weeks, but the way she'd asked that said she wanted to do more than meet for dinner. "Yes."

Dazzle returned from another tour of the house. He chased his tail twice then shot between Trish's legs, knocking her off balance.

Dazzle yipped.

Trish yelled.

Josh reached for her just as the four-pawed terror circled his feet, knocking him out of sync. The coffee table would hurt. Josh pitched his weight toward the sofa. His back hit the forgiving cushions a second before she landed on his chest with a thump, and he eased them both upright.

"Trish, are you okay?"

She lifted her head, laughing as she sprawled across his lap. "I am so sorry. Dazzle, um–" Trish gasped a breath. "–is just happy to see me."

Dazzle scurried past them, gone. A squeaky toy screeched from some other room. Trish broke into a fresh peal of chuckles. "Then again, he gets over my absence quickly."

Josh couldn't stop the laugh that came from deep inside. When was the last time he'd felt genuinely happy over anything? He had a hapless mutt to thank for the female in his arms. "You're pretty, but when you laugh ... you're breathtaking."

A mint-scented sigh squeezed out of Trish. Two pert breasts rubbed Josh's chest each time she inhaled, stoking the hot blood now pooled into his rigid erection.

Her breathing stilled. She stared at him, so close he could see each lash. He wanted to kiss her.

Not a wise idea in this position.

He'd led her to believe he'd keep this nonsexual plus, hello, he was on an op.

Time to remember Rule Number One: Never mix business with–

She leaned forward and kissed him.

CHAPTER 28

Josh was stunned for the microsecond it took to realize Trish was kissing him. Erotic pleasure bolted through him at the first touch of her lips.

She had her hands in his hair.

Man, she was hot and kissing him with passion that rocked him.

The need to taste Trish overpowered the voice whispering *Rule Number One* in his head.

Instinct took over.

He knew exactly what to do with a soft, willing woman in his arms. Knew what he wanted. Her.

This amazing woman who smelled fresh and powdery.

He cupped her face, taking over the kiss, hungry for more. When he slowed it down, she nipped at his lip and the race for satisfaction took off again. He didn't know when his hand moved, but he had that plump breast out of her low-scooped top and in his palm. He lowered her back over his arm until he had her stretched out on the sofa. A perfect position to drop his mouth down and scrape his teeth lightly over the thin material covering her other beaded nipple.

She gasped and let out a sound that said do-whatever-you-did-again.

I aim to please. He eased the dress off her shoulders, baring both breasts, and gave attention to both at the same time. "Jossshhh." She grabbed his shoulders, tensed up and arched with a quick intake of air.

She was incredible.

Kissing one breast, then the other, he used both hands to massage the soft mounds, gently rasping his thumbs across the tips.

She made sweet little cries and shivered.

Her reaction stroked straight through him.

Every time she gasped and tensed as if she leaped closer to

an orgasm, she felt his groin tighten and his erection get harder. She rubbed her hips against him.

He sucked in a sharp breath.

Another move like that and he'd have to be inside her, or this would get embarrassing for someone with his experience. He didn't lose control. Not with a woman or on a mission.

That's why he shouldn't be doing this.

Rule Number One.

He should end this now, but he'd have better luck stopping a locomotive at full speed by jumping in front of it.

Hell, he *wrote* damn Rule Number One.

It was his to break, because giving her up right now would be impossible.

Josh gripped Trish's perfect little bottom with one hand, pulling her closer to him. He groaned in pain and pleasure.

Narrow fingers combed through his hair, down his neck and over his chin, driving him mad with her frantic touch. She hooked her hands around his shoulders, fingers digging in to hold tight.

And he wanted her to. He forged ahead with the kiss, sending his tongue in to tangle with hers.

She kissed him right back, meeting his demands with those of her own. He loved the way she gave over to passion, holding nothing back. Her tongue mated with his as it moved in and out. He felt each stroke in his groin. In and out.

Exactly what he wanted to do.

With her. Right this damn minute.

His conscience roared *no!* She was vulnerable after what happened last night. She'd even told him she wasn't ready for this. She was sweet and sexy and trusting...the wrong man.

She might be making a bold offer, but she didn't know who she was dealing with. She thought he was an FBI agent with the task force and *that* was a lie.

He was here to watch over the bait for the Chessmaster.

Just thinking of that pissed him off all over again.

She dropped her head back from him, panting. "What's wrong?"

Her lips were puffy from being kissed. Her eyes were heavy with desire when she looked up at him, breasts heaving up and down with each deep intake and exhale. She licked her finger and traced it over his lips.

What's wrong? Nothing. He drew her finger into his mouth and sucked on it.

She closed her eyes and made an "mm" sound of pleasure.

He wanted to give her real pleasure, but if he accepted her tempting offer now, she might regret it later. *Would* regret it. He was touching her again just to watch her reaction. He tugged on her dress, sliding it further and leaned down to kiss her navel then kissed his way back up to her breast again and took the nipple into his mouth, stroking her with his tongue.

She arched up and called his name.

He wasn't sure how much more he could take, but he couldn't ride the fence any longer.

He was all in.

She rubbed up against him and his muscles clenched. Her body language begged for more. He'd be begging soon, too, but all she had to do was ask.

He'd give her anything at this point.

But he couldn't make love to her the way he wanted to and face himself later.

Besides, he had no condom. Taking this to its natural end without one was out of the question.

Josh moved back and slid his hands down to where her bunched up dress exposed the long legs now cupping his hips. He explored a little more and ran his finger along the thin elastic of her panties then dipped inside.

She was wet and ready. What he wouldn't give for a condom right now, but he would not deny her. He moved his fingers, teasing her, barely grazing the sensitive skin.

She gripped his arms and tensed. "Oh, uh, Jossshhh..."

Those sounds she made getting closer to climax drove him crazy. He fingered her wet folds, her breath hitched, missed. She shook with need, her body soaring closer, reaching for its limit. Josh caressed one of her dark pink nipples with his tongue, loving the way she whimpered when he stroked the hard nub.

Any second now she'd explode.

Pressure built beneath his zipper.

He'd been denied few things in his adult life. At this minute, he'd give up a lifetime of wishes to drive deep into her heat. He pushed a finger inside her then pumped it again and his thumb toyed with the spot that had her shaking.

A noise nipped at his attention.

He tried to listen but heard only Trish's whimpered pleas.

That was...until Dazzle flew down the hall again and into the living room, yapping and spinning around the table. The mutt batted the edge of the sofa with his paws as he jumped up and down then ran to the door. Once there, he repeated the whole process.

Trish tightened around Josh's finger and his erection pulsed in answer. She was begging him not to stop. Dazzle's yaps were getting louder and more intense.

The doorbell rang.

Damn media. No way would he leave her seconds from climaxing.

Pounding jarred the front door.

Trish arched hard, her taut body straining as he pushed her to the peak.

Pound. Pound. Pound. A muffled *"Trish!"* called from beyond the door. Dazzle batted the couch, yapping incessantly.

When Trish started to cry out with her release, Josh kissed her, gorged himself on her taste. Hated that they'd have to stop before he was ready to give her up.

She clutched at him, anchoring herself to him as she shuddered once more. Her labored breathing slowed.

His still chugged as if he'd run a foot race.

Josh kissed her damp face, his own brow beaded with the strain of resistance.

The doorbell rang over and over and over. *"Trish!"*

He growled, "Who the hell–"

"Oh, no." Trish slapped her hand over her eyes.

"Oh, no?"

Trish gave him a look of disbelief. "Not you. Her. That's Angel, my sister-in-law. She'll call Zane if I don't answer the door. Get up."

He did and took her hand, hauling her to her feet. "Can you walk?"

"Are you always so cocky?" But she would have stumbled if he hadn't held onto her. Damn right, he was cocky.

Josh kissed Trish's forehead instead of answering her and leaned close to her ear to issue quick instructions. "Go to your bedroom, put on a robe and wrap a towel around your head like you just got out of the shower."

"Trisssshhh!" yelled from outside the door with more pounding.

Trish tottered away, apparently not yet recovered.

Male satisfaction at seeing her boneless appeased some of the screaming in his loins.

Now the doorbell rang in between the pounding.

Josh straightened his clothes, all the while coaxing Dazzle to calm down and follow him into the kitchen.

"*Commminnng!*" Trish called out a minute later as she thudded back down the hall.

Not anymore. Josh curled a wry smile. Flipping on the lights in the breakfast area, he sat in a chair on the backside of the table. This way he could see the kitchen and use the tablecloth to hide his lap until his erection died down. That might take a while.

With no hope for true satisfaction, the only way to put this one to rest would be if he stood naked in snow. Not likely in south Florida.

Trish was making on-the-way-to-the-door noises.

He slouched back against the chair, arms crossed on his chest and legs sprawled to appear as bored as he could with his head slung back and eyes shut.

A door opened and closed in the front room, followed by a short, muffled conversation. Footsteps took off in two directions. One set back toward Trish's bedroom, and the other headed toward him.

"Hellooo?"

"Hmm." He straightened in the chair, stretching his body, pretending he was a mass of kinks. He blinked as if he worked to focus on the very attractive, very pregnant woman waddling up to him. He stood, banking on his loose khakis to save him.

"Hello." Josh arranged his face to present confusion. "Where'd you come from?"

"Trish let me in. Guess I caught her in the shower. I'm Angelina Jackson. Everyone calls me Angel. I'm Zane's wife."

Josh introduced himself and shook her hand. It was strong to be so delicate looking.

Zane had done well for himself. Angel was tall with strawberry-blond hair woven into some sort of braid. Based on what little weight she'd gained beyond that bulge in her middle, Zane would soon have his beautiful wife back to normal size *and* a new baby.

If he wasn't in prison.

Josh took a mental step back as some things clicked into place for him. What man would risk everything dear to him for money? Especially, a man who stood to inherit a fortune in a few short years. Josh knew from Zane's file that he and Trish's parents had been wealthy from the oil business and Zane stood to receive a bloated trust fund in the near future.

And Josh had figured out that nothing meant more to Zane than Angel and Trish. Jeopardizing his life with them made no sense, and Zane Jackson was a bright boy.

Josh sure as hell wouldn't risk losing Trish if she were his.

That thought pushed him off center.

He would never have what Zane had right now and should be running in the opposite direction as fast as he could. That reminded Josh that he had to leave soon anyhow.

"Are you going to be here for a bit, Angel? I don't want to leave Trish alone, but Heidi is supposed to come get her for lunch." He took a step toward the front door.

"Actually, Heidi's bringing lunch here for the three of us."

Perfect. "In that case, I'll head out." Before Trish walks in and one of them gave away what had just happened. He was trained to shield any reaction, but Trish wasn't, and he didn't want her to do or say something that Angel might notice and tell Zane about.

Angel said, "Don't rush on my account."

"I've got to go. Just traded off with Heidi this morning so Trish could sleep in undisturbed."

"Back to the office?" Angel asked in a casual way that wasn't supposed to sound as if she were fishing. But for what?

"I've got a lunch appointment." The way she nodded slowly and with a cool expression on her face gave him a strange moment of concern. Why would she care if he had lunch plans? She'd just said that she and Heidi would be with Trish. Maybe it was something else. "Did the media bother you outside?"

"No, the police were talking to them."

He yawned to sell the whole nothing-has-been-going-on scene. "Must have dozed off."

A smile quirked at the corner of Angel's mouth. She glanced over at the magazine he'd supposedly been reading.

"I can see how '*Nail and Hair for Women on the Move*' would do that." Angel met his gaze with a taunting grin in place. "Especially when you read it upside down.

Well, hell. Josh knew when to quit. "Please tell Trish I'll call later."

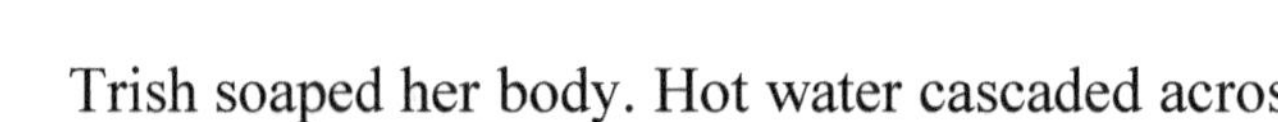

Trish soaped her body. Hot water cascaded across skin that still tingled from Josh's touch. Had that really just happened? Good grief, Josh could kiss. He should have to register his mouth as a sexual weapon of mass destruction.

That's all he'd need to rule a female universe.

Just those lips, and maybe that bulge under his zipper.

What would have happened if Angel hadn't shown up?

Trish had no doubt she and Josh would have finished what they started. She was uber happy, but he couldn't be. She'd gone after live-in-the-moment sex with a guy who was safe.

And she'd encouraged him by walking around in a flirty dress and no bra. She'd figured at the least, she'd test a few limits.

But the minute she'd fallen on the sofa on top of Josh, she couldn't think about anything except wanting him closer to her. To climb inside his skin.

Correction. Him inside her.

That he hadn't jumped all over her blatant offer surprised her. He'd given everything to her and asked nothing in return. Men didn't do that. Not the ones in the past. Josh kept tearing down all her preconceived notions.

Just like he'd said. She might enjoy herself with him if she'd let go of those notions. Therein lay the danger. She *was* letting go of those and every time she did, she found herself caring more for Josh.

He was different. Genuine. And he wanted her.

Now would be the time to decide if this was going any further or not. She'd never had a man think only of her. Josh had and deserved an indication of what this meant the next time they were together. That step toward intimacy had felt exhilarating and terrifying at the same time. She'd be lying if she said she didn't want to feel more with him, but she couldn't fence sit on this.

To encourage Josh, whether intentional or not, and not follow through would be wrong. Only a tease did that.

And she'd made the first move.

She finished soaping her body, hissing at the friction when her fingers washed over her breasts. She missed Josh's hands. And his mouth. And the parts she didn't get to see.

What would it be like to have him make love to her all the way? To take that step with a man while completely sober, without an accidental, tangled leg start or an interruption by visiting family?

Amazing.

What would it be like when he walked away?

She might not be as casual about this as she'd thought.

Trish flicked off the water and toweled down then tossed on jeans and a T-shirt. Seeing her airline ticket for tomorrow morning on her dresser brought up a new thought. Josh hadn't asked her about her flight. Had only said he didn't want her going alone. Was he really going to let her leave town while she was involved in a murder investigation?

He'd said she could, but that was last night when he might have said anything to keep from stressing her out.

She'd ask him tonight, but not until they reached an understanding about what was going on between them. First, she had to make up her mind about what *she* wanted between them. Could she spend a couple of weeks making love to him and still kiss him goodbye with no concern when he left?

She didn't think so. Not Josh.

And this wasn't some young girl infatuation. Josh stirred something strong inside her, something special she'd never felt with a man before.

For once, something felt extremely right, honest, and safe. But she hadn't known him long and might not get the chance to. There was email and phone calls and airplanes, right? Atlanta wasn't that far away. But he said he wasn't there often.

Don't start thinking that far ahead. Just worry about today.

Taking her life one day at a time had been easier before Josh entered the picture. She couldn't help it. He made her want someone in her life, and for more than just sex.

And that's what got you into trouble before.

It was true. Her inability to have casual flings had caused her to buy into all those perfect lies the guy back in Houston had told her just before he almost killed her.

But Trish was no longer that gullible young woman and would not judge Josh against a beast. If she told him how she felt and asked him to stay in touch when he left, would he?

His answer to that would determine what happened between them tonight.

She finished with her hair, but no makeup, ready to face Angel. When Trish walked into the kitchen, Angel sat at the breakfast table, flipping through a magazine. "Where's Josh?"

Angel glanced up then narrowed her eyes. "He had to leave. Said he'd call you later."

"Oh."

Angel was still staring at her with curious eyes, which meant Trish had given something away in her voice. Or she probably still had a flushed look the shower didn't fix.

Trish hurried over to hug her sister-in-law and spun the conversation back to Angel when she plopped down in a chair. "Are *you* doing okay?"

"Yes, I'm fine and so is the baby. I've had a little spotting that got Zane and the doctor all cranked up, but I'm staying off my feet most of the day."

"How'd you get my insane brother to let you out of the house, much less *drive* here, with you so close to delivering?"

"I didn't." Angel grinned with that mischievous look that had probably tied Zane in knots more than once. "I got a friend to drop me off, and Heidi's on the way here with lunch so I'll grab a ride back with her. When he calls, I'll tell him I was feeling lonely, and he'll get over my leaving home without checking in." Angel reached over and squeezed Trish's hand. "Are you okay?"

"I think so. It's been a little hairy lately." More like gut wrenching. She'd been scared out of her skin way too often.

Then there had been mind-blowing times like this morning.

"You're doing so great, but Zane and I are worried about you. What happened last night?"

Trish pulled her hand away to rub her eyes. "I don't know. I got tired of Big Charlie and his constantly irritating me about selling so I went over to have a come-to-Jesus meeting. We needed to reach an understanding." Of all people, she hated lying to Angel, but at least she could tell part of the truth. She *had* meant to confront Charlie.

Her sister-in-law had escaped a crazy man who'd sent thugs to hunt her down, so she'd been in dangerous crossfire and would understand Trish's need to take care of her own issues. Trish had been with Angel in Zane's apartment when a huge, scary-looking guy broke in while Zane was gone flying. Angel had fought the guy–before she was pregnant–and given Trish the opening to escape. Trish had been tipsy at the time. Zane eventually rescued Angel, but Trish was ready to quit drinking that day.

She'd put her life on track at that point and refused to look behind her.

But telling Angel the real reason Trish had gone to Big Charlie's–to confront him about being a stalker–could put Angel in danger, too, and stress her to the point of affecting the baby.

Trish would walk through the fires of hell to prevent that.

Angel grimaced and rubbed her side where the baby had probably kicked her somewhere like the kidneys. "Zane told me Big Charlie was stabbed. We're just relieved whoever it was didn't hurt you any worse than hitting you."

Death and blood had wandered through Trish's nightmares last night. Heidi had stayed downstairs on Trish's sofa and shaken her awake more than once.

Trish had to put on a strong front so when Angel reported back to Zane, he would calm down. "Yeah, well. Now that I think back on it, I must have walked in and not realized someone was behind the door. The killer must have panicked and hit me, then run, or he'd have taken the time to make sure I was dead. Or *she* would have. I shouldn't assume it was a man. I never saw a face." She'd managed to share that without her voice quivering, so she kept going. "I *will* be fine. Tell my brother I'm not going to break down or fall off the wagon."

Angel grimaced. "We're your family, Trish. None of us is waiting for you to stumble."

Dial back the defensive attitude. Trish rubbed her eyes and dropped a fisted hand on the table. "Sorry. I guess the truth is that *I'm* the one waiting on me to fail."

When Angel smiled with understanding, Trish added, "But I won't, so tell my brother I don't need babysitters around the clock. I'm perfectly safe here on my own today."

"Safe from crazy killers, but what about tall, sexy babysitters?" Angel arched an eyebrow, a direct challenge if Trish tried to lie to her.

How could her sister-in-law have figured out anything when

she hadn't even observed Trish and Josh in the same room? Trish had to shut this down, or Zane would really come unglued. "What are you suggesting? That there's something going on between me and Josh?"

"Is there?"

"Be serious. Zane claims Josh is gay." Nice divertive answer.

"I heard him say that, too. You haven't answered my question."

"I enjoy his company." She wanted to enjoy more of it and often.

Angel tapped her fingers across her rounded belly, trying to decide something. "Zane tells me little about what goes on at work, which is fine with me because it's his job, but I heard something that concerned me that I think you should know. I wouldn't bring this up now, but after meeting Josh this morning...."

Worry started churning in Trish's stomach. "What about Josh?"

"Don't share anything I tell you–"

"I won't," Trish assured her.

"Zane and Ben think there's still a mole inside the DEA."

"Really? What about Colbert?"

"They think he was just a link in the chain. I don't know everything, just that some new things have come to light. Zane was pretty upset about Josh being with you last night. If I weren't so close to delivering and hadn't had the spotting issues, he would have been *here* all night."

Trish argued, "I do *not* need anyone here besides Heidi."

"I understand," Angel quickly assured her. "But neither of us is going to change your brother at this point and if Colbert hadn't been killed–"

"Hold everything." Trish lifted her hand like a stop sign. "What happened to him?"

Angel looked up at the ceiling, muttering, "Hormones are going to be the death of me." When she lowered her eyes to face Trish again, she said. "Zane doesn't even know that I heard this."

"Wait. Are you telling me you got all this eavesdropping?"

"Yes. Zane thinks I'll be stressed out if I know what's going on. He can't get it through his head that having to *guess* what's going on bothers me more." Angel's sigh ended with a growl. "As soon as this baby is born, I'm straightening him out, but he's so wigged out over the birth I don't have the heart to yank him back in line."

Trish laughed. "I'm so glad he married you. If he'd picked some mouse to be with, he'd have been miserable, and I wouldn't have a great sister-in-law."

Angel smiled, her warmth filling the room. "That's why I had to come over. I never share anything Zane tells me, not even eavesdropping when he's on a phone call, but when I realized he was keeping you in the dark, too, I knew that wasn't right. I realize he can't tell things about his job, but I think you need to know what's going on. I believe you can handle anything if you know what you're facing."

"Thanks, Angel."

"Back to what I was saying before Heidi gets here so you and I are the only ones who know. I love her, too, and know I can trust her, but I already feel disloyal to Zane by telling you these things. So, whatever you do, don't share any of this with anyone."

"Deal, if you'll just spit it out." Today.

Angel scowled. "Don't mess with a pregnant woman who has forgotten what it is to go an hour without peeing and ... ouch." She flinched and rubbed her side. "And has a little terror kicking her kidneys nonstop." She took a breath. "Where was I? Oh, I know. Here's the down and dirty."

Sympathizing with Angel, Trish nodded patiently.

"When the DEA was moving Colbert, their transport was attacked, and everyone was killed."

Trish stopped short of saying "no shit." She might as well start now being careful around her niece or nephew.

Angel went on. "Zane was the one who pointed the task force toward Colbert, which is not a secret, but he's suspicious about how the information came through to him. It looked like the leak problem had been fixed until last night when some drug bust related to Colbert's activities played out in a strange way. Zane's words, not mine. No, I didn't hear any other details on that, so don't ask."

More nodding on Trish's part.

"It sounds like Zane and Ben have been looking for a second mole still in the task force. That's why I think Zane is bothered about Josh being around you."

Trish was stunned. "Whoa, you lost me with that right turn. How does Josh fit into this?"

"The minute Zane hung up from talking to Josh last night, he called back Detective Vickers and asked what your status was. Vickers said he'd released you into Josh's custody because Josh claimed you and Big Charlie were part of an ongoing FBI investigation."

Trish cringed at how that sounded but considering that Josh's FBI muscle card had allowed her to come home she was okay with it. "That's how Josh talked Vickers into letting me go and I'm not in a jail cell, so I don't see a problem."

"We felt the same way last night, especially after Zane had Ben check it out. Ben called back in half an hour and said the FBI had no information on Big Charlie or any case to do with him."

Way to go, Josh. "See?"

Angel lifted a finger from where her hands rested on her middle. "Ben's friend in the FBI called him back this morning and said there was *now* an active file on Big Charlie and *you*."

Trish wanted to brush it off as Josh being thorough, but she had a bad feeling she could be wrong. Her heart wanted to be right about Josh. "What does Zane think is going on?"

"This is where I had to do some speculating. I know Ben has a friend inside the FBI who's another techno genius like him, because that's who Ben contacted back when I had a run-in with the FBI."

"Run-in. That's putting it mildly." Angel had escaped an international thief bent on killing her. Thankfully, she'd stowed away on Zane's airplane and the FBI knew she was innocent of the theft, or she might not be alive, or free, today.

Angel was more than a survivor. She was a fighter.

Only someone who loved Trish like a sister would come here to share confidential information with her.

Angel continued, "I think Ben had this guy pull Josh's personnel file or something. Josh's file is not just classified, but in an electronic vault, which Zane said makes no sense if Josh is *only* a computer forensics technician. Ben must have agreed because he speculated that Josh could be someone sent in to work deep undercover."

"They think Josh is here hunting for the mole?"

Angel nodded. "I have no idea how any of that works, but it makes sense after Colbert was killed that the DEA would need someone outside the agency. I've asked Zane about his Special Ops work in the Air Force and one thing he told me was that an undercover operative used any, and all, weapons available to meet an objective. The really deep undercover will do it without concern over collateral damage, if necessary."

"And how does that have anything to do with me, Angel?"

"Colbert was seen talking to you for a long time at the party, then he stopped by ReSolution."

"But I didn't *date* Colbert."

"I know, but you said he called you a couple of times."

"He did and I politely refused." How had Trish been so firm with Colbert and a pushover with Josh?

"This is what worries me. Josh may be trying to get close to you just to determine if you know more about Colbert than what you shared with Zane after Colbert was arrested." Massaging her stomach, Angel pinned Trish with a questioning stare. "And if that man who walked out of here a half hour ago is gay, then I'm the next virgin queen of England."

"*I* didn't say he was gay. Zane did."

Angel had watched Trish closely and asked, "Are you sleeping with Josh?"

"No." Not technically since Trish had been the only one to get instant gratification this morning.

"Thank goodness."

Angel's relief raised a warning flag for Trish. "Why are you so glad we're not sleeping together?"

"Because he left here to have lunch with Leanne Witherspoon. Zane says Josh never spent time with anyone on the task force, male or female, but now he's spending time with you and going to lunch with Leanne. Ben heard Josh ask Rhonda out to dinner this weekend. Sounds like he's making the rounds with women who were in contact with Colbert."

Leanne wouldn't make a play for Josh because she knows I...

Trish halted that thought in midstream. She *had* told Leanne she wasn't interested in Josh or any other man right now. But that was before Trish realized she was interested. Very.

Had Leanne taken Trish at her word?

Had she told Rhonda?

If what Angel said was true, it colored everything Josh had said to Trish. Everything he'd done.

Was he going to see Leanne today with intentions of seducing her? Or had he already claimed that prize? What about that *appointment* he'd gone to last night? Could it have been one of those women? He'd hesitated when she'd asked him if the appointment was business.

Technically, he'd be right even if he'd slept with Leanne or Rhonda already.

Trish tried to draw a breath into her tight chest. And she knew why it was tight. She'd started falling for Josh and had exposed herself an hour ago.

Not just physically, but emotionally.

He'd gone from touching her to seeing another woman. Even if it was just lunch, the idea did not sit well with her, any more than being a checkmark on a list of suspects.

If he was here working undercover, Josh was not the man she thought he was, but playing a role.

Josh Robertson probably wasn't even his real name.

When she filtered the last two days through the lens of what Angel had shared, Josh's actions began to sharpen and make more sense. He hadn't *accidentally* happened along as Trish was going to Big Charlie's last night. Josh had been following her. Just like she hadn't been able to push him away that first night because he was so taken with her.

No wonder he'd been so irritated with her. He probably had orders to stick with her.

What a joke. And the joke was on her.

And what about this morning?

Had that moment on the sofa really happened spontaneously or was she so clueless about men she'd been seduced by a master who let her think she'd taken the lead? Had there been an ulterior motive behind *everything* Josh had said and done?

Sounded that way.

Just one big game to get her to lower her defenses so she'd trust him.

And she had, because she'd wanted to believe that a man as gorgeous and sweet and wonderful as Josh not only existed, but also wanted to be with her. That he could care for her.

How many times would she have to make a fool of herself with a man before she finally got wise?

She should have stuck to her guns and stayed away from all men.

Acknowledging the truth about Josh left an icy ball spinning in her stomach. She sat back, trying not to be nauseous over what she'd gained and lost all in one swift moment.

Angel said softly, "Are you *sure* nothing is going on between you two?"

Not anymore. Trish sat up and put some steel in her spine. "Absolutely. We had a few laughs and he's been a perfect gentleman, but that's to be expected from someone who knows how to manipulate a woman, right?"

"True," Angel said carefully then reminded her, "He's calling you later."

Oh, joy. The first response that came to mind involved serious adult language shouted at a high decibel, but she immediately changed her mind.

She would *not* lose her composure now, or later around

Josh.

Part of her felt as though she owed him a chance to explain himself, but the angry part said he could have simply asked her about Colbert at any point instead of playing on her insecurities.

If he could keep secrets, so could she.

If she ever allowed him to step inside her hemisphere again in this millennium, she wouldn't say a word about this. That way, he'd have no idea that she was on to him.

Angel's eyebrows lifted. "That's an evil smile on your face. What are you going to tell him when he calls?"

"I haven't decided yet, but that's not really going to be a problem as long as he can't find me to talk."

"Where are you going?"

"I have a convention in Atlanta tomorrow. I'm supposed to leave super early in the morning, but they offered me an extra night if I wanted to come in this evening since I'm one of the speakers. Josh thinks I'm leaving tomorrow, but if I can get an earlier flight out tonight, I'm going. He'll probably be too busy with Leanne to notice I'm even gone."

"Will you be safe?"

"They arranged shuttles from the airport to downtown and sent out the schedule. I'll be in the middle of a thousand convention attendees, surrounded by people constantly and I *am* capable of protecting myself."

A busy convention didn't seem like the right setting for the stalker who had yet to show his face, but Arnie's voice niggled in her head, about how pickpockets and predators work in the middle of crowds for good reason. Okay, so she'd be careful. She'd be on high alert, and she'd watch her back. But she was going. Without Josh. She laid her hand on Angel's arm. "Please don't say a word to Zane either."

Angel made the zipping motion across her lips.

Trish was proud of how she'd explained all that, sounding confident and secure, not as if her heart had been shattered with a sledgehammer.

CHAPTER 29

Josh walked into the task force offices behind Leanne Witherspoon, who was poured into a black skirt that fit her toned body like a second skin. She slowed and glanced at him over her shoulder as he headed toward the hallway that led to the conference room—aka Zane's office for the moment.

"Thanks for lunch, Josh." Leanne drew out his name and gave him a parting smile that a woman sent a man she intended to get naked with later. She strolled into her office and closed the door.

Where was his raging hardon now?

Not a flicker of interest.

Lunch had been a waste of time, too. He had to give it to Ryder. The FNG had nailed it after dinner with Leanne when he'd said she was extremely loyal to the task force, including Zane Jackson and the other charter pilots. Josh should be feeling arrogantly smug since Leanne had begged off on a second date with Ryder, yet made it clear that her schedule *could* be adjusted to accommodate Josh.

She'd made herself available for lunch with no hesitation and said he could call her this weekend.

Peeling her out of that black suit should be his top fantasy, but his body kept shifting the image to a peach-colored dress, dark curls, and luminous brown eyes.

Now I get aroused?

Shit. Not the way he wanted to meet with Zane, who believed Josh was gay.

Coming toward him was Rhonda Sutter, who took her time getting to him, but when she did, she paused. "I'm going to have to pass on dinner for Saturday. I've got a lot of work to catch up on after traveling this week."

Work or other activities? "Not a problem. I'll be around all next week."

Leanne had called Rhonda the productivity Nazi, then joked

that Rhonda was probably a closet dominatrix.

He didn't care if she was a nun, only whether she had information he needed or was involved with the leaks. Of the women Josh had been tasked to investigate, Leanne was proving to be the most accommodating, Rhonda the most reluctant, and Trish the most frustrating. That last bit of opinion might be Big John and the twins talking, though.

"You weren't at the meeting we had last night." She gave him an imperious lift of one eyebrow meant to demand an explanation.

Other than the boss, Mac, Josh did not have to account for his time or performance to anyone on the task force, least of all Rhonda. "That would be because I had somewhere else to be." Pleased to see that he hadn't satisfied her curiosity one bit, he took an about-face in the conversation and dished it back at her. "How's the High Vision case coming on the *DEA* end?"

Her face closed down. "We're making headway."

She didn't like being questioned, huh?

Then don't wake the bear.

Josh gave her a nod, mostly as a thank you for killing the erection that had started when he'd thought of Trish and moved on. The conference room door was open, so Josh tapped on the doorframe and entered.

Zane lifted his head from a file he was reading. "Shut the door."

Josh did, then turned around. "What'd you want to see me about?"

"Have a seat." Zane sat back with his arms folded over a chest that belonged on a linebacker.

Not one to follow orders from anyone except Sabrina, Josh didn't move. "Not sure I'll be here that long."

They did the staring standoff until Zane said, "Are you hunting for a mole in this task force?"

That was the last thing Josh had expected to hear from Zane. "What makes you think that?"

"Because we still have one."

Josh tried to come up with just one reason Zane would be

telling him this if Zane *was* the Chessmaster, but he couldn't. "If that's the case, should we even be talking in here?"

"I do a sweep for bugs in any room I use, every time I come in, and I've got a gadget a friend of mine created that jams a receiver." Zane's hard gaze didn't waver, but his tone was more reasonable when he said, "If you'll sit down, we can talk."

Josh took one of the chairs across the table from Zane. "Why do you think there's still a mole here?"

"Because of the way that bust went down last night for one thing, and the fact that you're here for another."

This might be interesting if not for the sick feeling that his cover had been blown. "Me?"

"I won't tell you how I know, but as I understand it, your file at the FBI is locked in an electronic vault that only two people have access to. Sounds like you're a dark ops undercover operator."

Josh was careful not to let his relief show. Zane still believed he was FBI, but not a computer specialist. He could work with that, but now he faced the question of how to play this with Zane.

Would the mole bring Josh in and confront him like this?

This called for a gut check and his said no. Josh made a show of blowing out a big breath and scratching his head. "Damn. Don't know what I'm going to tell my superiors. I've never been blown before."

"You're not blown now. I want this bastard, too, but I'm limited in what I can do as a contractor to the DEA and with a pregnant wife about to deliver."

Josh said, "I met Angel, by the way. Sweet lady. You're a lucky man."

"Thanks." Zane's eyes warmed at the mention of his wife. "Nothing is more important to me than Angel, the baby, and Trish."

"I can understand that, but you have a reason for telling me so what's on your mind?"

"Trish has nothing to do with this mole. She never knew

Colbert beyond talking to him at a holiday party here at the office. I don't want you using her in your investigation."

Josh didn't either. Now he just had to find a way to keep her out of the crossfire between Sabrina's plans and the Chessmaster. Failing to tell Zane about the Chessmaster would make this new working relationship tricky at some point, but Josh couldn't divulge his real role or what he knew about the stalker, who could be anyone on this task force.

But he could quiet Zane's concerns about Trish even if it meant lying through his teeth. "I have no reason to believe Trish is involved."

"Why were you at Big Charlie's last night?"

If Zane caught him in a lie, this fragile deal would fall apart, and Zane clearly had resources. "I told Trish I was on my way to her shop when I saw her heading away and tried to catch her. The truth is she'd canceled on dinner and said she had an appointment. I followed her out of curiosity and am glad I did."

That got through to Zane when nothing else might have, because the big pilot rubbed his forehead and mumbled, "She scares the shit out of me sometimes." He dropped his hand. "There was no FBI file on Big Charlie or Trish until this morning. Why'd you create one?"

Damn, Zane was seriously connected for a pilot, and his connections were fast. "If my people hadn't created that file, Detective Vickers would have stirred up a hornet's nest with FBI personnel who aren't aware of my status, which would have destroyed my cover. Then Vickers would have picked up Trish and taken her into custody since her fingerprints are all over the murder weapon."

Thick muscles in Zane's neck pulsed. "She couldn't have done that."

"I know it and so does Vickers. I spoke to him early this morning. He said it doesn't exonerate her from being a person of interest, but he had no reason to bring her in and wouldn't fight the FBI for custody." Josh waited for judgment, but there were limits to how much he'd tell Zane.

"To help find this mole, I'll make whatever I have access to available to you."

Evidently Josh had said enough—or the right things—to satisfy Zane about his identity. "I need you to not tell *anyone* what I'm doing here."

"Agreed."

"What about your wife?"

"The less she knows about this the less she'll worry. I don't want any of this around her."

Josh would feel the same way in Zane's boots, but he also saw the stress that Zane's overprotective tendencies caused Trish. She wouldn't do anything to hurt her brother, but she was clearly not going to let Zane or anyone else make decisions for her.

He admired that even when it caused him headaches. She had grit and a streak of loyalty a mile wide for those she loved. He could admit to himself he was envious of those she deemed worthy of that commitment.

He couldn't tell Zane about Trish's stalker, aka Chessmaster, but he had to give Zane a reason for Josh staying close to her. "We need to keep an eye on your sister. I know she had nothing to do with Colbert, but someone killed him who may not be as informed."

Zane's deep tan lost a shade at that. "I'll call in a favor. Get her in protective custody."

Wrong response. "She won't go for it."

"I don't care."

"Really? You don't give a damn about how she feels or what's important to her? You honestly only care about making *yourself* feel better?"

Zane slammed a fist on the table and started to rise, then deflated. "Shit." He sank against the back of the chair and swiped his hand across his face. "I have to live with not being there for her when she needed me. The world is an ugly place. I see it first-hand every day."

"Me too. But she's already seen her share. Take the choice away from her now and you'll destroy her self-confidence when she's working like hell to establish herself." Josh caught himself, but he'd already argued more strongly than he'd intended. It should have been to keep Trish free and available for Slye's operation, but he'd meant what he said.

Stowing her somewhere away from her business right now would be devastating. He understood Zane's need to tuck Trish into a safe little hole and would help him put her there if not for the damage it would do to Trish's self-esteem. She was fighting to hold on to ReSolution, which stood for her future as a person. Not the money. Not celebrity status on the television show, but an icon of her independence and rebirth as a valued person.

But if she had to remain free, Josh was going to be closer than her shadow every minute he could. Starting with tonight.

He'd stay the night. The Chessmaster would have to go through him to get to Trish.

But could he do it without finishing that sofa tango they'd started earlier?

What had he just tried to remind Zane? She was a grown woman capable of making her own decisions. He'd remind her that he was leaving in two weeks. If she gave him the green light again, he was hitting the accelerator.

And that had nothing to do with this case.

Just the fact that he wanted her.

One question nagged at the back of his mind. If he got what he wanted, could he walk away in two weeks?

Josh stood. "With this whole custody thing, I'm in a position to keep Trish safe without her knowing she's being protected."

Zane got to his feet, standing a couple of inches taller than Josh and carrying another thirty pounds, none of which had gone to fat. He took Josh's measure slowly. "You're not gay, are you?"

"No."

Zane put his hands on the table, leaning forward in an aggressive stance and said very quietly, "If you lay a hand on my sister, I'll break you into so many parts it will take tweezers to put you together."

"Trish will be safe." But no promises about where Josh put

his hands. He walked out, checking the time. Closing in on 1500 hours. He cleared a text from Ryder that the team was meeting at three at their temporary headquarters.

Heidi had said she'd text him if Trish needed him before four. That gave him time to catch up with his team and get to Trish's house.

Salazar had been found with a slit throat this morning.

He'd clutched a black-and-gold pawn that appeared to be from the same set as the one Trish had. The tracking device had been cut out of his back and laid on his chest.

The Chessmaster had figured out that Salazar had been in on the trap. Josh took that action as the Chessmaster getting agitated and taking out pawns.

One note had called Trish a pawn.

His phone buzzed with a text. Heidi's message was simple.

Trish at shop. She knows about lunch w Leanne. Doesn't want to c u.

CHAPTER 30

"Are you sure about traveling now with..." Heidi lowered her voice. "You-know-what going on?"

Trish put down the inventory sheet she'd been trying to finish before getting out of here. She wanted to leave home by five to reach the airport early to go standby and that gave her an hour if she and Heidi left soon.

"I know what you're saying, Heidi, but I've spent the last seven months being careful and playing it safe." And training with Arnie. "Where has safe gotten me? The police are still keeping a suspicious eye on ReSolution after the drug tip. I got knocked out and implicated in a murder, and the television producers aren't returning my calls." She hadn't heard from Senator Dixon's office, so she hadn't called. Best to let a sleeping dog lie.

"Have you talked to Josh?"

No. Just the idea of hearing his voice hurt so much she wouldn't play the voice mail he'd left on her phone. She wanted to be the strong I-can-live-without-you type, but every time she thought about not seeing Josh again, it crushed her.

"*Did* you talk to him?" Heidi repeated.

Trish glared at her as an answer.

"He may have a perfectly good reason for having lunch with Leanne. They do work together."

"He asked Rhonda out to dinner, too. He's been here a while. Why all this *now* and not before?"

"I don't know, but I think you need to tell him you're moving your flight. I'm pretty sure he intended to go with you."

Like hell. Thankfully, this conference and the hotel had been sold out for a long time and she had VIP status as a speaker. "Well, he's not going. He's not my keeper." *He's not my lover or the man who makes me smile or the one I thought I could trust.* She'd thought he was all that this morning. She'd hoped he *would* go to Atlanta with her until she talked to Angel.

"He sort of *is* your keeper since you're in his custody."

Trish wanted to tell Heidi how all that was a sham, no more real than Josh was. "You know I've been training. I'll watch my own back. I'm just as safe, maybe more so, in Atlanta." And Josh wouldn't be there to make her want to do crazy things like climb into the same bed with him.

"Okay, but I'd feel better if at least *I* was with you. You did agree not to go alone."

That was when Trish thought she was dealing with an honorable person. "I know our business has died from all the bad press, but I don't want to close the shop this weekend. Everyone will take that as a sign that I'm quitting. If you and Bunko will keep an eye on ReSolution, that would be the best help."

"Uh-oh," Heidi worried out loud, eyes wide and looking past Trish.

"What?" Trish turned to see what Heidi saw.

Josh was striding toward them with a look of we're-going-to-talk on his face. How could anyone that angry look gorgeous at the same time?

"Things are going to hit the fan," Heidi murmured.

"And me with no fan." Trish started backing away. She couldn't handle a confrontation with Josh and not let him see the damage to her heart. "I'm going to my office, and I don't want to be bothered," she rattled over her shoulder. Hiding might be cowardly, but she still had the headache from hell and was not up to facing Josh yet. She shut her office door with a decisive click and had just sat down behind her desk when Josh blew in like a tornado.

"Can't you knock and ask before walking in?" she demanded.

"Not when I know you'll tell me 'no.' We need to talk."

"No, we don't."

"Oh, yes. About lunch..."

She jumped up. "What you do is none of my business. You don't owe me an explanation." It wasn't his fault her heart was twisted into a pretzel. He'd probably slept with plenty of women to get whatever information he needed. Why not Leanne? Trish wished she could feel that cavalier about it.

"Just hear me out," he said.

"I don't want to hear it."

Josh clenched his teeth. He would *not* lose his temper. Trish could be the most exasperating female sometimes–most of the time–but he was trained to deal with difficult people.

Surely, he could manage one contrary woman. "Tough. I'm talking. You're listening."

Trish flicked an index finger back and forth. "No. Here's how this works. I *don't* sleep around, and this morning was a mistake. Mine. I gave the signal that I wanted you."

Damn right she'd wanted him. "No argument there, because I wanted you, too."

Something flickered in her eyes that he'd like to call hope, but it disappeared too quickly for him to be sure. She strangled a pen in her right hand. "Regardless, I know better and also know that I'm a far cry from the type of woman you would get involved with."

Warning! Loaded comment. *Open mouth. Insert foot.* Move forward with great caution. "And what *type* is that?" he asked, carefully.

"Leanne, for one. And there's nothing wrong with her. I think she's adorable. Senator's daughter, gorgeous, everything any man could want," Trish said with indifference as if she didn't care, but the disappointment leaking into her voice countered that. With arms crossed, she was anything but receptive. "However, you have been exceptionally kind to me..." she continued.

Kind? What the hell did she mean by that?

"Hold everything, Trish. Just because I had lunch with Leanne doesn't mean there's anything between us. We work together. And, for your information, she's far from the kind of woman I would be interested in." *Like you. She's nothing like you.*

"Whatever. As I was saying, I appreciate what you've done for me. I would like to remain friends–"

Ah, shit. Not the I-want-to-be-friends conversation. What had happened since this morning? How had she heard about his lunch date? Getting that information would take this conversation too far off track. He'd find out later.

Okay, so he'd had lunch with Leanne on the heels of leaving Trish after giving her an out-of-body-experience orgasm. He could see where she might misinterpret his actions, but this was drastic.

"–and I want to return the favor," she finished, sitting up and putting her folded arms on the desk. All prim and proper again.

He liked her mussed up and relaxed.

Her offer did not sound like any favor he was going to appreciate. "Return what favor?"

"Of being friends. When I get back from Atlanta, if Leanne doesn't suit you, I'll help you find the right woman for the sort of friends-with-benefits relationship that will. Your job probably doesn't allow for much time to meet women."

He couldn't decide if he was stunned more by Trish thinking she was going anywhere without him, what she *wasn't* saying, or her ridiculous offer to help find him a woman.

"We never discussed final plans for Atlanta. You don't *think* you're going without me, do you?"

She turned into a ball of defiance. "I *never* agreed to your going to Atlanta with me."

"Then you're not going."

"I'm speaking at a trade show. I have reservations and am expected."

"By yourself? With a lunatic stalking you? Are you nuts?" Yes, of course she was. First, she offered him to another woman–*dammit*–then she had some hair-brained notion about going out of town on her own.

"I'm *not nuts*. I'm in *business*. And how I run *my* business, and my life, is none of *your* business. If someone wanted to take a shot at me, they could have done it at any time *here*."

Trish stood up and stormed across the room, to within one step of him. Heat, anger and–God help him–a delicious scent radiated from her. The woman turned him on when she smiled, when she was quiet, when she raged at him.

Hell, she rocked him in his sleep.

"Listen, Trish. You can't leave until I say so. That's final."

"So now you're going to pull your badass FBI card on me?" she asked, her voice low and full of menace. She carried the Jackson genes, for sure. With another hundred pounds she'd be a serious threat.

"No, I'm pulling the I-haven't-told-your-brother-anything-about-the-stalker card. Haven't told him *yet*."

"You wouldn't." She paled.

He felt like the biggest jerk for using his ace, but her safety was more important than her anger. He'd soothe her later.

"Yes, I would," he assured her.

"You promised not to. I trusted you."

Ah, man. She was killing him with that wounded puppy look. He hadn't broken her trust. "Like I said, I haven't said a word to Zane so don't look at me like I've betrayed you." Josh lifted his hand to her cheek, but she stepped back, her message very clear.

Off limits.

Okay, so he had a *lot* of soothing to do. "I said I wouldn't tell Zane, but *you* promised not to take any chances."

She studied him for a minute. "Okay, you're right. I did agree not to take any chances. I'll keep my end of the deal if you'll keep yours."

He paused at her quick agreement, but now was not the time to push her any harder. She'd settled down, even appeared mildly content. He might be able to fix her ruffled feathers over a nice dinner tonight, but right now he was running late for the damned meeting with Ryder and his team.

What was another minute if he could just touch her? "I've got to run, but I'll swing by later. Okay?"

Her smile was tight, but a smile. She nodded.

"We still have unfinished business."

She shrugged.

Whipping her into his arms for a satisfying kiss was next on his "to do" list, but she wasn't giving an inch until after some major peacemaking. What had she heard about his lunch that had set her off?

He'd find out what was going on in his little hothead's mind then get back to the spot where they left off this morning.

When she'd kissed him.

But he couldn't fix this now.

Josh opened the door and strode to the front.

Trish followed him out. He'd just passed the register where Heidi tabulated figures when he heard Trish say, "Heidi, can you come to my office? I've had a change of plans."

That was more like it.

An hour later with the team meeting over, Josh hadn't been able to shake the nagging feeling that something wasn't right. Trish had thrown in the towel, just as any sane, cooperative woman would have.

The exact reason he felt justified in being concerned.

Trish Jackson, part sweetheart, part sex kitten, part hellion on wheels, didn't capitulate that easily. Still, she was willing to do anything to keep Zane from finding out about the stalker.

Even agreed to change her plans for the trade show.

Josh slowed his Porsche as traffic bogged down on A1A. Annoying shards of light glinted off the side mirror as the sun prepared to depart for the evening. The little voice in his head continued a non-stop commentary, telling him she'd agreed too quickly. Had he missed something?

What exactly had she said?

"Okay, you're right. I did agree not to take any chances. I'll keep my end of the deal if you'll keep yours."

She hadn't *specifically said* she wasn't going to Atlanta.

Josh snatched his phone from the top of the console and dialed ReSolution. When Heidi answered, he asked for Trish.

"She's not here."

The back of his neck tingled. He felt something coming he would not be happy about. "Where'd she go?"

"To pack for her trip. You know she has that trade show in Atlanta."

The little vixen. Josh pounded the steering wheel. "No, well, yes, but not really. I thought she changed her plans."

The stalker would never get a chance at Trish. Josh planned to wring her neck as soon as he got his hands on her.

"She did," Heidi said, giving him a moment of relief until she explained, "Trish was supposed to fly out early tomorrow, but she decided to go standby for a flight tonight. I just got a text that she made it on one leaving in fifty minutes."

The airport was forty-five minutes away ... if he caught all green lights and pushed speed limits.

Neither was a possibility with him sitting in parking lot traffic on the ocean side of the road.

CHAPTER 31

"What. Went. Wrong?" The General barked.

Standing in an apartment near South Beach that had more taste than character, The Chessmaster could tick off a list of things that had caused the High Vision contraband exchange to fall apart.

But The General would only want to hear the bottom line.

"Salazar tried to draw me into a trap. Someone with the task force had to be working with him."

"High Vision is extremely unhappy, which means I am, too."

And you think I'm dancing around? "I'm making changes that will take care of the problem. The next shipment will slide through untouched."

"What changes?" The General didn't yell, but he ground out his words.

"I took care of Salazar. I'll find the person who helped him and deal with that, too."

"What about Jackson? Think he was the one helping Salazar?"

"No, he wasn't back in time from a flight to have been the one."

"How long before Jackson's gone?"

Was The General finally realizing that the Chessmaster was waiting until the last possible moment to take down Jackson and his sister? "As soon as you bring in the unit to test."

"I can't have any screw ups on this sixth shipment."

I didn't screw up you rat bastard. "There won't be."

The Chessmaster disconnected the call and placed another one to someone in security at Miami Airport. "Has Trish Jackson passed through yet?"

"Yes."

"That's all I need."

CHAPTER 32

Trish had removed her necklace, earrings, watch, shoes–twice–and had her shoulder bag searched by the time she found her coach seat on the airplane. She'd just gotten comfortable with her e-reader when the flight attendant walked up and told her there had been a mistake with her seat, to please follow her.

What else could happen today?

Trish bundled up her things and dragged her carry-on back down the aisle, worming her way forward between passengers stowing luggage in the overhead bins. The flight attendant stopped in the twelve-seat first class section, empty except for one passenger on the far side in the third row.

The flight attendant said, "We're sorry for the inconvenience, but thought you wouldn't mind swapping for this seat."

Second row. Window. First class?

"I'd love to. Thanks," Trish said, confused, but not complaining. She stowed her carry-on in the overhead and sat down into her new seat with a sigh.

This was more like it.

An attractive, early-thirties man with mahogany skin, short black hair, and smiling gray eyes entered the cabin. He wore a lightweight brown leather jacket and business-casual clothes. First, he visited with the senior flight attendant then stuck his head in the cockpit and joked with the pilot, then he moved to Trish's aisle and took the seat next to her.

Not that she didn't appreciate the unexpected upgrade, but weren't there enough available seats in first class without him sitting next to her? He seemed to be a crew person, so maybe they were expected to fill in the single seats.

She didn't care. The guy had a great smile, and everyone seemed to like him.

"Going to Atlanta for business or pleasure?" he asked, dimples flashing at her.

"Business. To a convention. What about you?"

"Well, this started out as business, sort of, but it's taken a pleasurable turn. I'm Hugh Cavanaugh, but everyone calls me Hugh." He winked and extended his hand, flirting. After the week from hell and finding out Josh had been playing her—and might be making time with Leanne—Trish's female ego could stand a little stroking.

That wouldn't change the emptiness she felt in her chest at the loss of Josh, but the distraction would be nice. Especially with someone attractive.

Staying away from men hadn't worked, so maybe she needed more experience. No harm in flirting when she was surrounded by plenty of people, and it was going nowhere.

She returned Hugh's smile and shook hands. "Patricia, but everyone calls me Trish."

Over the next two hours, she discussed ReSolution and antique appraising, enjoying the freedom of being so far away from everything going on back home that she could pretend her life was as fine as she made it sound.

Hugh explained that he was employed by the airline they flew on, providing him with the opportunity to jump a flight when he needed to, like today.

When they reached the Atlanta airport, she deplaned ahead of Hugh and wished him a nice trip. Loneliness swamped her when she walked away, not because she'd taken an interest in Hugh, but he'd been so nice that all she could think of was Josh. She wheeled her little suitcase to the shuttle area and watched for the special service the convention had arranged. The airport bustled with activity outside in the brisk evening air.

Trish had just found her seat on the shuttle to the hotel when Hugh dashed up and jumped in.

He sat right next to her. Empty handed.

"No luggage?" she asked, suspicion creeping up her spine.

"I don't have a layover, just making a quick stop at the hotel and if everything goes as I expect there, I'll head out right away." He beamed a sexy smile at her. "Wouldn't mind a layover, though."

She began to worry about the coincidence of Hugh's ending up at the same hotel. But thousands of people were staying at that hotel and not all would be attending her retail show. Still, she shifted around in her corner seat, so that she had a view of the shuttle door, but also faced Hugh and could see if he made any sudden move. By the time the shuttle parked under the hotel canopy, lights outlined the dark streets.

Would the stalker be so bold as to sit right next to her on a trip? Hugh didn't give her the creeps, but how many times had an axe murderer been described as a nice person who everyone liked?

And what about her misreading Josh?

Like she needed a reminder?

She wouldn't drop her guard, but to be honest too many terror-filled days could have her imagining things. She would not allow this spineless, faceless stalker to undermine her confidence. Every man was not out to kill her, and she was being very careful, staying in crowds of people at all times to maintain a bigger bubble of space around her than usual. No reason to get nervous.

Except for Hugh jumping on this bus.

Josh might disagree, but she hadn't broken her word.

She'd love to see his face when he realized she'd beaten him at his own deceitful game.

Ever the gentleman, Hugh helped her from the shuttle when it reached her hotel and he accompanied her to the check-in desk, chatting with the staff as if they'd been friends for years. Still, she moved her suitcase to her other hand so it would roll between them, to give herself a little more distance. He didn't really concern her, but this was no time to get chummy with a stranger from an airplane.

She saw him glance down at her suitcase, then he winked at her and moved a half step further away, as though he sensed her caution. Nice. Hugh was adorable and charming, but still, all she could think about was Josh.

Damn him for waking up her heart then breaking it.

The line to check-in was daunting, but the hotel manager

spied Hugh and came around the desk to shake his hand. "Mr. Cavanaugh. So nice to see you again."

Trish waited for old-times week to pass. This obviously was not Hugh's first visit, which helped to ease her misgivings about the coincidence.

She tried to dismiss him again by saying, "Thanks for your help, Sug. I've got to get in line."

"That's not necessary." Hugh guided the manager's attention back to Trish when he suggested, "Let's take care of the young lady first."

Really? Trish took a step back and Hugh cocked his head to the side just a little. She swore she saw something flicker in his eyes that bordered on surprise and maybe ... *respect?*

Hugh was a frequent customer at this high-end hotel. Good friends with the manager. First name basis with airline pilots. She clicked through her checklist for assessing a person and he passed every test. *Except Arnie taught you there's no such thing as coincidence.* Okay, fine. But she could see no obvious danger in taking advantage of a small break. "Thanks. I am kind of tired." Feeling a little guilty over getting ahead of that long line, but not enough to turn down the perk, she gave the manager her name and placed a charge card on the counter.

"Oh, Miss Jackson, yes. Your room is ready." The manager fell all over her. He handed her charge card back with a keycard to the room and called for someone to go with Miss Jackson to make sure everything was acceptable.

Miss Jackson this and Miss Jackson that.

Thank you, Hugh. She could get used to the royal treatment.

Okay maybe she'd been pissed and pushed the edges of her promise to "not take chances" when she'd decided to travel alone. She'd been training this past year so that she *could* take care of herself on her own. But Josh hadn't given her enough credit to think she could even make it to Atlanta on her own. He'd made one heck of a show of concern over her safety, and she'd bought it. Had found it, and him, endearing.

But she felt smothered enough at home in Ft. Lauderdale. She didn't want somebody playing bodyguard here.

Hugh told the desk manager, "Your people are slammed. I'll show Miss Jackson where her room is on my way up to the restaurant."

Her comfort level took a nosedive. *Not okay, not okay, not okay.* She opened her mouth to state flatly that she'd rather go alone, but the look of relief on the manager's face, and the big smile he gave Hugh made her stop short. The manager said, "That would be a huge help, if Miss Jackson approves." Both men turned questioning looks at her.

Shit. There were cameras all over the building. And the manager knew she was here, knew where she was going and who was escorting her. No stalker would be stupid enough to try something under those circumstances.

And she'd leave Hugh at the elevator. She would not let him follow her to her room.

Her heart thumped hard all the same, and she chose the elevator that was already half full, rather than the empty one. Once again, Hugh cocked his head sideways at her. She swore he was sizing her up.

On the eighteenth floor, the entire group of people exited the elevator car and the door closed before Trish could tell Hugh goodbye. With the noisy, laughing group going down the hallway toward her room, Trish figured she was as safe as she was going to get. And she'd really did not want to offend Hugh after he'd been so nice. Maybe she'd call the manager, make an excuse, and request a room change so nobody knew her room number except hotel staff. Hugh took the handle of her suitcase and continued charming her all the way down the corridor. When she paused by the door, and said thanks, he returned the handle of her luggage and backed away.

Perfect gentleman. She'd likely been paranoid for no reason, but still, she would not unlock the door while he stood there.

Once he walked away, she keyed the lock and took two steps through the doorway and froze, shocked at the layout.

She wheeled around and yanked the door open, headed for the hallway. "There's been a mistake," she called out, and

Hugh turned around. "I booked a standard room, not a suite."

"No mistake, Trish," a male voice boomed from behind her.

CHAPTER 33

Trish tensed at that voice behind her.

Coming from the suite she hadn't booked.

Hugh smiled at her and tipped his head in a parting salutation. "Nice meeting you." He strolled away quickly though, like he didn't want to be a part of whatever transpired next.

She pivoted and dropped the suitcase just inside the room, letting the heavy door slam shut as she barreled across the room. "What are *you* doing here?"

"I'll answer that as soon as you tell me why *you're* here?" Josh snapped right back in a voice so sharp it could slice through bone. He stood over by the plush, high-back sofa and two side chairs with his feet apart and arms crossed as if braced for a battle.

She was ready to give him one. "I have business in Atlanta. You don't."

"Not exactly correct. Where you go, I go."

"I can take care of myself."

"I know you've had some training. But knowing the moves and using them in real situations is not the same."

Now he sounded like Arnie. And how did he know she'd had training? Had Zane told him? Or Heidi? "I know that, but my point is that I'm not defenseless." She rubbed her aching head. "Look. You can have this room. I have my own room, which I plan to stay in. *Alone.*" Hard to believe she'd been missing him the whole way here, but she'd been missing the Josh she thought she knew. Not this undercover operator.

"Wrong again. If you want to remain in Atlanta, you're residing *here*. With me."

She considered everything she knew about Josh to this point. "Did you confiscate my room?"

"Yes."

"How'd you do all this in so short a time frame?" This would be impressive for Zane who could fly his own airplane, and her brother was just one step short of a superhero in her book.

"FBI?" Josh said as if reminding a child that he had the master badge.

One more slick move by him and she would not be held responsible for her actions. Trish stalked around for a moment and finally gave up. "But how did you get here *ahead* of me?"

"It wasn't easy." With Josh standing that way she started to see the dangerous undercover operative she hadn't looked for before. "Once I had you covered, I called in some personal markers and hired a Learjet."

"What do you mean by *had me covered*?" Who hires a Learjet that fast? No wonder he'd beaten her to Atlanta. Good grief, how much had *that* cost? She felt her heart squeeze at the trouble he'd gone through. The trouble she'd put him through. But she was still pissed at him.

"Do you think the airline just *moved* you to first class because they like you?" Josh's calm tone was countermanded by his clipped words and taut jaw. She'd studied those blue eyes enough to read an inferno blazing behind them. He was furious.

"So, Hugh works for you?" she asked.

"No. He's a friend I've known a long time who has connections and exceptional defense skills in addition to being an ace pilot. I managed to get a few others into place quickly. Good thing for you or you would have been yanked from the flight."

"You're kidding."

"No. I'd have told them you were a threat if I had to."

Her skin chilled at how close she'd come to being removed as a criminal.

Everything that had happened in the last twenty-four hours hit her at once. She felt wounded that he would have humiliated her that way and failed to keep the pain out of her whisper. "Would you really have done that to me?"

They stared at each other for the longest time. An angry standoff until he finally said, "I would have done far worse to keep you safe."

Josh kept his arms folded so he wouldn't yank Trish up against him where he could feel her heartbeat. He was sure nothing could have abated all his righteous anger until he'd heard the deep hurt in her voice.

What the hell had he done that was so wrong?

Lunch with Leanne? He didn't believe for a minute that having lunch with a coworker had upset Trish that much. His intentions hadn't been as a coworker, but anyone watching him with Leanne should have interpreted it that way.

Trish asked, "Does anyone at the task force office know you're here?"

"Zane does. Don't give me that look, Trish. I haven't told him anything about the stalker. Zane found out from Heidi that you were on the way here when he called right after I did."

"Wasn't a secret. My brother just forgot."

"When he found out, he went ballistic when he heard you'd left town alone. Then he called me demanding to know how I let that happen if you're supposed to be in my custody." Getting Zane off his back had cost Josh precious time. "Once your brother stopped yelling into the phone, he ordered me to, and I quote, 'stick to Trish like tar on an asphalt roof.' Are we clear now?"

He leveled her with a glare she should have no problem reading. Starting this minute, they were inseparable.

Trish didn't deflate, exactly, but she looked away and he had the distinct impression she'd just given up. Walked out of the room mentally, even though her body was still here. She dumped her shoulder bag on the sofa and walked over to the window overlooking the twinkling city.

"Why didn't you tell me you were coming here tonight?" he asked. "You gave me the impression you weren't coming here until Saturday morning."

"I just wanted to leave early. Wanted to get out of town."

Was the hurt in her voice? Why?

He alternated between wanting to shake some sense into her for scaring years off his life over the last couple of hours and dragging her to bed so he could burn off the adrenaline still pulsing through him.

Trish leaned against the window edge. All her fight fizzled from her. He had no reason to feel guilty for making sure she was safe, but he did. Wouldn't change anything.

If he knew Trish was here, the stalker probably did, too.

Josh was not letting her get away from him again.

"Trish, if you want to get unpacked and freshen up, we'll grab some dinner. I assume you haven't eaten since lunch."

Damn. The minute the word "lunch" popped out of his mouth he wanted to suck it back in. Somehow, he would clear up the Leanne fiasco, which shouldn't *be* a fiasco.

But tonight, wasn't shaping up to offer any opportunity.

Twisting around, she sent him a hostile gaze that couldn't be spoken in polite company if that look had been translated into words. Then she returned to staring at the nighttime view, dismissing him.

Josh crossed the room and placed a hand on each of her shoulders, determined to repair some damage.

That lasted two seconds.

She spun away from him, lips taut and unyielding. "If we're sharing this suite, there are ground rules. The first one being that you keep your hands to yourself. The second being that I'm here for *business*, so don't interfere."

"Fine, if that's the way you want this. But we never did get lunch cleared up."

"Yes, we did. You have your job and I have mine. The two don't need to conflict or intertwine."

No chance of intertwining with a woman having a ... a fit of jealousy. Could that be right?

Well, hell. He hadn't done anything wrong. She was just jealous. Very jealous. Sorry bastard that he was, for some reason that lifted his spirits.

Josh pressed his lips together to keep from grinning at that possibility. She wouldn't be upset if she didn't care.

But he didn't want anyone to care about him. Right?

So why did the idea of Trish's reaction feel like a gentle caress to his heart?

He was not examining that any time soon, but now he had renewed hope of soothing Trish. Letting her know the direction of his thoughts would be unwise, though.

Keeping with the tone she'd set, he warned, "I'll stick to your rules as long as you stick to mine."

She waited, silent as a smoldering ember.

"I want to know your schedule each morning," he said. "You go nowhere without me. You take no chances."

"I've already agreed not to take any chances *and*–" She stopped him with a finger she wielded like a weapon. "I was *not* in any danger at the airports or here in the hotel. There will be over a thousand people around me most of the day tomorrow."

He would not snap at her. "You're far more at risk in a crowd than alone. If I was the stalker, this would be the perfect situation for getting to you."

Her face softened, erasing frown lines. She raked a hand through her hair. "Shit. You sound like Arnie, and I know you're right. I just don't want a bodyguard. Especially..."

Especially me, he mentally finished.

She was sad and hurting.

Right now, he wanted to wrap her up close and hold her, but that wasn't going to happen until he could figure out what the problem was. He asked again, "Want to eat?"

"No." She yawned. "I want to take a shower and go to bed." Trish walked toward one of the two bedrooms, stretching as if she were stiff.

Watching made *him* stiff.

He'd forgo dinner for bed, with her, in a flash. Lifting her small suitcase, he carried it to her semi-dark room and put it down. Light filtered in from the living room.

She stood with her back to him. Did she think he'd just walk out and leave her be? Maybe he should, but he was better known for doing what he shouldn't. Like right now when he shouldn't be thinking about giving her a full body massage.

Josh put his hands on her arms, careful not to spook her.

She turned around and put her hand on his chest. "Leave."

He covered her hand and rubbed her cold fingers. "Talk to me, Trish."

"Okay. Leave. Now."

Any massaging tonight would be a one-handed date.

CHAPTER 34

Trish climbed out of bed Saturday morning, still exhausted.

How was she supposed to sleep with Josh on the other side of a wall?

She'd almost folded when he'd tried to get her to talk last night. But that would have been impossible without asking him if what had happened at her house yesterday morning had only been about getting close to her for an investigation.

He could easily say his lunch with Leanne had to do with task force business, but Trish couldn't shake the feeling that there was more going on.

And she couldn't let go of the feeling she was being used. That he only wanted to be with her to get information.

Leanne might be fine with that, but Trish was not.

After calling room service for coffee and taking care of her bathroom needs, she'd just slipped her arms through her short silk kimono when someone tapped at the door and called out, *"Room service."*

Trish rushed across the sitting area and looked through the peephole to see the guy with the tray, then threw the bolt back, grabbed the doorknob and pulled.

The door had barely opened when a hand hit at eye level, slamming it shut.

She yelped and jumped back, banging into a solid wall of Josh. "What are you doing? You scared the fool out of me."

"That has yet to be seen," he muttered.

Trish scooted from under his arm and turned to face him.

Nothing covered his golden body besides a pair of partially buttoned jeans. His blond hair poked out at odd angles. Everything about him said he'd just climbed out of bed, except for the intensity of those deep-water blues he was using to stare a hole in her.

"Don't *ever* answer the door," he warned in a rough morning voice. "I'm the only one who opens it."

"I checked first. It's room service."

"You don't know that's who it is." He picked her up at the waist and moved her aside then opened the door, took his time assessing what he saw and stepped back.

A startled hotel waiter entered and placed a tray on the glass coffee table. Josh tipped him well then flipped the lock back in place behind the departing waiter.

"See?" she said. "Just coffee." Before he could respond with more than an annoyed look, the phone on the end table rang. He snatched the receiver away from her reaching hand and spoke.

"I can't answer phones either?"

He ignored her and spoke into the receiver. "Josh." Silence. "Sure, hold on."

She took the phone he offered her. How did anyone know she was in *his* room?

"I see you caught up with Josh." Heidi, thank goodness.

"How'd you know I was in this room?" Trish asked suspiciously, giving Josh the evil eye for infiltrating her circle of friends. A very small circle.

"Josh called to let me know how to find you. I feel much better that you'll be safe with him."

Trish disagreed. Danger came in many forms. Josh with no shirt, looking imposing and deadly was sending her hormones bouncing in every wrong direction.

But Trish was not admitting that with him standing so close. She told Heidi, "I don't anticipate a problem here."

"Wish I could say the same, because we have one here."

"What's wrong?" Had the shop been broken into again?

"More of an inconvenience than a problem. There's a gas leak in our building. We're shut down until the city finds it. They evacuated us and said we couldn't come back until Monday."

"Crap. As if business wasn't bad enough already." Trish gritted her teeth. "You and Bunko might as well take the weekend off and enjoy yourself."

"You take it easy and try to enjoy yourself, too."

Fat chance of that happening. Trish finished the conversation and hung up. A cup of coffee, complete with the right amount of cream, appeared under her nose. Josh waited for her to accept the mug. She didn't.

"Trying to get on my good side?" Trish asked.

"Is that possible?"

"Normally, I'd say yes, but highly doubtful at this point."

Josh set the cup on the table and stepped close enough to invade her personal space. She backed away, but he kept coming until retreat had her rear pinned against the door.

He threw a hand just above her head and leaned in intimately. His early morning musky scent invaded her senses. "We're going to clear up this misconception you have about yesterday."

"There is *no* misconception and there is *no* reason for us to discuss it." She pressed her lips together. He wasn't the only one who could pull off annoyed and dangerous.

"You are one stubborn woman," he grumbled then sighed. "Leanne and I were having a professional lunch."

"Oh, sure. What was the tactical question? Your place or mine?" Oh, crap. Had she really just said that?

A muscle in Josh's jaw ticked, confirming she had absolutely spouted those words. Since she had, what was his blasted answer?

He shook his head. "I guess there's only one way to fix this."

No chance. She had his number. Josh could talk until he was blue in the face and still not change her mind.

Trish picked up her chin. "Give it your best shot, Sugar."

"Whatever you say." Josh snatched her into his arms and covered her mouth with a kiss that shot straight to her girl parts. He scooped her bottom with one hand, lifting her completely off the floor, and cupped her head with the other.

Holy lip lock.

When she sighed, his tongue slipped between her parted lips, dueling with hers. He tasted like toothpaste and hunger. She understood the hunger part. Trish gripped his shoulders, trying to remember why she hadn't wanted to do this.

Must have been momentary insanity.

He lifted her up against the bulge in his pants and she considered begging. Heat flamed low, burning her up with needing him to touch her everywhere. The harder he kissed the hotter she got until she was panting.

Josh tore his mouth away and dropped her on her feet.

Her glazed eyes cleared. What ...

"That should be a good start." He turned and walked into his bedroom, shutting the door.

Wait a minute. Where was Josh going?

Confusion crashed around Trish. She wasn't fighting mad anymore. He'd shut down that emotion and cranked up her hormones to full throttle. She stared at the closed bedroom door and blew an errant curl off her forehead.

"Damn." She picked up her mug and sulked her way to her bedroom. What had *that* been all about?

Hadn't she told him to keep his hands to himself?

He needed to stick to the rules or do a better job of breaking them.

Trish pinched the bridge of her nose. What in the world was she thinking? Did she have no self-respect?

Apparently not when it came to Josh, because her heart wouldn't let him go, faulty organ that it was.

The hell with him. Trish jerked a brush through her tangle of curls. She was only a job. He could tag along all he wanted, but his hands better stay in his pockets.

The next time Josh had an impulsive idea like kissing Trish, he'd go ahead and just shove a knife through his eye instead.

Had to be less painful than kissing her and walking away when his body screamed to feel her beneath him. He washed his face and reached for a plush towel, drying off quickly.

He had to be ready to walk out of the suite on her heels.

But touching her again was not on the schedule today.

The only reason he'd kissed her this time was because he couldn't take another minute of accusation riding her gaze when he hadn't done anything wrong. No, that hadn't been the *only* reason, not after spending most of the night checking on her. He'd stood in her bedroom doorway for over an hour at one point, watching her breathe, so damned glad she'd arrived safe and alive.

She'd whimpered on and off with nightmares.

He'd wanted to hold her and let her know she didn't have to fight her demons alone. Not when he was around.

When she'd raced out to answer the door this morning, he'd barely stopped her in time. She shouldn't have left her room with nothing on but that silk napkin with sleeves that hardly counted as clothing.

No complaints, but a man could only resist so much.

Then she'd tasted like liquid sex when he'd kissed her. His hands could still feel her tight bottom through the slippery material, and he'd known without a doubt that she hadn't been wearing anything else. Just a thin silky barrier between him and the body he hadn't been able to get out of his mind since that first kiss.

Josh peeled his now-snug jeans down past his aching erection and flipped the shower on, cold. What would be the greater challenge for the next two days?

Keeping Trish safe from danger or from his thundering libido that only raged for one woman.

CHAPTER 35

Chatton latched the case on her binoculars and put them into her backpack. She wiped a stream of perspiration from her face. Bloody hot days in this country. But she'd be returning to London soon, leaving Miami's humidity behind.

She called the local number from Wayan's file and waited through several clicks until a man answered, "Time is of the essence."

She replied in code, "Tomorrow shows great promise as does the fourth."

The connection ended.

She'd fulfilled her obligation to Czarion by ensuring delivery of the three boxes and informing their man that he could pick them up Sunday at four in the morning.

The General had better come through on his end.

He wouldn't be in touch until he had confirmation she was on another continent. By then, whatever was inside those three boxes she'd planted in the High Vision container would be successfully delivered and tested.

The test involved killing. She was sure of it.

How many deaths? And why?

The General knew she'd try to find out what was inside those boxes by following the person who picked them up.

Whoever was claiming the three boxes would be a skilled operative–the male voice on the phone–who would neither come through the front gate of the shipyard nor allow anyone to trail him.

That's why Wayan and The General would expect to see her in Europe on the telly during a time frame that prevented her from being in the US when the three boxes were picked up.

Two hours on either side of 0400 in Miami Sunday morning.

It would be a tight timeline. She smiled at being tested.

CHAPTER 36

Trish walked into the hotel suite and tossed her convention bag on the sofa, glad to be out of the crush downstairs after all day surrounded by people. One very long Saturday.

This was not going to work.

Josh had to find another hotel room. He could have the one she was *supposed* to be in right now.

"You didn't tell me what Heidi called about." Josh tossed out that topic when he strolled in behind her.

Trish searched her mind to revisit the phone call about the shop, after which he'd smothered her with a kiss. All brain cells had gone on holiday at that point. "ReSolution is shut down for the weekend, at least, with a gas leak. Business has been slow with the Big Charlie news, but we're still losing our best days."

"Sorry your shop is going to lose the revenue." He sounded genuinely disturbed over her loss.

If he could offer understanding, she could be appreciative. "Thanks, but it's not your fault." She started for her bedroom.

"You going to ignore me all night, too?" Josh asked

Only to be civil, she turned around to face the body she'd tried not to notice all day. "What are you talking about?"

"You act like I'm invisible."

Oh, she'd seen him just fine. His black slacks, black knit shirt, and fawn-colored jacket fit as if each piece had been tailored–a distinct possibility with him. He should save his money.

That body could turn rags into a fashion statement.

If he didn't like being ignored, she had a topic. "Who are you, Josh?"

That turned him into a statue. "What do you mean?"

"I'm having a hard time believing that someone who is a computer tech with the FBI makes the kind of money that you've thrown around in two days or has the luxury of following me around."

He shrugged. "My family has some money."

"Fine. I got it." She turned to leave.

"Trish, stop." He caught up to her and grabbed her arm, careful when he turned her around. "Now you're pissed that my family has money?"

"No, I'm pissed that you act as though you want me to be open and trusting, but I know nothing about you. I can't trust what I don't know."

His jaw muscles flexed while he stood there holding her gaze with his fathomless blue one. "What do you want to know?"

"The truth."

"I don't know what you mean."

If she could tell him what Angel said this would be so much simpler, but Angel had only shared so much because she wanted to protect Trish. Breaking that confidence was not the way to thank her. "Where did you go night before last when you left my house?"

His face shuttered. "I can't discuss my work anymore than Zane can."

"Where'd you grow up?"

"On the streets in New York."

She believed him, but something had changed from then until now. "Where are your parents?"

That muscle in his cheek jumped again. "I never knew my parents."

"You said your family has money and now that you never knew your parents. That's a contradiction." But she sensed that he was telling the truth yet still hiding something.

Josh must have caught something in her face that gave away her thoughts. He lifted his hand to brush his fingers along her face and cup her cheek. "My life isn't my own sometimes. I've been as honest as I can be with you, but my work requires a certain amount of discretion."

"In other words, I'm not to be trusted with personal details."

"That's not ..." He ran his hand over his head, ruffling his hair. "I was adopted. I don't talk about my parents."

She nodded, but understanding what he said didn't mean she could allow herself to get any closer to Josh.

He lowered his head and kissed her, a gentle touch that felt as though he was trying to tell her something with the kiss that he couldn't say with words.

When he lifted his head and looked into her eyes this time, she saw regret. Her heart ached with the need to tell him how much he meant to her and see if that was what it would take to get him to meet her halfway on trust. She was dangerously close to falling all the way over that cliff alone and facing a world of pain once he left.

Someone beat on the door.

With resignation heavy in his voice, he said, "I'll find out who it is."

Josh opened the door and Heidi came in, big grin on her face. "Hey, Trish."

When they finished hugging, Trish asked, "What are you doing here?"

"Josh invited me and Bunko up for the weekend. He thought you might like the company."

"What about a room?" Trish asked.

"He said he had an extra one. We just unpacked."

The only extra room Josh had available was hers. But she had no problem giving the room to Heidi ... and Bunko.

Together. They were here together. Nice.

Trish cut her eyes to Josh, who dropped a casual shoulder against the wall, amusement in his eyes. She didn't take her eyes off sexy mystery man when she asked Heidi, "And how did you get here?"

"Oh, that was the coolest part," Heidi said. "Right, Bunko?" The normally shy, sometimes grim, Bunko chuckled. "Way cool."

"We flew up on a private jet." Heidi matched Bunko's reserved smile with her patent, cheerful one.

Trish raised both eyebrows in question at Josh who sent her a no-big-deal shrug. Just when she felt like she had a handle on him, he threw her a curve.

Unsure what to say in the face of all he'd done she just said, "This is quite a surprise."

"Maybe it won't be the last one *tonight*," he murmured.

An hour later with Heidi and Bunko gone, Trish still battled her thoughts. How was she supposed to hold on to her anger after Josh had flown her friends up here to keep her company? She'd tried to let go of it, and had been doing a bang-up job, until Heidi informed her that Josh made it clear he wanted more eyes on Trish.

Bottom line? He hadn't done it because he wanted to do something nice for her. He'd had his own motive. And his protectiveness rivaled Zane's.

Even knowing that, and much as she wanted to fight against being smothered, Josh's concern warmed her. Practicing self-defense with Arnie *had* given her a level of comfort, but some days she didn't want to fight alone.

She wanted to know she had a safe port in a storm.

That she had more than a safe port. She had someone who cared for her. She wanted it to be Josh.

Even now her silly heart believed he was here with her for more than information on the mole, but she still didn't know who Josh was.

She wrapped her arms around her middle and stared out her hotel bedroom window at a sparkling Atlanta that burst with nightlife. She wanted to feel that alive and stop worrying over every step she made – or more like every *misstep* she tried to avoid.

Maybe she should just stop wondering what was really going on with Josh.

He claimed lunch had only been business and he couldn't talk about his nighttime appointment.

It wasn't as if she couldn't accept that, because her own brother couldn't discuss his covert pilot work with the DEA. But Zane didn't avoid talking about the rest of his life the way Josh did.

Zane now shared his life with a woman he loved.

There was the difference.

Josh had no intention of getting that involved, and he'd played her–he'd used her for his investigation. But Trish had already made the colossal mistake of falling for him.

A whisper of footsteps approached from behind her in the dark room. She glanced over her shoulder and recognized Josh's blonde hair and broad shoulders then turned back around. She could tell by the way he moved against her kimono that he only wore a shirt and shorts. His arms came around her and she battled mentally over what to do.

Push him away or pull him closer?

She wanted a man who trusted her enough to tell her the truth. Josh hadn't trusted her enough to ask her straight out about Colbert.

He nuzzled her neck and kissed a path up to her ear then leaned around to kiss her cheek. He paused, his voice coming out in a low rumble. "Still mad at me for some unknown reason?"

Was she still angry with him?

After all he'd done to protect her, she owed him some honesty. "I'm not angry–"

His sound of disbelief forced her to correct her statement.

"I *was* angry," she corrected and was rewarded with another hot snuggle against her neck. Her skin came alive, waiting for him to touch her.

But she had to have answers first. "Now I'm just confused and need to know something."

His thumbs that had been moving in a soothing stroke over her hands became very still. "What?"

"Were you sent here by the FBI to find out more about Colbert?"

He took a moment before asking, "What makes you think that?"

"Answering me with a question is a diversion tactic. If you aren't going to tell me the truth, then just say so."

Josh dropped his chin onto her shoulder. She could feel his slow inhale and exhale against her back as he considered his next words. "I am doing some additional research regarding

Colbert."

She hadn't expected him to admit that and felt a flutter of happiness at his honesty. She wanted more. "What about me? Am I part of that research?"

"Trish–"

"Truth."

His chin lifted off her shoulder and he kissed the top of her head. "You were."

She'd asked for honesty and had gotten it. "Oh."

"Don't read the wrong things from that. I'm not *here* in that capacity right now."

"So, you didn't, uhm, the other day on the sofa, that wasn't ..."

"You think I was seducing you for information?"

She was actually happy to hear the indignation and shock in his voice. "Yes."

"No." His thumbs started grazing back and forth again then he added, "The only research going on that day was how long it would take you to climax."

Her heart twirled around at that.

His hands lifted to cup her breasts and use those same thumbs to stroke her taut nipples.

"Are you researching again?"

His hands stilled and his forehead came down to rest on her head. "I'm trying to keep my hands off you but giving up oxygen would be easier."

Her resistance cracked at that. To have Josh desire her as much as she did him destroyed the last of her hesitation.

She whispered, "What if I asked you to ... keep going?"

He moved his cheek back and forth over her hair. "I want to more than you can ever know, but I'm not staying in Miami."

He was telling her the truth. That he would be gone. She should accept that and walk away, but she wanted this with Josh. Wanted to feel him and be with him for whatever time she could have. She was already in over her head. Spending the night in his arms wouldn't change that. She would take what he'd give until he left without asking for more.

She waited until she could speak without giving away her heart in her words. "I know you're leaving soon, but you're here tonight and I want you."

His lips came down on her neck and she leaned her head aside to give him better access.

He walked backwards with her until he sat on the bed where he lifted her into his lap. "Josh, we can–"

"Shh. Stop thinking for now and relax."

Was he crazy? His fingers were touching her everywhere, had her wound tighter than a banjo string. No longer needing to hold her up, his free hand drifted down to part her kimono and touch between her legs.

He groaned and whispered in a husky breath, "You're so hot and wet. I want you more."

She should answer and say how much she wanted this with him, too, but his finger slid inside her, and she lost her breath. His thumb barely brushed over her and she tensed. "That feels amazing ..."

His fingers on her breast moved in harmony with how he was stroking her between her legs. She leaned back against him, exposed and safe in his arms.

She could feel the thick ridge of his erection behind her, moving with his heartbeats. He whispered, telling her what he wanted to do to her and how good she would taste. How wet she was. He changed the rhythm of his fingers plunging inside her and touched the place that unleashed the tight coil inside her.

Bright lights burst behind her eyes. She came apart, calling his name. He held her in his arms, stroking her gently through the aftermath until she drooped limp as a rag doll gasping for air.

Josh was breathing just as hard and, speaking of hard, yes, he was. He spoke close to her ear. "You just blew my mind with how fast you came. I want to be inside you. Now."

She didn't think she had enough energy to nod.

He touched her stomach, massaging his way down until his fingers slid into her again and convinced *her* she wanted him inside her, too.

"Tell me what *you* want," he whispered, still stroking her.

"You. Now."

He scooped her up in his arms and kissed her all the way to his bedroom where he laid her down, shed his clothes, and knelt over her with his powerful legs on each side.

She'd only *thought* what she'd felt was impressive. Josh, naked and fully aroused was a sight worthy of worship.

He leaned over, reaching for his nightstand and came back with a condom he ripped out of the package and rolled into place.

She couldn't think beyond watching him. She forgot to breathe.

He had beautiful, roped muscles that flexed as he moved, curving, and shaping his masculine body. He lowered that amazing body until he was covering hers and the kissing started again. She ran her hands over his skin, pausing to tease the hard nipples on his chest and he bit her gently.

She shivered at the erotic feeling that invaded her. When she cupped his balls, he hissed and warned, "Careful. You have no idea how much I need you right now."

But he had no idea how much she *needed* him right back.

His mouth captured hers, hungry and demanding until he changed direction and dropped lower to suckle her breast.

She reached up and grasped his sides, desperately hanging on to him through the chaos he raised in her body. But when he pulled away, he backed up until his knees were by hers. He kissed the insides of her thighs, his fingers moving ahead of his lips, caressing her into another erotic fever.

Then he used his tongue on her and she bowed off the bed. "I'm going to ... uh ... again ..."

The power of her orgasm shocked her. She felt tears sting her eyes and had no idea what she was saying, just floated, suspended in time.

No past. No future. Just now.

Then Josh was back, kissing her breasts and her neck.

That was not helping her regain her equilibrium. He

couldn't do that to her again. She wouldn't survive.

But neither would she complain about dying this way.

She reached down and grasped his thick erection, stroking up and down.

He moaned. "Killing me."

"Only fair," she countered. "What are you waiting for?"

He lifted his body and stared down into her eyes. "To be sure you're ready."

She knew he didn't mean wet because that was obvious. He wanted to know she had this–him and her–straight in her mind.

Did she? No, not really.

But would that stop her right now? Not a chance. "I'm ready."

"Keep your eyes open," he ordered quietly. He pushed inside her slowly, watching her face as she adjusted to him.

Even if she'd wanted to close her eyes and shut out his face, she couldn't. His gaze held her pinned in place, refusing to let go. His biceps bulged as he held his weight off her and moved in a slow, easy rhythm. His skin glistened with perspiration.

The man had ridiculous control and she'd had none. She pushed up on his next stroke and forced him deep inside her.

His eyes blazed with an intensity that should scare her.

It inspired her instead.

She curved her arms up under his and hooked his shoulders. "Stop holding back on me. I want to feel you deep inside, feel every ... hard ... stroke–"

Power snapped in his body. He pushed again and again, faster now. Veins stood out on his forehead.

She didn't believe she could come again, not until he reached between them and proved her wrong when she lost the ability to think.

Josh had almost gained control again until Trish whispered, "I want to feel you deep inside, feel every ... hard ... stroke–"

His orgasm went nuclear, blinding him to everything except

pounding into her sweet heat. When he was finally spent, he collapsed, unable to hold himself away from her physically or emotionally.

He'd made a lot of mistakes in his life, but this one might top all of them. He could not want a woman this much. Not with the life he led. Chelsea had been the cog that fit neatly into a spot he'd created.

Nothing about Trish was neat or simple.

She couldn't fit into a life wrought with danger and deceit.

Trish's fingers stroked up and down his back. "I know this is going to end soon and I'll never see you again."

He brought his elbows in and pushed up to search her face. Eyes soft and more relaxed than he'd seen on her in days, she shielded thoughts behind that walled-up gaze. His heart banged in denial. How could he never see her again? He'd rather take a knife in the gut.

Still, she'd only pointed out reality.

Fuck reality. He'd figured out a way to make it work with Chelsea. *But Chelsea didn't survive, did she?* his nasty conscience reminded him. He wouldn't let Trish put herself in danger. She was ... important.

Someone who deserved more than a friends-with-benefits relationship, but his life didn't allow for more. Would Trish be willing to meet up on occasion to spend a couple of hot nights together?

Would *he* be satisfied with that?

No.

That was reality. The kind Josh had never allowed to intrude on his shallow existence. He swallowed, at a loss for words or ideas, but he didn't want to give her up when this was done. They could find a way to make *something* work. "When this is over, and we find the stalker–"

She lifted a hand to his lips. "Josh, please don't."

"What?" Don't what? Don't touch her, don't kiss her, don't act on this attraction neither of them could deny?

"Don't say something that will make me hope for what I can't have. I'll take what we can have now and be content. I understand that you can't share everything about yourself, but for more than this I need all of you."

Meaning she wanted to know about his life, his family. Things he couldn't share so long as he stayed in this business.

He reached over and brushed the back of his finger along her cheek. He'd been on the verge of saying they would talk about seeing each other after this was over, but Trish was right. He had no intentions of sharing all those details. Uncle Ty had to be shaking his head, wondering what kind of fool thought he could live in the shadows and have a woman like Trish.

A man who wanted to fill the empty hole in his chest.

Her eyes moistened before she closed them. Her silky black lashes fluttered, stark against her creamy cheeks. "I'm not up to talking any more tonight. I should go to my bed."

She might as well have said alone at the end because he heard it in his mind.

Just like the way he was destined to spend the rest of his life.

Alone.

CHAPTER 37

Ryder paced back and forth, caged in a hotel room. He should tell Sabrina he wasn't cut out for surveillance. Stick him in miserable weather where he had to sit in the same spot for hours waiting on a target to enter his crosshairs and he was fine, but this private eye shit made him twitchy.

"You're supposed to be grabbing some sleep," Dingo said without looking up from the laptop on the desk. He was taking his turn at watching several hidden security camera feeds Ryder had installed in parking decks near the task force offices and inside the task force reception area.

Nick had the current shift covering surveillance at the shipping docks, where a container for High Vision had cleared customs yesterday and no one had collected the contents yet.

DEA had inspected the container. Bunch of parts for lab equipment.

Dingo clicked a couple of keys and suggested, "Watching movies puts me out."

Sleep had been an elusive quest for a long time. Ryder lived in a perpetual state of unrest, crashing for fast naps when he needed them. He didn't answer Dingo, who could talk to a stump.

"Reading helps you sleep," Dingo offered.

No. Spending a night screwing the eyes out of someone like Leanne might help me sleep. But that wouldn't happen and even if it did, he'd only get a few hours of respite.

"Yoga is good, too, if you know how to do it."

Lucky me that Sabrina sent along a sleep therapist. Ryder's cell phone buzzed. He snatched it out of his pocket before the second buzz, recognizing the number, and answered with his real name. "Van Dyke."

The man who owned Kearn Industries said, "I got your message about meeting. Does this have anything to do with your father or are you finally going to accept my offer of employment?"

The things Ryder did for his brother. "This is about the contract Hubrecht wants to discuss with you."

"I've already given him my answer, but if you'd like to meet, I'll listen to what you have to say."

Meet? Shit. Ryder had hoped to avoid that, because Kearn was known for being a master at negotiating in person. He preferred face-to-face contact and would fly across the world, sure of closing a deal.

And return home successful.

But Ryder wanted no part of the business he'd grown up around, in any form. If he accepted Kearn's cherry deal, Hubrecht Van Dyke would go ballistic and bust harder on Terrence. If Ryder accepted Hubrecht's standing offer, Ryder would walk back into the snake pit of Van Dyke Enterprises he'd joined the Army to escape.

"Have you changed your mind, Van Dyke?"

"No. I'm in Miami. Give me a time and place."

Of course, Kearn wanted to meet *now* at his home in Belle Glade on the south end of Lake Okeechobee, just as Terrence had thought. It would take every bit of an hour to make the drive if he didn't get caught behind someone on the two-lane parts of Highway 27. Ryder checked his time. Closing in on ten-thirty. He was off for the next three and a half hours. He ended his call and turned to Dingo who didn't wait to hear what Ryder had to say.

"Sounds like you have somewhere to go. Be back by oh-two-hundred to take your shift watching the containers, mate."

Ryder did appreciate *that* about Dingo. No bullshit. He started to ask if Dingo was sure but figured if Dingo hadn't been he'd have said so. "Anything changes, call me. I'll head straight back."

Dingo nodded, apparently not wasting his therapeutic advice on the terminally indifferent.

Ryder spent the drive up to see Kearn with the music at ear-bleeding level, the only volume for listening to *Theory Of A Deadman* music. His meeting went pretty much as expected, with Kearn offering Ryder more than he was making with the Slye team and plenty of fringe benefits but signing on with Sabrina Slye's group hadn't been about money.

He'd needed to be out in the field using his skills to do something he considered productive, not boxed in an office where he couldn't breathe and expected to schmooze assholes who sucked up too much of the world's oxygen.

Kearn had understood about Ryder's rejecting the position, but not so much when the conversation turned to Hubrecht. Kearn said he refused to do business with a man who would sell his own mother for a deal.

No argument there.

Ryder turned out of Kearn's long driveway in night as dark as a bottomless hole, procrastinating over calling Terrence, who was waiting anxiously to hear the outcome. Cellular service would be spotty on the drive back through the Everglades Wildlife Management area. Might as well get this over with.

When Terrence answered, Ryder kept it short. "Kearn won't deal with Hubrecht or you. I tried my best to get him to meet you for lunch or something, but he said he didn't trust Hubrecht not to show up without any warning. I think he would probably work with Van Dyke Industries if he knew he'd be working with just you. Sorry, bro."

"I understand. Thank you for trying." Poor Terrence sounded kicked in the jewels. "I ... was excited so I told Father, but I'll explain it didn't work out."

Ryder clenched the steering wheel, even more miserable now that Terrence had to go to Hubrecht with his tail tucked. Ryder had nothing better to offer than, "Sorry."

"It's okay, really. I appreciate your getting involved at all. Where are you now?"

"Just leaving. On my way back to Miami."

"Will you be home any time soon?"

Home to Terrence meant the Hubrecht mansion in Atlanta. Not for Ryder. He'd never felt at home there, growing up as the adopted bastard child. "Don't know my schedule for a bit.

I'll call when I'm back and we can …" Ryder stalled, trying to come up with an idea. Grab a beer? Terrence probably couldn't drink with all the medicine he took. "Grab a burger," he finished.

"I'd like that." Terrence sighed heavily for someone who lived in the lap of luxury. Some laps were less comforting than others. "I suppose I should go inform Father and get it over with."

"Sorry, man. Good luck with the old bastard."

Ryder fought with a bout of guilt after hanging up, but he'd given the meeting his best shot and missed the mark. In fact, he'd spent longer than he'd intended and had barely an hour to make the return trip, but at one in the morning he'd have an open road and no one from the team had called or sent a text.

In the middle of the dark, lonely drive through the Everglades, he felt a jolt in the front end as if he'd run over something. He pulled off the road on a stretch of empty highway, far from any businesses or streetlights. His black pickup truck blended right in. He flipped on the emergency blinkers and grabbed his flashlight to inspect the tire on his front driver side.

Flat, dammit. He rolled up his sleeves on his way to the rear of the truck where his spare was ... not hanging under the bed?

His spare was gone? No fucking way.

He ran the beam of his flashlight under there again, but the bracket that had held a brand-new tire hung empty.

Damned thieves.

Cursing a streak all the way back to the cab, he reached over and lifted his cell phone ... that had no signal at all.

Call it paranoia, but instinct kicked in and he was instantly alert. He palmed his HK. When would someone have stolen his tire?

CHAPTER 38

Trish flopped on her side again, tired, but not enough to sleep soundly. She'd battled the half-asleep stage of insomnia for the past four hours. A buzzing near her head pushed her from groggy to wide-awake.

Her cell phone vibrated on the nightstand. Maybe Angel had gone into labor. Trish swiped up the phone, noted the time was just before two in the morning–as in Sunday already–and she needed sleep.

She didn't recognize the phone number, but it was a Miami area code, so she punched the talk button. "Hello?"

"Resting well in your snazzy suite?" The mechanical voice buzzed through the lines.

Thump, thump, thump. Her heart went double time.

"Did you think I wouldn't notice that you left town?"

"Who are you?" she pleaded. "What do you want?" *Dear God, please make this stop.*

"Oh, I do want something and you're going to help me."

Trish rolled onto her back and scooted up to sit against the headboard, her shaking legs bent at the knees. "If you won't tell me what you want, I'm not listening to you anymore." Trish moved the phone from her ear to switch it off until she heard, *"Wrong move, Trish!"*

She clutched the phone back to her ear and squeezed her eyes shut. "Why are you doing this?"

"A good chess player never gives up, even an alcoholic would know that."

"Chess? I don't understand what you're talking about."

"You will, you will. In the meantime, don't let lover boy come between us."

Josh. This maniac was threatening him.

Trish hissed, "I refuse to play your game."

"You don't have a choice. By the way, in chess this is called check."

Josh kept the bedroom door ajar in his vigilance to watch over Trish. The fourth time he sat up to check the clock, he heard soft footsteps padding across the living room.

Should he stay put and give her privacy?

The distinct tinkle of ice hitting glass ended his debate.

He stepped into his jeans and quietly eased into the joint living area. Ambient light filtering through the window from outside cast the room in soft shadows.

Trish stood at the wet bar he hadn't given a thought to since arriving. She stared down at the counter, a glass with ice next to a miniature one-shot bourbon bottle.

Cap off. Empty.

Josh closed his eyes, fighting a wave of disappointment–for her, not himself–so strong he felt it in his knees. He looked at her again. She hadn't moved and this time he could see the glass was still full. Relief swamped him.

"You don't want to do that, Trish."

"How do you know? You're not an ... an alcoholic."

Simple words, but each one slashed his heart.

"You're right," he said, swallowing against the tangle of emotions he struggled to contain. "I have no idea about the battle you fight each day. But I know the warrior in you who won't quit. I know the woman who turned her world around, the one who trains hard physically and mentally so she can kick ass at everything she does. The one who loves her brother and life too much to give up now."

Trish's head snapped up at the mention of her brother. She wrapped a hand across her eyes that slid to her mouth. She set the glass down.

Josh searched for something to take her pain away, but nothing as simple as a word could heal hurt that deep. When she drew a deep breath that came out sounding full of misery, he gave in to the gut-wrenching need and crossed the room to wrap his arms around her.

When Trish turned to him and threaded her arms around his waist, a dam of emotions broke inside him. He hugged her as tight as he could without hurting her and rubbed a hand up and down her back to soothe her. Her body shook but that was the only sign of the internal battle she waged.

What had happened? Why now after all she'd been through?

He had the sudden insight that it could be him. His presence. His fault. *Shit.*

He waited, holding her until she quieted. Trish raised eyes glistening with tears on thick eyelashes.

Josh kissed her forehead. "What's wrong, sweetheart?"

"I got a call." Her fingers tightened on his arms. "From the stalker."

Just five minutes–that's all he wanted with the bastard terrorizing her. "What did he say?"

"Same stuff like the notes." She worked a hand free to rub her nose.

Josh wouldn't release her. Couldn't. He reached over and snagged a paper towel for her. "Tell me exactly what the caller said."

She hesitated a moment then recited the call, stopping to think a moment then finishing.

He had the feeling she'd edited the words, but he wouldn't push her now. She might have sounded hesitant because she was rattled and not sure of what she'd heard.

"I don't know what he, she, *it* wants. The voice always sounds synthesized or mechanical. Nothing makes sense. All these references to chess."

Another move by the Chessmaster, but he couldn't tell Trish about that. He had the feeling something about the call tonight had pushed Trish further than the notes or the text had. Something she wasn't admitting.

If Josh had his hands on the stalker at this moment, he would choke whoever it was to death. "This is going to end, sweetheart." He just worried about *how* it would end.

She stepped out of his embrace, hands fisted and eyes flashing with fire. "Get dressed."

"For what?" he asked, a little wary.

"Just do it." She stalked into her bedroom, tossing over her shoulder, "Shorts or warmups."

Not sure what to say to that, he changed to shorts, a T-shirt and running shoes then met her in the living room where she showed up in an athletic bra, pink tank top, and workout pants ... carrying a pair of pink-and-white kickboxing gloves. Whoa.

He followed her to the gym on the top floor of the hotel where one lonely soul ran on a treadmill at two in the morning.

Trish stretched, then looked around and zeroed in on a heavy bag hanging at the opposite end of the room from the treadmills.

Josh did a few stretches but kept Trish in view. He was glad to know *he* wasn't her target. She warmed up slowly with a jab, jab cross, changing the rhythm and hitting at face level, then chest, then bending her knees to strike at groin level. *Ouch.*

He stopped stretching and circled her, watching her technique. "Good form."

"How did you know about my training?" Jab, cross, jab jab. Sweat formed on her forehead.

Shit. He considered it for two seconds, then said, "I saw you. With Arnie."

She paused and looked at him. Not a word, but a stare that loaded him up with guilt.

"I told you I was investigating–"

"*After* I asked you."

He took a deep breath, but held her gaze, letting her see that he was being straight with her. "Yeah. I followed you the morning you met up with Arnie in the warehouse."

She took a few seconds to process that, then nodded. "So, you know a lot more about me than I realized, and you know I'm not just talking when I say I train." A tiny muscle in her jaw jumped when she clamped her lips tight.

"Yes. And you have good instincts. The best instincts can be fooled by trained operatives. We're an evil aberration, but your instincts are sound. I wanted you to know ... Arnie missed it, but you didn't. When you felt like somebody was watching you, you were right. You would've nailed me. Looked right at where I was hidden. It was ... impressive."

Her cheek muscle softened.

He wasn't sure how much she'd talk about her war with alcohol, so he asked, "This..." he gestured at the bag. "Does it help, when you want to drink?"

"Usually." She turned back to the bag and started punching again, picking up a little speed every five to six hits until she was punishing the thing. Fine dark hairs clung to her damp neck.

Josh moved to a weight bench a few feet away and did a few arm curls while he let her battle her demons, watching as she worked through her kick combinations, then moved back to punches and turned up the heat, attacking with rapid bursts until she finally grabbed the bag and leaned her head against it. Breathing hard. Muscles quivering.

The runner at the other end killed the treadmill, wiped it down, and walked out, leaving them alone.

Josh gave Trish another moment then walked back to where she stood. "Done?"

She pushed away from the bag and turned to him with eyes brighter than before. "Never. This beast will always haunt me, but it won't win. Every time I've gotten that close to letting the alcohol win, I've gone to the gym to fight the beast inside me."

When she lifted her hands to undo her gloves, he reached over and tugged one arm to him. She raised her eyes to his, thinking, then finally relaxed while he pulled the glove off first one hand, then the other.

The he lifted both hands to his lips and kissed the red knuckles. Who was this woman who drew him in more by the minute? The scent of her warm body, damp with perspiration, called out to his, reminded him of what they'd shared hours ago. He let go of her hands. "You amaze me."

She stepped up close to him and kissed him, holding herself back as if she thought he'd be turned off by a sweaty woman. Really? He pulled her sweat-slick body into his arms and kissed her back.

He wanted to promise her everything would work out, but too many unknowns still existed. With Trish next to his heart, the world felt right.

Now, if he could just keep her safe.

Her tongue played with his in a sensual dance.

It felt like weeks instead of hours since they'd made love. He missed her that much when she wasn't near him. He wanted her even closer, skin-to-skin, in his bed.

But he was not going there after what she'd been through tonight.

She pulled back. "Now we both need a shower."

Could she mean ...? "I'm not complaining."

"Then you won't mind washing my back?"

Damn, the woman read minds, too.

CHAPTER 39

Pacing the living area of the suite, Josh straightened his tux, glad he'd had the forethought to pack for any situation. And equally thankful that Sunday was practically done. Trish just had a cocktail party in the hotel ballroom before they gave industry awards.

That phone call hadn't broken her, but it had pushed her hard. And Josh's team had gotten nothing from the tap on her cell phone. The only sound that had come through to them had been loud static and the call hadn't lasted long enough to triangulate.

Chessmaster was a sophisticated traitor.

Trish sailed out of the bedroom draped in a shimmering-white gown, backless again. How did she expect him to protect her while she was dressed like a gift begging to be unwrapped?

"Would you mind hooking the clasp at my neck, Josh?"

Not as much as he minded her parading through a room full of men in that outfit. She swiveled around in front of him, holding the neckline in place with a hand at each shoulder.

He fingered the clips. His eyes roamed down her bare back to where the glittering material hugged a choice derriere before falling to her ankles. He finished clipping the catch and pressed a kiss to the top of her head.

"You're beautiful." Josh forced his hands not to finger the black curls arranged with sparkles.

"Thanks." She turned around, her eyes skittish and having a hard time landing on any one spot. "For last night, too."

Something had shifted between them during the early hours of the morning. He felt the change and knew she did as well. Hell, he'd slept for the first time in two years without seeing Chelsea's dead eyes.

He'd had Trish in his arms.

He wasn't going to analyze what that meant, exactly, but he wouldn't try to pretend Trish wasn't the reason.

Hopefully this meant she would listen to him when it came time for him to leave Miami, but Trish's nerves were tapped out from dealing with the stalker. Josh wouldn't load her emotional plate with anything else right now. When they returned home and the world no longer encroached on their privacy, they could discuss their relationship.

He could make this work with a woman whose brother had been in covert ops for years. Trish would understand if Josh explained there would always be parts of his life that he couldn't share but that had nothing to do with how much he cared for her.

Josh traced her neck with a finger. "I want you to enjoy tonight but be careful."

"I will, but don't panic if I step away from you."

He wouldn't panic, but he might hurt someone if they got between him and her. When they exited the elevator downstairs, Trish stopped and dug through her purse.

"What are you looking for?" he asked.

"Nothing." She smiled, but her eyes told another story.

Trish groused at herself for being so addle-brained. Josh had distracted her again. The last place she remembered seeing the pepper spray camouflaged as a lipstick holder had been on her vanity.

Josh threw her another speculative look. "Has anything *else* happened you want to tell me about?"

Other than the stalker now threatening to harm you? No.

"Nah, I'm just tired, Sugar." She gave him her best life-is-perfect smile. If Josh knew about the whole conversation she'd had with the stalker last night, he'd have her bundled up and on the next airplane home.

Then Zane would get involved.

She'd end up living in some safe house for God knew how long. She'd had enough of living like a hunted animal. The stalker wanted her. Here was as good a place as any, especially with Zane and Angel out of the picture.

This way, Trish had only Josh to protect.

And she'd seen a bit of his warrior side already. He could hold his own. She was no slack either.

He took her arm and led her toward the party, parking her near one of the six hors d'oeuvre tables spread around the ballroom. "I'll be right back."

She watched Josh as he filled a plate of munchies only because she enjoyed the way his hands moved.

She could trust Josh with everything. Except her heart.

Gunter and Olivia swept up as Josh returned to Trish's side. Gunter moved like a bag of potatoes with feet, but Olivia really did sweep through a room. She probably spent hours in front of a mirror perfecting her moves.

"My, my, you two are becoming quite a pair," Gunter said with more sarcasm than normal.

"Gunter, don't start on me," Trish warned.

"Oh, I understand," the German drawled. "He's here to keep an eye on you, right? Custody and all that."

"How would you know that?"

"The police interviewed me as well and when I inquired about your status, I was informed that the FBI had authority over you."

Olivia was either oblivious to the conversation going on or didn't care since it was not focused on her. "How chic to have a personal bodyguard, Trish. Does he rent out?" Olivia asked, wiggling her well-stacked little body in Josh's direction.

Josh cringed. God love him.

Gunter sniffed at Olivia's statement. "He's a computer geek, Liv. Bodyguards don't touch their clients unless they're in danger."

"Well then, as Trish's bodyguard, I feel the need to pull her from the line of fire. Excuse us." Josh smiled at the odd pair's sour faces. He took Trish by the arm and guided her over to a small round-top table covered with black linen.

"I'm sorry you're catching their abuse, Josh." She sat in the chair he held out for her.

"Those two would have to do a lot more than that to bother me. But I won't have them ragging on you." Josh glanced around. "This is wide open. There's Heidi across the room heading this way. You should be safe here. I'll go get us a couple of club sodas and be right back." He looked down at her. "If you're okay with that."

"Thanks. I'd like that."

His smile of appreciation took her breath.

She kept him in sight as he crossed the room, unable to drag her eyes away. His long, elegant stride drew the eyes of every female he passed. She stretched her neck, trying to follow his form as he melted into the crowd. Olivia, the blonde, half-pint cougar goddess, apparently had her hottie radar tuned to high, because Trish saw her whirl like she was on a spindle to watch Josh as he walked toward the food tables. Olivia set a beeline course to intercept him. Trish just shook her head.

Leanne and now Olivia. The man was a blonde magnet.

So, what if he was?

Trish had to give him up when she returned home. Fair enough. Just not right now. She had thrown all caution to the wind last night to have this little bit of heaven that would disappear soon.

A twenty-something, blonde, Meg Ryan type in an ultra-short, red spandex dress fell into step behind Josh, headed for the bar. Based on the way she was checking out his butt, Trish knew exactly what was on *that* blonde's mind.

Across the room, Heidi had someone engaged in conversation, but her friend's gaze kept flitting away. Was she searching for where Trish had landed? Trish stood and waved until she caught Heidi's attention, then sat down again.

Gunter appeared from nowhere. "Having a good time?"

She managed not to jump or snap at him, but she was on edge enough lately without people sneaking up on her. "It's been a nice convention. What about you? I saw you across the room yesterday but couldn't get over to talk to you."

He sniffed, a sound that matched the disgusted look on his face. "I've made a few worthy contacts, but nothing earth-shattering."

Heidi showed up wearing silver spandex tights with a faux tiger skin sweater. "Hi Gunter."

"Heidi."

Trish detected irritation in Heidi's voice. Why?

Fingers tapping on her hip, Heidi asked Trish, "Where's Josh?"

"Getting some drinks."

At the mention of Josh, the disgust on Gunter's face dialed up another level. "He's becoming a permanent fixture."

Something in his tone pricked Trish's temper. Or maybe she was taking out her tiring weekend on the easiest target.

"Yes, he is," Heidi said, smiling. She turned her head back and forth, searching the crowd. "Our men should be back soon. Bunko said he was getting drinks, too."

Our men? Trish glanced between Heidi and Gunter, trying to figure out why Heidi seemed to be purposely poking at the older man.

"On that note, I'm off to find a drink for myself." Gunter ambled away, blending into the crowd.

"Thought he'd never leave. He really gets on my nerves some days," Heidi grumbled.

"He's even getting on my nerves tonight, but what was with all that *our men* thing?"

Heidi's entire body brightened with excitement. "I didn't want to talk in front of him, because I checked our emails for ReSolution, and I have *news* for you."

"What?"

"Dixon's campaign manager contacted you. He said the Senator is still on to film the segment for *Treasured Past* on Tuesday."

"Are you serious?" Trish couldn't believe she might finally be getting a break.

"Yes, I am. In fact, he said the Senator also agreed to allow the television producers to do some additional filming of the Senator's private collection in Chicago. Dixon agreed so long as *you* flew up tomorrow to participate. His campaign manager apologized for any inconvenience, but he said they're planning on it and the studio is booking your ticket tonight since they have the information from your application file."

Trish rolled her eyes. "As if I wouldn't cancel everything just to do that. *Oh my God!* This is amazing!

It took a moment for Trish to realize her phone was buzzing in her purse. After a day of attendees grumbling over cellular calls not going through down here on the conference level, she'd forgotten about her phone, but text messages came through on and off. Trish was so caught up in being excited over Heidi's good news that she just stared at the phone display, not comprehending at first.

Go to your room and wait for further instructions.

Don't push me to make others pay.

The stalker was here?

Trish looked up, searching the room. What did she think? That the stalker would be standing nearby, holding a phone, and staring at her? But the message didn't have its usual taunting quality.

And the number was an Atlanta area code.

Was the stalker using a local disposable phone?

She couldn't spend time on questions she couldn't answer, not with Josh, Heidi, and Bunko's safety to worry about. If she told Heidi she was going to the room, then Heidi would call Josh immediately.

"What's up?" Heidi asked, turning to follow Trish's gaze.

Think fast. Trish shoved the phone back in her purse. "I've got to find a bathroom."

Heidi turned back. "I'll go with you. Josh wouldn't want you to go alone."

"No." That had come out too harsh. "If you aren't here, he'll panic that something has happened. I'm just going to the bathroom, Heidi."

"Can you wait a sec until one of the boys gets here?"

Trish put her hand to her stomach and grimaced as if she had intestinal pain. "I have to go now. Security is everywhere. Just sit tight and I'll probably be back before Josh gets here."

Doubtful since she was headed to their suite.

"I'll be there right behind you as soon as I find one of the guys." Heidi pulled out her cell phone.

Now would be a good time for the poor cellular service to work in Trish's favor.

She stood and took off toward the restrooms, then made a direction change as soon as she was out of Heidi's sight and hurried to the elevator lobby. No one could enter that lobby without showing their key card to security, then they had to use the card to activate the elevator. With her suite six steps from the elevator, she felt competent enough from her workouts with Arnie to make it there unharmed.

Then she'd hunt for her pepper spray first thing.

But why did the stalker want her in her hotel room? Was this another game like the night she had to sit in the car for over an hour?

The minute she passed through security at the elevators, her phone rang with a blocked number.

Worried the stalker would retaliate against Josh, Heidi, or Bunko for Trish's being slow to comply, she answered it with a breathless, "Hello?"

The call dropped before she heard a word.

When she stepped off the elevator onto her floor, her phone rang again with a blocked number. She was quick on the button. "I'm here."

A robotic voice said, "*Tick tock, tick...*"

The call died again.

Damn! She rushed to the room and shut the door quickly behind her. Her hands were shaking so hard she almost dropped the phone.

She stood waiting, but it didn't ring again.

For once, she begged silently for the stalker to call her back.

Josh waited impatiently for the bartender to serve the two couples ahead of him. Heidi was with Trish in the middle of the room. She'd told him that Heidi and Bunko were also recovering alcoholics, which was why Trish had been adamant that night at her shop when she told police that her employees didn't drink. He'd told Trish that she had good instincts, and after spending time with Heidi and Bunko, he'd figured out that Trish was also a good judge of character.

He'd been right to bring in friends she could trust. No one would bother her tonight with three of them watching out for her. Even knowing that, worry ate at him.

Olivia sidled up next to him. "Lookee here, lookee here. *I'm* glad to see you at this boring event even if Gunter isn't."

"Oh?" Just what was the platinum diva up to?

"Maybe with you in the picture, Gunter will give up on Trish. I sincerely hope you keep her."

Keep Trish? Olivia finally said something Josh agreed with. "What have you got against Trish?" he asked, tired of the witch's caustic digs.

"Of all women, I don't get why Gunter is interested in *her*."

Josh started to tell her it was because Trish epitomized everything a woman like Olivia would never come close to being. Instead, he said, "Trish is a terrific woman. She's attractive and witty, works hard and cares for the people important to her. I don't see how any man wouldn't want her."

But those other men couldn't have her.

Olivia fanned her hand, dismissing his remarks. "Regardless of all that, Trish looks just like Gunter's ex-wife. You'd think he'd want someone different, like *me*."

"Then why don't you work harder to get him and leave Trish alone?"

"Am I bothering Trish? How lovely." Olivia smiled and pranced away.

Josh picked up the two drinks and fought his way back through the crowd. Something about what Olivia said pricked a memory he couldn't pull up but had a distinct feeling the information was important.

CHAPTER 40

Trish ran across the hotel suite living room and into her bedroom to find the false lipstick holder with the pepper spray. It had fallen off the nightstand. She grabbed it off the floor and wedged the gold tube into her evening bag, then dashed back into the living room.

The hotel room phone on an end table rang.

Had Heidi had enough time to go the bathroom and find Trish missing?

The phone rang again.

Could be Josh if Heidi had found him. If Trish didn't answer, he might come up looking for her. She grabbed the phone on the third ring.

"Avoiding me, Trish?" the mechanical voice asked

Her hand shook. "I didn't hang up. The call dropped."

"Don't let it happen again."

"Like I have any control over the cell service?"

The stalker ignored that. The mechanical voice said, *"Having fun? No? Party girl like you should be enjoying yourself. Don't worry. I'm having enough fun for both of us. In fact, you may not have any worry at all soon."* Harsh mechanical laughter crackled across the line.

Trish clenched the phone, wanting to choke the stalker. She'd had it with being a victim and hiding in fear. No one was pushing her off the wagon. A buried fury came steaming to the surface. "You're a coward to send notes and make phone calls. If you're so bad, come and get me."

"I won't have to. You'll come to me because losers always run from their fears. And you will lose, starting with your silly little shop, then I'll turn my attention to those you love."

Trish slammed the phone down, unwilling to spend another minute living this way.

And neither would she stay in this hotel room.

Closing the door behind her, she rushed toward the elevator.

The hotel alarm went off. A booming, automated voice announced a fire alarm, to take the stairs and exit the hotel.

Doors banged open.

People spilled into the corridor, rushing for the stairs.

Trish fought against the panic rising in her chest. That phone call, and now this. *You'll come to me.*

Josh hurried back to the table where he'd left Trish.

Heidi stood there, but no Trish.

What the fuck?

"Where's Trish?" Josh asked, keeping his voice calm.

Bunko walked up and handed Heidi a Coke.

Heidi said, "Glad you're here. She had to go to the bathroom."

Fuck. *Don't panic yet.* "Why didn't you go with her?"

Josh caught a hard look from Bunko who obviously didn't care for the tone he'd taken with Heidi. "Sorry, Heidi, I just don't like her to be alone."

"I know and I was only waiting for you to get back so I could go with her." Heidi picked up her purse from the table, grumbling, "I should have grabbed Gunter to stay around so I could go, but that guy gets on my nerves. He's such pain in the butt. No wonder he's divorced."

Josh froze as the understanding washed over him. The first time he'd met Gunter, the annoying German had said he got rid of everything that reminded him of his ex-wife.

Olivia said Trish looked just like Gunter's ex-wife.

"Stay here." Josh slammed the drinks on the table.

"What's wrong, Josh?" Heidi called out in a worried voice.

"I don't know yet, but I want to find Trish. Now." He left at a run for the bathrooms, stretching his gait and ignoring all the shocked faces at his lack of decorum.

He hadn't reached the hallway leading to the ladies room when fire alarms started shrieking.

The crowd turned into a noisy herd that bordered on panic. Security ordered people to not take the elevators. Conference attendees down here on the basement level clogged the stairs, terrified of being trapped below ground, and trying to reach street level.

Josh burst into the bathroom, ignoring the gasps and evil looks of women rushing to exit. He bent to check under the stall doors, looking for the sparkly silver shoes Trish had stepped into just before they'd left the suite. Nothing. *Shit.*

He raced out of there, searching all around him until he was convinced Trish must have been closer to the stairs than he was when the alarm went off. He joined the push for the stairs, jostled and shoved by a sea of frightened people.

Trish would be busy doing the same, rushing for the stairs.

Then she would be outside, exposed.

Josh trusted his gut, and his gut said this had FUBAR written all over it.

———*m*———

Caught in a wave of humans pouring onto the street, Trish clutched her bag and moved away from the building. With no wrap or jacket, she shivered against the chilly evening air.

The bulging mass drove Trish further from the building. A cacophony of stricken voices yammered all around her while she stepped from one small pocket of open space to another, trying to maintain the bubble of space around her. Fire engines screamed in the distance.

Police directed gawkers and guests to keep moving away from the hotel.

Trish searched the glass-covered tower for a blaze but saw none. No smoke. Not the first sign of a fire.

The burgeoning crowd forced her down the sidewalk until she had to back down a side street.

She reached for her phone to call Josh and Heidi.

A sharp tip stabbed her ribs.

Knife. She wasn't in the right position to defend against that, and she couldn't run in this narrow gown. Not yet.

Annoyed and ready to let someone share in her misery,

Trish half-turned until the knife shoved harder. A craggy voice warned, "Keep your hands at your sides and move when I tell you unless you want to die right here."

From the corner of her eye, scraggly gray hair, thick makeup, and a bulky flowered dress came into view.

Pruneface? What was she doing here? The hag tugged her arm, forcing her to take a step.

She had the pepper spray but couldn't get to it, or to her phone that was now buzzing with texts and ringing with calls. Trish felt she could take the woman if Pruneface didn't have a blade ready to cut her if she made a wrong move. What did this bitch have against her?

"What do you want?" Trish asked. Could this old crow be the stalker behind a terror campaign?

"Shut up and walk." Pruneface stood up straight now, as if her curved spine had miraculously healed itself. She yanked Trish away from the crowd with more strength than expected. "I also have a gun. Make a sound to draw attention and I'll kill you and anyone who tries to help you."

Trish kept moving on shaky legs. She cut her eyes to the side at three men across the street who were walking the opposite way toward the hotel. Paying no attention. No help there unless she wanted to get them killed, too.

With all the noise and excitement going on back at the hotel, no one would notice two women in an empty side street.

Trish's pulse thrummed with fear, but she'd had enough. Frustration and anger battled to the surface. This was the moment she'd been training for with Arnie. She only wished she were wearing clothes she could better move in, but she would not go down without a fight.

———— *◆◆◆* ————

When Josh ended up outside, he muscled his way through the crowd and searched for Trish.

He'd lost one woman to a human predator.

He couldn't fail Trish.

Thousands of guests were pouring out onto the street,

pushing him toward the first cross street. He kept turning, looking in every direction for Trish while he called her cell phone over and over.

He'd just glanced down at the cross street when he had to look again. A pair of women walked along two blocks farther away.

One wore a shimmering white gown.

They disappeared around a corner.

He took off after them.

———*m*———

Trish tried stomping on the woman's foot to get loose. She got choked for her efforts.

Pruneface lost her wig in the struggle and shouted in a much deeper voice, "If I didn't have to get rid of your body, I'd kill you right now."

Trish recognized that voice.

Twisting, she stared at a person she'd believed was her friend. "Gunter?"

"Took you long enough to figure it out." Covered in heavy makeup and wearing a bulky dress, he peered at her through bright, insane eyes.

Trish searched the street, hunting for help, but no police officer miraculously appeared. They would be helping with the hotel crisis.

Gunter held her arm in a tight grip and moved the knife to Trish's throat, pricking the skin. "I don't want to have to carry you but make a sound and I'll cut your throat then drag you to my van." He yanked her along.

"Why are you doing this?"

"You're a blood sucker just like my ex-wife. That damn shop of yours is ruining mine, then they want *you* for that miserable show. I've been on Las Olas longer. I'm the pro, not you."

Gunter's shop was *near* Las Olas, not on the street, but that wasn't relevant when a madman had a knife close enough to end her life. "How am I a threat to your business? I'm struggling to make it."

He hauled her along faster. The dress he wore slapped at boot-covered ankles. His voice snarled and lifted hairs along her neck. "You stole my customers. You and Charlie were going to team up. Finish me off."

What was he talking about? She stumbled, but he kept her upright, taking her farther and farther away from Josh.

At least Josh was safe, but he'd never forgive himself if Trish let Gunter kill her. She trembled at the thought of dying, but Josh was right.

She wasn't ready to give up the life she'd fought so hard to own.

Gunter's mind had left the room, but if she kept him talking, he might make a mistake and give her an opening to escape.

"You're wrong about me and Charlie teaming up. He didn't even like me."

"Oh, sure. Think I'm as stupid as you are? Charlie had plans for you."

"No, he didn't."

Gunter muttered a string of words that made no sense. "He told me. Same day he made me a pity offer. That miserable pig."

"Told you what?"

"About bringing you into his empire to manage his Florida stores. Don't act so coy. He was standing right in front of me when he called you. Whore that you are, you couldn't wait to go see him."

Oh, dear God. That had been the day Charlie tried to guilt her into selling by telling her that Gunter's deal depended on Charlie's getting ReSolution. Trish never had a chance with arrogant Charlie manipulating everyone.

Gunter dragged her into a parking lot where a handful of vehicles were parked and no attendant. The tip of his razor-sharp knife pricked deeper into her side.

Trish came up with another argument she forced out between panting breaths. "But Charlie is dead."

"Yes. He. Is," Gunter said in a bragging voice. "Using your

letter opener was a nice touch if I do say so myself."

"*You* killed him?"

"Of course, I did." Gunter's smarmy laugh crawled along Trish's skin.

"But ... you were with Olivia," Trish said, thinking out loud. Vickers would have checked his alibi.

"She's another stupid bitch, but she's good for an alibi."

He'd stalked her and set her up for murder and hit her over the head. Trish wanted to scream at him and bash *his* head with a brick, but until she got her hand on a weapon, she'd keep her voice calm. Someone had to remain sane here. "So, all this stalking and game playing has been about getting rid of my business?"

"And you."

"The pawn."

Gunter laughed, a high, hysterical sound. "Yes, you're my pawn."

"Where're you taking me?"

"Somewhere that you can never be a problem again."

Trish shivered hard from cold and shock. She hated giving him any satisfaction, but she couldn't prevent her voice from shaking when she offered the only thing that might save her life. "What if I ... give you ReSolution?"

"I don't want your miserable piece of shit."

He just wants to kill me.

There was no hope of talking him out of this. They were headed toward a van parked facing a tall brick wall along one side of the lot where the light hardly dented the darkness.

She dragged her feet, forcing Gunter to slow down. He moved the knife, pricking her neck. She hissed at the pain.

Her time had run out. If she got in that van, she would never get away.

Drawing on all the frustration she'd suffered from being stalked, she snarled, "I've never been anything but nice to you, you crazy asshole."

Wrong choice of words.

"You bitch! You'll beg for death before I'm done with you."

Gunter flipped the knife and cut a gash under her chin.

Blood ran down her chest. She cried out at the metal hitting bone.

"Stop where you are!" a male voice yelled at them from across the lot.

Josh?

Gunter wrenched around at the order, bringing her with him as a shield.

Any doubt about Josh being a deadly warrior disappeared when Trish faced him. He moved toward them at a steady pace, with both hands locked around a huge gun and a feral expression she'd never seen on his face.

Gunter reached back with his free hand as he changed his knife position to lay the long blade horizontally across her throat. She clamped her lips to keep from crying out and distracting Josh.

In her peripheral vision, she saw Gunter lift his own big-ass gun into view.

Pointed at Josh.

CHAPTER 41

"Let her go," Josh ordered, continuing to step slowly toward Trish. She was white as her gown. The wrinkled face that tipped into view for a split second had to be a guy ... a guy covered in an inch of makeup. And wearing a dress? Crazy didn't begin to describe that image, especially since he was holding a knife at Trish's throat with one hand and a .357 Magnum in his other hand.

If the guy was a little taller, Josh could take a shot, but Trish's head shielded the stalker's head.

The creep spoke in a deathly calm voice. "You have ten seconds to leave, or I'll shoot."

Josh had experienced gut-clenching fear only one time before, and a woman's life had been at stake then, too. The terror clawing his chest this time was tenfold. He forced himself to think only about controlling the situation.

That might have worked if Trish had been a trained operative and not a frightened woman who thought and reacted like one.

The crazy bastard chanted, "Eight ... Nine ..."

Trish's eyes had widened. Her hands flew up to grab the stalker's knife wrist. She shoved her head back, slamming the guy's nose. All that happened in a nanosecond as she swung her body at his gun arm, throwing the shot wide just as it blasted from the muzzle.

Josh raced forward, weapon raised and his heart trying to explode in his chest.

The stalker swayed, off balance. Josh stopped in his tracks, less than ten feet away. Trish leaned further to the left, shrinking into herself, ducking as low as she could with the knife at her throat, and the stalker's head swiveled into view for a mere second.

Josh had a clear shot and took it. The explosion cracked the air.

Trish and the stalker fell backwards into a heap as Josh ran toward them.

Josh slid to a stop, down on his knees next to Trish.

Part of the stalker's head was gone. Blood covered Trish from neck to waist.

Josh shoved his weapon into his waistband and reached for his phone. "Hold on, baby."

She clutched her throat, staring straight ahead. The knife had cut her.

He punched one button on his phone and used his free hand to feel for her pulse. Thready, but there.

The minute Sabrina answered, Josh started rattling orders, giving her the location for an ambulance. She would get help here faster than he could with 9-1-1. He tossed the phone down and ripped off his jacket to wrap Trish in.

He lifted her off the guy.

Her hand still covered her throat. He clamped his hand over hers, not willing to lose one drop of her precious blood.

She stared at Josh as if she didn't see him. He could not watch the light die in those brown eyes.

"You're going to be okay," he told her in a hoarse voice. "I've got people on the way."

Trish's eyes focused on him. Her lips moved but no words came out. She lifted the hand not clutching her throat and caught Josh's lapel. He leaned down close to hear her thin voice.

"I ... love ... you."

Her arm fell away. Her fingers beneath his relaxed and her eyes rolled up in her head.

"*No, Trish, no!* Please don't die," he begged.

CHAPTER 42

She's alive.

Josh kept telling himself that as he waited alone in a corner seat of a very small sitting area in Grady Hospital. One of the emergency room doctors still worked on Trish. The antiseptic air reeked of the dried blood soaked into Josh's shirt, but none of it was his.

Because Trish had risked her life to protect him. His hands trembled.

She's alive, he reminded himself again.

The knife had not cut a vital artery or the muscles or tendons in her throat. The knife. *Gunter's* knife. The old German guy she'd considered a friend. Gunter was the stalker.

Trish had a deep gash under her chin that took internal and external stitches. And she'd have a bandage where the knife had sliced across her throat, but it had gone just through the skin.

A sliver of space between life and death.

She had some cuts on her arms and on the fingers that she'd shoved between her throat and the knife blade. All of those were minor.

If Trish hadn't gotten her hands on Gunter's wrist his weight would have dragged the knife deeper across her throat when they fell backwards together. Josh had Arnie to thank for the training he'd given Trish. She'd defended herself from an attacker. But Josh would bet money that Arnie hadn't taught Trish to risk her own life to save someone else.

Josh had seen her for a few minutes only because of lying through his teeth and flashing his FBI badge.

He wanted Trish to spend the night in the hospital.

She wanted to go home.

He'd stood firm until she'd looked up at him with the same determination he'd seen in her eyes when she'd put that glass of bourbon down. Then he'd caved, sending Heidi with Bunko to pack up their room and be ready to leave as soon as the doctor signed Trish out. Josh had someone from Slye to pack up his and Trish's rooms and deliver their things to the airport.

Every second dragged by, torturing him until he had her back.

I love you.

He couldn't breathe, thinking about what she'd done. Gambled her life to shove Gunter's weapon aside. *I would sacrifice all for the ones I love.* Her words played over and over in his mind. He swallowed, humbled by a love he hadn't earned and didn't deserve.

But wanted.

Sabrina came walking toward Josh with a purposeful stride and carrying a dark gray flannel shirt. Her gaze warned he was in for an earful, but when she reached him, she took a long look.

She tossed him the shirt. "My FBI contact is getting his ass chewed over having a covert FBI operative on a mission in Atlanta that his superiors were not aware of, but he's jockeying around to fix it. Lucky for you, he owes me. *I've* dealt with Atlanta PD."

What a mess. Josh yanked out his cufflinks and jammed them in his pants pocket, then shed his shirt and undershirt. Sabrina took those and handed them off to someone in the hall, probably to burn.

By the time she returned, he'd buttoned up and smelled better. He told her, "Thank you. For the shirt, too."

Sabrina was a volatile energy even standing still. Questions boiled in that Latin gaze and Josh owed her answers.

But not right now.

With a second look at him, the questions settled to a simmer. She sat down next to him. "Who was the kidnapper?"

Sabrina had been on hand when Josh answered questions for the police. She knew the general information about Gunter. What she was asking for had to do with the Slye case in Miami.

"He *was* stalking Trish, and she thinks he's the one who left the notes, but this guy isn't the Chessmaster. I wish it *was* Gunter, so we'd have the traitor. But as it is we don't even have a lead on the Chessmaster or Rikker." Before Sabrina could ask about Trish, Josh gave her the rest of his report. "Trish is not involved with the Chessmaster either. She has no clue what's going on with the DEA."

"What about her phone?"

"We never expected to be able to triangulate the calls since they were extremely short, but we put a tap on Trish's phone that should have yielded information. When Trish finally got a phone call from the Chessmaster, there was static interference preventing anyone from listening. Pretty high tech."

"We searched Gunter's room for the electronic filter and any other evidence. Nothing."

Josh thought on that. "I doubt he had the capability or the equipment to place that call, or to place the notes that were found inside Trish's home and her locked car. I think Trish has been stalked by two people." A chilling thought.

"That makes sense."

Josh dropped his head back. "We're screwed. We have no idea who the mole is or how to find Rikker."

"We *would* be screwed if I hadn't found out the last shipment came in this weekend on a container ship. The container's been cleared through customs."

Josh sat up. "How'd you find out?"

"My informant."

Fucking Gage Laughton, but Josh was too exhausted to rally any anger. Besides, how could he fault Sabrina when she was coming through with intel they had to have? He still wanted Rikker but finding the Chessmaster took precedence. No one was hurting Trish again. "What was in the container?"

"Boxes of medical equipment for a new High Vision lab. Ryder is spending tonight watching from a distance, far enough away that Rikker won't see him."

"You don't think someone from High Vision will claim the contents first?"

"My contact doesn't think so."

"And you trust him?" Josh didn't want to start an argument now, but he needed to know where she stood with the CIA. The only CIA agent Josh would've placed faith in at this minute was his uncle, but Ty was dead.

"Trust someone with that bloody agency? No. But we have nothing right now and every detail about the last shipment was spot on. If Ryder catches sight of Rikker anywhere around the container, that will confirm the intel."

Josh couldn't really argue with that. "Did he give us anything else?"

"Yes. He received a tip that whatever was planned would happen very soon, no specific timeline yet."

A weary young man in blue scrubs, with a head of scattered, short, brown hair came into the sitting area, then straight over to Josh and Sabrina who stood to meet him.

The doctor said, "Miss Jackson still wants to go home. I'll release her, but I don't want her doing anything strenuous for the next twenty-four hours."

Nothing strenuous, like fighting off an attacker. Josh told the doctor in a firm voice, "She won't be lifting a finger."

The doctor went over the usual processing procedure that would take another twenty minutes, then he shook hands with Josh and left.

Sabrina waited until it was just her and Josh again. "What are you going to do now?"

From anyone else, that was a simple question. From Sabrina, there were all kinds of land mines to dodge. "I'm taking Trish and her two friends back to Miami. I'll let Trish think Gunter was her stalker for now. If she gets another message, she'll tell me." *Because I won't be far from her.*

"You won't have any problem leaving her alone?"

"She has a housemate and a dog. Her brother will probably cover her up with security." Josh lifted his shoulders, doing his best to convince Sabrina he was taking all this in stride and not so eaten up with worry he couldn't think past getting Trish out of here right now. "I'll stay near Trish in case the Chessmaster contacts her again, but we'll need everyone mobile on short notice."

She took her time deciding, but finally said, "I agree." After a glance in the direction of where they had Trish, Sabrina said, "I'll send someone else to cover her, if you want."

Sabrina wasn't challenging him to admit he was too close to Trish and this case. She was offering personnel from her Slye teams to watch over Trish and give Josh peace of mind. He considered taking it, but then he'd have to explain who they were to Trish. Also, Sabrina's resources had to be available to get Rikker.

Josh said, "She's fine, but thanks."

Nodding, Sabrina lifted up and kissed his cheek. "I owe her for saving your sorry hide. I won't forget."

When Sabrina left, Josh returned Zane's call now that he had definitive news. Once Zane calmed down, Josh could hold the phone at his ear again without his eardrums getting abused.

"You're sure Trish is okay?" Zane said, for the tenth time.

"Shaken up, a few stitches, but relieved more than anything." Josh downplayed it for Trish's benefit. She'd be mad as a hornet if Josh upset her brother more than he already was.

"I don't know which one of you two I want to strangle right now. Since I love my sister, my first choice shouldn't be hard to figure out."

Josh thanked the gods he was nowhere near Miami this second since that hadn't sounded like an empty threat.

"However," Zane went on. "You've kept her alive. I find myself having to thank you. My wife would never forgive me if I wrapped your leg around your neck."

Thank you, Angel. "Trish is stubborn, independent, and hell-bent to run her own life. You of all people should understand that. You two are cut from the same cloth." Josh moved the phone from his ear, expecting a torrent of verbal abuse. When a deep sigh blew through, he eased the phone back to listen.

"True. Angel keeps telling me I'm not giving Trish room to breathe. Damn, I don't know what to do with her. I just can't lose her."

"Neither can I," Josh said. And he meant it.

Silence answered him for several seconds. He'd expected that to raise Zane's hackles as well. "Then take care of her."

Would wonders never cease? "I plan to."

Zane grunted. "Tell her to call me when she gets home."

Josh ended the call just as an orderly wheeled Trish into the room. The muscles in his chest tightened when he took in her pasty skin and the bandage around her neck.

She smiled up at him and his heart started beating again.

She's alive.

CHAPTER 43

Josh kept checking on Trish, who looked so alone sitting in the passenger seat of his Porsche. She'd slept most of the flight home, cuddled against his chest, and he missed the contact. When he parked at her house, she stayed without being told while he circled the car.

That was telling. She had Heidi and Bunko to stay with her and Zane had someone keeping surveillance on Trish's house. Should he call Sabrina back and accept her offer, too? If he did, he'd leave the team short. Trish would stress out if Zane showed up, since Angel's due date had come and gone.

Bunko had parked first in the drive and was carrying luggage inside, with Heidi pulling Trish's little bag.

Josh got Trish out of the car, and she planted herself in front of him like a barrier. Arms crossed. "What are you doing tonight?"

"This isn't about Leanne again, is it?"

She frowned at him. "No. Just tell me if you're going to be in any danger." Her eyes were shiny with banked tears.

Ah, hell. How would he be able to walk away if she cried? "Don't worry, sweetheart. You know I can't talk about any of this, but I'll be fine."

"You'd better be." She rubbed her nose and sniffled.

Walking away from Trish was getting more difficult–almost as much a test as seeing her lying on top of Gunter with blood covering her neck and chest. Josh's heart knotted at recalling that image.

She was fiercely loyal.

The woman had no concern for her own safety.

Had fought an insane killer to protect him. She deserved a man who would do no less for her. And he would, if he could stay with her every minute, but that was the problem. He didn't want to give up what he did.

Why had he thought he could make a life work with her? He couldn't closet her away somewhere safe and bring her out every time he wanted to be with her. Trish was life itself. She needed room to grow and spread her wings.

Around someone with a normal life.

And his would never be normal.

But she was his right now. He reached for her, and she dove into his arms. He held her heart-to-heart close and kissed her with something that felt more real than anything he'd ever experienced.

Was this love? He understood his parents' love for each other, but they shared everything. No secrets between them. Trish had asked Josh about his life, and he'd cloaked the truths in camouflage, just as he'd always vowed to do. *Had* to do to protect his parents from his enemies.

Trish hadn't said another word about love since she'd lain in his arms bleeding.

Shock had probably wiped the words from her mind.

But he had them tucked into a special corner of his heart where he could hear her say those three words over and over during the nights he would miss her once he left.

That would be every night he'd spend without her.

He ended the kiss, slowly lowering her to the ground. "I still don't like you flying again so soon after having stitches."

"I've dealt with much worse. I can fly in a few hours."

Hearing that didn't make it right or better. "Go inside and keep the doors locked. Zane has someone watching your house and Bunko said he was staying on the sofa tonight." Or Josh wouldn't be leaving.

She swallowed and pulled up that steel will of hers. "I'll call you when I land in Chicago tomorrow."

Josh had argued and argued about her leaving town, but she'd countered that she'd be covered up with security around the Senator. And she'd be home by the end of the day so the Senator would be able to film his segment for the television show tomorrow. Trish would be flying back with the Senator and his entourage, security and all.

Talking about it had taken a toll on her and Josh wanted her in bed and resting, so he'd given in. He'd contacted Detective

Vickers who'd been surprised to learn Gunter had confessed to killing Big Charlie, but glad that *Josh* had heard the confession so they could close that case.

Josh hadn't heard a word of it, but he believed Trish's version. Olivia Lackey had flown home early from the convention, but Detective Vickers had sent men to the Miami airport to arrest her for lying as Gunter's alibi.

Olivia would confirm Gunter's admission. She was no match for being interrogated by Vickers.

Trish was free and clear, but he didn't want her in Chicago when he couldn't join her. "I wish you would stay home tomorrow." *Today*. Monday was already here.

"Stop." She got that stubborn look. "Bunko and Heidi will be with me all the way to security at the airport. Dixon's people are meeting me when I arrive, and I'll be with him until I come back tomorrow night."

Sounded safe enough, but she wasn't seeing what Josh saw. She still had a bump from getting hit over the head and even if she wore a turtleneck to hide the neck bandage, she had another one covering the stitches under her chin. "I promised the doctor you'd take it easy."

"I'm not even packing luggage. I'm carrying my shoulder bag and a book. I seriously doubt that Senator Dixon or his people will let me do anything beyond talk to him." She gave him another smile meant to comfort him and joked, "Go do your top-secret work, but you better not come back with a scratch."

He should tell her the same thing. "Either I'll be at the airport to pick you up or Zane will."

"Oh, good Lord, he's rubbing off on you. I. Am. Fine."

She might say that, but her eyes still held a vulnerability that grabbed him by the throat. He kissed her again, worse than a teenager not wanting to leave his first heartthrob.

Trish felt like a first. And she definitely made his heart throb, along with other parts of him.

Josh waited until she was in the house, locked up tight, then climbed back into his car. He pushed the speed limits, anxious to find out what the team had and maybe even get back to Trish tonight.

Dingo and Ryder were in the hotel suite-turned-headquarters when Josh walked in. "What have you got?"

Ryder stood from where he'd been hunched over next to Dingo who sat in front of the laptop. When he turned to Josh, his roadmap eyes bled exhaustion. He told Josh, "I was on watch at the container at oh-four-hundred this morning–"

"Late taking your shift," Dingo groused.

"I explained that," Ryder said, cutting his eyes at Dingo with a promise for pain if Dingo brought that up again.

Josh would be the first to admit to not giving the FNG a fair shake, but no one slacked off and ran late on a Slye team. "Then explain it to me," he told Ryder who turned a black scowl on Josh.

"I was on time coming back from a meeting and had a flat with no spare. Someone stole it off my truck. Satisfied?"

"Did you call?"

"Couldn't. No signal where I was in the Everglades. I got lucky with a trucker who stopped to help me out with his radio, or I wouldn't have gotten rolling as fast as I did."

Dingo gave Josh a that's-his-story shrug.

Josh lacked the patience or desire to be diplomatic. He took in Ryder's bloodshot eyes again and asked, "Were alcohol and women involved?"

"Fuck. You." Ryder folded his arms, looking insulted and unwilling to defend himself further.

"Fuck *this*. You're Sabrina's problem, not mine. What'd you find out at the container storage?"

Ryder bumped up his glare to blistering. "Rikker. Maybe. So, while *you* were playing bodyguard, I was getting you a chance at the guy who I understand is at the top of Slye's Most Wanted List."

This was the problem with having a team that Josh hadn't hand selected. He ended up with Prick of the Month. "Go on."

"I was using IR binoculars and picked up body heat moving across the top of the containers. When the intruder got to the

High Vision box, he disappeared inside, then came back out with what looked like a couple of small boxes. Maybe three."

Josh swung to Dingo. "Thought we had someone inspect that container."

Dingo kept his eyes locked on the computer that had a mix of security screens on the monitor. "We did. Everything checked out as equipment for a lab."

"You want to hear this now or plan a lunch date?" Ryder asked.

Drawing a slow breath that Josh needed to hold his temper, he told Ryder, "Continue."

"There was no way to ID the intruder at that distance and in the dark, but he fit the build of Rikker, and he's clearly trained. He put the boxes in what must have been a watertight bag because I kept him in sight through the enclosed area until he reached his exit point at the end of a dock. The water."

"You *lost* him?"

"Do *you* have the ability to shift into Aquaman, or x-ray vision for someone underwater?" Ryder rubbed his eyes and blinked. "Nick was in the air, circling the zone on standby with a helo. He covered that area back and forth but never saw the guy surface. Still out there."

"*Fuck!*" Josh kicked a chair into the dining room table.

Still scanning the security feeds, Dingo lifted his index finger and launched into his TV announcer voice. "But wait, there's more. For just nine-ninety-nine you get a deluxe op that comes with a surprise gift."

Where was a good belt of scotch when Josh needed one? "*What?*"

Ryder's eyebrows rode high on his forehead. "You're testy for the only one getting any action on this job."

Sabrina would not have to deal with Ryder after all. Josh would take care of the FNG and dispose of the body. "You haven't seen testy. Drag this out another second and you'll find out that I passed testy hours ago."

Blowing out a gruff blast of air, Ryder rubbed his eyes again then pointed at a gray metal briefcase lying on the sofa. "That was inside the locked cab of my truck when I walked back, after Water Man disappeared. My truck has a custom security system that changes every time I lock it. Takes more than a common criminal to gain access."

Dingo muttered, "Maybe that's who got your spare tire."

Ryder sent him a death glare, then shook his head and continued the briefing as Josh walked over to the sofa. "All we did was open it. Haven't touched a thing inside."

Josh popped the catch and opened the case.

Inside was a small electronic tablet with a note on top that read: Engage the program. Track the boxes. Stop the test.

Two boots stepped into Josh's view. Ryder said, "That's convenient."

The last convenient tip had ended in the capture of Colbert and Salazar, both of whom were later murdered.

This convenient tip smelled like a trap, but it was their only lead for Rikker. If that's what this really was.

CHAPTER 44

"Everything is on schedule for today." The Chessmaster studied the Monday morning traffic moving through downtown Miami eight stories below and spoke into a new sat phone. Change was important when dealing with jackals. "Your man must be ready no later than sixteen hundred hours."

The General stated, "He will be. He needs twenty minutes to construct the unit and have it ready to activate. Are you sure your timeline is firm?"

"Yes. Even if it changes, we'll still have several hours of notice."

"High Vision wants to resume shipping next week," The General ordered in his get-it-done voice.

"Not a problem."

The General had the misguided notion that he was in control of the Miami project. Once the unit was successfully tested, the Chessmaster would step from the minor leagues into major league power. All The General wanted was to appease an associate with a new weapon.

The Chessmaster had far greater aspirations. Knocking The General off his arrogant pedestal would be a personal pleasure, but he had to be kept content in the meantime.

"I want the problem solved in Miami *tonight*," The General reiterated with more force.

"I've told you it *will* be. You're the one who cautioned me against doing anything drastic in the beginning or this would have been handled sooner. My way."

Not true. The Chessmaster had enjoyed putting Trish Jackson through torture for drawing Zane's attention to Colbert when she'd schmoozed Colbert at the holiday party. Then Colbert went sniffing after Zane's sister. Idiot. If he hadn't started thinking with his dick, he'd still be alive and running interference for the Chessmaster.

The General was getting *nothing* until the weapon his man was constructing functioned successfully.

"What *is* your way?"

"I'm loading evidence into the task force computers that will have to be found by specialists so that it doesn't appear planted. But they'll go looking as soon as they receive a tip after tonight's disaster. If your unit does its job, I'll do mine, then Zane Jackson and his two friends in the DEA will land in adjoining prison cells."

"What about his sister?"

"She'll be onboard for the test." Literally.

As soon as Trish was out of the way, Zane would be arrested for his role in her death, based on ghost information a forensic computer tech would discover. That would lead the tech to investigate everyone Zane was close to, starting with Ben and Vance, who would be fingered for their roles in killing a US Senator.

Josh Robertson *might* disappear before he got his due. A hardened agent would, but he'd followed the Jackson bitch to Atlanta. From all signs, Robertson had made the unforgivable mistake for anyone in his line of work. He'd gotten personally involved.

The Chessmaster hoped that was case, and that Robertson showed up during the test. Neutralizing him in the ensuing chaos would be a breeze.

The General only *wished* he could strategize at the Chessmaster's level. This time tomorrow, High Vision would have what they wanted. The General would have what he wanted.

And the Chessmaster would show the Orion Hunters exactly who held the power in this country.

CHAPTER 45

I can't take another minute of this.

If Trish had to smile at one more person, her face muscles were going to lock up until she looked like Batman's Joker.

Not that she wasn't thrilled to be alive after last night, or that she didn't appreciate the attention from Senator Dixon's staff, but her face hurt. She blamed it on being tired.

Mentally. Physically. Emotionally.

Yeah, especially that last one.

Close-up, full-color views of death had taken their toll. She'd been repeating her AA mantras constantly. One day at a time. Easy does it. Breathe.

Big Charlie was dead. Gunter was dead.

She could've been dead, and would've if it hadn't been for Josh. Which was why she shouldn't be complaining about her good fortune now even if she had been showing her pearly whites all day since arriving just after eight this morning, with only two hours' sleep.

Smiling was a small price to pay, really, after Senator Dixon had flown her up to Chicago in first class and she'd been given the royal treatment when she landed. She'd had no idea what a hectic pace a senator maintained and felt a little guilty for asking him to do the *Treasured Past* television show, but not guilty enough to cancel.

Dixon's campaign manager *had* clarified that there was no way Dixon could have made this commitment if a trip to France hadn't been canceled at the last minute.

That had freed up two days.

"Would you like some coffee, Miss Jackson?" Lawrence asked, dropping back from the cluster surrounding Dixon as he made long strides toward their gate.

Trish smiled at the senator's personal assistant who was joining her, Dixon, and three more of his staff on this flight.

"No thanks." She eyed the Starbucks with lust as they passed the airport stand, but Lawrence would have to slow the whole entourage down to get coffee for her when they were cutting it close to make this earlier flight. The Senator had someone he wanted to meet while he was in Miami. Tonight was the only time he had available.

Tilting her chin down to hide the bandage, she tried to avoid the people taking photographs. Some called out to the senator and waved.

His constituents seemed to like him, and Trish liked him now, but it had taken all day for her to warm up to him. Leanne had been right about Dixon. He had an engaging persona when he stood at a podium, but in an intimate setting he did come across as aloof.

When she reached the gate, the flight was already boarding. A group of at least fifteen women were dressed for fun in the sun wearing shorts, Hawaiian shirts, sandals and crazy hats. Additionally, each one had a matching scarf with a logo for a children's literacy foundation.

Trish recalled a conference going on in north Miami this week that had to do with literacy. She bet that's where they were headed and in spite of her aching jaw, she smiled at the way they were cutting up with each other.

Several recognized Dixon, who clicked his robotic, obligatory smile into place and spoke politely, wishing them a good trip. Minimal interaction.

Trish thought he could do more.

Not that her opinion mattered when he had plenty of skilled handlers who knew way more than she did about how he should handle his constituents.

Onboard, she was surprised to find herself seated next to the senator in the middle of his entourage, and waited until they had taken off to say, "Thank you for letting me sit with you going back, and for doing this television show, Senator Dixon."

He gifted her with a genuine smile, filled with warmth. "I enjoyed today, too, and when we're away from all the hoopla you can call me Ron."

This man probably lived in a fishbowl existence of nonstop hoopla. "This will be a tremendous help for my business and for the television show, but I hope you enjoy some satisfaction as well."

"Oh, I will. Donating proceeds from this to the local women's shelter you suggested is valuable to me. Plus, the publicity they'll receive."

"This will help you connect more with the female voters, right?"

Ron stared at his hands a moment and said, "That's always important in politics, but I've supported shelters like the one in Miami for a long time. It's been a private endeavor."

"I'll admit that I've read a few articles, so I'd feel a little familiar with you."

"Did they help?" His easy smile teased her.

"Not really. I feel like I met the real Ron Dixon today. I'm glad you support the shelters. Why don't you mention it in interviews?"

"Because of my mother. If not for a shelter like that one, she wouldn't have survived when she ran from an abusive man to protect me. She's close to ninety and doesn't understand that women today would be as proud of her as I am. She feels humiliated by that time in her life and doesn't want it discussed."

Trish felt a deep admiration for this man who was not using a personal strife to further his career. "Can I ask you something?"

"Sure."

"I know zip about politics, but why didn't you take advantage of campaigning a little with that group of women that got on this flight?"

"Some people would take offense at being bothered on vacation."

"I don't think they're on vacation. I'm pretty sure they're headed to a conference in Miami. They were all wearing scarves that supported childhood literacy."

"Really?" He seemed genuinely surprised to have missed that about the women.

"You could always take a walk down the aisle and say

hello."

He didn't say anything, but she could tell that might be more activity than he wanted on this flight.

The flight attendant's next announcement instructed everyone to shut down electronics in preparation for takeoff and that this flight would arrive on time in Miami at twenty minutes after six this evening.

"I'm going to catch the devil," Trish mumbled, pulling out her book when Dixon turned his tablet off.

He asked, "Why?"

"I forgot to call home to tell them we were taking an earlier flight. After all that's happened this week, my family is smothering me and thinks I can't take a cab from the airport."

"You certainly will not take a cab. I'll have my driver drop you."

"Thank you." She still should have contacted Heidi to let her know Trish would arrive close to seven tonight instead of after nine.

But she'd be extremely safe riding with a senator.

Trish just wished she'd had a moment to herself today to call Josh. Did he miss her? Would he come by tonight?

Or would he finish up his investigation and just disappear from her world forever? Zane had once told her how some undercover operatives spent years gone.

Had that been why Josh never acknowledged her words after she'd left the hospital? Maybe he didn't want a woman saying she loved him.

Whether he wanted her to or not, she did love him.

Enough to not make him admit he'd heard her and to let him go when the time came.

He'd said either he or Zane would pick her up at the airport. She might just pass on the senator's generous offer if she could reach Josh by phone.

CHAPTER 46

Josh sat at the dining room table in the team hotel suite, trying to keep his attention on the six-inch wide electronic unit mounted inside the briefcase.

Wondering why he hadn't heard from Trish all day.

Wondering if her neck was bothering her.

Or if she missed him.

He'd gotten confirmation that she'd arrived and was met by Senator Dixon's staff, which included security. She was safe. Josh had to believe that, or he couldn't function.

He still had to decide what he was going to do if this monitor in front of him started receiving a signal.

Would it lead his team into a trap?

Or would an attack happen while he sat here staring at a static map of Miami? The map had appeared as soon as he opened a program that was unlike any he'd seen before.

And he'd seen plenty.

He wanted to dig into the backside of this program and see what he could find, but the risk of hitting a hidden oh-shit electronic tripwire set to destroy the software was not worth the gamble.

Sadly, this represented their only chance at finding Rikker.

"What time is it?" Ryder asked the room in general when he walked in looking marginally rested and as if he'd slept in his clothes. Probably had. Combat naps.

"Seventeen-forty-eight," Dingo answered, but he was no longer tied to the laptop. Ready to move out the minute they had a target, the Aussie had on his dark cargo pants and a brown long-sleeved T-shirt over a body shaped by weights and rowing. Nick released constant sighs from taking his turn studying the security camera feeds on the laptop monitor. No one had gotten twitchy or acted suspicious in the task force offices so far.

Ryder crossed the room to Josh. "Nothing yet?"

"No." Josh stood. "Your turn."

Ryder sat down and turned the briefcase toward him. "The purpose of this briefcase might be simply to keep us out of the way."

"I know."

"Or a map to a trap."

"I. Know."

"Could be–"

Josh grabbed his forehead to keep from strangling Ryder, who had thankfully fallen silent. Then the FNG muttered, "Shit."

Jerking his hand away, Josh looked down where a light had begun blinking. "That's near the Miami airport."

Trish was flying in tonight, but not until closer to ten. This whole thing could be a scam to divert the attention of Josh's team, which would mean someone knew he and Ryder were not agency people. Or maybe this had been sent for the DEA.

Hell, he wasn't freaking clairvoyant. It came down to a fifty-fifty chance that this could hand him Rikker or kill everyone on his team.

Standing up, Ryder said, "Decision time. What's it going to be?"

CHAPTER 47

Rikker carefully unpacked each of the three boxes, following explicit instructions on where to cut the packing tape and which flap to open in specific order.

He carefully integrated each of the three pieces with his base unit. With the exception of those parts shipped in the High Vision container, everything else he'd needed had been easy to acquire.

With the sliding glass doors to the patio open, he could hear the low roar of jets passing overhead on the way to landing at Miami International. Some developer had practically stolen the land for this neighborhood, then built decent two-story homes, figuring families would deal with a little noise in exchange for a bigger house than they could normally afford.

That's what the listing realtor had said, all pleasant and bubbly until Rikker had sliced her throat.

The real selling points on this house for Rikker had been the extra-high privacy fence and deep back yard.

He couldn't wait to finish assembling this unit and take it outside.

Weather was perfect. He'd have a straight shot to Flight 819 on approach in twelve minutes.

CHAPTER 48

"Might have to shut down the airport," Josh told Sabrina through his Bluetooth. He spun the wheel on his Porsche, taking a sharp left.

Ryder rode shotgun with the briefcase open on his lap.

"Can't do that without a clear threat," Sabrina said. "What if we send people fleeing and that's exactly what someone wants?"

The two right tires lifted a few inches then dropped down. Josh whipped between two cars, passing through with no more than a hand's width of clearance. "I didn't say we should do it yet, but it's on the table. See if you can get someone in the tower. I sent Nick for now."

"He'll get in."

"Maybe." Or he'd start a riot. Never knew with Nick.

"Call you back."

Ryder dictated another turn to watch for.

Josh slowed enough this time to keep all four wheels on the pavement.

Dingo flew overhead in a helo. His voice came through Josh's commo unit. "I have eyes on you."

"Copy that," Josh answered, in communication with Dingo and the other two by radio. The minute Josh and Ryder confirmed whether this "test" was definitely a threat and not some hoax, Josh would alert Nick who would rally airport security.

If they didn't arrest him.

Nick had a tendency to bring out the wrong kind of reaction from law enforcement.

"ETA?" Sabrina asked when she called back on Josh's cell phone.

Josh said, "Ryder?"

Eyes locked on the small monitor, Ryder said, "ETA five minutes."

Josh relayed that information then told Sabrina, "You find

someone with the FAA to get Nick in that tower."

"I've got someone with better resources working on it."

Just the way she said that told Josh she was talking about Gage. "This op has FUBAR stamped on it already. Think involving the agency is a good idea?"

"He was right about the container and Rikker picking up the packages," she tossed back, confirming Josh's guess about Gage.

With the team hearing Josh's side of the conversation and Dingo knowing what Josh meant by the reference to *agency*, Dingo spoke up. "I don't like it none better, mate, but we don't have many choices left now do we?"

True. Josh told Sabrina, "He fucks us over again, I'm going after him."

"You won't have to."

"Slow down," Ryder said, putting his phone away and focusing on the briefcase.

Josh ended the phone call and eased his car down to forty miles an hour. He kept slowing as Ryder gave him directions into what looked like an attractive middle-class neighborhood.

"One of those houses down on the right."

Josh pulled to the curb. It was just after six, the dinner hour in many neighborhoods like this one. Older homes, but well maintained. A few kids and dogs played in yards and along the street. Real estate signs poked out of three yards. "You sure this is right?"

"This is where the signal is coming from. I'm betting it's that house with the realtor's "For Sale" sign. Fifth one down on the right."

Hell of a place to run an attack out of, so maybe this was only a hoax. Josh told Ryder, "We walk down to the house. You cover the front. I'll insert through the back."

Ryder did a weapon check and reached for a lightweight black jacket in the backseat.

Josh had the flannel shirt Sabrina had given him at the hospital to cover his weapon. The shirt made him think of Trish, who he couldn't be thinking about right now.

I love you. She deserved someone to love.

Not a man who had lived so long in the dark that he would extinguish the light around her.

He hadn't been happy about her going to Chicago, but with this new development around the airport he was glad she wasn't arriving for another three hours. If he didn't have answers by the time she called to say she was leaving, he would either convince her to stay there or have security pull her aside.

She was not coming near this airport until he knew it was safe.

When they headed down the sidewalk, Ryder grumbled, "Kids everywhere. They keep popping out from behind bushes and cars. Fucking nightmare if we have a situation in that house."

Josh agreed but had no words of advice beyond protect the civilians at all costs. Nothing Ryder had to be told with his military training.

At the corner of the yard with the realtor sign, Josh peeled off from Ryder, walking as if he were considering the house. Ryder took the front walk, easing up to the windows to look in. He gave Josh a shake of his head. Nothing obvious.

Josh continued around the house to the tall privacy fence that surrounded the back yard. In his ear bud, he heard Nick's voice. "I'm in the tower, but I may need help getting out. All clear right now."

That didn't sound good.

Since Ryder would know Josh couldn't make a sound right now, Ryder answered softly. "Copy."

Jet engines rumbled overhead with incoming flights.

Josh peeked through a crack in the wood fence. He could see a figure squatted in the back yard, focused on something his body shielded from Josh.

Nick's voice boomed in Josh's ear. "A flight on approach is having major electrical problems. The pilots say the plane is losing control. The engines are powering down."

At that moment, the figure in the yard turned enough for Josh to ID him. Rikker. Josh drew his weapon.

He tested the latch on the wooden gate. Unlocked. He opened it and stepped into the yard, wanting to kill the bastard, but he had a duty. "Get away from whatever that is, Rikker."

The former CIA agent glanced calmly over his shoulder while he kept his hand on the strangest looking mechanical device Josh had ever seen. "Hello, Carrington. Willing to risk killing millions by shooting me?"

Was it a fucking bomb or what? "Get up."

"Blood's on your head. I'm moving slowly." Rikker kept a hand on the backside of the unit as if he couldn't let go. "If I move my hand, everything goes boom."

Shoot him? Knock his hand loose? Would either of those choices kill people?

Josh told Ryder, "Keep the front covered." He walked over to see if Rikker pressed a button.

Rikker used that moment to yank up a hand that held a 9mm Browning Hi-Power. Josh dove away, rolling and firing up at Rikker to keep from sending a stray bullet into the next yard.

Kids screamed out front.

Rikker dove away, too, and he was up on his feet as quickly as Josh, but Josh got a kick in that sent Rikker's weapon flying. Rikker made a counter move that knocked Josh's away.

At least that should take care of any stray bullets.

"The airplane is on a collision course," Nick said in the ear bud, pounding the words in a low voice. "They say something is screwing with the plane's electrical system. Won't be able to control the landing. Six minutes."

Rikker was throwing chops and hits.

Josh deflected, hit, jabbed, and kicked, knocking Rikker back.

"Stop whatever the fuck is killing that airplane!" Nick shouted this time.

"Getting there," Josh snapped and took a hit to his back. He spun and dove at Rikker. Shooting him would be so much easier, but Josh couldn't put a personal vendetta ahead of the lives of millions and he needed Rikker to stop that damn machine.

"We got company out front," Ryder said, calm but tense.

Rikker collided with Josh, slamming hits against his ribs. They hit the ground and Rikker came up with a decorative rock he bashed against Josh's temple.

Stars burst behind his eyes. Josh shoved up, but that had given Rikker the extra second he'd needed to escape.

Josh grabbed his weapon and started after Rikker.

"*The fucking plane is going to crash!*" screamed in his ear bud.

"Eight men out front with an armored truck...no open shot," Ryder called through the ear bud. "Fuck, fuck a *fucking* duck! Rikker grabbed a kid to shield himself to the van ... Dropped the kid. He's gone."

"*Four minutes,*" Nick yelled.

Josh roared and unloaded a full magazine of 9mm hollow point rounds into the mechanical device that popped and squealed, then stopped making any noise.

Ryder came running into the yard. He looked at the gut-shot machine and shook his head. "Remind me to never go on bomb detail with you."

The machine started ticking.

They both dove for the exit just as it exploded.

CHAPTER 49

Josh spit dirt out of his mouth and looked over at Ryder. "You okay?"

"Yep. You?"

Nodding, Josh pushed up and turned to see what had happened. Not a bomb, but the unit had self-destructed.

"Flight 819 has power coming back on," Nick said, updating them. "But the pilots are warning the tower to clear everything they can. They may crash yet."

Josh looked up to see a jet wobbling overhead with lights flashing on and off. *Fuck. Don't crash.*

Ryder stepped up. "I called Sabrina on my way back here. She's got a cleanup crew on the way."

Josh kept watching that big chunk of steel lumber its way toward the airport. "You tell her we lost Rikker?"

"Yes. She said we'll get him."

That's what Sabrina had said two years ago. She had to be disappointed. Josh was gutted over having Rikker in his hands and losing him. Nothing to be done right now.

Josh looked at the melting machine. "What the hell could that be?"

Ryder studied it and looked up at the flight that was still coming down crooked and faster now. "A laser unit of some sort?"

Josh's phone buzzed. He pulled it out, his eyes glued to the plane as it wobbled. He felt sick. That jet was going to crash. He hadn't killed this machine fast enough.

When he glanced at his phone all the blood drained from his head. Heidi had sent the message:

Trish caught early flight 819. Can't get there in time. Can u?

The airplane hit the ground with a boom and metallic noise that went on and on.

Nick shouted something about it crashing, but Josh couldn't hear past the roar of blood pounding in his ears.

Trish was on that flight.

CHAPTER 50

"You can't go running in there," Sabrina yelled at Josh through the speaker on Ryder's cell phone.

"They let me in or I'm going through them," Josh shouted back at her. He punched the accelerator on his Porsche, taking every corner on two wheels, only slowing when he reached the airport terminal.

"You said you could do this and not get involved again."

"Not the time, Sabrina."

He whipped his car to the curb next to where passengers were dropped off. Sabrina was still barking orders at him when Josh and Ryder jumped out of the car. Josh spared a second to tell Ryder, "This isn't Slye business, and I may land in jail over it."

Ryder ended the call, "I'll have someone to play cards with."

Josh took off at a dead run with Ryder keeping pace.

Someone yelled about his car, but he was already inside the glass doors and rushing past passengers unaware that a plane had just crashed. At security, he flashed his FBI badge, shouting that there was a "situation" he'd been called in for.

But he wasn't making any sense.

Ryder stepped in, calmly showing his DEA badge and in seconds he had Josh pushed through. When Josh turned, Ryder yelled, "Go. I got this."

Damn, he owed the FNG. Josh raced through the terminal, looking out the windows where a plane rested off the side of the runway. The nose had broken open and part of a wing was missing.

Sirens screamed along the runway, racing toward the airplane.

Ryder and Nick were talking in his ear bud, but Josh didn't catch it until Nick said, "Did you hear me, Josh?"

"What?"

Nick told him where to meet him to get out to the tarmac.

Josh made several turns and met up with Nick who raced alongside him, yelling instructions and using his FAA badge–*where had that come from?*–to get them finally outside.

Holy shit, there was a huge crack in the first-class cabin where Trish would have been flying.

Josh forced his knees not to buckle and kept moving.

Emergency vehicles were everywhere. Foam was being sprayed.

Nick held his ear and muttered, "No word on casualties."

Passengers were sliding out of an exit. A female flight attendant and an older guy were helping passengers slide out. Josh's heart thudded against his breastbone. He was frantic to get inside there and find Trish.

He tried pushing past emergency personnel but got shoved back. "*Trish!*"

Nick put his hand on Josh's arm. "We'll get–"

Josh roared, "*Trish!*"

He saw a gap and raced forward, hunting an emergency ladder, any way into that airplane. Ground crews were shouting to get back.

Nick caught up to him and said, "There's a bit of luck."

"What?"

"Senator Dixon was on this flight. Everyone thinks it was a terrorist attack to get him."

"Dixon. Where?"

"The old guy helping those women onto the slide."

That's when Josh really looked at the dark-haired flight attendant giving a hand to passengers. She had wild black curls. She looked over at that moment and saw him.

The old guy said something to her, and she nodded, then stepped out to slide down.

Josh caught her at the bottom, grabbing her into his arms. She was shaking, but dammit she was alive. He clutched her to him, kissing her face, her hair. Anywhere he could touch her.

Tears soaked his shirt. She gripped his back.

People kept coming down the slide.

Josh moved Trish out of the way, so no one fell into her.

She lifted her head. "I should help."

"You've done enough. I want you out of here."

"They're not going to let me just walk away."

The hell they wouldn't. "I'll tell them you're in my custody."

"I'm going to end up with a rap sheet if this keeps up," she muttered.

Josh turned to Nick, who was watching him with a curious smirk. Nick glanced around, then his low voice came through Josh's ear bud. "Go on and get her out of here before she can't leave."

Josh whispered, "Thanks." He guided Trish away, but she made him stop. "What's wrong?"

She turned around. "I don't want to leave Ron."

The jealousy that slammed Josh came out of nowhere and practically blinded him. "Who the fuck is Ron?"

Cocking her head at him with a surprised look, she said, "Senator Ronald Dixon. Told me I could call him Ron."

He was losing his freaking mind. "Sorry, sweetheart."

Her knowing look said she'd figured out what had caused that. She gazed over at the plane. "He looks fine, and everyone is fussing around him. I tried to get him to leave, but he wouldn't. Not until all the others were out."

"He'll get a hell of a media event out of it."

"Yes, he will. I'll talk to him tomorrow."

Josh pulled her up against him. "I want you out of here now. I've had all I can take of watching you almost die."

She reached up and grabbed the collar of his shirt, pulling him down. He kissed her, pulling her hard against him.

His phone vibrated with someone trying to reach him.

Chaos raced around them, but nothing mattered except the steady beat of her heart against his chest. He finally slowed the kiss and held her more carefully. She still wore bandages and had been through a plane crash for God's sake.

When he lifted his head, he brushed his thumb over her damp cheeks. "I thought I'd lost you."

Trish looked up into his eyes, her beautiful brown ones full of so much love he didn't deserve. "I'm not going anywhere."

He put his palm against her cheek and dropped his forehead gently against hers.

His phone was vibrating over and over.

She whispered, "You better answer that. You might need to save the world or something."

Without letting go of her, he lifted his phone into view. "Your brother sent me a text."

Her fingers tightened on his shirt. "Does he know about this yet?"

"No, but it's not going to take long." Josh stroked her hair as he finished reading. "He wants me to come into the office. Has something important to show me on the mole. Must be on the computer. Wants to know if I'm picking you up from the airport because Heidi sent him a message, too, that you were taking an early flight."

"Don't tell him until I get home. I don't want to deal with my brother upset right now. I just want to go home."

"I don't want you alone." Josh typed a text.

"Heidi will meet us there."

Josh thumbed a message back to Zane that he was at the airport picking up Trish to take home, and he wanted protection at her house.

Zane sent back that Leanne should be in the area. She had a meeting near the airport. Zane said he'd ask her to take Trish home so Josh could come in now.

Must be extremely important.

Once the phone messages had been handled, Josh walked Trish through the terminal against the tide of hysterical passengers trying to figure out what had happened or why all the flights had been canceled all of a sudden.

When they reached baggage claim, Leanne came rushing up to hug Trish. "Are you all right?"

"Shaky, but I'll make it, Sug."

"What about Senator Dixon?"

"He's fine. He'll be a hero by tonight."

Leanne nodded and hugged Trish again. "Let's get you

home."

Josh pulled Trish into a long, hot kiss. He didn't want to give her up, but she needed to get out of here. If the goal had been to crash an entire airplane and kill all the passengers, plus any others if the airplane had fallen outside of the airport, Trish might be retaliated against as if this were her fault.

With the Chessmaster, who knew?

Trish held his face and kissed his chin. "I'll wait up for you."

Leanne said, "I left my car on the curb, but we need to go. They were towing a Porsche that looked a lot like yours, Josh."

He slapped his forehead.

Ryder walked up in time to hear Leanne's announcement. "No problem. Nick drove my truck here instead of his rental."

Josh followed Leanne and Trish, watching until Trish climbed into Leanne's four-door Lexus and drove away. His phone rang and it was Heidi. When he answered, Heidi started yelling before he got a word in.

"Was Trish on that flight? Zane is going apeshit and so am I."

Josh tried to calm her down. "Trish was on the flight, but she's safe. I just sent a text to Zane."

"You couldn't have."

"Why not?"

"Zane can't find his phone. It's been missing for almost an hour. Angel went into labor. He's losing his mind over Trish and Angel both."

"Where is he?"

"The hospital."

"The hospital?" Josh looked at Ryder and they stared in the direction that Leanne had just driven off.

Ryder pointed. "Truck."

Josh raced right behind him and told Heidi. "Stay away from home and don't tell Zane anything, Heidi."

"Why?"

"Because I think the person who's been stalking Trish just drove away from the airport with her. I don't want anyone to spook her kidnapper and cause her to harm Trish."

Josh stuffed the phone in his pocket and jumped in on the passenger side of Ryder's truck while it was backing out and taking off. "I have no idea where Leanne is headed."

"I do."

"How would *you* know?"

"While you were following Trish around, I put tracking devices on everyone's vehicles. Even yours, but we need my laptop from the hotel suite."

CHAPTER 51

Chatton enjoyed the breeze that ruffled her hair as it blew past the outdoor café in Milan. She made a point of smiling for the paparazzi that followed an international car racer from Belgium. Today she was Sassone, a French model on the arm of the sexy driver.

The General and Wayan would be watching this live news feed. She'd told them to watch the telly last night and today if they wanted proof she was nowhere near the US.

She'd attended highly publicized events since arriving. Easy to do with a celebrity like the one she'd entertained last night. All night. She had no doubt that, since she'd arrived, she'd been under surveillance by The General, Wayan, or both.

Neither could blame her for the failed test that ended with a US Senator being hailed a hero.

She hadn't opened the three boxes. The General's man who'd constructed the laser unit wouldn't have noticed the meticulous job she'd done of loosening the two-finger wide, corded strapping tape. She'd sliced out tiny strips of cording and replaced each one with a paper-thin, quarter-inch strip of electronics, conformed to fit the ridges of the tape.

Once activated by a cut through the hair-like wires running through the tape, the tiny electronic piece acted as an EPIRB, an emergency tracking beacon. She'd inserted a continuous piece of wire under the edge of the tape that circled each box. It was amazing what a skilled person could do while inside a container at sea.

But the attack on Flight 819 had been only a test. What was Wayan *really* planning to do with a laser unit like that? And why had The General arranged for the test to be on US soil?

She did enjoy a worthy challenge as much as she loved a good puzzle.

CHAPTER 52

At Leanne's insistence that she rest on the drive home, Trish unclipped her seatbelt and laid her head back. Yes, she was breaking the law, but she trusted Leanne to drive her a few miles. After surviving a plane crash, she'd take her chances for a moment of comfort. She closed her eyes and felt herself dropping right off to sleep.

She rolled her head to one side and came awake, looking out at the dark night flying past her window. Not her neighborhood, where they should've been well before dark.

Trish shook off the groggy feeling and sat up, looking around. Not a light in sight except for a pair of headlights coming from the other direction, then gone as the car passed them. "Where are we?"

"Headed to Naples."

That meant they were traveling west ... through ... Alligator Alley? Trish looked to her right. The headlight glow bled over the shoulder of the road where the land dropped off into wide canals. The ditches on each side were deep. Cars that ran off the highway here sometimes sank into the murky water, and the people were never found. The place was full of snakes, alligators, and scorpions.

She might be tired, but this had "screwed up" written all over it.

She turned to Leanne. *Ah, shit.* Leanne had a gun in her left hand, resting in her lap and pointed at Trish.

"Just sit back and we'll be there soon," Leanne said.

She was awfully perky to be holding another person at gunpoint. "What in the Sam Hill is going on?"

"I'm taking you to trade with a man who will fix the mess you made today."

That made zero sense. Was Leanne serious? "I didn't do *anything* today. I was in a freaking plane crash and your dad's friend might not be alive if I hadn't convinced him to go to the back of the plane and visit a group of convention women."

Leanne's head should have spun around a few times because her next words sounded possessed. "He was *supposed* to die in that crash, you interfering idiot. So were *you*."

Woops. Trish took a moment to process that. "I thought we were friends."

Leanne snickered at that. "You're so far beneath me intellectually, it was a strain to talk to you every time you showed up at the office. If not for you, Colbert would still be alive."

"Colbert?" Trish backtracked mentally for a few seconds and the truth sank in. "*You're* the mole in the task force."

"Look at *yoouuu*. You didn't even have to buy a vowel to figure that out, but what about the chess references?"

The black rook. References to being a pawn. "You're the stalker?"

"What? Please tell me you never thought that German moron had the ability to mount a stalking campaign like that. I'll really be insulted."

"The chess piece and the electronic voice wasn't Gunter," Trish marveled out loud. So, Gunter had become Pruneface only to irritate her, but he'd also tried to cut her throat. And now Leanne with a gun. How in blazes had she landed on everyone's hit list?

"You're not going to spend the next hour whining, are you?" Leanne dimmed her lights for an oncoming car, then flicked back to bright. *She stalks and kills innocent people but is a considerate driver.* Leanne sent a smirk Trish's way. "You should appreciate all the benefit you got from this."

"I might need a vowel to understand what you're talking about by *benefit*."

"The television show?" Leanne cocked an eyebrow when she cut her eyes at Trish again, then went back to watching the road. "Who do you think had an Amber Room panel for the show, huh? Think something that rare from the fifteenth century just walks through the door every day?"

Leanne had told Trish about the show and nudged her to try out. She'd been pulling strings and manipulating Trish from behind the scenes the entire time. "Is that panel even real?"

"Yes, it's real. It's not the one the Czarion are searching for, but it's from the original Amber Room. It's been in my family for many generations. Cost me a small fortune to get it brought here."

"What's Czarion?"

"No one you'll ever meet."

Trish glanced around the car, familiarizing herself with the interior for when she had a chance to escape.

Leanne sighed and spoke as if she were instructing Trish. "If you're going to try to escape, you shouldn't be obvious about it. Need I remind you that I'm a fully trained DEA agent? I can take down a man twice my size. I wouldn't even have to muss my hair to deal with you."

Trish was sick of being insulted, terrorized, and reduced to the level of a victim. "If you're so smart, why did you need me to help you kill Dixon? What'd he ever do to you?"

"See, that's how simple you think. As if everything revolves around liking and hating or being angry or hurt. I cared about Dixon. He was like an uncle to me."

Trish would hate to see what Leanne did to people she didn't like. Her gaze strayed to the gun in Leanne's lap.

Oh, wait. That's right. She didn't like *Trish.*

Got it.

So much for having good instincts. But Josh had said even the best instincts could be fooled by a trained operative.

"Dixon was genuine, intelligent, and a great chess mentor," Leanne said as though taking a mental stroll down memory lane. "I have him to thank for my love of the game." She smiled. And in the next second her face twisted with fury, then smoothed out in a chilling calm, the kind Trish imagined would be on the face of an imprisoned serial killer with no remorse. "But later this year he intends to announce his candidacy for president. With him out of the way in a tragic plane crash, the path would have been open for my father to be the leading candidate in their party."

Oh. My. God. This was about putting her father in the White House.

"How could your father kill people for a political position?"

"My father has nothing to do with this. He's the most honorable man in this country."

If that was true, clearly it didn't pass through to the next generation.

Leanne's voice could ice over a fire. "Say another word about him and you'll make this trip in pain."

"My mistake." Leanne was behind all of this? She could claim she was doing it for her father, but people like Leanne were self-serving. She must imagine herself as the first daughter who would reign like a first lady.

How many would she kill to get what she wanted?

Trish kept her tone non-combative with a touch of worry, hoping to keep Leanne talking. "How was this going to work?"

Evidently appeased for the moment, Leanne returned to lecture drone. "Once Dixon died, my father would have led the memorial for him and the investigation into the plane crash. That would have played well in the media."

"Weren't you concerned about getting caught in the investigation?"

Leanne spared her a look that questioned Trish's ability to find her way out of a room with one door. "Not when all the evidence they'll find on this terrorist attempt will indict your brother, Ben, and Vance."

"What?" Trish leaned toward her.

Leanne shoved the gun across her lap. "I really want to kill you. If not for the value of handing you over to a man far more ruthless than I am, you'd already be dead. Don't give me a reason to change my mind."

Trish eased back in her seat. She had to stop Leanne from putting the blame for that crash on Zane, Ben, and Vance. "How are you going to blame Zane? He isn't even a DEA agent."

Leanne's sigh sounded as though she indulged a child. "The DEA already has an email from Zane's computer that had a cryptic reference to Colbert and his drug runner connections. It was beautifully done, if I do say so myself, so that once they start investigating this crash and find evidence of Zane and his cohorts communicating covertly about it, the DEA will start digging deeper and find a few more buried electronic treasures. All it will take is a few clicks once I get home from dropping you off."

Holy crap. What kind of crazy did it take to do all of this? Trish had no idea, but she did know one thing.

She could not let Leanne get back to a computer.

Trish's heart banged against her chest as hard and fast as she'd pounded that heavy bag at the hotel. Leanne was trained.

So was Trish.

But Leanne was DEA trained and had a weapon.

Tough shit. Trish was Arnie trained and capable of going for the throat of anyone threatening her family. *What would Arnie tell me to do?* Use everything at her disposal.

Starting with her brain.

Trish made her left hand tremble.

Leanne's eyes whipped over at the movement then up at Trish's face that crumbled, lip quivering. Trish slowly lifted her shaking hand to her lips, moaning, "What am I going to do?"

"Pitiful." Leanne chuckled, moving her attention back to the highway and shaking her head.

The minute Leanne tilted her head to the left to glance at the side mirror, Trish made her move. She lunged, shoving the weapon toward the dash with her left hand as she used her right hand to wrench the steering wheel and yanked it hard to the right.

Leanne pulled back to the left, but at ninety-plus miles per hour, tires screeched, and the car spun out of control.

Momentum tossed Trish backwards.

Leanne stomped the brake, throwing Trish against the dash, and landed a fist to Trish's jaw.

Trish used the dash as a brace and flung a fist to Leanne's nose.

While they fought, the car careened over the side of the shoulder, diving down into the canal.

Trish's shoulder bounced against the dash when the car slammed the water that gushed up over the hood and windshield.

Then everything stopped at once.

She looked over at Leanne who was leaned forward against the steering wheel. Dash lights still lit the interior and the engine continued to hum.

The car had hit at an angle, leaving Leanne's side out of the water and Trish's sinking into the canal.

"God, I want to kill you."

Trish whipped around at the sound of Leanne's voice to find the crazy bitch awake and with a murderous glint in her eyes. She had the damn gun again. "We're going to get out and I'm going to find us a ride. If you try *anything*, I will make you wish you'd never drawn your first breath."

Trish just shook her head. "What fucked you up this bad?"

"Shut up and get out."

Leanne opened her door, keeping an eye on Trish as she backed out and leaped away to the bank. She called out, "This water's full of moccasins and my door will sink to the water in about thirty seconds."

Trish struggled to pull herself up to Leanne's door. She didn't make much progress until she heard something splash in the water. She knew it was irrational, but a reptile with big teeth scared her more than Leanne with a gun. She scrambled out the door and leaped to the bank, then climbed up to the pavement.

Not a car in sight, but an almost-full moon shed enough light to see where she walked.

Leanne shoved the barrel of the gun against Trish's head. "You deserve to die."

Not as much as you do, bitch. The only thing in Trish's favor right now was the element of surprise, and the fact that Leanne still wanted to keep her alive.

What would Arnie say? *Watch for an opening and attack.*

When Leanne pulled the gun away, Trish took a step and spun around, kicking Leanne's wrist to knock the gun loose. Didn't happen. Dammit.

Trish punched Leanne twice, aiming for the throat but catching her jaw and her chin, then she ran. Leanne staggered, spun around and came after her.

Fight dirty, and fight to win.

Trish ran for the shoulder, stopping at the last minute and turning back toward Leanne, praying for the right timing.

Leanne was nearly on her when Trish dove toward Leanne's legs. Leanne couldn't stop her momentum and flew forward, off the shoulder and down onto the rocky bank.

Leanne landed hard on her back and the gun flew out of her hand as she rolled toward the water's edge, screaming obscenities. Trish heard the splash when Leanne landed in the water.

Trish hesitated for a few seconds. Could she outrun a woman with five inches on her and a much longer stride? No.

What would Arnie say?

When your enemy is down, strike hard.

But Leanne was a human, after all.

A human who tried to kill a US Senator and wants to send your brother to prison.

Trish started down the bank.

The water splashed. Leanne pushed up on her knees. Her body jerked backwards. Eyes rounded in horror, she screamed, *"Alligator!"*

Terrified, Trish looked around for the gun, but Leanne clawed at the bank, fighting to hold on and slipping backwards even more. Trish raced down the bank and grabbed Leanne's arm, sitting back and shoving her feet in for purchase. *Dammit.* She wanted to stop Leanne, but not this way. She strained to hold on as Leanne cried and screamed, her body jerked back and forth.

Trish saw the alligator's eyes, reflecting yellow in the moonlight. He was huge and had Leanne by the thigh.

The whump, whump, whump of a helicopter came out of nowhere. Wind from the rotors buffeted Trish and a floodlight blinded her as it swept the area.

She turned her face away from the flying dirt and debris. The crack of a gunshot made her drop onto the rocks but still, she held onto Leanne's arm. The alligator jerked once. A second shot killed it.

Leanne was sobbing and moaning.

Trish couldn't let go. She risked a quick look around. The helicopter landed on the highway and figures were running toward her.

"Trish!" She heard the shout over the noise of the rotors.

Josh.

He came for me.

Trish's heart did high jumps.

He scrambled down the rocky bank,

"Are you hurt, baby?"

"No, but Leanne..." Trish couldn't breathe.

Ryder appeared on her other side with a mean-looking rifle in his hand. "Let me have her." He took Leanne's arm from Trish.

Josh pulled Trish back from Leanne and the alligator. Ryder used the muzzle end of his rifle to push the alligator's jaws open and pull Leanne free, but her leg had been severed. Blood turned the murky water black and spread onto the rocks at the water's edge.

Ryder looked up at Josh and shook his head. Dead.

Trish said, "I tried–"

"You couldn't save her from that." Josh pulled her into his arms. He was trembling. I'm so fucking glad you're alive."

"She's the mole."

"I know. We figured it out about the time she drove off with you."

That meant his job was done.

Josh would be leaving Miami.

CHAPTER 53

Sabrina's cell phone rang as she'd just pulled off her clothes to step into the shower. She wrapped a towel around her body and answered it. "Slye."

"I just opened the box with what's left of the laser weapon used on the airliner." Gage stopped there, offering no hint of whether he was angry or pleased.

"We don't have Rikker."

"I know."

How could he know? She'd find out later. "But we will."

"I know that, too."

This time, she let the silence grow until he said what he had on his mind. Talking to him with no clothes on brought back memories of erotic phone calls when they'd been on opposite sides of the world.

There were times when their conversations had been as languorous as their bed play. This one needed to end before it began to live and breathe.

He gave in first. "Have I earned back any of your trust?"

"You scuffed the surface. Takes more than a shot at Rikker."

"That's all I needed to know. Enjoy your shower." *Click.*

CHAPTER 54

"What do you think Leanne meant by Czarion?" Ryder asked, driving along the beach highway toward their hotel suite headquarters.

"I don't know. Never heard of it." Josh had hoped for closure with this mission, not to open up a whole new set of questions. He still wanted Rikker, but he accepted, now, that finding the agent would not fix what had happened with Chelsea.

Like Sabrina tried to tell him. Chelsea was gone and Josh was still here. If it had turned out the other way around, he wouldn't have wanted Chelsea so focused on finding Rikker that she'd let her life slide by unlived.

"What are you going to do about Trish?"

Josh tensed at just hearing her name. "Nothing."

"After all this, you're just gonna let her go?"

When did the FNG decide Josh and he were BFFs who talked about relationships? "Look, I appreciate what you did at the airport, and your help finding Trish." Josh waited for Ryder to look over and he said, "I mean it."

Ryder nodded.

"Trish needs to be with her family and live a normal life with a man who can *have* a normal life."

"She told you this?"

She didn't have to.

Ryder raised an eyebrow. "I see. So now you read minds?"

"No." Josh really did owe the son of a bitch. Maiming Ryder at this point would be dishonorable.

"How would you take it if someone made your decisions for you?"

Not very well. Which was exactly, he realized, why Trish was always fighting Zane so hard.

Shit. Josh had the sudden insight that he'd been doing it too. The very thing he'd told Zane would undermine Trish.

Was he shortchanging Trish by deciding for both of them? "I can't bring her into this world."

"Her fucking brother lives in this world. What would be any different with you?"

"I made a vow to someone to never get involved with a woman as long as I'm in this line of work." A vow that felt as hollow as the inside of his chest. That vow had made sense in his life at one time. Back then. Not now.

"Is that someone going to keep you company in your old age?"

"No. He's dead."

"Are you saying you're willing to walk away from Trish for some vow to a dead guy? You're a dick, you know that?" Ryder grumbled, turning the truck off the main highway.

Maiming the FNG was back on the table. But damn if he didn't have a point. "Got any other pearls of wisdom or is that it?"

Ryder pulled into the hotel parking lot and left the truck running. "Yeah, I got one more. If I had someone like Trish who was in love with me—or did I misunderstand the way she was looking at you?—I sure as hell wouldn't quit on her."

Josh had *thought* his moment with Trish had been private when he and Ryder had dropped her at home. He'd kissed her, several times, and it would have turned explosive if the FNG hadn't been there and Trish hadn't been in a rush to get to Zane and Angel at the hospital.

Ryder turned off his truck. "Or is she not worth the trouble it would take to keep her?"

That struck so hard Josh should have doubled over. The idea of giving her up sucked all the air from his lungs. He realized in that moment just how much he *would* do to keep her.

Trish was worth everything.

Breaking a vow to a dead man was the least of what he would do.

Josh waited to feel a moment of guilt, but instead he felt a strange calm blanket him at accepting that.

Ryder tapped his fingers on the steering wheel. "Your loss."

It would be. Josh would never get over wanting to keep her, but Trish would want to know everything about him, including who his parents were. He wanted to continue with Sabrina and Dingo, but he didn't feel the passion for what he'd always done. Like seducing women. He only wanted one woman.

Lots of wanting and not enough having.

Ryder hadn't gotten out of the truck. Worse than a dog after a squirrel. He wouldn't give up. "Life's short, especially in our line of work. I signed on with Sabrina for freedom. I can accept or turn down an assignment. I can have a life. That's all I want. The only thing that would make it any better would be finding a woman who likes the outdoors as much as I do. I find that, *I'm* not turning her loose."

The FNG was starting to grow on Josh, but there was also the question of Trish tying herself to a man who spent more time in the bleak underbelly of the world than in the light. Would she be willing to do that? Did *he* still want to do that?

If not, could he tell Sabrina and Dingo goodbye?

He had a decision to make.

Josh didn't want to talk about it anymore with Ryder. He wanted to pack up and find Trish. "I know what you're saying. I've always had to do the right thing and I'll do it this time."

They both got out and Josh caught up with Ryder in front of the truck.

Sirens screeched.

Cars pulled up around them, coming from every direction.

Ryder's hand moved toward his weapon.

Josh warned, "Don't. This is the real FBI. Let me find out what's up and see if I can get us out of here."

A crowd of FBI personnel wearing black windbreakers and with weapons drawn had Josh and Ryder encircled in seconds. "Hands in the air."

Josh complied, but said, "I'm FBI, too."

Agent Theron showed his badge and checked Josh's, then turned to Ryder. "Ryder Van Dyke?"

"Yes."

"You're under arrest for the murder of J. K. Kearn."

Josh turned to Ryder whose imperturbable face was slack with disbelief. Ryder asked, "Kearn's dead? What happened?"

The agent started reading Miranda.

Ryder ignored him and met Josh's gaze. "Didn't do it."

Josh couldn't stop this train wreck right now, but he gave Ryder a nod that he hoped conveyed their team rule. *Slye never gives up their own.*

What the hell had the FNG gotten into?

CHAPTER 55

Trish smiled at her brother as he put down the sack of carryout food and sat on the edge of Angel's hospital bed, staring at his wife and daughter with such a look of raw love that Trish wanted to cry. But a happy cry. "Aren't they beautiful, Zane?"

He raised the happiest proud papa face to her that Trish had ever seen.

Her sister-in-law gave a little headshake. "Jacey is beautiful, but I've spent twelve hours in labor. I haven't brushed my hair, or my teeth and I still have a baby belly."

"Let me tell you what I see," Trish said. "You have that new mother glow. Zane has always loved your hair because he's constantly touching it like he is right now."

Zane laughed sheepishly. "She's right."

"And as for a little pooch at your middle," Trish continued. "You'll be out running that off before you know it."

Angel heaved a relaxed sigh. "True. I can't wait to get back in shape."

"Which is why my baby gift to you is one of those cool three-wheel jogging strollers."

Angel's eyes lit up. "Really? I was thinking about one."

"Yes, ma'am." Trish nodded, happy to see that she'd chosen well. "But when you need to go on those really long runs, Heidi and I will have an auntie day."

"You're going to be the best aunt, but a very busy one." Angel grinned. "Hey, what happened with the filming?"

"Senator Dixon is rescheduling."

"Oh, honey, I'm sorry." Angel looked heartbroken. "Did you lose the competition?"

Trish's smile came from deep inside her soul. "Xavier had a much sexier Hollywood celebrity, but he embarrassed her by not really being an expert."

"Who?" Angel's eyes lit up at the possible gossip.

"The producers aren't revealing the name. I just heard that around the studio."

"You've been back?"

"Yes. I *am* one of the two new consultants."

Zane grinned. "Way to go, honey. I never doubted you."

Angel rolled her eyes at her husband and winked at Trish, who'd already forgiven her brother for worrying himself into a frenzy over her.

Trish checked her watch, but only for show. She had nothing to do for three days. Heidi had run her off from ReSolution, claiming Heidi and Bunko had everything under control. Trish was warned to not return without a tan. "I need to get moving."

"Wait," Angel said, shifting the baby in her arms. "What about Josh?"

Trish shrugged. She didn't think she could say he was supposed to leave today, and she never expected to see him again. Not without crying, anyway, so she kept her lips pressed into a campaign-worthy smile.

If Josh's decision was to walk away, then so be it.

She'd made a deal with herself that she could love him enough to let him go. He held a part of her she'd never be able to share with another man, but she was not the woman she'd been before meeting Josh. She'd survived murders, assaults and lunatics. All without taking a sip of alcohol.

To still be sober after all that gave her the confidence she'd been only pretending to have until now.

Zane got that dark I-hate-any-men-around-my-baby-sister look. "Josh *is* gone, right?"

Angel gave him an elbow.

Zane oomphed. "Hey. Just watching out for my kid sister."

"What makes you think Trish needs it or that Josh can't take care of her?" Angel countered.

Trish was lucky to have Angel. She'd become Josh's biggest fan when Trish had shared what really happened in Alligator Alley. She had *not* told Zane the whole story. He'd find out soon enough. Hopefully when she wasn't around.

Zane had been out getting coffee and making Angel's snack run, so the two women had been able to talk freely. But Trish had also told Angel that Josh was protecting someone, and until he could share that world with Trish, she couldn't live in the shadows of his.

Neither would she live in any other shadow, even if it was the shadow of her own brother's fear. She was done with that.

When Zane had come back into the room carrying a sack of contraband goodies that smelled suspiciously like pizza, Angel's personal poison, Trish had bided her time.

"I just heard back from my buddy Randall," he said as he started unpacking the sack. "He said he'll be at your house at seven tomorrow evening." He set down a Styrofoam cup of coffee and looked at Trish. "He'll meet with you to get your regular itinerary, then check out your house and let me know what kind of security system you need. Plus, he's just hired a new team out of Tennessee. They're former Army Special Ops, which is perfect. He says they can follow you from home to work in the mornings, then back in the evenings, and they'll set up a new, state-of-the-art system in ReSolution and one at your house.

He kept talking as he pulled out a pizza slice-shaped box from a local mini-mart chain. Trish walked over to Zane and put her hand on his chest. She heard Angel snicker behind a bite of pizza. Zane stopped talking and both eyebrows shot up. "Problem?"

"Not as long as you pay attention to what I have to say." She really loved this big idiot. "This is the last time we're having this conversation, because I'm done with being coddled and smothered. Why do you think I train so hard with Arnie? I can take care of myself. I need your love, not your protection. Got it?"

"Trish–"

"Stop right there. Do you really want me to move across the country, far away from you, to prove I can stand on my own two feet without you—or any security you hire—standing guard over me?"

Zane started making a growling sound, then tipped his head back and stared at the ceiling for a minute. Probably praying for the patience to deal with the women in his life. Trish reasoned that it was good for his character.

Without warning, he grabbed her into one of his bear hugs. "You're right and I hear you. I love you, Sis. I just don't want you hurt."

Too late. Mainlining pain drugs wouldn't help the ache cutting her up inside. She hugged Zane back. "I love you, too, crazy man. I'm leaving now and I don't want you calling constantly or coming by. I'm fine and you have your hands full watching out for your girls."

She kissed his cheek, stepped over and hugged Angel and kissed her niece on the head. If only someone could bottle that new-baby smell.

Outside the hospital, Trish walked to the end of the sidewalk.

A silver Porsche was parked off to the side.

Josh climbed out.

She marveled at what a chameleon he was, from techno computer guy to chic designer male to warrior toting a gun.

He walked over to her. "Hi."

"Hi. Thought you were gone."

"I couldn't leave yet."

Josh wanted to kiss her goodbye. That was all.

She shouldn't kiss him again. It would be just one more painful memory she'd miss for the rest of her life. But was that going to stop her? She put her hands on his shoulders and lifted up to kiss him. He met her halfway, kissing her with a tenderness that threatened to buckle her knees.

A couple walked by, talking about prescriptions.

Trish broke the kiss. She couldn't stand here forever. This was a hospital. "Why are you here?"

His eyes were softer than she'd ever seen them. "I have something to tell you and we don't have much time."

Then just say it fast. So, she could leave while she could still keep it together. She put on her best face of understanding, ready for his goodbye. "I'm all ears."

"No, you're all heart and sweetness."

Her heartbeat stuttered, but she held silent so he could talk.

"You asked me about my family, and I only told you pieces. I did run the streets as a kid, with two other friends. I work with them now." He went on to explain how a CIA field operative had watched Josh and his band of thieves surviving on the street. Josh looked like the man's nephew, who'd been kidnapped and killed, so he convinced his grieving brother and sister-in-law to take Josh in as a foster child.

That led to his adoption, and to his uncle training him in intelligence work. Josh looked past her. "I was not an easy child. I wanted to be back with my friends Sabrina and Dingo, but my adoptive parents loved me enough to be patient until I realized what a gift I'd been given. Not being adopted but being loved."

Trish brushed a lock of hair off his forehead. "I'm thankful your parents and uncle protected you so well and that your uncle gave you elite training. But I see now why you believe you can never have someone in your life, someone who loves you, and that makes me sad."

Josh would protect those he loved and not want to put a woman at risk from his world. And she wouldn't want him to give up what he did. But living every day had all kinds of risks.

She'd been in just as much danger in that hotel room years ago.

And she'd been in just as much danger over the past few weeks from people she'd thought were her friends. If Josh would only realize that she could take care of herself.

Some things would never change, like Josh and Zane being overprotective males. She would not make this any harder on Josh or herself.

She lowered her hand to touch his cheek. "Thank you for telling me that. I can accept what you're saying. I hope you'll always be safe."

"Is that all you have to say to me?"

"What else is there to say?" God, this hurt too much. "Goodbye?"

He leaned close so that only she could hear him. "I want to hear the words you said to me in Atlanta."

Did he mean ...

"Three words, Trish. They're mine. I want them."

A tear trickled down her face. "I can't do this. I understand that you live in a world of mystery and secrets for your job, but I can't–" She got stuck on the word "love" and changed it to, "–care about someone I'll never really know."

"Say it, Trish."

Another tear joined the first one. What the hell? It was all she could think about day and night. "I love you."

"I love you, too."

"Don't do this to me, Josh. I don't think I'll ever get over you."

"I don't want you to."

"That's just wrong." She swiped at her cheeks.

He wiped her tears with his fingers. "I love you, sweetheart. Get used to hearing it."

"When? When will I hear it?" She held up her hand and retreated a step from him. "Once a year when you surface out of the blue?"

"What if I told you I would give up what I do?"

Trish shook her head. "I thought I couldn't be with someone who kept secrets from me, but I've realized that's not the problem. I'd never ask you to give up your work. It's all you've ever wanted. It's who you are, Josh. I'm not afraid of what you do, and I don't need to know the details of your work, but I *am* afraid of loving someone who doesn't trust me with the rest of his world. And you're afraid to have a real relationship because of your work."

He stalked her, refusing to let her escape. "You may not want to ask me to change what I do, but I'm *going* to make changes, starting with shifting my work from the field to intel, which means I'll be able to tell you how much I love you pretty damned often. Like daily."

Could she believe his words? Did *he* believe his words? "Why would you change your life that much now?"

He touched her hair, twirling a curl around his finger. "I loved being an operative at one time. I thought I still wanted to do this, but my heart hasn't been in fieldwork for a while. It took meeting you to realize I don't have the passion for living this life anymore–or for some of my assignments."

He dropped his head and inhaled near the bit of her hair he was fondling. Drew in a deep breath, almost like he was breathing *her* in, and let out an even deeper, contented sigh. Little quivers started in her belly as he went on. "I work with a private security team. They deserve my best and I'll always give that to them, but in a new capacity that will allow me to work down here. I told them this morning and they're good with it, relieved if you want to know the truth. I may be gone a couple of days a week, sometimes, but I'll be down here with you every other minute of my life."

She had to look shell-shocked because she was. "You're serious." She squelched the belly quivers. This had to stop.

He took her hand in his. "I've never been more serious in my life."

She started shaking her head. "I still don't know who you are."

"That's why I want you to go to dinner with me."

He was insane. She'd fallen in love with an insane man who wanted to give up his world of cloak and dagger. "It's only ten in the morning, too early for dinner, and I have things to do."

"Liar. Heidi said you're free for three days."

So now he expected her to just vacation with him for three days and *then* what? The fact that she was considering it said she might be just as far off her rocker as he was. She shook her head again. "I thought I could be with you then give you up, but I can't. It will be even harder to do this in three days. Just go now."

He put his finger on her lips. "If you have dinner with me, it will change everything."

"How?" she asked around his finger as it traced her lips.

His eyes turned dark blue, and he muttered, "I'm going to get this done then I'm going to get us both naked."

"Get what done?"

"Take you to dinner. In Seattle."

"Why? What's there?"

"My parents. I want them to meet their future daughter-in-law." Josh wrapped his arms around her. "That is, if you'll have me. Will you marry me? I should probably warn you if I don't hear yes, I'm going to push for the answer I want, even though you hate being pushed. You're mine and I'm not giving you up. Ever."

"You want me to meet your parents. Real parents? I thought you couldn't share their identity."

"I made a vow to my uncle to protect them—and protect myself—back when I thought I could live without love in my life. But I can't. I called my parents and told them about you. They trust my judgment and I trust you."

She caught her breath at his admission. "Just who are you, Josh?"

"Joshua Ike Carron, the heir to Carron Technology."

"They're ... you're ..."

"Obscenely wealthy, which is why we can go straight to the airport. I'll buy you whatever you need, but first I need your answer." He took a breath and his eyes held something Trish had never seen before. Vulnerability.

He'd kept his family shielded from everyone, and now he was sharing them with her. Here was the trust she'd been looking for.

And here stood the man she wanted in her life.

She snuggled up to him. "Yes, I'll marry you."

"And you love me." He dropped his forehead to hers.

"And I love you."

DEDICATION

For Cassondra Murray who was with me every step of the
way

***Thank you for reading my books. If you enjoyed this story,
please help other readers find this book by posting a review.***

To find out about new releases, sign up for Dianna's
private newsletter list (emails are NEVER shared) at
AuthorDiannaLove.com/connect

———*m*———

For SIGNED PRINT copies of Dianna's books visit
www.**DiannaLoveSignedBooks**.com where you can preorder
new books.

E-book and international fans:
You can also order a set of signed bookplates for your print
books and/or signed cover cards just for the cost of postage at
www.DiannaLoveSignedBooks.com (click MORE)

**The Slye Team Black Ops romantic thriller series is
'completed' (great for binging!)**
Prequel: Last Chance To Run
Book 1: Nowhere Safe
Book 2: Honeymoon To Die For
Book 3: Kiss The Enemy
Book 4: Deceptive Treasures
Book 5: Stolen Vengeance
Book 6: Fatal Promise

An excerpt of *HONEYMOON TO DIE FOR* is next.

HONEYMOON TO DIE FOR

Bianca enforces the law and Ryder is a deadly rule breaker she's convinced is guilty of murder and tied to a terrorist group who cost her someone dear. Ryder is just as motivated to get out of prison and find the real killer who set him up.

Slye agent Ryder Van Dyke is locked inside an Atlanta penitentiary facing the death penalty after being framed for murder. When his last hope for freedom disintegrates, he's offered a commuted sentence – if he helps the FBI nail a bigger criminal, his father. Only Van Dyke family is allowed inside his father's compound. To prove his innocence or tap his Special Forces skills to disappear if he can't, Ryder accepts a deal to take an agent inside his father's home as his wife. FBI analyst Bianca Brady spent two long years substantiating that his father is guilty of funneling weapons to terrorists. Now all she needs is the proof, but she hadn't expected to marry a criminal who hates her after her team put Ryder in prison.

Bianca is the last person Ryder will trust, but he'll take any gamble to avoid life in a cage. While the unlikely pair navigates a minefield of deadly secrets and assassination attempts, as well as unexpected chemistry, they set off a series of attacks neither anticipated. When it's clear Bianca is the killer's target, Ryder is forced to make a choice to give up his freedom or risk the life of the woman who has stolen his heart.

Bianca and Ryder dodge bullets and race against the clock to unmask a terrorist who can prove Ryder's innocence and stop the monster before he can kill again, but at a sacrifice neither saw coming.

CHAPTER 1

Predators inside the prison yard grew tense and quiet. They'd caught the scent of a weak prey—the overweight, middle-aged prison guard named Boyd. Sweat streamed down his face and his deep-brown skin had lost two shades.

Standing alone with arms crossed over his orange jumpsuit, Ryder Van Dyke kept an eye on Boyd *and* the other twenty Atlanta Federal Penitentiary inmates milling around during their hour of yard time.

The standard mix of killers, rapists, and thieves.

Present company excluded.

Ryder had never harmed a woman. He *had* stolen and killed, but only to protect the innocent. Actions he'd taken to preserve national security while on black ops missions for the Army before he was honorably discharged.

Operations that had resulted in saving thousands of lives.

Had that weighed in his favor when someone framed him for murder?

Hell, no. In fact, being an elite marksman—a sniper—was one piece of the circumstantial evidence that had put him in here. But he had a two o'clock meeting this afternoon with his attorney that he hoped meant positive news.

Forty-three minutes from now.

He eyed the guard and the players in the yard.

Ryder couldn't ask to go back inside early. Not at this point. If the guards picked up on something in the yard after he left, the other inmates would accuse *him* of snitching and turn on him even though he had no idea what was going down.

No, he was stuck until they were all called inside.

Survival to this point had been iffy. He'd spent the past four months, twenty-nine days and thirteen hours in this shithole. Given a choice, he'd have taken a bullet between the eyes instead of getting locked away in a space so small it would drive a dog crazy. He was lucky to have survived this long, and almost hadn't that first week.

The predators, led by the Beast, had turned on Ryder the second day.

Facing an undetermined stay here, he'd had only one option to stay alive. Take on the meanest bull in the yard—the Beast— and bust his balls, if he could, to make the rest think twice before testing him.

Ryder had ended up taking on three, and had hobbled away with cracked ribs, a bruised ball of his own, and peeing blood.

But he'd been upright.

The other three had left on stretchers.

Cost him thirty days of solitary confinement in the SHU, Single Housing Unit, aka the Hole.

A safe place. Physically. A wasteland of invisible land mines mentally.

The space would have been suffocating for an hour. He'd touched two walls when he stretched his arms across the space and the COs, Corrections Officers, controlled the fluorescent light that stayed on nonstop. Seconds turned into endless minutes that blurred into insanity while he waited to get out. His palms dampened just thinking about that thirty days.

When Ryder's breathing hitched, he ran his hand over his forehead to wipe away perspiration that stung his eyes. He drew a deep lung full of air. *Stay calm.*

In the past, he'd adjusted to any situation, but there was no way in hell he'd ever get used to being locked in a cage forever.

Movement in the yard tapped at his awareness. Shuffling around was normal. Choreographed moves were not and, all at once, it seemed as if everyone had new dance steps.

The predators were twitching.

Ryder eyed the sickly guard.

Fifteen feet away, Boyd panted in between wheezes from his two-pack-a-day habit. With a cool, late September breeze scurrying through the dirt exercise area, the temperature wasn't causing the excessive sweat that soaked Boyd's steel-blue uniform. Did he have the flu? He fisted his left hand then opened his fingers as if trying to work out a muscle issue before he gripped his rifle again.

Now Cherry Man turned toward Boyd. Bad sign that. Wide as a refrigerator, if they were produced in the color of burned oil, and just as hard to knock down, Cherry Man had been convicted on six brutal rape accounts. He gave a tiny head nod to the Beast.

His full moniker was the Rajun Beast. He'd climbed out of the Louisiana swamps and killed a two-hundred-pound man with his bare hands during a botched robbery attempt.

Rumor was, that hadn't been his first B&E *or* his first kill.

Cherry Man and the Beast moved slowly toward Boyd.

The rest of the jackals eased along behind their vicious leaders. All but four inmates who migrated away from the pack to the opposite side of the yard. What were they up to?

Ryder assessed the threat.

The Beast wouldn't be thinking to grab a sick guard's rifle and shoot his way out. He was a homicidal maniac with plenty of self-preservation instinct. Six weeks ago, Boyd had reported the Beast for harboring a homemade weapon. The Beast had been dumped in the Hole. He had the ruthless patience of a crocodile, waiting for a chance to make Boyd pay, and this was shaping up to be the perfect opportunity.

Fuck. Ryder had to keep his nose clean so he didn't make it any more difficult for the attorney hired by Sabrina Slye, his former employer, to get his ass out of here. If not for Sabrina calling in favors, he wouldn't even be getting yard time.

He still couldn't believe Sabrina and her team of operatives continued to stand behind him even with a potential murder conviction.

His family sure as hell hadn't.

Except for his brother, Terrence, who'd visited three times and offered to bring in Van Dyke attorneys. Accepting that would have just put Terrence at further odds with their father, the one man Ryder did not want to owe.

Besides, aid bought with Hubrecht Van Dyke's checkbook would only play into the prosecutor's case against Ryder.

Smart money said to keep as much distance from the Van Dykes as possible. That same smart money also said Ryder should stay away from Boyd, who was looking worse by the minute.

Boyd leaned back against the wall, grimacing with each breath he took and white knuckling his weapon. His hand went for his radio, hesitated, then he drew a raspy breath, straightened up and pulled his hand back.

He was a decent guy who showed up and did his job without attitude. He'd actually dragged Ryder away after the fight with the Beast and his lackeys, before someone else could attack Ryder's broken body.

People who'd never been in a prison might assume Boyd's action had been standard protocol for a guard. Not even. The guards could have left Ryder to the other thugs, until his entire body had looked like hamburger, but Boyd had been standing close enough to know Ryder hadn't started that altercation.

Ryder spent thirty days in the Hole with nothing but time to think about that one act of consideration.

Forty-three-thousand, two-hundred minutes.

No clothes except underwear. Nothing but him, a bunk too short to sleep in, a toilet, and whatever rodent came by to steal a bite.

Dots swam in front of his eyes.

He squinted. *Stop thinking about it.*

Instead, he focused on Boyd.

What to do? Take the risk of saving a life, or live with the guilt of not lifting a finger?

Ryder began moving toward the guard with subtle steps as he searched the yard to locate all the players in the macabre show unfolding around him. He should back away, but his damn DNA was hotwired to his conscience. His odds floated right around toilet level. Interfering with the Beast's plan meant facing the Beast *and* Cherry Man.

The second guard in the yard was still observing what had turned into an intense four-man conversation.

Ryder looked back at Boyd, who sagged. *Stubborn bastard, radio someone to relieve you.* But Boyd had missed too much time recently while he cared for a diabetic little girl he was raising alone.

He was afraid to take another day of sick leave and risk losing this job in a sucky economy.

Ryder didn't want to know all that, but he did.

Don't take your eye off the goal, his common sense warned. Half an hour until the Slye attorney showed. Six minutes until exercise hour ended.

Come on, assholes, call us in early.

The predators closed the gap between them and Boyd to thirty feet. At five steps from the guard, Ryder paused because everyone else had stopped. Maybe he'd misread something and let his mouthy conscience interfere when he should be listening to his common sense. Just a couple more minutes and the Beast would lose his chance at whatever he was up to, this time at least.

Boyd looked right at Ryder then his face drooped on one side and his skin paled two more shades.

One of the inmates whistled a birdcall. A signal.

The foursome over in the corner cranked up the volume on their rumble-in-the-making discussion, which hadn't reached the point of an argument. No worse than a loud debate about sports. So far.

Whatever the Beast had in mind was on.

Ryder wasn't surprised at the crazy inmate going after vengeance, but how much was this going to cost him? The Beast had to pay the other inmates—and Cherry Man would not be cheap—plus he'd face whatever disciplinary action the warden dealt out.

When the other guard took a step toward the four noisy men, Ryder relaxed. That guard would call the end of exercise time and...

Boyd's left arm fell slack at his side. The rifle slipped in the grasp of his other hand. His knees buckled and Boyd slid helplessly down the wall, moaning.

Ryder took another cautious step. Sweat trickled into his eyes. Why wasn't the tower calling the other guard?

Because the four men in the corner had everyone's

attention.

Everything happened within seconds.

A shrill birdcall split the air, then a shouting match erupted between the four men, but no contact or the tower would shoot. The second guard stalked over, weapon raised, and ordering the men to separate.

At the same moment, sixteen predators rushed Boyd.

Ryder cursed his stupidity and lunged for the guard, hoping like hell he didn't draw a bullet from the tower.

Bullets popped the ground around them. Sirens screeched and bullhorns shouted to break apart.

The guards *might* hesitate to shoot into a crowd *if* they realized a guard was at the bottom.

Boyd's pain-filled eyes locked on Ryder with a glimmer of hope that one person was not coming to hurt him.

Reaching the guard first, Ryder slammed his foot down on the rifle as he squatted to unclip the guard's radio. He got his fingers on the radio, then was body tackled to the ground. Feet and legs were everywhere. Dust boiled the air. Ryder choked and coughed. He sucked in the odor of stinking bodies. Fists punched *his* body and a sneaker-covered foot bashed *his* face.

What the fuck?

The bigger the pile, the easier it was to cover up whatever went on underneath.

Sirens wailed and shots were fired.

Ryder yanked the radio free and dragged it toward his mouth. Calling medical aid for Boyd might save both their asses.

Two huge hands grabbed Ryder's forearm, knocking the radio loose and yanking his hand into the pile. His palm landed on cool metal. He closed his fingers to jerk his hand away. Another shoe kicked his jaw, knocking him dizzy. His captured hand slammed down on something. He couldn't breathe with the weight on his back. Stars crowded his vision. The inmate pinning him down rolled off. When Ryder felt his arm slip, he wrenched his hand back and found it empty. He shook his head to clear the ringing.

Gritty voices shouted orders. More shots erupted close by. Someone screamed.

An inmate clutching a rifle fell across Ryder. Guess that was the one who'd grabbed Boyd's weapon. The pungent smell of fresh blood stained the air.

Ryder shoved his elbows to his sides and pushed up to hoist the limp body off his back.

Boyd's arm stuck out of the pile with his banged-up Timex watch. His fingers flexed. Ryder grabbed Boyd's wrist, trying to drag him from the pile. If he could keep the guard alive then he had a chance to prove—

Another shoe heel slammed Ryder's kidneys. He fell down on his side, curled in pain. He tasted blood in his mouth.

More guards shouted as they poured into the yard, locked and loaded.

Inmates grumbled and cursed as they unpiled.

Clutching his gut, Ryder lifted his head and looked to his right.

Boyd's face was turned to him, eyes wide and blank. Blood trickled from where a homemade shiv had been jammed into his throat.

A vile laugh drew Ryder's gaze up to find the Beast grinning at him.

This hadn't been about payback to Boyd, but to Ryder.

There would be only one set of prints on that metal shiv.

Fuck.

CHAPTER 2

"I got the new springs in that antique platform rocker." FBI Special Agent Bianca Brady paced back and forth on the manicured grass, fighting off the gut-wrenching ache that lived in her chest. "It turned out great. It's goin' to Millie Fryer. She needs it for rockin' her new grandbaby."

Bianca held a red velvet cupcake with "26" on the top, printed in red icing. Sara Lynn's favorite.

"The upright freezer just needed a new cord. It went to a raptor rescue center in North Georgia. Daddy's proud o' that." Bianca continued with her progress report as she looked up into the brown leaves clinging to the giant oaks scattered around the area, at a few lingering patches of color in this part of the Appalachian Mountains, anywhere but toward her best friend.

"I've got an entire pallet of Raggedy Ann dolls in the garage. They didn't even hardly get wet when the Wal-Mart roof leaked. The boxes are toast, but the dolls don't need much except new dresses. Sewin' is *your* job."

Or it had been.

Bianca stopped in her tracks. She couldn't slide back into her native mountain speech pattern. Not even here.

She finally gave up and sat down on the ground, crossing her legs as thunder grumbled closer. "I better not leave here wet this time, Sara Lynn."

Leaves rustled as the chilly, early October breeze kicked up, but no other sound. Not even a bird chirped.

She hated the silence more than anything.

Missed the times when Sara Lynn would give her a shove and say, "Don't be a wus, BB." *BB* for Bianca Brady. Sara Lynn had started that in grade school and she was the only person Bianca allowed to get away with that, or with calling her a wus.

She missed Sara Lynn spending hours with her in Daddy's barn, refurbishing old furniture, appliances, toys—anything that could have a second chance—to give to somebody who needed it.

Bianca had a knack for seeing the value in something discarded and enjoyed the challenge of bringing it back to life. Her daddy had taught her how to work with her hands and use all kinds of tools.

Sara Lynn thought Bianca could do anything.

Bianca reached out and touched the cold granite headstone, squinting back another tear. "I thought I could do anything, too, as long as I had my best friend beside me. I hate celebrating your birthday here, dammit." A tear slid down her face. "God, I miss you so much."

Sara Lynn would swat her for taking the Lord's name in vain.

"I'm not holding up my end of the business right now, but I'm a bit busy. I'll get back to it when this job's done. I miss fixin' things almost as much as I miss you."

Sara Lynn claimed Bianca was drawn to all things damaged and abandoned, including people.

She'd only said that because Sara Lynn had been an outcast until the day Bianca met her in fifth grade and claimed Sara Lynn as her best friend *ever*. Bianca still didn't understand why others had never looked past the maroon birthmark that covered more than half of Sara Lynn's face, her full figure or her kinky orange-red hair to see the loving soul inside.

Or the mind capable of running a Fortune 500 company.

The day Bianca handed Sara Lynn a small dollhouse Bianca had cleaned up and repaired in her daddy's backyard shop, Sara Lynn had burst into tears at the gift.

Bianca's throat tightened at the memory.

Even after high school, Sara Lynn had always been there with her, spending nights and weekends refinishing discarded furniture in the tiny living room of their ground floor apartment. When they had a load ready, they'd run it back to Thatcher for their neighbors.

When Bianca was recruited out of college to work as an analyst at Quantico, Sara Lynn moved home to work for her church. But Friday afternoons at five, Bianca would head south on I-81 to spend her weekends with her best friend.

Until two years ago.

Bianca fingered the charm bracelet on her wrist. The six charms and bracelet links were shiny once again.

She'd rubbed a blister on her finger the first time she polished the second-hand jewelry and gave it to Sara Lynn for her sixteenth birthday.

The tear slid down Bianca's face. She wiped it away and sat up straight.

This should be like any other day on the calendar, but it would never feel that way unless she could turn back time. If she had that ability, she'd take back the words she should never have uttered that sent Sara Lynn to her death.

Swallowing against the knot stuck in her throat, Bianca said, "I brought your favorite cupcake." Sara Lynn was one month younger than Bianca. She placed the birthday cupcake on the ground in front of her best friend's headstone and tucked her birthday card underneath.

Thunder rumbled louder this time and the wind intensified.

She had to get through this and admit she was failing Sara Lynn. "Now that the party has settled down, I'll be honest with you. I have a favor to ask."

Was that rain falling in the distance?

She took in the clouds still piling together and lowered a narrowed gaze at the headstone. "I'm wearin' my good clothes today, but I'll make this quick if I'm holdin' you up."

Sarcasm was lost on Sara Lynn.

Bianca got back to her point. "Our investigation is stuck. I've searched everywhere for evidence on this case, but we still don't have any way of proving how the terrorists in your attack got their hands on those *specific* weapons."

Your attack.

As if everyone were allotted their own personal death squad when Sara Lynn had been nothing more than a warm body in a humanitarian group to those terrorists.

There were attacks—somewhere in the world—every few days now, but the one in Istanbul two years ago had taken Sara Lynn from Bianca and eight more victims from their families and friends.

A few wet sprinkles tapped against Bianca's arm. She sighed and hurried on. "I promised you I'd see this through and I will, but I need help. I'm thinking you've got some pull and ... since your current Boss sees everything..."

Understatement of the year.

No flash of inspiration hit her.

Why should God help her when it was Bianca's fault Sara Lynn was dead?

She took a shuddering breath. "I am so sorry I talked you into going to Istanbul. I really thought it would be a great opportunity and it sounded low-risk." Her voice cracked. "I'm more sorry that I got sick and couldn't go with you. We should've been together, just like always."

Bianca's cell phone buzzed. She scrubbed at her eyes and checked the display. "Really? I take one day off..." Another round of thunder boomed. She cleared her throat, sat up straight so she could sound professional, and answered, "Special Agent Brady."

"Murdock wants to see you in the Atlanta office pronto," Murdock's assistant Quinten said.

Pointing out that Bianca had taken a vacation day she'd put in for months ago was not a wise career move at this point. Not when Jason Murdock, her boss at her temporary assignment and FBI Special Agent in Charge in Atlanta, wanted to see her. "I'm about five hours north of Atlanta, but I'll head back right away. Can you tell me what he needs? I have my laptop so I can send him something immediately."

Water pinged her head and arms. Bianca glared at the headstone.

Quinten said, "No. Murdock wants, and I quote, 'his expert on the Van Dyke Enterprises case' located ASAP."

Bianca jumped to her feet. Did that mean they'd had a break in the case? "On my way. Please tell him I'll be there by three."

Rain gushed down as she ran for her Ford Explorer. She turned her face up to the heavens. A regular frog strangler. "So *not* funny, Sara Lynn!"

Bianca dove into her truck and slammed the door. Soaked. Oh well, her hair and clothes had five hours to dry.

Rain pounded the roof of her sport utility, as it had every time she'd come to visit her best friend's grave.

Sara Lynn had to be laughing right now. She used to hoot at Bianca for fussing over her hair getting wet. Assuming Bianca was worried about her looks for some boy, Sara Lynn would say, "A man who *really* loves you won't care 'bout no wet hair, BB. Just let it go."

Bianca and Sara Lynn were going to be each other's maids of honor, but Sara Lynn wouldn't be getting married now. And neither would Bianca. Not after what she'd been through in her one serious relationship.

Sara Lynn had been there for her through that hell.

Bianca was here for her friend now.

The deluge of water came down so fast and hard, it blurred the cemetery, dredging up a memory of days long gone.

Sara Lynn would always stop whatever she was doing when they were inside, and the noise was deafening from hard downpours hammering the tin roof. Bianca would grouch about having to deal with a muddy yard. Sara Lynn would smile and look up at the ceiling with reverence, then say, "You can't have rainbows without a little rain."

I miss your sweet take on things, Sara Lynn. Bianca wiped the water off her face and cranked the engine, heading back to Atlanta.

And Sara Lynn, now would be a good time to ask your Boss about that favor.

AUTHOR'S BIO

New York Times **Bestseller Dianna Love** once dangled over a hundred feet in the air to create unusual marketing projects for Fortune 500 companies. She now writes high-octane romantic thrillers, young adult and urban fantasy. Fans of the bestselling Belador™ urban fantasy series will be thrilled to know she has a new spinoff series - Treoir Dragon Chronicles, which is also completed. Dianna's Slye Team sexy romantic thriller series wrapped up with Gage and Sabrina's book–Fatal Promise–perfect for bingers! She also has HAMR Brotherhood romantic thrillers and a new League of Gallize Shifters paranormal romance series. Look for her books in print, e-book, and audio. On the rare occasions Dianna is out of her writing cave, she tours the country on her BMW motorcycle searching for new story locations. She lives in the Atlanta, GA area with her husband, who is a motorcycle instructor, and with a tank full of unruly saltwater critters.

Visit her website at www.**AuthorDiannaLove.com** or www.**DiannaLoveSignedBooks.com**

A WORD FROM DIANNA…

No author creates without a great support team and I have the best, starting with my husband, Karl, who has always believed in me and makes it possible for me to do what I love.

Steve Doyle has spent many hours sharing his vast knowledge gained as a Special Forces soldier, especially when it comes to all forms of weapons. Additionally, he reads every story and his feedback is a tremendous help. Any mistakes made or adjustments for fiction are my own, because every one who helped me went above and beyond the call to give me the best information.

One of those people who helps me ferret out important details is my assistant and intrepid traveling companion, Cassondra Murray, who is in the trenches with me every day whether it's reading early rough drafts or proofing final edits or juggling the massive amount of office work that happens behind the scenes of producing a book.

Much appreciation goes to award-winning author Mary Buckham who brainstorms with me during the year when she isn't writing on her own Invisible Recruit series.

Thanks also to enthusiastic early reader Joyce Ann McLaughlin who makes me smile with her fun comments and keeps me straight with her sharp eyes.

Judy Carney's first copy edit read catches all those things you scratch your head over not seeing and she smiles the whole time, making it a pleasure to work with her. I want to shout out to Hope Williams who is an early reader as well when I need it.

Thanks to Kim Killion for another rockin' cover and to Jennifer Jakes for formatting the pages and exorcising gremlins.

Thanks also to Leiha Mann, Su Walker and the RBLs for supporting all authors!

A special thanks to Tina Rucci who recently went through

the story and caught things that were missed years earlier.

Dianna